the Blackgloom Bounty

the Blackgloom Bounty

Jon F. Baxley

Five Star • Waterville, Maine

First Edition
First Printing: April 2006

Published in 2006 in conjunction with
Tekno Books and Ed Gorman.

Set in 11 pt. Plantin.

Printed in the United States on permanent paper.

Library of Congress Cataloging-in-Publication Data

Baxley, Jon F.
    The Blackgloom bounty / by Jon F. Baxley. — 1st ed.
        p. cm.
    ISBN 1-59414-451-6 (hc : alk. paper)
    1. Magicians—Fiction.   I. Title.
    PS3602.A974B57 2006
    813'.6—dc22   2005030201

This book is dedicated, first and foremost, to all of you aspiring authors who toil in obscurity, hoping your works might one day stand beside this one in the great domain of literature. Trust in yourself, give of your time and expertise to others and keep the faith that all things are possible. Do that, and you *will* succeed, even if no one ever reads a word of your writing. And remember, if conjuring images in other people's minds was an easy task, *everyone* would be an author.

I would also like to extend my personal homage to Fran Baker and Nancy McCulloch. Without your help, guidance and support, my work might well have languished in obscurity for all time. In addition, a special thanks goes out to all of you on the worldwide web that have aided my crusade from eBook to print publication. I hope to see your works on the shelves next to mine someday.

Esse Quam Videri (To *be,* rather than to seem.)
Jon Baxley

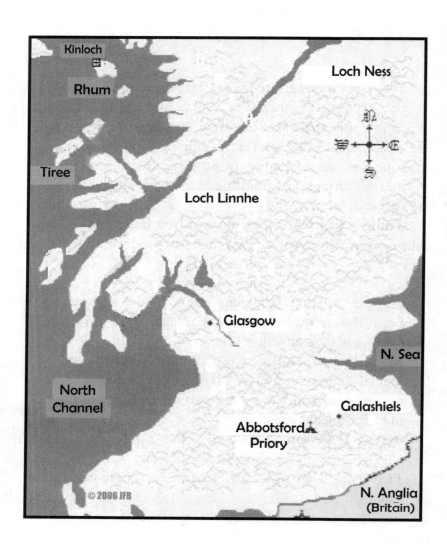

Prologue:

Britain, Spring, 988AD

It came to him in a dream. Or was it a dream? Merlin's image seemed so real. Then the image spoke, and Kruze knew he was not dreaming.

"Kruzurk Makshare, the time has come to avenge me," the image said, gliding closer to the back of the wagon.

"Merlin?" the old man questioned aloud. "Is it really you, or have I passed to the other side?"

The silky, colorless image floated into the wagon and settled less than a foot from his face. It hesitated, as if studying the craggy lines of the old man's hideous features. "It is I, Merlin. Has it been so long that you have forgotten your teacher?"

"Merlin? It is you!" Kruzurk swore aloud. "It's been—how long—sixty, no seventy seasons. It's true, then, what they say about your powers of making. I never really believed that you could . . ."

The image interrupted, saying, "Kruze, my old friend! I have little time, and much to say. My powers have weakened from the long stay on the other side. There is no need of magic there, you see. But I must ask of you a boon. It will take great courage, and I can think of no other better suited for the task."

"Merlin, you need only ask."

"Avenge me, Kruzurk," the image said. "The Seed has gained great powers. He must be stopped. All that you

7

will need is contained herein."

A tightly rolled black oilskin scroll appeared in Kruzurk's lap. "The powers of light be with you, old friend, for I can help you no further."

As the image seemed to dissipate in a sparkle of moonlight, Kruzurk cried out, "It will be done, Merlin—upon my magician's oath, I swear it!"

Chapter 1:

The Beginning

"On with you, now!" the old man cried out, his voice becoming distant and hollow in the damp evening's clamminess. "Pull my ladies!" he shrieked. " 'Tis but a waine strip you've ta complete afore the light fails. On with you, now! Pull, ya big-butted sisters of perrr-dition."

Daynin waited patiently at the edge of the field as his grandfather finished plowing the last three rows for the seasonal planting. The boy amused himself by slinging the small gray stones for which his adopted shire had been named. Already his keen eye and quick release had felled two of the fat, hairy rodents that scurried in and about the deep ruts his grandfather's plow had furrowed only moments before.

His amusement was cut short by a loud snort from one of the two great Rhone mares on his grandfather's team. Quickly, the other mare snorted and joined the revolt against the heavy strain the team had encountered in the last row of the field. The old man slapped at the horses' backsides with a heavy leather thong that Daynin had grown to know all too well.

"Curse ye, get on!" the old man bellowed.

Daynin was unaccustomed to hearing his grandfather swear like that, and in none of his fifteen previous planting seasons, had he ever seen him strike one of the animals in anger. "Something's wrong," he whispered aloud.

The sound of the lash on bare horseflesh caused the boy to shudder. He agonized for the mares, knowing how badly that thong could sting when wielded by a man as stout as was Ean McKinnon. Sixty planting seasons and three terms as bowman in the service of Scottish lords had done little to weaken the stocky, stone hard features that Daynin had come to know and love above all others.

"Bring a staff and come 'ere, boy!" came a shout from across the rows.

"What's wrong, grandfather?" Daynin shouted through the thickening darkness. Staff in hand, he was already halfway across the field.

"I'll be a blaggard's whore if I can tell ye, boy. A bloody great stone is buried here, where none has ever been afore. Agnes and Matildy cannae barely budge it. Some black evil it is that's left this here booty in my field."

Upon reaching the far side of the plowed field Daynin could see, square in the middle of the last furrow, an upturned edge of what appeared to be a great round headstone. The few curious markings that were visible in the failing light gave little evidence of the stone's meaning to the two McKinnons.

With Daynin's help and a mighty heave from the mares, they dragged the stone from the furrow and cast it aside for the night. Ean and his grandson, both tired from the long day's work, talked little of the stone on the way back to their hovel. Daynin asked at supper what his grandfather intended to do with the stone, and was met with a brief, pointed rebuke for reminding the elder McKinnon of the stone's annoying presence.

The next day was market day for the village. Daynin had little to do except wander around and investigate all the wonderful things the traveling merchants had brought to

Hafdeway to sell. He stopped at one wagon and stared for a long time at three magnificent books on display in the back. The ornate covers and beautifully inscribed writing fascinated the boy. He had not had the pleasure of being so close to a real book in a long time.

When he reached out to explore the cover of one book, a thin wooden stick struck from nowhere, slapping across his knuckles with the swiftness of a black snake. Tears welled in Daynin's eyes as he rubbed the stinging flesh on his hand.

"Look ye, brat, but touch ye not!" came a harsh admonishment from inside the wagon. "Lest, of course, ye be the Duke's heir and have brought me ten pieces of silver for the pleasure," the gruff, squeaking voice continued.

"But I was just . . ." Daynin protested.

"Just is dust when profit I must, says I," the voice interrupted again.

Daynin peered carefully around the tailgate of the wagon to see whence his admonishment came. A mop of long, unclean, stringy hair growing from a too-small head, sitting atop a too-small body met his eyes.

"Nosey bit o' work, ain't ye, sprite?" the hairy head asked.

The shock of seeing the head talk, seemingly without the benefit of a mouth, temporarily struck the boy dumb. He stepped back from the tailgate and briefly considered running away. Strangely, his feet wouldn't respond to the warning his brain screamed at him.

"Rat got your tongue, boy?" the hair demanded.

"Uhh, no, I—uhh, I just uhh . . ."

The hairy head turned and screeched, somewhat less loudly, "There ye go using that just word again. Ain't no profit in that word, boy. You got to be pure, or sure, elsewise you ain't fit for nothin' but cleanin' up horse

11

droppin's in the middle of the road. Remember that, lad! Remember what old Boozer tells ye, 'cause there's profit in it, if'n ye'll listen and mark it well."

Daynin's eyes grew large as the screaming in his head exploded again. His feet still refused to move. The ugliness of the heavily scarred face staring down at him from the wagon was almost more than he could bear.

The boy's eyes dropped, preferring to stare instead at the mud and animal dung caked on the wagon's axle. Words totally escaped him. The horror of the man's face and of the whole situation made him hope he was dreaming and not really there.

"Ye never see'd a face like this afore, have ye, boy? Never see'd a face spoilt like this one, eh? Here, give us a good look at that sweet cherub smile of yours," the hairy face said. A long bony hand reached down to cup the boy's face in its palm.

Daynin cringed at the touch of the hairy thing's rough skin. He noted a strange color in the hand—a kind of bluish white flesh tone. The hand slowly pulled his chin up, forcing his eyes to meet those of his tormentor.

"Please, I only wanted to look at the . . ." Daynin pleaded.

"Manuscripts? Truly it is with everyone. And what happens if I let every curious bloke touch me books? 'Ere long, the covers get tore, the pages bespoiled and then me books are as worthless as three-day-old pig guts. What's yer name, cherub? What is it they call you, or do you *just* go by boy? Eh—speak up!"

"Daynin's my name, sir. I live just, er, uhh, half a league outside the village."

"Daynin, eh? Bloody curious christenment for these parts, says I."

12

"I'm not from here, m'lord. My grandfather brought me here from the highlands of Scotia. He is a McKinnon, of the McKlennan clans."

"Then what need have ye of books, master McKinnon? 'Tis common knowledge that highlanders are a wild lot and have little need of education. Their swords do most of their talking, so I'm told."

Daynin rankled at that notion. He thought of the books in his father's house, and how they had smelled as the great fire engulfed all that he had known of life in the highlands. His mind flashed to the blood splattered snow and the image of his father's still warm brains melting a hole in it. Gone was the clan of McKinnon, killed one and all by the order of men he knew not. All gone, save for Daynin and his grandfather, and they alive only by the grace of good providence and the luck of being caught out in a late winter's storm.

He had never forgotten that scene, the smell of the burned flesh, the agony of finding all of his kin murdered in one bloody afternoon. He seethed with anger at the loss of the books his family had cherished so much.

"I have to go," Daynin replied sheepishly. "I have chores . . ."

"Run away if ye must, lad, but stay, if me books you wish to muse."

"But you said . . ."

"Not many have the stomach to stay and chat with old Boozer. Let alone make an argument with 'im that has the looks of the devil's own nightmare. You got the grip, boy, and that's rare these days. What say you, now? Have ye a readin' eye, or was ye only lookin' outta curiosity?"

"I can read," Daynin replied, matter-of-factly. "Latin and some Greek, but it's been a long time."

The Boozer held up a small sign and said, "Then read this, and I'll let ye spy me books. If'n ye can't, I'll swat ye again for bein' the liar."

"*Boozer's Books and Magical Items,*" the boy read out loud.

"Hanged if ye ain't a reader!" the hairy one declared excitedly. "Sit down and tell me what the village of Hafdeway is doin' with one as bright as you."

Daynin reluctantly agreed, his mind having finally convinced his feet that he was in no mortal danger for the moment. He jumped up on the wagon's tailgate opposite the Boozer and began to describe how he and his grandfather managed their harrowing exodus from the highlands.

The Boozer listened attentively for a while. Then the boy's story reached its climax at yesterday's finding of the great stone in his grandfather's field.

"Headstone, says you?" the Boozer asked excitedly. "Rounded like and wider than a man is tall, with strange markings on it?"

"Yes, that's right."

"Gimme the lay of those markings, boy. If they weren't Latin, tell me what they looked like."

"Like that," Daynin replied, pointing to an ancient astrological chart the Boozer had hanging inside his wagon.

The old man's head twisted around rapidly, as though not connected to his body by a neck. "*Runes,* says you!" he spat out. "On a bloody great stone, buried in a highlander's field. Friar's Rush, boy, *that* ain't no headstone! No wonder 'twas never found. The legend says a highlander's field—but it don't say the field is *in* Scotia," he crowed.

"What are you *talking* about?" Daynin replied.

"Every mage for a thousand years has been lookin' for that sacrosanct slab of infernal sedition, and it took a cherub like you to find it. Luck is indeed with you, boy. The powers of all the heavens is alayin' out there in that field right now. You could well have discovered the Scythian Stone!"

Chapter 2:

The Taking

"What do you mean?" Daynin begged. "What is this Sa-Si-than Stone?"

"Scythian, boy, SSScythian," the Boozer hissed. "The legend says it has the secrets of all the heavens writ down for 'im what finds it. Take the Stone to the Great Circle at Briarhenge, and ye can read where the sun will be at the equinox. Supposedly, ye can even predict when the sun and the moon are gobbled by that great black demon in the sky. Imagine it, boy. To be able to say when the sky'll go black for a time. No one's ever done that in our day. But it's said the Scythians could do it, and they were worm meat long before the Norsemen came. That stone's the only record, and there's those that'll pay a Duke's ransom, or slit your gullet to possess it."

"My grandfather said . . ."

"Words is words right now, boy!" the Boozer snapped. "We got to be haulin' out there to get that Stone. Quick now, you get down and throw my goods in the wagon, whilst I hitch ole Abaddon to the trace. Go on! Daylight and prosperity's a burnin'."

Daynin did as the Boozer ordered. The old man's excitement was rapidly becoming contagious. The boy could feel his heart beating faster as he loaded the wagon, carefully placing the Boozer's books last on top of the heap.

"What do we do with it once we get the Stone?" Daynin

asked, as the wagon jounced heavily over the last remaining ruts of his grandfather's field.

"Do? Why, with it, boy, we can do anything we want!" the Boozer exclaimed. "Once we've got the Stone and can read it, the very powers of the heavens'll open up to us. Think of it, boy! The magic I know now will pale in significance compared to that of the Scythian Stone."

Daynin turned abruptly to stare at the Boozer's gnarled profile. Fear swept over him again. He wished to be back at his grandfather's hovel, safely asleep in front of the fire. "Are you a sorcerer?" he asked sheepishly, as if afraid to hear the response he knew was coming.

"Magician," the Boozer proclaimed. "There's a world of difference. Sorcerers are them what's evil with nothing but evil intent. You know what a sorcerer would give to have the power of the Scythian Stone?"

Daynin shook his head, "no".

"Anything they had, boy, that's what. The Stone'd make 'em legitimate, you see. Not just some evil crackpot who does bad things for the fun of it, but genuine knowledge and power, that's all. If this is the Stone, we're gonna be real careful who we be tellin' about it, wager on that!"

The magician pulled the wagon to an abrupt stop a few yards from where the Stone lay. He climbed down and hurried over to examine it. Within seconds, he seemed to be convinced. "Help me turn it over, lad. If they's runes on the backside, it's treasure we've got and not some mislaid headstone."

The back proved to be full of the same mysterious encoding as the front. Even the edge of the stone was engraved all the way around with more of the intricate carvings. The Boozer could barely contain his excitement. He danced a strange jig around the upturned stone, chanting words that Daynin had never heard before.

The old magician grinned and brushed the dirt off his hands. "There it is, boy. That's a handy bit of work, eh? You didn't think my rigging would lift the Stone's weight did ya, now?"

Daynin smiled and shook his head. "No. I've never seen such a contraption. Is it magic?"

"Of course it's magic, you bean-headed plowboy, but not the way you think. It's ropes and pulleys, that's all. Best magic there is—common sense and leverage. Remember that, boy. Now, let's get this plunder over to your grandfather that he may have a say in its future."

It was mid-afternoon when the wagon rolled up to the modest hovel that the McKinnon clan called home. Daynin's grandfather stormed out of his front door, ready to argue or fight with the unwanted visitor until he saw his grandson's face appear from under the wagon's cover.

"Can ye not see it's well past the dinner time, boy?" he bellowed. "You shoulda been home from the market long ago. We've got seed to ready!"

Daynin jumped down from the wagon, expecting to be clouted for his tardiness. Instead, his grandfather seemed transfixed, staring up at the wagon's driver. "This is my friend, grandfather," Daynin blurted out.

"Boozer's me name, kind sir . . ." the magician said as he climbed down clumsily from his lofty perch, ". . . and magic is me game. That is, it was, until your young cherub of a grandson, there, told me about you and the Stone."

"What stone?" the elder McKinnon demanded.

The Boozer replied, "Sure it is I am you've unearthed a treasure of immense significance in your field. Have ye ne'er heard of the Scythian Stone, Ean McKinnon?"

"Aye, that I have," McKinnon answered. "And so I've heard of a thousand other such treasures. I give 'em as little thought as flies on a boar's ears. They be nothin' but old fool's tales and myths."

"Then take a spy in me wagon and see a myth come to life," the Boozer countered. "There be nothing but truth in this tale, and we brought it to you so's you can help us make a disposition of the spoils."

"Spoils!" McKinnon scoffed. He poked his head in the wagon and shook it mockingly. "Nothin' here but that bloody headstone."

"But grandfather," Daynin pleaded, "the Boozer says it's a treasure, and I believe him."

The elder McKinnon pushed the boy aside and stormed toward his front door, saying, "Then take it to the Duke and collect your reee-ward. That is, if ya live long enough. Be gone with you, now, ya scaggy nightmare. I'll hear nothing more o' this tripe." With that, he stormed inside and slammed the door.

The Boozer remounted his wagon. "Come on, lad," he said. "There's some spice in what your grandpere says. We'll take it to a man I know what can say for sure if it is the Stone, and the worth thereof."

"But I can't leave the village," Daynin protested. "I have to help with the planting tomorrow. You don't understand . . ."

"I understand aplenty, boy. I understand that with the spoils you can get from this here Stone, you can take your grandpere and go back to Scotia in the style of a real genteel highland clansman. 'Course that probably ain't much to be considered, you bein' the great landlords here in Hafdeway and all. I mean, you'd have to be leavin' this here great and mighty estate behind and such."

Daynin's ears burned at the very thoughts the Boozer

was implanting. "Go back to Scotia?" the boy questioned aloud. "Back to McKinnon land?" Daynin practically flew into the wagon. "I'll go, but I have to be back by first light."

"First light it is, boy," the magician agreed. The cackling inside his ugly, hair covered head seemed so loud, the Boozer feared the boy might actually hear him celebrating. *It's working,* he thought. *Better than e'er I thought it would. Now, on to Tendalfief!!!*

After a long, jolting silence on the road to Tendalfief, Daynin finally summoned enough courage to ask the Boozer the question he'd held onto all afternoon. "What happened to uhh, to your uhh . . ."

"Me kisser? Burned in a cauldron, boy. Seethin' with all manner of slime and black bile. Warn't a pretty sight, you can pledge on that one."

"But what happened? Did you fall into the cauldron?"

"Manner o' speakin', 'twas so," the magician replied. "Only I had a little help from a man I trusted. Seed was 'is name. Seed of Cerberus. Vilest of the vile, he turned out to be. He was an apprentice to Merlin himself, just like me, afore Merlin found out the boy was a demon seed, that is. By then it was too late. The Seed stole all of Merlin's charms of 'making' and then his 'chants' to boot. I tried to stop him when I found out what he planned to do. This here mess was my reward. The Seed pushed my head into a vat of boiling goo, then cursed me with an evil spell. Lucky for me he hadn't yet learned any *powerful* spells. I might've ended up a cockroach for life. But my hair's been dirty ever since, for if I wash it, spiders and roaches come a crawlin' out. And if I cut it or shave it, great oozing scabs appear."

Daynin's heart leapt into his throat listening to this horrendous tale. He cringed at the thought of spiders, and felt a great pity for the Boozer, cursed as he was. "Is there no way to lift this curse?" he asked.

"Sure there is. They's always a way to reverse a curse, boy. But ye got to get right in the face of the one what put the curse on ye, and make him take it back. That's the only way, short of killin' the curse maker."

"Have you ever tried to go back to, uhh, wherever this Seed is? To get the curse lifted I mean?"

"Can't do that. The Seed never leaves Blackgloom. He'd likely lose his powers if he did. There's no way in or out of there, save by the use of sorcery."

"What is Blackgloom?" the boy asked.

"Bloody great fortress north of Insurlak. Surrounded by trees so tall ye cannot see the tops. Trees of a girth so great that three men can't link arms around one. And guarded inside, it's said, by demons and beasts of which nightmares are made. No place for the faint hearted, wager that."

Daynin's curiosity grew with each new facet of the old magician's story. He asked, "Then no one's ever been there?"

"None what's lived to tell of it, boy," the Boozer snapped.

"Lights ahead!" Daynin cried out after another long stretch of silence.

"Aye, that'll be The Never Inn. We're just ten leagues from Tendalfief and the Al Cazar. Then we'll know if we be fools or finders."

"What's the Al Cazar, Boozer?"

"He ain't a what, master McKinnon, but a who. He's the biggest cheese in the north of Britain. His mage'll know if the Stone's real, and may even make us an offer for it. We'll have to be keepin' a sharp eye after that. Once the word gets out, every blaggard for a hundred leagues'll be after the booty we've got. Have ye knowledge of weapons, boy?"

21

The question came as a mild shock. The idea that they might have to fight for the Stone had never entered Daynin's mind. "I'm good with stones, and a fair to midlin' archer," he said. "I can bring down a squirrel at a hundred paces."

The Boozer pulled the wagon to a stop near the barn of the inn. He held out his hand to the boy and said, "Take this silver and get us some cheese. Bread and a tankard of ale, too, if you've enough. It's a long ride to Tendalfief, and I don't want to be stoppin' on this here thieves' road tonight."

Chapter 3:

The Meeting

Daynin opened the huge doors of the inn very cautiously and peeked inside. A roaring, poorly vented fire filled the top third of the room with light smoke. Blackened lanterns cast eerily dancing shadows from the dozen or so figures moving about within. In one corner stood a large harp, seemingly out of place in the hazy den of iniquity.

"Close the gate, you weedy little dolt!" the barkeeper growled from across the room. "Leave the cold outside where it'll do the most good."

Sheepishly Daynin entered the room, quickly shutting the great doors behind him. He felt a flush of embarrassment coming over him as he made his way to the bar. Off to his left, he caught just the swirl of a long skirt moving across the darkened side of the room.

"Some cheese, and, and bread, and a tankard of ale," he stuttered, holding out the coins in his hand.

"A tankard says he!" one of the bar's scruffy patrons scoffed. "And would ye be needin' a room for the night, Sir Puke?" he added, bringing a round of heavy, raucous laughter from the small crowd.

"Leave him alone, you crowbeat blaggards!" came a resounding rebuke from the shadowy corner.

Daynin turned to see from whence his honor had been defended. "Who are you?" he asked of the mysterious figure.

"Never mind, boy," the shadow answered. "You just get your goods and be off. The Never Inn's no place for the likes of you. Especially at this time of night."

Daynin realized the voice, though deep and somewhat hardened, was that of a young woman. He stepped toward the corner and was stopped in his tracks by another strong rebuke. "Get thee hence, swineboy, before I lose my patience and let these blaggards have their turn with you."

"I just wanted to thank you for—for, uhh, helping me. I'm Daynin McKinnon of Hafdeway. My friend and I are on the way to . . ."

"To hell, sooner or later, as are most of us! That is, if you're lucky and don't get that scrawny little throat slit right here, tonight. Now be off with you!" the woman warned. "You've no business in a place like this."

Daynin backed up to the bar, still facing his mysterious benefactor. He tried desperately to see some semblance of a face, but the smoke and darkness made that impossible. He did make out some detail, along with one shapely ankle that protruded into the light, and he liked what he saw. He was at a loss as to what course to take then, as his curiosity had completely overcome his fear of the situation.

The tavern's doors swung open just then, and in marched the Boozer, looking for all the world like a deranged demon in the hunt for its prey. The room fell coldly silent for several seconds while the magician sized up the situation. "What's keepin' ya, boy?" he roared. "Time's a wastin'. We got no time for the dillydally. Did you get my ale?"

"Uhh, not yet, m'lord," Daynin responded, attempting to cast the manly image of himself as servant rather than plowboy for the benefit of the shadowy female enchantress. "Ale, innkeeper!" he ordered loudly.

The heavy clump of metal on the spiral wood stairs above the room announced the arrival of a new player to the scene. "Play, woman!" a harsh, gruff voice demanded from the stairs. "I didn't bring that harp here for an ornament, you know. Get over there and earn yer keep."

Daynin swirled about to catch a glimpse of the woman, but was attracted instead to the thump of riding boots on the floor of the inn. He saw the long black hauberk first, its tiny, intricate rings of iron a flowing masterpiece of smithwork. Then his eyes met the heavily gold inlaid belt with a magnificent silver dirk protruding angrily at the man's waist. He had not yet gotten to the stranger's face when his inspection got interrupted.

"What're you lookin' at, pup?" the black hauberk growled. He pushed a chair out of his way and strode rapidly toward the corner where the woman had yet to move.

Before Daynin could answer, the magician intervened. "He looks at nothing, my lord," he said apologetically. "He is but a foolish boy. May I buy you a tankard of ale for your trouble?"

The hauberk roared, "Woman! I told you to play! Now make that harp sing, or there'll be the devil to pay for you this night." With that, he stormed into the darkened corner and shoved the woman out into the light. "Do what I tell ye, now, or the lash'll be your reward."

Young McKinnon was instantly struck through by the woman's beauty. The bodice front of her dress fell away from her as she attempted to get up from the floor. Even in the poor light of the inn, he could see the round fullness of her breasts heaving with each breath. Her long black hair glistened from the sparkle of firelight, her skin reflecting the yellow glow of the room's lanterns. She was a dream come true for Daynin. He had never before seen such a beautiful woman.

25

"Let's go, boy," the Boozer urged, so as not to intervene further.

"No!" Daynin replied. "He can't treat her that way! It's not . . ."

"It's none of your business, lad. We've a trek to make, remember?" the old magician urged again, this time jerking on Daynin's leather frock sleeve.

Daynin jerked his arm free and took two steps to where the woman had just come to her knees. He held out his hand and asked, "Are you all right? I mean, are you hurt? Can I help you?"

"Help her at your peril, boy," the innkeeper snapped. "She belongs to the Marquis, there, and he's as apt to break your head as look at you."

The woman pushed herself to her feet, her eyes meeting briefly with Daynin's. He realized she was no woman, at least not in years. The marks on her face and hands belied her true age, but he knew her eyes were those of a very frightened young girl, not much older than was he. He smiled, and received the barest hint of a smile in return.

The Marquis' great shadow descended upon them like a demon's breath. Daynin's eyes flashed from the woman's face to the black hauberk just as the blow fell upon her. The Marquis struck her in the back of her head with his heavy studded gauntlet, stunning the woman and splattering blood on Daynin's face and arms.

In a heartbeat the boy reacted in anger for the first time in his life. Perhaps the memory of his family's fate at the hands of black-armored slayers had done it. Or perhaps the passion of a young man long held in abeyance to the harsh injustices of the Duke's realm came to the fore.

Regardless the cause, the result was the same. He grabbed blindly at the Marquis to stop the assault. His hands found the hilt of the man's dirk. With the precision of a trained assassin, he pulled the blade free and jammed it to its limit into the seam of the hauberk. Instantly, blood gushed from the deep wound, the Marquis toppling forward onto the boy like a great oak felled by lightning.

Pandemonium reigned in the room. The innkeeper climbed over the bar with a short, studded board in his hands. Several of the patrons drew their dirks in anticipation of more bloodletting. Everywhere there was confusion. The woman screamed, then swooned as a scarlet river of blood she must have thought as her own spread rapidly on the barroom floor.

Boozer jumped between the innkeeper and the boy's unprotected back. He, too, drew a large dirk from under his cloak, and that, combined with his naturally fearsome features, served to stem the tide of the others. They stopped in their spots or backed away quickly, preferring not to be added to the casualty lists for the inn that night.

"You best be takin' your leave, afore the Duke's men hear of this," the innkeeper warned. "The Marquis was the Duke's cousin, you know, and he'll not take lightly to his kinsman's murder, bastard that the Marquis was. And take that wench with ye as well. She's been nothin' but trouble since she's been here. Good riddance to ye all!"

"Help the woman to the wagon, Daynin," the magician ordered. "We'll be headin' back to Hafdeway now. Be quick with ye, boy!"

The magician's wagon was thundering down the track toward Tendalfief before Daynin came to fully realize what had happened. The woman lay stunned in the bottom of the wagon next to the Scythian Stone, still bleeding from the gash in the back of her head. All Daynin could hear was the Boozer lashing out at Abaddon, urging the old horse onward through the gloomy darkness.

The heavy jostling of the wagon finally broke through the stupor where Daynin's senses had gone. He reached over to touch the girl's fine black hair, now lightly matted with blood at the base of her skull. She moaned slightly as she tried to turn her head.

"Best be still," Daynin cautioned. "You've a bad knot on your head."

"Owhhhh," she said, after running her fingers across the bump. "That *bastard!* I'll strangle him with his own lash the next chance I get."

"Then you'll need a spade to do it. He'll be feedin' the worms 'ere you see him again," Daynin said, somewhat boastfully.

She sat up, holding her head as if it were a melon balanced on a fence post. "Owwww! Charon's Cross! I'll make that felon pay," she swore.

"I'm trying to tell you," Daynin insisted, "the Marquis crossed over to the other side this night. He'll not be bothering you nor you, him, ever again. At least not as a mortal man."

"The Marquis is dead?" she begged. "By whose hand, and for what price was this deed of heaven's justice done?"

"Is that important?" Daynin evaded. "Isn't it enough that the man is dead? He paid the ultimate price for his misdeeds, that's for sure."

"*You* killed him!" she said with a finality of recognition. "You've condemned yourself to the gallows and me in the bargain. Damn you!"

"The man gave me no choice. He would have killed you if I hadn't . . ."

She pulled up her sleeve and snapped, "Do you not see these bruises and scratches? He's beaten me before, but I've lived to tell of it. Besides, he owns me. It's his right. I'm indentured to him for life."

"Not any more," Daynin scoffed with a large sigh. "Might I at least know the name of the person I've chosen to share the gallows with?"

"Sabritha, if it matters. And after this night, I doubt it will. We'll all be hanging from an oak tree before the cock crows twice. And who might you be, anyway, sir knight of the barroom?"

Daynin could feel the flush of embarrassment flooding his face again. "I already told you. I'm Daynin McKinnon of Hafdeway. And that is the Boozer, a traveling magician. We're on our way to . . ."

"I don't give a render's puke where you're going!" she growled. "If we don't head for the border of Scotia, *right now*, we're going to be crow's food when the Duke's men catch us. The Marquis was Duke Harold's cousin, you know. Not a liked man, to be sure, but a Marquis . . ."

Daynin interrupted. "Are those lights in Hafdeway, Boozer?"

"Tendalfief," he replied. "We can't go back to Hafdeway just yet."

"Tendalfief!" Sabritha cried out, then shuddered with the pain echoing in her head. "The Al Cazar is the sheriff of Anglia. You've saved 'em the trouble of looking for us, you old fool! Turn around now, before it's too late!"

Daynin pointed toward the back of the wagon. "It's already too late," he whispered. "There are soldiers behind us!"

Chapter 4:

The Entangling

"Quiet! Both of you," the Boozer demanded. "No one here knows of the Marquis' death, yet. We'll do our business and be gone by daylight."

Hardly had old Abaddon pulled to a stop before three heavily armored gatemen surrounded the magician's wagon. "What's yer business here at this hour of the night, hawker?" the sergeant of the gatewatch demanded.

"I must see the Al Cazar," the Boozer answered, very solemnly. "I have something of great value he will wish to see."

One of the gatewatch held his torch higher to get a better look at the visitor, then jerked it back down, wishing he'd not seen the horrible apparition the torch presented. "That's what you hawkers all say," the sergeant mocked. "You be gettin' down from there and we'll see what this here 'something' is."

The Boozer was not about to play his only card on a lowly gate guard. "I am sent here as a personal emissary of Duke Harold's," he boasted. "If you value your commission, sergeant, I suggest you go and wake the Al Cazar."

The Duke's name had the desired effect, as the heavy gates of Tendalfief swung open slowly, allowing the magician's wagon to enter. The fort stood as silent as a graveyard, its magnificent stone edifices rising at a steep angle to the level of the rocky hill upon which the great keep had been built.

Tendalfief had long been the only stone fortress in the whole of northeastern Anglia and was frequently the sight of bloody engagements between the Duke's men and the wild highland clans of Scotia.

The hollow "rrhuuump" of the gates closing behind him caused the Boozer to wish he'd never made the vow to Merlin's ghost. That was especially true now that he had the blood of an innocent man staining his sacred vow. He mused to himself, *once the Al Cazar knows of the Stone, it won't take long for word of it to reach Blackgloom and the Seed. Then will I know if my plan has succeeded.*

Daynin had listened curiously to the conversation between the gatewatch and the Boozer. Something about it bothered him, but he couldn't quite decide what. Then it struck him. "Boozer," he whispered, as the magician wheeled the wagon into the stables area of the keep, "you talked differently with the gatewatch than you have before."

The Boozer laughed and then said, "Aye, you got the grip, that's for sure. Don't much fly between them ears, says I. Solid as a rock you are, boy. Sure, I talks different with them what's got the authority, boy, because they make the rules. The rules say that if ye be smarter or better educated than the next man, he's got to bow down to you. That blaggard of a gatewatch would've kept us waiting all night, if I'd let him. But you see how fast he moved when I talked down to him. That's the lay of things, boy, and you best be learnin' that rule right now."

"What happens if the Duke's men come looking for us?" the boy asked.

"They'll be lookin' toward Hafdeway, I expect, since that's the clue I gave 'em in the tavern. But it won't matter, 'cause nobody could've got here faster than we did, and we'll be out of here by first light with any luck at all. You just tend to the wench and keep her quiet. Let me do the talkin' and there'll be no trouble."

Climbing down from the wagon, the Boozer thought to himself, *this boy was a wise choice, after all. It's obvious he has the grit for the task ahead of us. I don't know what will become of him after that, but I'll do the best I can by him. I swear that to you, Merlin, and to the magician's guild. That is, if I'm still alive on the morrow to make good on any of my pledges.*

A light, cold rain had begun to fall outside, pattering quietly on the wagon's oilskin cover. Daynin wetted a cloth in the rain, and placed it gently on Sabritha's neck. Her skin felt warm to his touch. He began to worry that she was seriously hurt or that she might not recover from her wound.

"You've the manner of a blind ox when it comes to healing," Sabritha blurted out, rather unexpectedly.

Daynin recoiled from the surprise onslaught. "I-I'm sorry," he stuttered. "I didn't know you—I thought you felt hot. I just wanted to . . ."

"To what? Touch my skin? You're not the first to want *that*, plowboy. But most are willing to pay, and pay handsomely. What are *you* willing to pay, huh?" she jabbed.

"Nothing!" he shouted, involuntarily pulling his hands away to prove his innocence. "I was just trying to help. I would never—I mean, I wouldn't do that to you—I wouldn't, I couldn't . . ."

"You never have! That's what you really mean, isn't it?" she parried.

Daynin seemed confused. He replied, "Never have what?"

"Been the Duke's minstrel, of course," she laughed, then

continued, "been with a woman, you rock-headed son of a bean planter."

Daynin feigned confusion. He shuffled his position in the wagon, making a pretense of looking out for the Boozer, and allowing himself an escape from the conversation. "Boozer's been gone a long time. I hope this Al Cazar can tell us what we need to know, so we can get out of here."

Sabritha sat upright, leaning her back against the Stone. "What is it that's so full of importance the old man had to bring us here anyway?"

"That," Daynin said, flatly, pointing at the Stone.

"A headstone? He's risking our necks for a headstone?"

"No. It's—it's something special. We've come here to find out how special. Boozer thinks the Al Cazar may even want to buy it."

Sabritha ran her hand along the edge of the Stone, feeling the runes around the rim. "Never seen a headstone with runes like these. Is it magic?"

"We'll soon find out," Daynin answered. "The Boozer's coming with some men. Now keep quiet, and say nothing about last night."

"Whatever you say, your worship," she said mockingly.

"Open the wagon!" the order came.

Two men-at-arms threw open the back of the wagon, and stopped, as if frozen in time. Sabritha's presence surprised and instantly delighted them both. "Hold!" one of them bellowed. "We've got a wench bestored here, and a sightly one at that!"

"Step aside!" the Al Cazar ordered. He leaned into the back of the wagon, apparently more curious to see the woman than the Stone. "You failed to tell me you brought us a treat, old man. We may indeed have some bargaining to do, after all."

"Good morn, your lordship," Sabritha purred.

Daynin's anger flared once again. This time his tongue did the work, rather than a dirk. "Quiet, wench!" he snapped. "The Al Cazar is an important man. He has no need of your diseased services. Now move aside, so the Stone can be got."

"Diseased is it?" the Al Cazar repeated, stepping back quickly.

"Aye, m'lord," the Boozer joined in. "Something she picked up in the north, I'm afraid. You know how nasty those highlanders are."

The Al Cazar stepped back further, his interest in the woman obviously diluted with a twinge of fear. "Get the Stone," he ordered.

"Get back, wench!" the man-at-arms ordered, fear evident in his tone as well.

An elderly mage stepped forward with a large leather-bound manuscript while others unwrapped the Stone. He waved for a torch to be brought closer, and opened the book to a pre-marked spot. He studied the writing in the book for several seconds, then compared it to what the Stone contained. He ran his hands across the face of the Stone, carefully tracing the etched runes with his fingernails. He stopped, turned the page in his book and repeated the process twice more.

"M'lord," he whispered, "I believe it to be genuine. It appears to be the Scythian Stone." The mage turned to the Boozer and asked, "Where did you find this?"

"In a highlander's field, just as the legend says," he replied.

"Bring the Stone inside," the Al Cazar ordered. "We'll examine it further in good light."

The Boozer stepped between the mage and the Stone.

"A moment, if you will, m'lord," he said firmly. "We've a bit of hagglin' to do afore the Stone leaves the wagon."

"Haggling!" the Al Cazar exclaimed. "Name your price, old man, and be quick about it. Throw the woman in the deal and it's a Duke's ransom you'll be getting."

"It's not just silver I be needing, your lordship. 'Tis a pardon by your hand for any and all crimes committed here in Anglia that I would wish for me and my mates. We've, uhh, had a minor scrape or two with the Duke on occasion, and you bein' the high sheriff, why, I figure you could grant us your pardon. 'Course, I realize your word don't carry the weight of the Duke, but, 'tis better'n a sharp stick in the eye, as you might say."

The Al Cazar thumped his mailed hand into the Boozer's chest, boasting, "The law's the law, merchant. And I make the laws in Anglia, not the Duke. But your pardon'll only be good for past crimes, understood?"

"Clear as a fall day, m'lord. Now, as to the price. Five thousand talens should about cover it, I expect. And the woman's no part of this deal."

"Five thousand talens!" the Al Cazar roared. "Why not five times five thousand, you witch-faced trammel? There's not that much silver in the whole of Anglia. Maybe a year or two in the dungeon will lower your demands, eh? Or a week on the rack, perhaps?"

"Your lordship knows the power of this Stone," the Boozer said, quietly. "You said yourself it's worth a Duke's ransom . . ."

"Duke's be hanged if there's one I'd give more'n a thousand for, and that's if he be blood kin, old man. You'll take seven hundred and be on your way, or you'll be my guest till the rats feed off ya."

The Boozer turned to flip the cloth covering back over

the Stone and said, "A bargain made fair by the details, your lordship," his voice flat and unemotional. "When can your mage draw up the pardons?"

"By first light, and we'll need the names," the mage replied.

"Done!" the Boozer agreed.

Daynin couldn't believe his ears. Seven hundred silver pieces split three ways, as the Boozer had agreed to include a share for his grandfather, was more than the boy had ever hoped to earn in his life. And now he would have it all in one lump sum. A vivid image of the highlands lit in the back of his mind. A brief image of something much closer that he could now afford, also made his head swim.

"If you don't mind, your lordship, I'll be keepin' the Stone in the wagon until morning," the Boozer said. "Not that I don't trust you, you see, it's just that the Stone is quite heavy, and I wouldn't want any risk to come to it."

"First light, old man," the Al Cazar warned. "I'll have an extra guard posted at the front gate, just in case."

The Boozer climbed into the wagon and waited until all the men of Tendalfief had departed. He pulled Daynin very close and whispered, "We got to beat it out of here, boy. We got to make a break, or we're goners for sure. This Al Cazar's no man of his word, and besides, I think he's hot for the woman. I want you to open this keg and grease up the wheels on the wagon, so's we can make a run for it. I'm gonna spy us a way out."

"But—I don't understand!" Daynin protested. "I thought the deal was made. Why do we have to run for it?"

"Gut feelin', lad. He means to slit our throats for that Stone."

Sabritha agreed, though her council seemed unheeded. "The old man's right, Daynin. The Al Cazar would sooner part with his mother than seven hundred talens."

"What do you know about that kind of plum?" Daynin scoffed.

"Never mind that, now," the Boozer interrupted. "Get out there and grease those wheels, so's we can make a run for it. I'll be back in a while."

The magician removed a small bag from under the wagon seat and disappeared into the gloomy darkness. His black cloak and diminutive size made him all but invisible in the light rain and haze of the fortress.

Daynin finished greasing the wheels and took a large handful of grain to feed Abaddon. Having accomplished all he could to ready the wagon, he climbed back in and settled down to wait. In minutes, he was fast asleep.

In the wee hours of morning a heavy rain beat down hard on the wagon's cover, drowning out the sound of a dark shadow as it crept closer and closer. The shadow reached its long bony fingers through the open canvas front, feeling for the soft human flesh it knew to be inside. Slowly, the tip of its fingers crawled unseen onto the boy's neck. Another instant, and the shadow's prey would be struggling for its last breath.

"Ahhhhrghh!" Daynin screamed. "No!" he gurgled, desperately trying to gain some air through his throat.

"Shut up and go back to sleep!" Sabritha scolded.

Daynin sat up and felt for his neck. His eyes were so wide that Sabritha could see them in the dark. "The Marquis! He was *here!*" Daynin moaned. "He—he was—he had no skin. He tried to *kill* me."

"Bad dream, that's all. Now go back to sleep."

"I may never sleep again," Daynin whispered, his throat still aching from the phantom's attack.

Outside, he could hear a loud commotion stirring toward the main gate. The clatter of horse hooves on stone mixed with garbled voices, though not loud, seemed definitely out of the ordinary for that time of the morning. Daynin peered out from under the canvas, instantly recognizing the distinctive yellow and red standard of the Duke fluttering across the courtyard. "Sabritha! The Duke's men—they've found us!" he whispered, almost choking on the words.

Chapter 5:

The Eluding

"Damn!" the woman replied. "The Al Cazar betrayed us. That weasel eyed son of a skunk. Where's the old man? We've got to run for it!"

"I don't know where he is," Daynin answered. "He never came . . ."

Just then, the wagon lurched forward, throwing both of its passengers to the rear in a confused heap. Daynin fell face first into the woman's lap, unable to cushion or redirect his fall. He looked up at Sabritha, a deep crimson tide of embarrassment flooding his whole body.

"Closest you been to a woman since you was birthed, eh, plowboy?" she jabbed laughingly.

Daynin was speechless. The momentum of the wagon was so great, he could not easily escape from his unsightly position. It hit him what Sabritha had just said, and another wave of embarrassment washed over him. He put his hands on her thighs and tried to push away, but fell forward again, face first, into her lap.

Sabritha laughed uproariously and said, "If this wasn't so funny, I'd kick you all the way back to Halfwitway, or wherever it was you said you were from."

"Hafdeway!" Daynin screeched. He finally managed to right himself, his mind instantly jumping from her warm lap to their more immediate plight. By now the wagon roared across the cobblestoned courtyard at breakneck speed. He still had no idea who or what was guiding it, but the image of his dream's dark shadow suddenly popped into his head.

"Onward, Abaddon!" the Boozer hollered. "Drive for that gate, my weathered old friend!"

Finally able to look out, Daynin couldn't believe his eyes. The frail little man sat astride the horse's back, lashing him for all he was worth. The magician's long dirty hair and flowing robe made him look for all the world like a demon unleashed. The gatewatch must have thought so, too, for they scattered like a batch of chickens when the wagon roared through. The gate stood wide open, its portcullis raised just high enough to allow the wagon's escape. A squadron of the Duke's men, still horsed outside the gate, reeled in terror at the oncoming spectre. They, too, scattered to avoid being run over by the hairy demon.

As the wagon passed through the group, the magician cast his bag to the ground. Its effect completed their escape. Before the gates of Tendalfief disappeared into the darkness behind them, Daynin watched with great amusement as the Duke's horsemen tried in vain to control their animals.

"What was in the bag, Boozer?" Daynin cried out.

"Wasps, boy. No armor in the world'll keep a mad wasp out. Those troops will be licking their wounds for a week," he shouted over the roar of the wagon. "That's leverage, boy, at its best. Mark it well."

A half league away, he stopped to dismount Abaddon. Daynin had to admire the agility demonstrated by a man of his age. "How did you know to run for it when we did? How did you know the gate would be open?"

The magician climbed onto the seat and handed the reins to Daynin. "Simple, my boy. Leave nothing to chance and risk becomes your ally. I put a hard clout on the head of the gatekeeper. When the Duke's men came, I opened the gate. The rest was a matter of momentum."

"But how did you know the Duke's men were coming?" Daynin persisted.

"Because the Stone would have been unloaded otherwise. Why unload that which you intend to move anyway? Simple deduction."

"I'll have to hand it to you, old man, you sure made the Duke's men look like a gang of drunken minstrels," Sabritha said, laughingly.

"Aye, but they'll be untangled and after us by daylight," the Boozer warned. "We've got to run for Briarhenge. The more people and roads the better. They'll have a hard time tracking us once we reach the Great Circle. Then on to the border. We'll be out of the Duke's reach there."

"The border?!" Daynin yelled. "But I *have* to get back to Hafdeway."

The Boozer put his hand on the back of Daynin's neck and said, "You best be forgettin' about that for now, lad. There's nothin' but a gallows waitin' for you there. We get the booty for the Stone, then you can go back as someone else—a prince of Scotia mayhaps, or some such ruse. But your life as Daynin McKinnon ended in that bloody tavern."

"But what about my grandfather? He won't know what's happened to me. He'll probably come looking for us. Then I'll never find him."

"Never is a word that losers use, boy, and you ain't no loser. We've got time and momentum on our side. And we've got the Stone. Now lay on those reins and let's get on to the Circle. We'll mingle with the pilgrims, then disappear like we were never on this earth. Upon that, you have my pledge as a member of the magician's guild."

"That certainly makes me feel secure," Sabritha said

sarcastically, instantly drawing a quiet, but angry, look from Daynin.

Just before daylight, the magician's wagon passed through the first encampment south of Briarhenge. Pilgrims from the whole of Britain had come for the Rites of Spring festival at the Great Circle. Thousands of travelers, hundreds of wagons, and more animals than could be counted were clogging all the roads leading into Briarhenge.

Sunrise over the forests of Briarhenge seemed more brilliant than any Daynin could recall. Perhaps he realized how narrowly they had just escaped from an eternal darkness. Or maybe it was the realization that five leagues from them lay the border of his ancestral land, and safety.

While his mind raced along through images of the night's escapades, it kept stopping at the same place—with Sabritha. He thought of her coal black hair, her long, shapely legs, and the beautiful smile that seemed to beckon his closer attention. He remembered how she had laughed at him, then why. A hint of flush came over him, thinking about being in her lap. The one thing he recalled most vividly about the night was how Sabritha had *smelled* when he was close to her.

Daynin had nothing to compare it to. He thought of the tea berry soap his mother had often used, but Sabritha's smell was wonderfully different. There was a mixture of wood smoke and heather to it, or perhaps lavender and clover. He could not decide which, but he knew, somehow, that her smell would be with him forever.

Wheeling the magician's wagon around a sharp bend in the road ahead, his reverie abruptly stopped. Standing square in the middle of the track was a man so large that, at first, Daynin thought him to be a tree. He slowed the wagon, realizing that he could not pass the man on either side. A quick glance into the back of the wagon told him that the Boozer and Sabritha were both sound asleep. Rather than wake the old man, he decided to stop.

"Hold!" came a shout from the stranger in the road.

"You're blocking the road!" Daynin replied. "Move aside!"

"A moment of your time, kind sir, if you will," the stranger said.

"I've no time to stop," Daynin replied, sharply.

From out of nowhere, another man, small, wiry and covered with hair, appeared and jumped onto the side of the wagon. "Mayhaps this here blade'll be changin' yer mind, boy," he slurred.

A long, lancet of a knife flashed in the corner of Daynin's eye. He froze in terror. With the man less than an arm span from him before he could react, Daynin stuttered, "Wha-aat do you want? We have nothing! We uhh, we're pilgrims. On our way to the, uhh, Circle."

"Pilgrims, aye," the wiry little man hissed. "It's pilgrims we seek, boy. Them what's got the goods to make our days some'at easier here in these woods. Now, you be easin' them reins down and we'll be havin' a look in this 'ere wagon of yours."

The tree man grabbed old Abaddon's trace chain and steadied the animal while the knife man climbed inside the wagon. Another man came out of the woods on the right side of the road and disappeared around the back of the wagon. Daynin could do little but submit to the knife man and his woodland band. He could only hope that the magician would once again display his wit to help them escape this new threat.

The Boozer awoke to find the third man climbing into

the back of his wagon. He reached for his dirk, but was stopped by the knife man climbing through the front of the wagon.

"Hold yer piece, there, old sot," the knife man ordered. "We'll be lookin' through yer plunder, here, and that ain't worth dyin' for. You just take out that there frog sticker and hand it over, and nobody'll get hurt. Otherwise, this here blonde haired cherub'll be feedin' the worms some'at sooner than ye might wish. Understood?"

"Yes," the Boozer snapped. He glanced at the woman, completely covered by a blanket, obviously realizing that she, too, was at risk. He pulled his dirk very slowly and handed it to the knife man. "We've nothing of value here, but if it's food you want, I can give you whatever we have."

"Value's in the eyes of the beholder, as it were," the knife man said. He climbed over the Boozer and began to rummage through the bundles and bags at the front of the wagon. He pulled a large woolen cloak from the pile and tossed it out of the front of the wagon. Next he took a small wooden box without opening it and disposed of it similarly. Finally, he reached for the blanket.

The man in the back and the knife man both whooped at the same instant. "Value, says he!" the knife man hollered. "Guess where he comes from, they don't hold much with women, eh, Tom?"

Tom's eyes were as large as silver talens, his filthy face broad with a smirk of delight. "Maybe she ain't worth nothin' to them, Blackjack. But wenches is hard to come by in these parts—especially them what's got the looks of this 'ere beast."

"Leave her alone!" Daynin snapped. "She's very ill. That's why we're bringing her to the Circle—to find a healer."

"Or to bury her," the Boozer added. "That's to be her headstone, there in the back. The mage at Tendalfief told us to keep her away from others. She's got a fever, so he told us. If I were you, I would . . ."

"Ohhhh, ohhhh," Sabritha groaned aloud. "Where am I? Is this the other side?" she moaned, adding her part to the charade.

The two bandits fell back in horror as the woman reached out and flailed her arms at them blindly. Tom tumbled toward the open back end, while Blackjack grabbed for the Boozer to steady himself in the close quarters. "Damned pilgrims! Ye've all got some kinda disease. Get thee gone from here, afore I light up this whole pestilent wagon."

Before the knife man could extricate himself from the front of the wagon, a great commotion erupted in the back. Tom had suddenly been jerked completely out of the wagon by an unseen adversary. A brief struggle ended in a loud "thump" as poor Tom's head received a bashing from his attacker's staff.

The tree man at the front of the wagon ran to help Tom, but was met half way by Tom's attacker. Blackjack grabbed his plunder, took a quick look at the lopsided battle at the side of the wagon, and charged off into the woods. The tree man went down from one swing of the stranger's staff, collapsing in agony on the side of the road with his kneecap shattered. In a matter of seconds, the fray was over.

Daynin had watched in amazement as the stranger dispatched his much larger opponent with nothing more than a hickory staff. He cheered wildly when the giant went down, urging Boozer to come and watch the spectacle before it ended. Sabritha, too, scrambled for a better vantage point, but missed most of the action.

"Who are you?" Daynin cried out excitedly. "Where are you from?"

"Never mind that," the stranger replied. "We should go before they come back with more men. Everyone in the wagon, now, quickly!"

Sabritha jumped back into the wagon hurriedly, offering her hand to the stocky, tartan-clad stranger. A musky, but not unpleasant odor accompanied the highlander. Her eyes lingered on the man's muscular frame as he climbed over her in the close quarters. Perhaps it was the shaggy mop of blondish hair that caught her attention, or the flash in his eyes.

Whatever it was, Daynin didn't like it. He lashed at Abaddon, and off they went until reaching the edge of the next encampment. Feeling safe there, the Boozer ordered a stop.

Chapter 6:

The Joining

"We owe you a debt, stranger," the Boozer exclaimed.

The stranger jumped from the tailgate and walked to the front of the wagon. "These woods are full of blaggards and cutthroats," he said, a heavy highlander's accent more evident, now, in his rolling words. "You should'na stopped when you did, boy. Don't make that mistake again. You cannae trust anybody on this road."

"Where're you going?" Daynin asked, as the man walked away.

"Back to Scotia," the stranger replied. "My business is completed here."

"Then travel with us," the Boozer offered. "We're headed for Insurlak, and would be grateful for your company."

"I travel alone," he replied, "and you've a sickly woman with you."

Sabritha poked her head from the front of the wagon, and said, "I'm not sick—just bored. I'll wager you'd make the trip more interesting, eh?"

Daynin's ears burned hearing that conniving tone in her voice. "Fare thee well, stranger," he bellowed, raising the whip to snap Abaddon into stride again. "We thank you for your help."

Sabritha grabbed Daynin's wrist and stayed his motion. "We're in no hurry," she insisted. "Join us, stranger. It's a long walk to Scotia."

The man seemed to hesitate, then agreed. The woman's beautiful smile was more than he, or any man could resist, it seemed. Daynin waited for him to climb onto the tailgate once more, then angrily snapped the reins, jerking the wagon forward abruptly.

The Boozer grabbed the reins to steady both the boy and old Abaddon. "Yer time'll come, boy. Best be patient," he said.

Sabritha's sharp tongue couldn't resist the temptation. "That would indeed be a trick of magic," she sneered, quickly disappearing toward the back of the wagon to engage a more likely prey.

With the morning rushing quickly toward its midday axis, the road to Briarhenge seemed to sprout all manner of men and beasts. The Boozer became impatient with the slow moving traffic. *Mustn't be in too big a hurry, now,* he counseled himself. *The word should reach Blackgloom by nightfall tonight. By tomorrow at the latest. Then I'll know if the Seed has taken the bait. After that, my patience will indeed be tested.* He glanced at Daynin seated next to him and added, somewhat sadly, *As will yours, my young friend.*

"You've not said a word all morning, stranger," Sabritha said. "Are we not worthy of your conversation?"

"Worthiness comes from one's values when applied to another's plight," the stranger recited, almost as if from a manuscript. "Even though I didna seek your company today, yet here I am. Neither did I seek to fight a pitched battle this morning, yet so I did. Now it's my desire to rrrr-ide with you to Scotia, but that doesna mean I wish to converse whilst we're about it."

The hair on the back of Sabritha's neck stood up at the stranger's mild rebuke. Not to be outdone, she snapped back, "No need to be haughty, sir highlander. I'll have you know that I am a personal friend of the Marquis of Greystone."

"Then you've no knowledge of his demise?" the stranger replied.

Sabritha's anger at the man's verbal saltiness was quickly overshadowed by her concern for his knowledge of the Marquis' death. She could not believe the word had spread so far, so rapidly. "Demise?" she dodged. "The Marquis is dead?"

"At the hands of a straw-haired plowboy, so I'm told—in a drunken brawl over some sprightly wench. The Duke's men're searching every village from Wingsdale north to Tendalfief. When they find 'im, they'll hang 'im for sure. Him and his cohorts in the deed, that is."

"Cohorts?" she asked, continuing to feign ignorance.

He stared at her, as if to decide the depth of her interest in the matter. "Curious, m'lady. Of such matters, most women make little note."

Sabritha avoided the stranger's gaze by crawling over the Stone to the back of the wagon. She decided to change the direction of their conversation, and quickly. "Have you been away from Scotia for a long time?"

"Aye, too long," he answered, wistfully. "I hate this cursed country and the Saxon swine who rrr-ule it. With any luck, I'll not have to venture here again."

"Soldiers!" the Boozer gasped from the front of the wagon. "Sabritha, under the blankets, quickly! And you as well, Daynin."

"That's the first place they'll look, old mahn," the stranger said, with a knowing tone in his voice. "Let me take the boy through the woods and we'll meet you at the Widow's Bridge over the Tweed."

The Boozer hesitated, then apparently realized the stranger knew exactly whom it was he was traveling with—and that the stranger was right. "Go with 'im, boy. Ye've no chance here if they search the wagon."

"But Boozer," Daynin pleaded, "I don't *want* to go with him!"

"Come on, boy, we've no time to waste," the stranger ordered.

Before they could move, the Boozer stopped them. "Wait," he said. "They're not searching the wagons. There's just a big crowd ahead. Daynin, you get in the back and hide with Sabritha. Stranger, come join me here in front. We'll bluff our way through whilst the soldiers are busy."

The stranger did as he was asked. The instant he reached the wagon's front seat, he knew what the hubbub ahead was all about. "It's a flogging," he said. "Probably some poor pilgrim caught stealing food. Or one of my kinsmen in the wrong place at the wrong time."

"Highlander it is, eh?" the Boozer probed. "I thought so. Damned few of your countrymen would wear the tartan so boldly in the Duke's realm."

"The Duke's realm, indeed," the stranger scoffed. "Only by treachery and deceit, it is. Otherwise, 'twould still be the land of mah kinsmen. And someday 'twill be so again, have I and my mates anything to say of it."

"Do you know who the boy is?" the Boozer whispered to the stranger.

"Aye. I do now. Like as not, he's the one that laid low the Marquis of Greystone. And you'd be the scarecrow that helped 'im in the deed."

"But how did you hear of it so quickly? It was only . . ."

"I was there, old mahn—in the inn, that is—upstairs. And your boy there did a deed 'twas meant for me to do. I was sent by mah kinsmen to take the Marquis, or to kill 'im, whichever. We planned to trade 'im for one of our chiefs held captive in Tendalfief. I've been following you ever since to see if the boy's deed was a fluke or a task given 'im by others."

"It was a fluke, trust me, but why does it matter? Where's the profit in pursuing him?" the Boozer fished.

"It's said your boy's of Scotian blood. If that be true, the honor of avenging mah kinsmen is his, and I intend to see that they know about him and what he did for us. If I can get him to Donnegal, his deed will help us raise a hundred more like me, then a thousand, then ten thousand. With that many clansmen, we can make these bloody Anglish pay for two hundred years of tyranny in the highlands."

"That may not be so easy, my friend," the Boozer continued. "I must warn you, this boy has a task ahead of him even the stoutest of hearts would do well to avoid. I can tell you no more of it, as that is all I know for sure."

"It matters not, old mahn. The clans must know that even a farm boy can face the Duke and live to tell of it. To that end, I'll follow 'im to the very gates of hell if need be."

The Boozer shook his head and cracked a wry smile. "Ye may be closer to that end than either of us wants to know, good sir. By the bye, what is it that we should call you, or would you prefer to stay a stranger?"

"McCloud, of the Dunlock Moor McClouds," he said, extending his hand. "Caelum's mah given name, but it's seldom used where I come from. Most call me Cale, as was my father's name, and his father afore him."

The throng gathered about the soldiers seemed unusually quiet as the Boozer's wagon passed by on the road. Suddenly a unanimous groan went up when the first "crack" of a whip split the still morning air. Cale shuddered at that sound, knowing well the pain that a nine-tail could inflict. He stood up on the wagon seat to see if he knew the unfortunate soul on the sharp end of the cat.

"Stop the wagon!" Cale ordered.

The Boozer jerked Abaddon to a halt. "What's wrong?"

Cale dropped down onto the seat and reached for his dirk. "I know the mahn being flogged," he whispered. "He's Toobar the Ferret. He helped me escape the Duke's dungeon when I was Daynin's age. Save for him, I would have grown no older. I have to help him."

"There's a score of soldiers, highlander. What do you think you'll accomplish by yourself? Wait 'til the flogging's over, then make your move."

"He'll likely be dead when they're through with him. You just be on your way and if we can, we'll catch up to you at the bridge."

The Boozer waited for a few seconds while Cale disappeared into the crowd, then decided his oath to Merlin would not permit him to risk further involvement. He urged the horse on as another loud crack echoed behind them.

Half a league down the road, a great roar erupted back in the village. The magician knew what it signaled, and instinctively lashed out at Abaddon to put distance between them and the problem.

The sudden lurch in speed brought Daynin to the wagon's front. "What's wrong?" he asked. "Where's the stranger?"

"Where we don't want to be, I'm afraid," the Boozer replied. He lashed the horse harder, scattering pilgrims in the road ahead. "Keep a sharp eye out the back, Daynin.

We've trouble on our heels."

No sooner had Daynin turned than the Boozer's warning proved out. "Riders coming—hard!" Daynin shouted. "Looks like soldiers, and they're chasing somebody—a man—and a boy—on horseback."

"Open the keg of axle grease and be ready to dump it when I say. That's our only chance to stop 'em this side of the bridge."

"It's the stranger!" Daynin screamed in recognition. "How much farther to the bridge, Boozer? The soldiers have almost caught up to them!"

The Boozer whooped, "There's the bridge! Wait 'til they're upon us, boy, then dump that grease so's to catch as many of the soldiers as ye can."

Old Abaddon's hooves clattered like hailstones when they hit the great stone bridge over the Tweed. It was the signal Daynin awaited. Cale and his companion were but a wagon's length behind them now. Sabritha helped Daynin tip the heavy keg as the Boozer shouted, "Now, boy! Do it now!"

Over his shoulder, the Boozer watched as the thick goop splattered heavily on the road, barely missing Cale's hard charging animal. The first two soldiers avoided the slippery mess as well, but the third went down in a confused heap, his animal losing all traction. The rest of the soldiers drew up and stopped well back from the bridge, fearing the same disastrous fate as their companion.

In a moment of unplanned joy, Daynin and Sabritha hugged each other and shouted, "We did it!" almost at the same instant.

The Boozer pulled hard on Abaddon's reins at the far side of the bridge. He turned the wagon broadside in the road, knowing the horsemen would be forced to stop or go headlong into the Tweed. The plan worked.

Cale's horse buckled first, throwing his much smaller companion under the wagon with the sudden stop. The lead soldier's horse slammed into Cale's fallen mount and collapsed like a puppet whose strings had been cut. The second catapulted the first and crashed into the side of the wagon, throwing its rider into the wagon cover. Cale and the first soldier immediately became entangled in close combat with their dirks. The second soldier lashed out at the wagon cover to free himself and quickly joined the fight. The little man under the wagon leaped onto the back of the second soldier to keep him busy while Cale continued the fight with the other.

Across the bridge, the Boozer spied a half score of dismounted soldiers forming up to rush the wagon. He knew the fight would be brief if those men were able to cross the bridge. Suddenly, his attention was drawn away from the battle to an enormous black cloud that had appeared overhead.

A heavy, deep rolling rumble seemed to stop all the action in place. Every head turned to watch the awesome spectacle unfolding above the bridge. The cloud churned and rumbled again; a monstrous blue black, snake-like funnel formed and danced across the sky. With an accompanying flash of brilliant lightning, the huge vortex darted straight down and engulfed the wagon and everything near it. A howling wind whirled violently, sucking the wagon, men, and horses high into the air.

As the cataclysmic event unfolded around them, the Boozer held on to the wagon and smiled, knowing the first part of his plan had succeeded. *Blackgloom can only be entered by the use of sorcery,* he mused. *The Seed has taken the bait at last! If only the rest of the plan works as well . . .*

The Bringing

The melodic chanting echoed from wall to wall in the dank blackness of the great chamber. The low groaning voice repeated the chant for the third time, "*Maelstrom mach, trochilics* and *gyre,* vortex to swirl, then to tire."

Every candle in the great hall wavered in unison from the change in air pressure outside. The huge swirling cloud descended upon Blackgloom's courtyard, its funneled vortex slowly spinning to dissolution. The Boozer's wagon and all that had been picked up with it dropped abruptly to the black cobblestone surface. Horses, people and wagon became a tangled mess as the cloud disappeared, leaving them all in a confused, disoriented pile.

The Boozer smiled inwardly. He shook off the effects of the dizzying delivery and looked around him.

The horses were first to move, clambering to their feet out of instinct. Cale was the first to notice the ring of fully armored paladins surrounding them, each guarded by a massive, drooling animal held in check by heavy chains. Daynin wrinkled his nose at the awful smell of the place. Sabritha gasped at the eerie yellow darkness of their surroundings. One of the soldiers cringed in terror at the whole spectrum of events to which he had unluckily been made a part. The other soldier lay motionless, having been crushed under the weight of two horses and a wagon wheel. Only the Ferret seemed to relish his new surroundings.

"I don't know where this is, but it beats the lash, that's for sure," the diminutive Toobar said, breaking the otherwise tomb-like silence.

"Dinna judge too quickly mah friend," Cale advised.

"Nor would I move too fast," the Boozer warned. "These ogrerats are deadly."

"Ogrerats!" Daynin moaned. "I thought they only existed in legends."

"This is the place such legends come from, I fear," the Boozer said.

Sabritha shook off her initial dizziness and peered from under the wagon cover. She stared at the ring of magnificent paladins, each adorned in black polished armor. "Well, well," she purred in mock-heroics, "there'll be no want of men here."

The Boozer shook his head and whispered, "I do not believe these are men. They are spectres, controlled by the master of this dark place. Legend says they have neither body nor soul. They do not relish life as do we, nor have they any compassion for it."

"What *is* this place?" Cale demanded.

"As near hell as mortal man will ever view," a hard, graveled voice answered from the air around them.

The Boozer stood up to see whence the answer came, but was quickly admonished by the voice. "Make not a move you'll regret, old man. My ogrerats will make quick work of one as skinny as you. Now! All of you, and I say this only once—you will do as my minions bid, or your flesh will feed my pets for supper. Simple. My house—my rules. No others apply. Cooperate and you may yet see your precious sun again. Refuse, and you will forever dwell in a black pit of pain."

The Boozer hesitated, then to help make his charade a success, demanded, "Why did you bring us here?"

"Quiet, old man!" the graveled voice boomed, its words

coming slowly and ominously. "You have something of great value to me. If it pleases me, you may live. If not, then you will satisfy me in other ways. *Take* them!"

Upon that order, the paladins moved as one. The ogrerats snarled and drooled at the prospects of fresh meat, pulling hard on the binding chains held fast by their keepers. The paladins formed a column and urged their captives forward with the points of their lances toward the gates of the inner keep. None of the prisoners resisted, though Cale had to be held back by Boozer's strong hands and knowing gestures.

The prisoners were disarmed and led down a series of steep, winding passages to the very bowels of the Blackgloom Keep. Sabritha was quickly separated from the men and shoved into one of the upper cells of the dungeon. Daynin, too, was taken from the group and locked in an upper cell. The rest ended up in a deep, circular pit, surrounded at the top by a narrow catwalk. Accessible only by rope ladder from the catwalk above, there appeared to be no way out of the pit. Three of the half dog, half giant rat "pets" of the Seed had been left unchained by the paladins, free to roam the catwalk and the nether reaches of the dungeon. Remains of the pit's previous inhabitants lay scattered all about the straw-covered floor. Light from a single slit of a window high above the pit gave the prisoners just enough of a view of their surroundings to horrify them.

Toobar did a quick reconnaissance of the dark pit, then said to no one in particular, "Damned poor hospitality in this inn, I must say."

"We're lucky to even be *alive,*" the Boozer snapped.

The Duke's soldier shook uncontrollably, barely able to keep his sanity. He began to whimper and utter Latin prayers under his breath.

Cale immediately began trying to scale the slimy pit

walls, but without success. "This is a bloody long way from Donnegal to die—for nothing," he whispered.

"We're nowhere near death yet, my young friend," the Boozer offered. The magician removed two small pellets from the lining of his cloak and rubbed them slowly. His palms began to glow a warm green color, the light spreading out gradually to illuminate the whole lower pit.

"There, now we can see what we're up against. Toobar, my little thief, find me a long, stout bone—one that won't break under your weight. Cale, take my cloak and tear it into long strands, then tie them together end on end—long enough to reach that window."

"Aye, then we'll climb out," Cale responded. "But what of the beasts?"

Toobar produced a tiny flute from inside his shoe and brandished it in the air as if it were a broadsword. He smiled and said, "Those creatures be no match for this little gem. Watch 'ere!"

He huffed and blew hard into the flute, but not a sound could be heard. Immediately, the ogrerats began to stir above them. Toobar blew again, and this time the ogrerats snarled and growled and shuffled around angrily on the catwalk. A third blow and all three of the horrible creatures took off up the stairs into the upper realm of the dungeon.

"They hear what we cannot," Toobar explained triumphantly. "Many a watch dog have I dispatched with this little tool. Makes thievin' a good deal easier, as you might say."

Cale slapped the Ferret on the back, practically knocking him down. "Ya dinna earn the name 'Ferret' without good reason, eh?"

"Quickly now, we've no time to waste," the Boozer ordered. "Make fast those strips. Hurry. Daynin and Sabritha are in great danger."

As Cale worked, a nagging question came to mind. "Boozer," he finally asked, "how is it that you know so much about this place?"

"I cannot answer that. You just have to trust me. And you must do exactly as I tell you. We will have but one chance to escape from here alive."

Cale couldn't contain his curiosity. "It's that stone in the back of your wagon, isn't it? That's what this is all about. That's what we've been brought here for." He threw down the cloth shreds to confront the Boozer face to face. Grabbing the old man's tunic and jerking him around he growled angrily, "You *knew* this would happen, didn't you?"

The magician maintained his composure and said quietly, "I told you not to come with us. I knew something like this *could* happen. That Stone is of greater value than you can begin to imagine—especially to the keeper of this place. He will do anything to possess its power. We are not important at all. The Scythian Stone is."

Cale backed off and stared in angry silence. "I've heard the legend of the Stone. I've also heard that it was destroyed by Norsemen because they feared its power. How is it that you came by it, old man?"

"We are here. It is here, and that is reality. If you do not help me, all of us will remain here forever! And that is no legend. Now, can I count on you, or do you wish to argue more while our chances of escape dwindle?"

Toobar stepped between the two to separate them. "Count on me," he boasted. "I've no wish to rot in this filthy hole."

"What is Daynin's part in this?" Cale demanded. "He is the reason I am here. For his sake, I will spend my life if that be the price of his freedom."

"I cannot tell you that, for I do not know. But if we

59

don't get out of here now, his life will mean nothing. Nor will yours. Now, let's get to work."

The upper reaches of the dungeon reeked of the smell of death from the cells below. Daynin's only escape from the nauseating odor was a small crack in the stone masonry that allowed outside air to penetrate. He leaned against the wall and pressed his face to the crack. He thought of home, and of the spicy porridge his grandfather made on Sundays. He could almost smell the flat bread cooking in the fireplace. Then he thought of Sabritha.

His mind jumped instantly to the wagon and his embarrassing episode in Sabritha's lap. He jerked his head from the crack, for a moment reliving that mysterious and wonderful event. He could feel the passion building in his stomach as the memory of her smell and of her soft, supple thighs engulfed him. Suddenly the room seemed less dark, less foreboding with her images all about him.

"Sabritha!" he cried out, his voice echoing time and again through the maze of narrow passageways outside the iron mesh gate. An ogrerat heard the cry and growled angrily somewhere in the darkness. In an adjoining passage, a much more intuitive pair of ears made note of the boy's obvious desires.

Exhausted from days without rest, Sabritha collapsed on the stone platform that lined one side of her tiny cell. She didn't hear the two paladins approach, but the creaking of her cell door brought her quickly back to reality. "What do you want?" she asked angrily.

The paladins clanked over to her in unison and swept her off the platform. Their cold iron gauntlets on her skin sent shivers throughout her body as she was lifted and dragged out of the cell.

"Where are the others? Where are you taking me?" she demanded.

There was, of course, no answer. The paladins dragged her up the steep, winding passageway toward the upper realm of the dungeon. There, in a well-adorned room with a large bed and a fireplace, they dropped her in a heap on the floor.

While Sabritha sat there pondering the warmth of the fire and her fate, an old woman entered the room. "Is there anything you require?" the scraggly voice asked.

Surprised by the visitor, Sabritha could think of nothing else to say, except, "Uhh—well, do you know where my friends are?"

The old woman put her serving tray down. Steam rose from a pot of tea as she poured Sabritha a cup. "Honey in your tea?" the woman offered.

"Uhh—yes, that would be nice," Sabritha replied, bewildered by the sudden show of hospitality. "Who are you?" she asked.

"Gretchin's my name, m'lady," the old woman purred. "I am here to serve you while you are our guest. I will be staying here with you for now."

Sabritha gulped down the cup of tea, quickly gesturing to Gretchin for another. "What about my friends?" she asked again.

"I know not of them, my lady," the old woman whispered plaintively. "But please. I have so few human visitors. Tell me of life outside these walls. Tell me how you came to be here. Tell me of sunshine and flowers and of all the wonderful things I've not seen these fifty years."

Completely taken in, Sabritha told Gretchin everything, including her growing desire to see Daynin again. By the third cup of potion-laced tea, she had told the Seed all he would need to know.

Chapter 8:

The Testing

"Sabritha! Wake up," Daynin pleaded. He shook her motionless body several times, then feared the worst. "Sabritha!" Her skin felt cold to his touch. Daynin began to panic. He shook her violently without result. He pinched her arm, and still there was no reaction. "God of life, if there be one, bring her back to me!" he begged.

He hesitated, then pulled the sheet back that covered her body. He placed his hand on her bare breast to feel for a heartbeat. Finding a faint rhythm, Daynin's own heart jumped with joy. "She's alive!" he cried out. He moved his hand slightly, then noticed the nipples of her breasts had hardened from his touch. He jerked his hand away and quickly pulled the sheet back over her chest.

"Day—nin?"

"Yes, Sabritha. Can you hear me?"

"Wha-a-at happened?" she whispered quietly.

The boy hesitated, then sat down on the edge of the bed, careful to maintain his distance. "I don't know," he replied. "Two paladins just brought me here from the dungeon. I-I thought—I was afraid you were—you weren't moving or anything."

"I feel so dizzy," she whispered slowly. She tried to sit up, and in doing so, allowed the sheet to fall away from her body.

Daynin admired her female beauty but turned quickly, as if to hide his embarrassment for having noticed anything.

"Sabritha, you—uhh—you don't have—uhm—I guess they took your clothes," he finally blurted out.

With that, Sabritha seemed to come fully awake. "No wonder I'm so cold," she said, reaching for the sheet. "You can look now, if you want to."

Daynin turned and smiled sheepishly, the blush still evident in his skin. He also adjusted his position on the bed in a vain attempt to hide the uncontrolled evidence of his desire. Sabritha smiled at Daynin's obvious predicament. "You know, you don't have to be ashamed of that. It's natural. And for a woman, it's very flattering to see a reaction like that from a man."

The word "man" surprised and delighted Daynin. "Uhh, I uhh, I wonder where the others are?" he said evasively. "We should try to get out of here if we can."

"Daynin, this place is too heavily guarded for us to go anywhere. Besides, what would you do if you could get out? We don't even know where we are. At least we've got a fire. And each other."

Those last words inflamed the passion in Daynin's stomach. He could feel the warmth of his blood coursing to one spot in his body. The excitement of the urge seemed to push all the air from his lungs. His head began to spin from the lofty heights to which his dreams were taking him. He tried in vain to forestall the intense desires he had felt for Sabritha since that first sight of her at the inn. He looked into her eyes, but images of her naked body completely obscured his vision. Words would not come to him. The blinding heat in his brain had all but taken over his senses.

"Daynin?" she said. "Daynin!"

He could barely answer. "Uhh, w-what?" was all he could say.

"Where are you?" she whispered, seductively. She

reached out and put her hand on his forearm.

He jerked it away as though it had been burned by a hot coal. Reality set in and again he blushed, the rush of blood to his face like that of a blacksmith's bellows on a fire. He jumped up from the bed and took several blind steps backward. His heel caught a crack in the floor and down he went, falling hard on the cold flagstones.

Sabritha lunged to try and catch him, but too late. She leapt from the bed to his side, seemingly unmindful that she was completely naked. "Are you hurt?" she cried out.

Daynin's eyes fixed on her chest as she leaned over him. Although stunned by the fall, he had hardly lost his senses *or* his urge. His hands seemed to have a mind of their own, suddenly, when he reached out to touch her sides. The feel of her warm, soft flesh caused his lower half to convulse. He shuddered, then pulled her down on top of him.

The taste of her lips was magic. One hand searched her body, feeling, touching, sensing with the ease of a practiced lover. The other sought the long black hair that covered her shoulders. Images of silk clouded Daynin's mind while his hands explored her skin, now afire with a growing passion at least as great as his.

Sabritha explored where Daynin had never been touched before. Her body moved in a slow, rhythmic motion, making his whole being quiver with her every touch. She kissed him again, sensing the imminent release of passion he'd only known in his boyhood dreams.

"Make love to me, Daynin," she whispered.

"But—Sabritha . . ." he could barely manage to say.

Sabritha kissed him again, then whispered, "We may die in this place, Daynin. Please. Give me one last taste of life."

Daynin rolled over, bringing Sabritha under him. He tore at the laces of his tunic, maddened by the difficulty of the task. She pulled at the cord of his breeches, trying in vain to loosen the tight pants. Daynin swooped down to kiss her chest, searching her body with his tongue, thence downward to her stomach. Suddenly, he stopped and pulled away abruptly.

Sabritha waited several long seconds before opening her eyes. He was staring back at her intently. "What's wrong? What's the matter with you?" she begged.

"I don't know," he answered, flatly. "There's something—I don't know . . ."

"Daynin, I *want* you. I want to *be* with you. Why do you hesitate?"

"I don't know. There's something wrong," he repeated, a trembling alarm in his voice.

"If you want me, too, there's nothing wrong with that."

"But you're not—the same," he whispered.

"Is it because you've never *been* with a woman?"

"No—well—yes, but that's not it. You're different, somehow."

Sabritha smiled and reached out for him. "Then you *are* a virgin, aren't you?" she said, her voice suddenly deepening.

"Yes, but, but, *you're not Sabritha!*" Daynin growled, recognition giving way to horror in his reply.

"Take him!" the voice from the courtyard boomed. Before Daynin's unbelieving eyes, Sabritha's image instantly changed to that of a shabbily attired, black-robed being whose long, bony face and hands appeared almost skeletal. Daynin realized it was the Seed just as two paladins stepped from the shadows of the room and grabbed his flailing arms.

"Bastard!" he screamed. "What have you done with Sabritha? Why have you *done* this to me?"

"A virgin proved by his own admission," the Seed

cackled aloud. With a sweeping motion of his arm, he ordered, "Take him to the Black Room, and bind him there. This virgin's blood will soon cleanse my Stone!"

"There! We've got it!" Cale hollered. He pulled the knotted rope tight, making sure the bone at the end did not slip out of the bars where he had skillfully tossed it.

The Boozer slapped Cale on the back for the accuracy of his throw. "Quickly, now, Toobar, up the rope," he said. "But beware of the ogrerats."

The little man blew his Egyptian flute once more, just to be on the safe side. He scaled the knotted rope with the skill of an acrobat and quickly gained the catwalk. He dropped the rope ladder for the others, then left to search the passageway for paladins. His three companions in the pit made it to the catwalk without a word. The soldier was last to climb, still deathly afraid of whatever came next.

"What now?" Cale asked, having decided that cooperating with the Boozer was his only reasonable chance of escape.

"We must find the others before it's too late," the old man answered.

Toobar reappeared in the passageway. "Paladins— coming this way," he said breathlessly.

"Against the wall, all of you," the Boozer said, motioning for them to take station against the circular wall where the paladins would not see them.

As the dark spectres entered the chamber, they each stopped at the edge of the pit, apparently confused by what they did not see. With one motion, Cale, Toobar and the Boozer shoved them from behind, sending them cascading into the pit. The paladins fell into a heap of clanking metal at the bottom and lay motionless.

The Boozer motioned for the group to follow. "The Seed

will soon realize what's happened. Quickly! To the upper dungeon."

"Who is this 'Seed'?" Cale asked as they ran.

"The master of Blackgloom," the Boozer answered. "He controls all but the ogrerats with his mind, so be careful you do not alert him to your presence. There's the way to the upper dungeon," he pointed out. "Go for the others. I must go this way. Escape if you can, but don't come back. One more thing—the Seed is limited on how many of the paladins he can control at once."

Cale grabbed Boozer's tunic. "Where are you going?" he demanded.

"Where you cannot follow. The evil in this place is far greater than I can begin to tell you. Hurry now, we have little time and much to do if we're to save the others."

The trio worked their way up the spiral passageway, checking each cell as they went. At the top of the dungeon, another paladin stood silent sentry next to an arched portal. There was no way to approach him without being seen, and it looked like the only way out.

"Let's rush him," Toobar suggested.

"We may not have to," Cale advised. He jerked an iron brad from his tunic and tossed it into the passageway. The paladin did not react. "Remember what the old man said? This one is not controlled."

Cale approached the sentry cautiously, then reached out to take his halberd. The sentry stood motionless, allowing Cale to take the weapon. "Help me with this," Cale ordered. Quickly, he donned the paladin's empty suit of armor.

Cale led the way through the portal, unsure what he might find on the other side. The great circular room stood empty. Passageways led off in six directions. He motioned for the others to go in front, acting as prisoners being led from one area to another. Two of the passages contained nothing but more empty cells. When they entered the third, they heard the distinct sounds of a woman crying.

"Where's it coming from?" Cale whispered. "I can't tell in this bloody helmet."

Just as they turned a corner, two paladins came straight for them, dragging a sobbing Sabritha in between. Cale froze in position to mimic his counterparts. Allowing the enemy to approach, he stepped in front of his two companions and delivered a crushing blow to the head of the left hand paladin, knocking its helm asunder. The other paladin dropped Sabritha's arm just in time to ward off a similar blow from Cale's halberd. The helmet-less body of the first paladin seemed to flail blindly at his attacker. Toobar grabbed for its sword, but was knocked flat from one swing of the paladin's mailed fist. The Duke's soldier turned to run, only to be speared by another paladin that appeared from behind them. Gutted, he fell without so much as a sound.

Sabritha screamed at the blood and gore splattering the passageway while Cale stunned the second paladin with a sharp blow to his helmet. He turned to face the new threat, but was knocked to his knees from behind by the headless paladin. Toobar recovered enough to reach for the legs of the headless paladin, felling him with a push. Cale looked up as the third paladin lunged toward him. He knew the battle might be over, for he hadn't the strength to resist another attacker. He brought his arm up to block the blow, but the paladin seemed to just stop in place. In an instant, the others did the same.

"We've won!" Toobar whooped.

"No," Cale answered. "Their master's been distracted, somehow. Remember what the magician said? Let's go while we can. This chance may not last very long."

Chapter 9:

The Conjuring

The Boozer followed the strong scent of bergamot and balm emanating from the floor above him. He recalled the Seed's fondness for the mixture of foul smelling oils in his early days as a magician's apprentice. Only now, the smell was heavily laden with the stench of death and decay that pervaded the whole of Blackgloom.

He scaled the last spiral of steep stairs carefully, not wanting to let the Seed know of his presence just yet. He gripped Merlin's black scroll tightly in one hand, a small crystal amulet in the other. Kruzurk Makshare was about to face the greatest peril of his life. He knew there would be no turning back once he had revealed himself. If his plan worked, he could put an end to an evil unlike any the land had seen before. If he failed, he knew the powers of darkness would prevail, perhaps forever.

A low, wicked chant was Kruzurk's first proof he had found the Seed's private and most secret of chambers. He crept silently to the entrance and peered through the inky yellow darkness. The glow of a large candle outlined the shadow of the Seed, kneeling and chanting before the Stone. The Stone stood against a wooden pillar in the middle of the room, supported by a strand of heavy rope tied to an iron bolt in the beam above it.

"Powers of darkness, powers of mine, make the Stone's secrets the Seed's to divine. Prince of all evil, from your well of fire, keen the gates open, bring me higher. Give me the power, great lord of the dark, with a virgin's blood, I'll make your mark."

Kruzurk shuddered at the horrible vows made by the sorcerer. He watched as the Seed turned to a large table. Daynin lay stretched across it, bound and gagged, unable to move. The Seed ripped off the boy's tunic. Kruzurk knew he could do little for Daynin, except watch and wait for the right opportunity to make his move. Hopefully, his chance would come before the Seed drew the blood he thought he needed to cleanse the Stone of any ancient spells.

The Seed turned back toward the Stone and repeated his ritual. Kruzurk knew, too, that he would do that thirteen times before the boy's blood was drawn, but he had no way of knowing how many incantations had already been uttered. From somewhere in the darkness of the room, Kruzurk could hear the labored breathing of an animal. A beast would be sacrificed on the eleventh chant, so he still had a little time to plan his move.

Sabritha sobbed quietly on the floor of the passageway, having all but given up to the dark powers of Blackgloom. Toobar tried in vain to reassure her that all was well, but she would not move. Cale tried to recover from the battle and the enormous effort it took for him to move in the heavy armor.

"We've—got to—get moving," Cale ordered. "Got to—find—Daynin—and get out—of this place."

"They took Daynin," Sabritha sobbed.

"Where?" Toobar asked.

Sabritha pushed herself from the floor, obviously trying to regain some of her composure. "I don't know. I don't even know *how* I know. I just know."

"Are you all right?" Cale asked her.

"They—they gave me something. I went to sleep. But I dreamed."

Toobar helped her to her feet, then asked, "What did you dream?"

"That someone else was me. That Daynin and I, we were in a room, and—I—I don't know. Something happened. They took him away. To a tower, where he—oh God! We've got to find him!"

"The old man said to get out if we could," Cale argued.

"But we have to *help* him, if we can," Sabritha continued. "It's—very important, somehow. More important than anything. Quickly, this way," she said, motioning for them to follow.

The Seed repeated his chant again, this time in reverse, as was the requirement. Kruzurk observed every movement, careful to note how long he turned away from the Stone each time. Those few seconds would be the only chance the magician would have to move unobserved across the room. He had to reach the Stone, as it would be his only protection from the awesome power the Seed could wield from his fingertips.

Kruzurk held his breath in anticipation of the next move. The Seed stood and turned to the table, allowing Kruzurk to move with the precision of a cat. The Seed opened a box on the table and drew a magnificent jeweled blade from it. The jewels in the handle sparkled from the candlelight, casting red and green reflections over the walls of the chamber. Kruzurk had managed to crawl half the distance across the floor toward the Stone before the ogrerat sensed his presence. He stopped when it began growling and snarling, jerking violently against its binding chains.

The Seed turned from the table and smiled at the beast. "Easy there, my pet," he whispered. "They are only colorful shadows on the wall. Come now, it is time for your part in this great moment."

Kruzurk crawled closer to the Stone, fearful that his heart pounded so loudly the Seed would surely hear him. The ogrerat growled and gnawed at its chains, doing its best to warn the master of the unseen enemy it knew to be present, but in vain. The Seed remained transfixed, rigid before his grotesque pet, with seemingly but one thought in his mind.

He raised the blade high over his head, chanting for the evil power the blade possessed. The tip of the knife glowed red, then white as heat traveled down to its grip. At the proper moment, the Seed stepped forward and plunged the blade to its hilt into the ogrerat's massive neck.

The beast let out the most horrendous of howls. Blood squirted from the gaping wound and the animal dropped to its haunches. The Seed took the ogrerat by its tusks and held its snout aloft as he finished severing the creature's head. Blood pumped wildly from the opened veins of the headless carcass, forming crimson rivulets on the flagstone floor. Kruzurk shuddered at the horror of the sight, but continued to crawl for the safety of the Stone.

The Seed brandished the beast's head above his own, gulping the thick red blood that gushed from the ogrerat's throat. He doused himself generously in the sanguineous flow, chanting the Latin death knell, *"Sic itur ad astra,"* like some mindless child at play in a horrible dream.

Kruzurk scurried behind the Stone while the Seed bathed himself in the ogrerat's blood. The magician knew the vile ceremony had almost reached its climax. He prepared himself mentally for the task ahead and prayed that the powers of light would be at hand to protect him, for he knew that little else of earthly value could.

"This way," Sabritha indicated, pointing to a long corridor that led to a set of steep, winding stairs. "He's up there, somewhere. I feel it," she said.

"Look out," Toobar cried out. "Ogrerats—behind us!" He reached for his flute and blew it for all it was worth, but without effect.

Cale turned and hollered, "What's wrong with you? Blow that damned thing!"

"My flute's bent!" Toobar screamed. "Must've happened in the fight."

Cale pushed Sabritha behind him and stepped out to face the first ogrerat, now only a huge, hairy blur as it charged out of the darkness. Toobar ducked when the beast launched itself from half way across the corridor. The animal slammed into Cale, sending him crashing against the wall. Cale's helmet flew off with the impact and he dropped his halberd. It was all he could do to jam his armored forearm into the beast's massive jaws to stave off its gnashing teeth. Sabritha grabbed the loose helmet and began beating the animal on its rock-hard skull, with no effect.

Toobar managed to engage the second ogrerat with Cale's halberd. That quickly proved to be a mismatch. The diminutive little man had neither the strength nor the skill to battle the monster for long.

Cale struggled to pull his dirk from its scabbard, but the weight of the ogrerat made that all but impossible. Sabritha ran to the end of the corridor, jerked down a lantern and poured its oil into the helmet. She ripped a shred from her gown and lit it from another lantern, then rushed back to the fight.

"Cale! Cover your face," she screamed. Hesitating only a second, she threw the oil on the ogrerat's back and ignited it.

The animal's fur burst into flame and it bellowed in agony, its scream releasing Cale's arm. Cale had the chance he needed to draw his weapon and in a flash, he slit the ogrerat from belly to throat, almost drowning himself in the creature's foul smelling innards. The huge animal groaned once more and collapsed on top of its killer.

Toobar was quickly losing his fight with the other ogrerat, but he had inflicted several bloody wounds on the beast in the process. Sabritha helped Cale escape from under the blazing carcass and get to his feet, though they were an instant too late for Toobar. With one mighty leap, the ogrerat toppled the Ferret, bending him over backwards and snapping his spine like a twig. The beast stopped only long enough to tear a great chunk from Toobar's throat, thus finishing its helpless prey.

Sabritha screamed again, then wilted against the wall. Cale had only time enough to unsheathe his broadsword as the animal catapulted from Toobar's lifeless body. Fortunately, the broadsword was well aimed, penetrating completely through the creature's neck, severing its jugular, and killing the beast instantly. Cale fell backward under the weight of the monster.

Just then, a horrible, unearthly wail emanated from the stairwell somewhere above them. The sound echoed time and again through every hall of the Blackgloom keep.

Chapter 10:

The Crushing

The Seed turned back to the table where Daynin struggled against his bindings. He held the ogrerat's head in his left hand and pulled Daynin's gag free with the other.

"Drink of the beast's blood, and your life will be spared. Come in to the darkness, and my power you'll share. Refuse this oath and your life you will give, for your heart I will take that my power shall live," the Seed chanted. "What say you, boy? Open thy mouth and receive the blood of darkness."

Daynin jerked hard on his bonds with one last effort to break free. Then he screeched, "Bastard son of a snake! I'll die before I become a part of this."

"See this?" the Seed boasted, shoving the ogrerat's head in Daynin's face. "Your head will soon be its mate on my mantle. Is that what you want? Or would you prefer to spend eternity here with the woman. Several women. All the women you want, in fact."

"Sabritha's alive?" Daynin asked.

"Alive and waiting for you. Or for me, if that be what you choose. She's a sprightly wench, that one. I like the fire in her. Took three cups of my potion to bring her down. That was a first."

"Bring her here that I might see she's alive," Daynin offered, "then if you swear to free her, I'll join you in this hell."

"Not that it matters, but she's on her way here as we speak. And you are in no position to demand a thing. Remember? My house, my rules. You will do as I say, or I'll put the woman's lifeless head in your lap."

"What of the others?" Daynin asked.

"Ah, the others. An old fool, a young fool, a thief and a coward. What a gang of rescuers. The last I thought of them, they were working their way out of the dungeon, but that's been tried before. Which reminds me—how did you know that I was not the real Sabritha? I thought I did an admirable job of recreating her, especially the way I made her body respond to you."

"She would never have acted that way toward me," Daynin lamented.

"Ah, but that's where you're wrong, boy. I've studied her thoughts. I've even talked to her about you. Of course, she didn't know it was me, at the time. But she told me all about you—how she owed her life to you."

Just then, the chamber's door burst open. "Cowardly son of the darkness!" Sabritha screamed from behind them. She hurled Cale's dirk at the sorcerer's unprotected back.

The Seed waved his hand in the air. The dirk seemed to bounce off an invisible shield that surrounded him. "See," he laughed, "I told you she was coming!" He turned and leveled both hands at the woman, chanting, "*Amal Matrach, Dein Bei!* Spirits—take her away." The spell threw the woman hard against the wall, knocking her unconscious.

Cale stepped forward and launched his halberd with all his might. The Seed slapped it down just as it reached him, causing the heavy spear to glance off the face of the Scythian Stone. The sharp point of the halberd splintered when it struck, cracking the Stone's corner in the process.

The Seed let out a deafening roar. His anger swelled while he gathered strength for one of his most powerful spells. Cale stood motionless, facing his enemy, sensing that he had only seconds to live. The Seed leveled his arms again and chanted in Latin, this time sprouting an enormous yellow blaze from his fingertips. Flames exploded across the room, engulfing its target. Cale could do little to withstand the attack. The paladin's armor became a flaming coffin, his body instantly turning to ashes from the terrible heat.

Daynin writhed in agony and screamed at his tormentor, "Stop it! I'll do what you ask. Don't kill them!"

Kruzurk knew his opportunity fast approached. The combined effect of the incantations and the spells the Seed had just cast would likely have drained the sorcerer of much of his power. Cale's death weighed heavily on the magician but he prepared to stand up to the Seed anyway. He hoped that Sabritha had survived, but decided that, too, was something he could not change. Daynin's life hung in the balance, and that was the one thing Kruzurk could do something about.

The Seed dropped to his knees in front of the Stone. He ran his hands along the cracked edge, and sobbed quietly, "It could only be broken by sorcery. It can only be repaired by the same." He began to chant a new spell, "*Nexus, vinculum and trennel.* Powers be free, funnel through me, and mend what could not be broken."

Kruzurk waited, knowing that the Seed's futile efforts to repair the Stone would serve to further weaken him. He could tell with each successive chant that the Seed's strength was failing. His great gamble might just pay off, after all.

The Seed finally turned away from the Stone. He stood up and grabbed the jeweled knife. "To hell with it," he cursed. "The Stone will work, even if it's cracked. And your blood will seal the bargain," he swore to Daynin.

He raised the dagger, poised to plunge it into Daynin's chest.

Then Kruzurk finally stood up. "Hold, evil one!" he demanded.

The Seed turned about, his eyes flashing with anger. "Roaches!" he swore. "You're like cockroaches, coming out of every crevice. That shall be your punishment for having interrupted my pleasure, old man."

"You are, indeed, an evil one. Just as Merlin said," Kruzurk answered, intending to draw as much anger from the Seed as possible.

The Seed raised his arms, bent on dashing the new tormentor with a spell, but he hesitated. "What do you know of Merlin, old man? He's been worm meat for more than seventy years."

"Do you not recognize a fellow apprentice?"

"No, and no one else will after I've turned you into a cockroach."

"It is I, Kruzurk Makshare."

"Impossible. I put a curse on him that would drive a man to madness."

"Yes, and I still carry that curse," Kruzurk said, shaking his filthy hair loose from under a tight mesh cap.

"So! You've come back to test me, eh?" the Seed boasted.

"No. To stop you."

"Stop me, indeed. I can crush you with one word, fool."

"I think not. Remember this?" Kruzurk said, brandishing the opened black scroll in his hand.

The Seed gasped at the unexpected display. "Where— how the devil did you get that? I thought I destroyed that, along with everything else before I left the guild."

"Merlin gave it to me. It is your apprentice bond. Signed with your own blood. Do you remember? You swore to uphold the magician's oath and that if you did not, you would kneel before the bearer of this document and recant your sorcerous ways."

"Ha!" the Seed laughed. "Those old crow-baits—they've no power over me, and I'll prove it!" Looking upward, he raised his empty hand into the air, and pointed the other one at the bond.

The oilskin scroll burst into flames, its contents dripping as the skin was instantly consumed. Kruzurk held the amulet under the flow of droplets, smiling and allowing a critical part of his ploy to reach completion.

He held the amulet aloft and laughingly taunted the Seed, "Only through sorcery can a sorcerer be quelled! Do you recognize this?"

Dead silence reigned in the chamber. Then the Seed gasped, "Merlin's amulet! And my blood is upon it!"

The Seed lunged at Kruzurk with his jeweled knife. Kruzurk dodged behind the Stone, knocking the blade aside with his arm. The Seed slashed again, cutting a small wound in Kruzurk's hand and causing him to drop the amulet at the base of the Stone. Slashing a third time, his blade missed its mark and cut cleanly through the rope that held the Stone in place. Kruzurk backed up, watching the heavy Stone begin to topple.

"Look out!" he warned, but too late.

With a deafening roar, the Stone crashed down onto the Seed, instantly crushing him like a mealy bug. Brains, blood and gore exploded all over the floor.

"You're finished, Seed! Dead by your own hand," Kruzurk crowed.

"Boozer—" Daynin whispered, his voice hoarse from screaming, "help me."

Kruzurk stepped to Daynin's side. He freed the boy's hands and helped him up on the table.

"What happened, Boozer?" Daynin asked, weakly. "How

did you—oh God," he gasped as he saw the gory scene around him.

"It's actually Kruzurk, or Kruze, as my friends call me. But never mind that now. You best see to the woman. She'll be needing you."

"But Booz, uhh—Kruze, I don't understand. How did you—how do we get out of . . ."

"So many questions, boy. As for the Stone, this one's a fake—carved by my own hand. No one knows where the real one is. I needed the fake to fool the Seed into bringing us here. Our whole journey was made for that purpose. We would never have gotten close to this place without it."

Daynin rubbed his shoulders to regain some circulation. Then it struck him, what Kruzurk had said. "This whole adventure was *planned?* You used us to get in here? Curse you, magician! Cale would still be alive if not for you!" he snapped.

"No, Daynin, he likely would not. Cale had already given up his life for a vow of vengeance against the Duke. Except for me, you would have never met with Sabritha, and the Seed would still be conjuring his evil over this land. Some things are worth dying for. I am truly sorry for deceiving you, but you have helped to rid the land of one of its greatest evils. For that, I and many others will forever be in your debt."

Daynin stumbled to Sabritha's side, more concerned with her life than his own at that moment. He leaned down close to her and put his ear to her chest. The rhythmic beat continued, along with the sweet smell of her body that with all his sorcerous ways, the Seed had been unable to duplicate.

"Sabritha," he whispered, "it's Daynin. The Seed is finished."

She reached out slowly to stroke his cheek. "Then take me home, plowboy. I've had all the adventure I can stand for a while."

Chapter 11:

The Plotting

D'Argent slammed his heavy gauntlets on the table and swore, "I tell you, Sire, I saw the whole thing with my own eyes! The magician's wagon, our men and horses—the whole lot was carried away by a boiling cloud with a great, huge, greenish black tendril. Never have I seen the like."

"Just picked up like some reaper's chaff in a wind storm, were they?" Duke Harold scoffed. "After the way those blaggard troops of yours let that boy escape from the Al Cazar, I should have had you flogged, then and there, Captain." As if to emphasize the point, Harold let fly his heavy tankard of ale, sailing it past D'Argent's helm, barely grazing his lieutenant, Geile Plumat.

D'Argent swept the helmet from off his head and bellowed, "Sire! I will not be treated like some gatewatch nawdry!"

Three strides and the Duke was in the Captain's face, his jeweled stiletto poised a mere blink from D'Argent's chin. "Twenty of your best men outwitted by an old fool and a boy and *now* I learn that towheaded son-of-a-Scotian whore is the very one who sent my own cousin to an early Hell."

Plumat stepped forward to mediate before things got out of hand. "Had we known they were the Marquis' assassins, m'lord . . ."

"Plumat, you and Captain D'Argent never seem to *know* anything until every barmaid in the village has passed the news amongst them. Has there been no trace of these people and my treasure since last you saw them at the bridge?"

Plumat took a long draw from the tankard of warm ale, hoping the blade poised at D'Argent's throat was just another of the Duke's errant threats. In all the time he had served the man, not once had the Duke ever drawn blood from one of his own. "No, Sire, we have *seen* nothing of them, although there *are* rumors of a Blackgloom keep in ruins and some kind of great treasure having been found there."

"Rumors? You think I should govern the north of Britain based on rumors, Plumat?" The stiletto found its way back into the hidden sheath inside the Duke's leather armlet. Captain D'Argent relaxed visibly. The Duke turned on his heel to face Plumat, the finest swordsman in his garrison.

"Of course not, Sire," Plumat offered, relieved at not having to witness the Captain's immediate demise. "But neither can we launch a war in Scotia to find some strawboy and a magician. You would be the laughing stock of Anglia were that to happen. King Ethelred would have to be informed and your holdings on the border reinforced. All that aside, from what our spies tell us, the Scythian Stone was destroyed, along with the great wooden keep and its hundred men-at-arms."

Duke Harold's face turned the shade of his scarlet tunic. The realization of having lost the Scythian Stone was almost more than his temper could bear. "This highlander and his wench bested a keep and a hundred men-at-arms? Then destroyed *my* magical stone in the process? I think not, Plumat. I think mayhaps your spies are a drunken lot with naught but wild tales to spin."

"Well, they *did* have a powerful magician to help them, Sire, or so I was told."

Captain D'Argent cleared his throat, probably overjoyed by the fact that he still had one. "Sire? There is considerable talk of that treasure the boy and the old man unearthed, so it must be true. Might I suggest we post bounties along the border for news of that? Those Caledonians up north would sell their mothers for a handsome booty such as we could offer."

"Aye, that's a plan worth its salt," Plumat agreed. "The treasure and the boy won't be far apart, you can wager on that."

The Duke plunged his fist into a wooden trencher on the table, still holding the Captain's uneaten supper of barley wisp and hen meat. Debris splattered all over the front of D'Argent's hauberk. "We? Are you offering to pay this reward, Captain?" the Duke demanded. He wiped his greasy hand on D'Argent's chainmail, then strode purposefully toward the round stone hearth in the center of the galleyway.

"We are merely brokering an alternative for you, m'lord," D'Argent's somewhat shaky voice managed to utter. "A plan which suggests, on the one hand, that you think little of this boy and his wench, and that you therefore choose not to traipse about the wilds of Scotia to find him. Whilst, on the other hand, the bounty you post sends a message to every great hall in the highlands that Duke Harold is a man not to be scoffed."

Turning his back to the roaring fire, the Duke's glare fell upon Plumat's narrow frame. "Plumat, *you* will go to the Scotian border. You will announce a one hundred talen bounty for information. You will post it on every hut, hovel and whore's haunt from the Tweed River Bridge in the east to the Solway Firth in the west. Is that clear?"

"Yes, m'lord," Plumat answered smartly.

"Then you will proceed to Galashiels across the border

and employ a squad of men. Hire only men from that area, so they may travel unnoticed in Scotia. You will pay them five talens each, with a further contract of twenty talens if they bring that boy back across the Tweed alive. Have him and the wench taken to Tendalfief. Those two will stand trial under the King's Eyre, and be hanged for their foul deeds. And while you are about it, offer a pittance reward for the old man—or wizard or whatever he is."

Plumat grabbed his helmet in one hand, and a cold hen's leg in the other. "It shall be as you wish, Sire. That boy will find himself facing your jurists before the next moon or I, Geile Plumat, will stand trial in his stead."

"Just do as I tell you, Plumat," the Duke growled. "I find no joy in the prospect of having you hanging from my gallows. Seize that towheaded boy and I will add two hides of land to your holdings in Cumberland. Bring justice to the slayers of the Marquis, and the Blackgloom treasure to me, and I shall grant you a Captaincy with a parcel of land from my own holdings there as well."

Plumat bowed from the waist, his risky gamble having won a great honor from the Duke. "Your command is my destiny, Sire. I leave tonight. The Blackgloom Bounty is as good as yours."

Daynin's first visit to the great cathedral compound at Abbotsford was seven years in the past, yet he could still remember every detail, every structure his father had pointed out to him from the top of the rocky cairn that marked the priory's southernmost boundary. Despite the years, Daynin could tell that not much had progressed on the nave of the church or the score of outbuildings. Money was scarce, as were the skilled masons needed to move the work along. *That is about to change,* Daynin vowed as he slowed

Abaddon and the heavily laden cart to a stop.

Abbotsford had been his father's greatest ambition. All of the precious McKinnon library was to be brought to the priory for safe keeping once the nave of the church was finished, so that others in the highlands might learn from the books and benefit from the knowledge they contained. That ambition, like many of his father's dreams, had been slain on the bloody slopes of Rhum on Daynin's twelfth birthday.

Not only had the invaders nearly wiped out the family McKinnon that night, they had also burned all the books, maps, drawings and a hundred years of McKlennan Clan treasures which were destined for the priory at Abbotsford. None of that could ever be replaced, and Daynin knew it. But he also reckoned the vast wealth they had just liberated from Blackgloom presented a way to resurrect his father's dreams. A dead sorcerer's horde could educate an entire generation of Scotian clansmen, so that one day Daynin's kinsmen might face the Britons on their own terms.

His father had taught him well the value of words and education. Daynin had seen it used firsthand in his adventures with Kruzurk Makshare. He had vowed upon the ashes of Blackgloom that only good would come of the treasure they unearthed from that foul place. Daynin would see to it that the cathedral was finished, and at least some of the books provided that his people so desperately needed.

"This is the place my father brought me when I was ten years old," Daynin half whispered to Sabritha, crouched beneath him in the back of the magician's cart.

Sabritha snuggled closer under the heavy flaxen blanket that had provided her only protection from the mist and cold since leaving Blackgloom. After several long days of jostling, she seemed to care little where they were or where they were going, perhaps longing only for a fire to warm her tired body.

"So this is where you're taking me? These are the great McKinnon lands you talked about? I see only rocks, gorse and more rocks. You highlanders seem to have a strange want for desolate and rocky places. I swear, if not for all the booty you and the old man took from the Seed, I might well have stayed behind where there were trees and people."

Daynin turned around to look at her, curled into a ball on top of the four large chests the cart contained. "I plan to give the priory some of the treasure, Sabritha. It is what my father would have wanted. I'm also going to have a stone raised for Cale and Toobar, even though I didnae know them that well. They paid a high price for our freedom and it should not be forgotten."

"Oh! Well, that just makes me warm all over, plowboy! If you had told me that before we left the Northumbrian forests, I would have saved us both a lot of trouble. Now, not only am I to be a beggar again, I'm destined to be carted around in this craggy wasteland with little more than a blanket to call my own."

"We're still many leagues from Rhum and what remains of Kinloch Keep. It may take a week or more just to reach Glasgow, where we will take a ship to Rhum. But you will not be poor, Sabritha. Trust me."

"Trust you? Oh, I *trust* you all right. I trust you to offer a long trip on a short rope for me, or worse, if the Duke finds us. And what ship? You said nothing about that! I thought your home was in Scotia, not on the ocean sea. I've no desire to become a sailor's wench, if that is your plan."

Daynin couldn't help but chuckle at Sabritha's surly attitude. She had been through a lifetime of nightmares since the last moon, to be sure. She had seen more death and destruction than a keep full of Caledonian mercenaries, and yet, she could still make him smile with her sharp wit and that tantalizing voice—not to mention her comment about being his wench.

"Rhum is a beautiful island off the coast of Scotia, Sabritha. A boat is the only way to get to it. We will be safe there, and with the part of the treasure I plan to keep to rebuild Kinloch, you will be very comfortable for a long time, I promise you."

Sabritha rolled on her side, grasping the blanket even closer. "I don't suppose I have a say in this. And I don't hold much stock in promises. All I know is, you better find me some place warm and in a hurry, plowboy, or I may freeze to death keeping your 'booty' warm."

Daynin's frosty cheeks reddened, then wrinkled. But, she was right. It was getting colder, the day nearly gone, and old Abaddon's stride had slowed to a half walk under the weight of the treasure creaking along behind him in the muddy track. The huge solid wheels of the cart were almost completely caked in mud, making progress all the more difficult.

Flipping the reins over, Daynin guided Abaddon off the track, his target the prior's hutch at the rear of the cathedral grounds. They would be welcome there, and mostly unnoticed, of that he was fairly certain.

Prior Bede had been the driving force at the great cathedral works for more than a score of years and a friend of the McKinnons for even longer. As Daynin pulled the cart to a stop near the swine bays, Bede appeared from an outhouse behind them.

"Hold! Who goes there? This is consecrated ground, I warn ye!" he growled.

"Your raspy voice has changed as little as your girth, Prior," Daynin cried out, laughingly. "You said the same thing to my father some years back. He paid as little mind to you then as do I, this frosty afternoon."

For a man of sixty, who was considerably more portly than the average inn keeper, Prior Bede danced lively around the muddy hog pits to get a closer look at his unwanted guests. "Who is your father? And what business have ye here? I've no booty, if that be yer game."

Daynin slid off the cart seat, flipping back his hood, and stepped forward to greet the old man. "Perhaps your memory is better for faces than voices, Father. It is I, Daynin McKinnon, returned to visit."

"McKinnon? Of the Clan McKlennans and Kinloch Keep? This cannot be. I was told you were all dead, slain by a band of Caledonian killers."

Sabritha pushed herself off the back of the cart, stretching her legs. "Good, we've finally reached a place with a roof over it. Can we hold this happy reunion inside, where I can get warm?"

"Caesar's Legions!" the Prior howled. "Ye've brought a female into my priory? This is no place for a woman. Get thee gone, now, or I'll be takin' a staff to both of you!"

"Speaking of Legions, Prior, I have something for you in the wagon. It is an illustrated copy of *Caesar's Commentaries*, complete with the seal of the *Ordre de la Rose Croix Veritos*."

"Aye, and I suppose you will be telling me next that the Bishop of York is on his way to personally bless me next week," the fat little man scoffed.

"No, Father. But when you see these books, you can invite him for prayers," Daynin parried.

The Prior stepped closer to get a good look at Daynin. "Are these books of yours written in that awful hand of the Burgundian monks?"

Daynin retrieved the first volume from his haversack and held it out. "No, Father, they are in the original Latin. You will have no need of a Burgundian translator to read them."

Both the Prior's attention and his demeanor immediately shifted from ire to desire with the realization of such an immense treasure within his grasp. He took the proffered manuscript and barked, "Come in, boy, and bring yer ancillae along. I have fish gruel and roots. We'll have us a draft and discuss yer needs whilst we sup."

Sabritha's face lit up with anger. "What did he call me?"

"*Ancillae*, it's an old word," Daynin hedged.

"Do I look haggard enough to be your aunt? That old fool is blind as well as rude."

One look at Prior Bede's surprised expression brought Daynin a chuckle. "It means *slave*, Sabritha. Female slave, to be exact. And I'm sure Prior Bede meant nothing by it. The Romans brought that word to this land a long time ago."

Sabritha slogged past Daynin and the Prior without saying a word. She was obviously anxious to get inside, despite having to share space with a man of The Cross. Having never understood their piety or their poverty, at the moment gruel and roots sounded very inviting to her, even from a humble prior's pot.

Twenty leagues to the southwest of Abbotsford stood the Lanercost Priory, a half day's ride east of the ancient Anglian shiretown of Carlisle. Unlike the Bede's modest holdings, Lanercost boasted the best collection of books north of York, and had always been a magnet for learned men from around the world. Kruzurk Makshare had been there for two days, quietly studying among the manuscripts when the terrible news reached him.

"Mediah, are you certain this writ is genuine?" Kruzurk asked, his eyes never leaving the damp and badly smudged scrap of parchment he had just been handed.

"Yes, I am, learned one. Writs such as that one have spread through the whole of northern Anglia, almost overnight." The other man leaned closer, so as to talk somewhat softer. "A friend of yours at Hawick across the frontier sent this one by runner as soon as they saw your name on the warrants."

"I am not concerned about me. But this writ includes Daynin and the woman, although these likenesses are hardly distinct. I was afraid this would happen once the Duke learned the truth about the Marquis' death at the Never Inn. Daynin and Sabritha are at great risk, and that is my fault."

"Aye, the Duke must know the whole story by now, Kruze. To offer a bounty of this size is unusual, even for the worst criminals. Such a prize is too great for all but the laziest blaggard to ignore. I fear for you here, so close to the frontier. With both Anglian and Scotian bounties after you, there can be no safe place to hide. You must quit this place, straightaway."

"Can you get me a horse, Mediah? A good mount—one I can ride for a day and a night, without falter?"

Mediah's eyes scanned the dozen or so scholars seated around the fire in the middle of the priory's central reading room. None seemed to have taken notice of their conversation, but he could not be certain they had not overhead his excited news. "A boat, uh certainly uh, Thomas," he said loud enough to be heard over the crackle of the fire. "I should be able to arrange passage to Normandy for you from Tynemouth, say, three days hence?"

Kruzurk winked at his olive-skinned cohort's quick wit, then waved a small pouch toward him. "Excellent. This should cover our passages, my friend. You will be going along, of course? I hear the tapestries at Bayeux are worth the trip, and being an artist, your ability with the brush should make for some interesting interpretations."

"You're most kind, m'lord. I will be delighted to accompany you."

Sabritha stepped through the low arched doorway and down onto the dirt floor of the priest's hovel. She seemed unfazed by the Spartan furnishings. It was the enormous hearth that drew her attention. It had an overly large opening with a cook pot hanging in it big enough to feed the Duke's army. The odor of gruel mixed with wood smoke hung in the air, pungent, full of garlic and onions. She hesitated, as though wanting desperately to grab a trencher and dip it into the bubbling stew.

The Prior's dark coif appeared in the doorway behind Sabritha, followed by his considerable girth. Daynin stepped through and closed the door, his haversack tucked snugly under his arm.

"Daynin, I confess I have little recall of yer last visit here, but I am very happy that ye survived that bloody business at Kinloch Keep."

"Thank you, Prior. If not for my grandfather, the Mc-Kinnon line would have surely come to an end that black night. I will never forget the smell of those books burning, mingled with the flesh of my kinsmen."

The Prior shucked off his cloak, splattering the room with moisture. "Aye, the books! That was a bounty I had great stock in receiving from your clan. We may never see the likes of those books again."

"Never is a long time, old friend," Daynin said. He hefted the haversack onto the table, flipped it open and stood back so the Prior could have a closer look.

Sabritha cleared her throat loudly, then asked, "Can we

eat now? Or are you two going to spy those books all night?"

Tears welled in Prior Bede's eyes, and not from the strong scent of garlic hanging in the smoky confines of the room. He reached out to run his chubby fingers over the gold inlaid backing of the largest volume. He stared at the book before him, then at the others. "This is too great a treasure for me to imagine. These texts are like none I have ever seen, and you say it's a complete set? Where did you acquire them?"

Daynin was almost ashamed to admit that they had been part of the Blackgloom Bounty, but he knew the Prior would never accept them if he didn't have the whole truth of their origin. "They come from a dark place, Father. Some would say a cursed place full of evils from which the worst nightmares must surely come."

The Prior lurched backwards instantly, throwing his hands up as if the fires of hell had scorched them. He made the sign of the cross in the air, then bellowed, "Beasts and boogers, boy! Ye've brought the devil's spoils into a House of God? What foul manner of deceit is this?"

Momentarily taken aback by the Prior's sudden swearing and animated gestures, Daynin stood there, speechless. He looked at Sabritha, but she could only shrug.

"Father, I'm sorry! Truly I am," Daynin offered. "I should have told you outside, but I refuse to believe these books are cursed. They contain knowledge, and knowledge is for good, not evil."

The Prior slumped back onto the stone hearth, his bald head now covered with beads of sweat. "I need beer. Fetch me that pail, girl, and be quick about it!" he growled.

Sabritha handed him the heavy, three stone's bucket and waited as the Prior gulped the contents without so much as a gasp of air. "I could use a draft of that myself, if there's any to be spared for guests."

"Guests is it, now, eh?" he snapped, wiping his mouth on his frock.

"Yes, Prior," Daynin said, stepping between them to take the considerably lightened bucket. He handed it to Sabritha and added, "If we could but stay the night, I have important things to discuss with you. I want to help you finish the nave, in the name of my father."

An enormous belch preceded the next words out of the Prior's mouth. *"Finish the nave?* Indeed, boy! Then I hope ye've brought more than manuscripts, because I can't pay masons and carpenters with words or books."

"Aye, that I have, Prior. You shall see—that I have."

Chapter 12:

The Scheming

Galashiels was its normal bustling place on market day, full of the usual assortment of tanners, tillers, taletellers and thieves. Plumat dragged the heavy rumpbag off the rear of his steed, staggering slightly from the weight of the chest inside as he hefted it over his shoulder. He waved for his escorts to stay mounted, then headed for the Sheepstow Tavern.

Plumat's stagger did not go unnoticed by the host of evil eyes watching him from inside the tavern. His black chainmail marked him as a nobleman, or a nobleman's thegn, even though his maize and scarlet heraldry could not be seen by the watchful coven inside.

"Mark this bloody henchman well, lads," came a raspy warning from one of the Caledonian clansmen. "He's got booty in that 'ere bag o' his, I wager."

"Aye, Scarba," old Jack Scurdie agreed. "Him and 'is lot be the ones who been postin' those writs 'long the frontier, fer sher. I seen 'em wi' me own peeper, I did." That brought a round of raucous laughter from the drunken lot, one-eyed Jack having been the butt of many a bar room skit by those still possessing both their eyes.

Plumat strode purposefully through the door of the tavern, brushing past a dozen well armed men, then slung his heavy load up onto the bar board. "Ale for the first ten men who can read, quencher!" he crowed loudly. "And a pail of beer for those who can't."

A small stampede of ragged, stinking bodies rushed forward, almost toppling the bar board from its barrelheads. A loud "hurrah" swept away the silence of the room while a hefty five stone's pail began passing from hand to mouth, not a single man having taken the offer of ale.

Scarba pushed his way through his mates to stand tipsy toed to Plumat. "What's yer doings 'ere, Sir Fancy, if I may be so bold?"

Plumat grimaced at the man's breath, which was almost as hideous as his pox ruined face and snaggle-tooth grin. "I've a handsome bounty to offer those who can handle the task."

"Task is it?" Scarba growled. "We be Caledonians 'ere, not some lot who be lookin' fer a stint shoveling swine guts. Eh, lads?"

Plumat allowed the grumbling and guffawing to die down, then replied, "I've a boy who needs finding, and I've come with bounty enough to make it worth your while. There be five talens in it for the taking, and a contract of twenty more when the boy is handed to the Sheriff at Tendalfief within a fortnight."

"A boy, says you?" grumbled a gaggle of men, almost at once.

Scattering a pile of silver talens onto the bar board from his rumpbag, Plumat declared, "Aye, and his wench, and the spoils they be hauling. And there's another ten in it for the head of an old man they call 'the Boozer' who poses as a magician."

"Magicians, mopboys and mizztresses," one-eyed Jack sang out, having had the last heavy draw on the pail of beer. He fell backward in a drunken heap against his mates, bringing another hearty laugh from the Caledonians.

"What'd this 'ere 'boy' do? Bespoil the virtue of some nobleman's daughter?" Scarba demanded, his finger poking ominously into Plumat's chest.

In the flash of a fly's flutter, Plumat drew his dagger and thrust it dangerously close to Scarba's left eye. "You cross me, blaggard, and there'll be *two* one-eyed drunks on the floor of this haunt before you can say 'aye m'lord'!"

That got the attention of the assembled masses. They backed away from Scarba to distance themselves from the carnage they knew a well armed man could bring when wielding a Kensian blade as long as a forearm.

Scarba went limp at the prospect of his imminent blinding. His voice changed instantly to that of a whipped dog. "Meanin' no harm, yer Lordship. I was just wonderin' what this 'ere boy is to you, and should we be needin' a gang to grasp 'im, or can a couple of me stouter mates do the job?"

Plumat shoved Scarba back, and with a flick of his wrist, stabbed one of the talens in its center. He waved it aloft and taunted, "This is all you need to worry about, knave. Bring the boy, and you get paid. Fail in the attempt, and this blade may find its way to your gullet. And another thing. I have cohorts who watch my back constantly, should any of you think me the fool and try to gain your bounty with a foul deed. Now, which of you is man enough to step forward and best a towheaded boy and his wench?"

Mediah the Greek and Kruzurk Makshare rode a measured gait for two full leagues to the east of Lanercost Priory before drawing their steeds to a gradual stop. The ancient boundary of Hadrian's Wall marked the turning point for their journey north, and was far enough east that any who might have followed would think they had continued on to the port of Tynemouth.

"Turn in here, Mediah," Kruzurk ordered, waving toward the remains of a half hidden Roman fort that would offer them a concealed view of the road. "We should wait here, to ensure that no one follows. The horses need a rest, too, that we may make our dash for the frontier before it gets any darker."

"As you wish, m'lord."

"Mediah, you need not address me that way when we are alone. I have no regal lineage. That moniker is only to fool strangers whilst we travel together, you know."

Mediah gathered his long robe, threw one leg over his steed's head and slipped to the gravel, grabbing the halter of Kruzurk's mount as he hit the ground running. "I know, m'lord, but it is the custom, even among my people. Besides, I owe you for saving me from that black hole of the Seed's dungeon. If you and your friends had not come along when you did, the Seed planned to skin me alive. He believed me to be a daemon spirit, you know."

Kruzurk dismounted, rubbing his sore backside to relieve the unaccustomed pain that was growing there. "I know, Mediah. One does not see many travelers as dark as you in this part of the world. Your rather exotic heritage would tell another tale altogether, I should think."

"My mother was Persian, m'lord. I'm told my line stems from one of Alexander the Great's cavalry commanders. My father came from Jerusalem. I know nothing of his lineage. But somewhere beyond Persepolis I have family, though I have never seen them. Those twelve years I slaved in the bow of a Silesian galley never got me any closer to them—or to home."

"Perhaps we can remedy that some day, Mediah. I would very much like to visit the classic Greece I have only read about all these years." Kruzurk rubbed his backside again and groaned slightly. "I also wish I had kept my wagon and old Abaddon. This riding through hill and dale like some knight errant is hardly to my liking."

Mediah raised his hand, cocked one ear to the light wind, and whispered, "Shhh!" He hesitated for a few seconds, then declared, "Horses. Three, perhaps four. Two furlong, coming from the west."

By then, Kruzurk could hear the rumble himself. They were heavy mounts, running at full gallop. He grasped his and Mediah's reins and herded the two horses toward the blind end of the fortress walls, out of sight of the road, and waited.

Sabritha's mind had wandered to the far reaches of a home she only vaguely remembered, and of a father she remembered all too well, but never really knew. His had been the one shining image she clung to on the darkest nights, the coldest days and through the worst moments of her life. She had thought of him that horrible night in the Blackgloom keep, when it seemed the light of morning would only be a promise attached to the end of a lingering, but certain death.

A shiver went through her, even as sparks jumped out of the fire behind her and singed the flaxen blanket she had draped over her shoulders. Three heavy draws on what remained of the Prior's beer bucket, combined with days and nights of riding in an open wagon had dulled her senses almost to a stupor. All but asleep, she sat upright on the hearth as a long, gratuitous belch from the Prior brought an abrupt end to the quiet.

"Yes, it *was* good stew," she said, mocking the Prior's disgusting mannerism.

The Prior waddled toward the door, turned and made the requisite sign of the cross, and chanted, *"Te Deum, non nobis Domine, nunc dimitis."* He waved a meaty paw toward Daynin and added, "I shall be in Prior Peen's hovel behind the chantry, if ye need me, boy. My brethren and I will decide in the morning what is to be done with that bounty. Until then, sleep well, if ye *can*, but do not go wandering in the grounds." His disapproving glance toward Sabritha was all too clear.

As soon as the door closed, Sabritha let fly. "That old sot! Who does he think he is?"

Daynin ignored her for the moment, his mind already trying to resolve their next problem. The hovel was barely large enough to sling a cat over his head, let alone for two people to share. And it had only one straw cot. Sleeping close to her had not been a problem before, but now it seemed like an overwhelming issue. He hadn't the first idea how to resolve it.

"What's wrong?" she snapped, angrily. "You look like a miller's mutt with no place to mess."

"There's only room for one on that cot. I should sleep in the wagon anyway. I don't want to leave the chests out there unguarded."

"Suit yourself, plowboy. I don't intend to spend any more time shivering out in the cold than I have to. As for the chests, I can't imagine even a thief would be out in this weather."

Daynin stopped almost in mid-stride toward the door. "Sabritha," he growled, his anger more than a little obvious, "if you call me 'plowboy' one more time, I swear I will leave you here with Prior Bede."

She swept past him and rolled herself onto the Bede's

cot. "I've been in worst places, I guess. But if it bothers you that much, I'll save that name for when you have made the biggest fool of yourself. And sleeping out in the rain tonight would be just such a time." She rolled on her side and held the blanket up, then motioned for him to join her. "Now get you into this bed and be quick about it, before I change my mind."

The ominous rumble of heavy hooves swept by the fort within a stone's throw, first one horse, then three more in rapid succession. Kruzurk breathed a sigh of relief that they had gone on, but couldn't help wondering who they were and where they were going in such a hurry so nigh to dusk. "Are they well and truly gone?" he whispered.

Mediah crept out onto the hard packed road and dropped to one knee. He placed one hand palm down on the damp earth. "Aye, m'lord. I believe they have gone on toward Tynemouth. There are no tracks on the trail north."

"Then we must be off. I want to cross the frontier before morning."

"The Hogshead ferry only operates after daylight, m'lord. It is the only way I know to cross into Scotia without risking a challenge by the Duke's men at the Liddle bridges. Unless you want to cross well to the east, that is."

Kruzurk threw himself onto his mount the way a man half his age might do, then winked at his companion. "Let me worry about the crossing, Mediah. We've no time to waste. Daynin and Sabritha are in great danger. We must find them before the Duke's men, else they come to a terrible end on my account."

Chapter 13:

The Seeking

Determined pounding on the thick oak door of the hovel roused Ean McKinnon from a deep, well earned sleep. Instinctively, he reached for his *sgian du,* knowing that such a door pounding in the wee hours before daylight could mean nothing but trouble for a clansman in the land of Anglia.

"Open in the name of Duke Harold!" a loud voice demanded.

Ean realized his ancient sock knife was woefully outclassed by armored men and much heavier weapons. If the Duke's men even suspected him of being a clansman, they would clap him in irons and cast him in some hell hole from whence he would never again enjoy daylight or the smell of freshly turned earth.

Another loud, clanging, "wham, wham, wham," echoed from the door, almost knocking the slide bolt loose. Ean jumped over his cot and threw open the concealed cellar door, hesitating only long enough to grab his tartan, short blade and a chunk of bread. He slid down the root cellar ladder, closing the trap door tightly, thus making it invisible to all but the most heedful eye.

Several heartbeats later, the door to the hovel fell under the crashing blows of the soldiers. "Make way for a Duke's Warrant!" the same gruff voice bellowed. "Search this haunt for any sign of the boy, then we'll torch it. We've two more of these dives to sift through afore the light breaks."

Ean felt relieved that his bad habit of letting the fire die overnight had spared his life, at least for the moment. The soldiers must have thought he was long gone. Since his grandson had left him, the old man had allowed everything to go to wrack and ruin, including the farm. But he couldn't dwell on Daynin's plight. The men above him were ransacking the hovel, swearing and bemoaning the absence of the boy, bent on destruction of the meanest kind.

With cat-like skill, Ean slipped down the ladder to the floor of the cellar and began moving the sacks of stored grain out of the way. He had to get through to the barricaded escape tunnel before the Duke's men found the entrance to the cellar and made it his grave.

The old man cast a last wistful glance around at the stacks of hard gained stores, shoved open the door to the tunnel and scurried down the dark passageway. Two hundred steps east of the cellar, he peeked out from the reeds covering the tunnel exit at the riverbank, making sure his escape was clear, then bolted for the woods. Soon, a bright glow on the horizon behind him announced that once again, a clansman's holdings had gone up in flames by the order of men he could only resist with his anger—for now, at least.

The horses lathered heavily from the brisk pace Kruzurk and Mediah had kept up since turning north toward Scotia. They were several leagues from the closest of the Liddle River bridges, and Kruzurk still had no plan for dealing with the Gatewatch he knew would be posted there in large numbers.

"M'lord, the horses are spent," Mediah offered, then added, "as am I, being unused to the bouncing of this wretched saddle."

A smile crept over Kruzurk's deeply lined face as he drew his mount to a slow stop, glad for a reason to become acquainted with his legs again. He dropped onto the marshy slope at the side of the track, then replied, "We need to plan our crossing anyway. Bring your horse and we'll rest on the other side of the marsh. No need to risk being seen here on the road."

Safely out of harm's way, the two shed their horses' trappings and led them to drink in a brook at the edge of the marsh. The whole place had small, round boulders the size of early fall pumpkins strewn about. Kruzurk noticed something else scattered among the rocks. Teller's mushrooms grew everywhere. Their distinctive black striped stalks had long been credited with the ability to make one see things that were not real, much as a fortuneteller might. An idea began to blossom in the old magician's head while he carefully selected a few of the larger specimens.

Mediah gave the old man a quizzical look before he asked, "M'lord, you have no plans to eat those, do you? I've been told they are poison, even to the touch."

Kruzurk laughed. "Aye, poison they are, if used the wrong way, my Greek friend. But an ally of immeasurable value when used the right way. I know how to use them. Now, go and empty our waterbags—I will need them shortly."

Hours later and the horses fully rested, Kruzurk woke Mediah from his fitful slumber sitting upright against a huge bog oak. The sun had just begun to cast its narrow shards of light through the ancient forest, mingling willowy beams with the morning mist and a light ground fog.

Somewhere in the distance, the evanescent cry of a sparrowhawk echoed over the glen, sending shivers through the horses and their riders. Both men sensed the uneasy atmosphere from the animals as they turned north toward the Scotian frontier and an enemy they couldn't begin to estimate in strength or cunning.

The tinny clanging in Daynin's ears seemed more annoying than real. He tried rolling over on the narrow cot to avoid the racket, but found himself entwined in Sabritha's arms. Her breath came slow and measured—the sound of one in a restful sleep. He wondered how anyone could sleep that way, let alone in a strange bed.

Determined not to wake her, Daynin eased onto his back to stare up at the cobwebs hanging down from the wattle and daub roof of the Prior's hutch. Glad now that the room had been so dark the night before as to make the ceiling indistinct, he squirmed slightly at the notion so many crawling creatures shared the hovel.

The clanging started again. This time he recognized the pattern. It was the morning call to prime.

The simple hand bell made a poor substitute for the set of Durham bells Prior Bede had already brought north from York, to eventually install in the cathedral tower. *The tower I will help build,* Daynin pledged in his mind, his determination to finish what his father had started even more ingrained now than ever.

A timid knock on the door brought Daynin to his feet. Sabritha groaned slightly, then rolled over to face the wall.

"Is that you, Prior Bede?"

"No, 'tis Novice Dunoon, m'lord, sent to fetch you," a very young and boyish voice answered.

"Where is the Prior?" Daynin asked, having yet to open the door.

"He waits for you in the refectory. Breakfast will be over soon. If you wish to share bread with him, you must hurry."

"Aye, that we will."

"Uh, m'lord, the refectory is a chaste area for the novitiate. The woman cannot go there, but you may bring her food later."

"Well, aren't *you* special?" Sabritha chimed in from across the room.

The hackles on Daynin's neck went up immediately. "Thank you, Novice. I will join you straightaway." He turned to the woman and snapped, "These are good people, Sabritha. They at least deserve your respect, even if you don't believe in what they stand for."

"*Witch* hunters and hangmen's helpers, that's all I've ever seen these black robed repressors do for people. Where are your priors when the poor need food, or a place to stay, or some measure of justice from King Ethelred's Eyre? There always seems to be a reason they can't do what needs to be done. And I won't even *talk* about the low regard they have for women."

"They are not *my* priors, but I respect them nonetheless." Daynin plucked his haversack from the table and turned to leave. "I'll bring you some bread and beer when I come back, and the fire needs tending while I'm gone."

"Why yes, your lordship," she mocked. "And would you be needing a bath drawn whilst I await your eminence? Or perhaps some roast venison for lunch?" Daynin was out the door before she could throw her shoe to finalize the tirade.

Plumat's lukewarm breakfast of barley broth and herbs hardly fit the cuisine he was accustomed to in Anglia or his native Normandy. He poured a hefty measure of beer over it, then stirred the gray mass with his knife. One taste was enough to set him off. "We cannot serve this bloody warrant soon enough!" he growled, stabbing the knife into the tabletop to emphasize the point.

Miles Aubrecht, Plumat's reluctant young squire, almost jumped out of his tunic at the sudden assault on the table. The night had been a long one, filled with unending drinking and the comings and goings of scores of Caledonian mendicants seeking a piece of the bounty Plumat had offered in the tavern.

Most of the drengs had been sent on their way, but enough passed the initial tests by first light to provide a troop of twenty. Plumat's second in command, Earl deLongait, had rounded up every horse in Galashiels to mount the cavalcade for rapid movement through the highlands. If they were to catch the boy before he disappeared into the vastness of northern Scotia, speed would be their only advantage.

To make the ragtag troop seem more formidable, Plumat ordered that tunics be issued to each of the bountiers, along with the distinctive scarlet hoods of the Duke's army. This despite the Duke's orders that plain Caledonians be employed to blend in with the locals for gaining better intelligence. Fifty leagues inside hostile territory and carrying a small fortune in silver, Plumat felt far more concern for his own well being than for any tidbits of information such blaggards might provide him. And besides, he knew with some certainty where the boy was headed. His army just had to get there first.

The elder McKinnon's age was beginning to tell on him. It had taken Ean nearly half the morning to circle around to the west of Hafdeway and avoid the Duke's patrols. He hoped his old friend Simon Troon could sell him what he needed to go after Daynin, for Ean knew by now the boy must be in terrible trouble that he should cause such a frenzied search by so many soldiers.

Simon's farm appeared peaceful enough from the edge of the forest, but Ean kept himself overly cautious now, what with the Duke's men seemingly behind every tree in the shire. He watched for a long time, then finally ventured into the clearing behind the house. A fast dash got him inside the gate and out of sight from the road. He knocked thrice, then once more, as was the custom between clandestine foreigners in Anglia.

"Bloody hell! Who comes a-knockin' at my door this 'ere time o' the marnin'?"

"Open the door you old Irish swindler—'tis Ean McKinnon."

The door opened a crack, allowing the smell of lard, tanned leather and larch pine to seep out. "Let me in, damn ya. The Duke's men are everywhere."

Simon pulled the door wider, poking his head out to ensure that no one could witness his larceny. "I can get forty lashes just for opening the door to the likes of you, McKinnon. You should'nae be here."

"I need your help, Troon. My grandson is under warrant. The Duke's men came looking for him before the cock crowed this morning. They burned my house and ransacked the neighbor's farm to boot."

"Bloody henchmen, these Anglish," Simon growled. He rubbed the stubble of graying beard, then stepped back to allow Ean entrance. All around him lay the trappings of his trade—freshly shaped longbow frames, untallowed draw strings and a host of the most prized arrows in middle Anglia.

To Ean, it looked for all the world like Simon prepared himself for war, but then he realized market day was on the morrow, and these were Troon's trade goods for the week. "I need a bow and a brace of arrows. I cannae pay you,

Simon, save for offering what's left of my farm, and that ain't much to be sure."

"Sounds like you'd be offering me naught but a pile of ashes, Ean McKinnon. For what you ask, I'd be needin' twelve talens without a haggle. That'd be the going rate for my weapons." Troon turned and spit into the fire, as if to put an end to the conversation.

Ean's shoulders drooped. The years and growing sadness in his heart were bringing him to the verge of banditry. He let out a noticeable sigh and said, "I've neither stoat ner vole ner farthing for ye."

Simon placed a gnarled hand on Ean's shoulder and said, wistfully, "Was it not you who sat with my dying Maggee Muldoon when I was forced into the Duke's service two winters ago? And was it not young Daynin who cut saplings for me when I came back, sick with the grippe from that bloody war? Without the two o' ya, I would have gone to the grave or at least the pauper's prison."

"Aye, I remember that. We nearly starved from the cold that spring. I was broke then, and so I am now. I cannae pay you for what I must have. But I *must* find Daynin, whatever the cost. Will ye front me the bow or not? I swear I'll pay you somehow."

"Front 'im the weapons, says he? And 'im off to fight the Duke gawd knows where," Troon scoffed, playfully. "I won't front you so much as an arrow feather, you old fart, but if ye've a mind to go that bad, I'll be loaning you the bow and brace, then be going with you to protect my property. When we find Daynin, you can work off the debt, if we're still alive to give a hoot about it by then."

The pathway leading through the back acreage of the cathedral was lined with scores of ancient, weathered stone markers—each the resting place of some nobleman or his family from a time long before the current cathedral grounds had been consecrated. Many of the markers were so old their inscriptions had given way to the scourges of time and the eternal winds of the highlands.

Some of the tombs had been carved from solid rock and adorned with columns and vaulted arches that bore the distinctive markings of Pictish and Scotian chiefs for whom the Abbotsford grounds had been a favorite resting place since the glory days of Dalriada. Others were etched with more recent crests of Anglian or Scotian lineage, both of whom were welcomed to the sanctified ground, provided the dead had left a sufficient endowment for their eternal stay.

Daynin shuddered as he walked past the long rows of mounds, crosses and cenotaphs that filled the landscape. He knew the priory could not exist without the endowments, but he never realized the vast scope of death the place represented. *The Blackgloom Bounty will change all that,* he mused. *With enough gold and a library of books to rival York, Prior Bede will never have to worry about the dead supporting his church again.*

The boy's agile mind slipped from his reverie of treasure to a wispy image that revealed itself a dozen strides ahead of him in the archway. It looked like his father, standing taller than the oak door behind him, waiting at the entrance to the novitiate for the boy to catch up. Duncan McKinnon had been an impressive sight in life, especially to lowlanders used to the more diminutive size of most clansmen. They, like Daynin now, were awed by Duncan's height and his enormous arms.

"Father?" he blurted out.

The image appeared to dart away, straight into the massive stone abutment that supported the wall of the church.

Daynin shook his head, then realized it was only an image from his past. That spot had been the last place he had ever seen his father smile.

A hand dropped softly onto Daynin's shoulder, startling him, and almost putting him to flight. *"Get thee gone!"* he screamed, his voice cracking in the process. He shoved the hand away and took three fast steps before he realized just how foolish he must have seemed.

"Daynin, it's Prior Bede. Relax, boy. These tombs have you spooked."

"Aye, Father," he said, a hard swallow clearing his throat. "I—uh—I thought I saw my father—just for an instant. He stood right there!"

"I cannae argue what you saw or did'nae see, lad. Some spirits are always with us, they being much stronger than most, or having a score to settle that won't let them rest in their crypt. Your father was a vigorous man in life, and few had more things left to settle than he. No reason to think he would be any different from the angry ones existing on the other side."

"You really believe there are spirits among us, Prior?"

"Daynin, there are things I cannae begin to explain any other way. We find a sepulcher opened here, on occasion, even down in the catacombs where no one except the brethren ever ventures. And mind you, some of these tomb closures are mighty heavy stones for the likes of mortal man to be shoving aside."

The Prior crossed himself and added, "Aye, some men are blessed by the number of things they can afford to leave alone. Wandering spirits is something I choose not to dwell upon, my son, and so should you. Now, let's get you some bread and hot wine, then we'll discuss the lay of that bounty you've brought."

Chapter 14:

The Revealing

For the startled villagers, the two mounted men trying to escape through their midst must have been both an amusement and a curiosity. Their horses were so heavily laden with weapons and supplies that the beasts could barely move, let alone maneuver in the crowded mudlanes of Hafdeway.

Being market day, the town was flush with every manner of two and four-legged impediment along with all manner of carts and stalls in great abundance. "Out of the way, you lot!" Troon bellowed in a vain attempt to clear the throng ahead of them.

Ean slapped his mount's rump, urging the swayback mare to push her way onward, only to be repaid by a sharp buck that almost dismounted him. "Damn ye lowland nag," he swore, then slapped the mare again, this time with the flat of his long bow. That did the trick. The mare cleared the way for Troon's much smaller Shetland steed trailing behind.

"Thataway," Troon urged, "to the right—that'll be the shortest route to Ravensport and the sea."

McKinnon prodded his mare to take the right fork leading away from the edge of the village. A quarter of a league onward and the two old warriors would be shed of the town and further scrutiny by the Duke's men. Ean turned in the saddle to make sure Troon was behind him and quickly realized they were not the only ones headed for the coast. A troop of black hauberks circled around the village from the south, bent on intercepting the main road by way of the mill bridge. That would put the troop square across the highlander's path to the sea, as no doubt the soldiers had planned.

"We've got to move, Simon. They're onto us!"

The tiny pony had barely enough height to keep Troon's feet from dragging, let alone support the weight of him and an armory on its back. "Get on with ya, Sparkle—make yer old pap proud," Simon squealed. He dug his heels into Sparkle's flanks, bringing a surprising burst of speed from the shaggy, mud-caked creature.

Nearing the edge of the forest, Ean heard the Duke's men shouting behind them at the same instant an arbalest bolt shattered a tree limb barely an arm's length from his head. Without looking back, he scoffed, "Damned Saxon fools—waste of a good crossbow at this range."

Troon didn't respond, having slumped precariously over Sparkle's neck. He held on with all the strength he could muster, biting his lip to keep from screaming in agony from the bolt that had just pinned his thigh to Sparkle's saddle.

Prior Bede drained the large chalice of wine, then burped with his usual gusto. "Ah-h, that's a day maker for me. Drink up, boy—we've a lot to do before the noon prayers."

Daynin's attention was fixed on that fleeting image of his father instead of anything the Prior had said. "Aye," he replied distantly. "Thank you for allowing me to share prime with you and the novices."

"Finish yer wine, boy, then we're off to the catacombs beneath the sanctuary. The brethren have selected a Promethean vault down there where they think your booty will be safe. We must find it, get it open, and then move your bounty in."

"*Your* bounty, Father," Daynin corrected. "What I leave here is for you to use the best way you see fit. My only two conditions are that the coin is applied to the building of the cathedral, and that the books are made available to any who want to study them."

Prior Bede stood up, wiped a beefy hand across his mouth, and swept a large candelabrum off the table. "It shall be as you ask, my son. And your name will be forever enshrined here for this deed of charity."

"Enshrine my father's name, Prior—not mine. I'm only doing his bidding. All the rest is up to you."

Silently, the Prior motioned for Daynin to follow. Together, they walked out into a gray morning mist, then through the back portal of the church. Just inside, they met a novice standing at the nexus of three steep stairwells leading down into the pitch blackness of the catacombs. Maintaining his rule of silence inside the sanctuary, the novice lit his candle from the Prior's, crossed himself, and started down the center wellkeep.

Both sets of candles flickered from a strong updraft of musty air as they descended the first circular turn. The light cast a host of willowy shadows on the abundant cobwebs. Suddenly, the stench of death became all too fresh for Daynin to ignore. He clasped his hand over his nose and mouth and whispered, "Forgive me, Father, but the smell down here is awful."

"Aye, that would be Father Michael, bless his soul. Not yet a fortnight gone to his rewards—he's a ripe one, I'm sure. Ignore the smell, boy. We'll be below it soon enough. These steps go down a long way."

Daynin swept his fingers along the curved wall, testing the dampness and reassuring himself that there indeed was a wall there since he could not see it very clearly in the gloom. "How far down do these steps go, Father?"

The Prior stopped, turned about and laughed aloud, causing him to jiggle the candelabrum and make the shadows dance in unison to the echo of his voice. "All the way to the Stygian River itself, if one believes the tales told of these catacombs. No one has ever gone lower than where we are going, at least since I've been Prior here. It would be an easy place to lose one's senses, if say, your candles were to burn out, or you had a bad fall."

A sharp, stinging shiver snaked through Daynin's spine, making him shake all over. "You—really don't know—what's down there—do you—Prior?"

"Saint Columba, boy! Could be the Pit of Acheron for all I know, though I've never actually seen any daemons traipsing through here, if that be your worry. Now stop those teeth from chattering and let's move on. We've a ways to go yet."

Daynin pulled the hood of his cloak tighter and bundled his arms against the seeping cold of the stairwell. His mind flashed to Sabritha and the warmth he had felt during the night while rolled up snugly against her backside. *I could sleep that way the rest of my life,* he mused. *She is so warm and soft . . .*

The candlelight suddenly illuminated a large open area below them. The novice stepped from the wellkeep and strode purposefully toward one of a dozen dark corridors that led off in all directions from the main room. Daynin searched for some sign of which direction they were headed, but could find none. Every crack, crevice and cobweb seemed to be identical. Even the wellkeep they had just left was not easy to identify in the dark circular domain. Again, Daynin's teeth began to chatter.

"Come along, boy," the Prior urged. "I think we're nearly there."

No sooner were those words spoken than the novice started gesturing toward an impressive Saracen arch at the end of the long hallway. Coming closer, they could see that it was adorned with a host of runes, pictographs, and angry gargoyles arranged in a pattern around the arch. In the center of the arch stood a huge oaken double door sealed by a bronze plaque bolted across its middle.

Prior Bede raised his candelabra to get a better view of the text, then just stood there shaking his head. "You're certain *this* is the vault the brethren chose, Novice John?" he asked, his voice incredulous at the prospect.

The novice obediently shook his head yes, then crossed himself. From inside his robe, he produced a sturdy iron bar with hooks on one end and a St. Columba's Cross on the other. He handed his light to Prior Bede and indicated that the bar could be used to pry off the bolts holding the plaque in place.

Daynin was momentarily taken aback by the vast array of characters, symbols and ancient words he saw, but the instant Novice John made clear his next move, Daynin shouted, *"No! Stop!"* His sharp tone echoed through the chamber like the scream of a thousand people all crying "top" in cadence. Even the walls seemed to wither from the sudden cacophony of voices.

Both of the robed men turned in unison at the outburst. "What the *hell* is *wrong* with you, boy? This ground is sacrosanct!" Bede barked, siring a hundred score echoes of his own.

Stepping between the priests, Daynin grabbed the

crowbar from John and pushed him away. "You can't open this vault! Did you *read* what it says?"

"Pictish palaver, that's all it is. That language is older than Saxon tyranny. Take no heed of it, Daynin."

"Father, this is not just some fool's warrant. It's a warning. Can't you *read* it?"

"No, I cannae read it and neither can anyone else, that I'm aware of."

"Well, I can," the boy growled. "This is a traitor's tomb, marked with a warrant to warn anyone who enters that they are in great peril. We can't open this—we just can't."

Prior Bede shoved his considerable girth against the boy, pinning him to the door. "Now look 'ere, boy. You came into this priory seeking help and shelter. I've given you that, and considerably more. All the other large vaults in these catacombs are inviolable. They are consecrated and pro-tected. This one is not. If this be the resting place of a hea-then, then so be it—that's why the brethren chose to use it for your heathen goods. Now stand aside, or take your bounty elsewhere."

"Can I at least read you the warning before you open it?"

"Read away, if that be enough to quiet your tongue. But this vault is where we store the bounty, no matter what the warrant says."

Daynin stepped back, and began to recite the pictographs. "Herein lie the reviled remains of the *raven feeder*—Brude McAlpin—descended from the royal blood of Fortrenn. This blaggard slayer of the Seven Houses of Scone deceitfully offered parlay and porridge to his rivals, then cast one and all into a pit, sown with deadly blades, that his scurrilous deed should advance an unearned station of royalty. Though first born of the Brude of Nechtansmere, beloved conqueror of the English, Vikings, and Caledonians, and savior of the lands of Dalriada, the spirits condemn any and all who venture beyond this entrance to lay praise, prayer or petition at the feet of Brude McAlpin, the uncrowned king of the Picts—known to all as the Great Deceiver."

"Saints of Argyle, boy. Where did you learn to read the language of the Picts? They were worm meat long before the Saxons raped this land."

"There was a manuscript at Kinloch, Father—written in two languages. It must have been intended to translate the original Pictish to Latin. I never realized it at the time, but these runes are as clear to me now as Latin or Greek. This warning is *not* something we should ignore."

The Prior motioned with his head for John to take the crowbar and proceed. "We've wasted enough time as it is. These candles don't burn forever, and I for one have no desire to be down here in the dark."

Trepidation spread over the novice's face. He crossed himself again, kissed the icon of St. Columba he wore around his neck and stepped forward to pry the first bolt loose. Six more rapid wrenchings and the heavy bronze placard fell with a resounding "clunk" at his feet.

"Go ahead, open it," the Prior ordered.

Determined to make one last effort to stop them, Daynin shoved the novice aside. "Don't *do* this, Father—please—I have a terrible feeling about this place."

Bede paid him no mind, moved forward an arm's length and forced the boy's back against the door. This time it opened just a crack. "There—the deed's done. The seal is broken, so whatever comes of this, we are committed. Now, let's get on with it before we lose the light."

Plumat sat impatiently on his steed watching his counterfeit troop of mercenaries attempt to mount up at the edge of Galashiels. Cauldron neighed nervously, chomping at his bit from all the delays. "Steady boy," Plumat urged. "These ragtags will be ready soon enough, and then you shall have your run, I promise."

Miles Aubrecht waited nervously on his mount as well, having never before been on such a dangerous expedition. He had no clue what risks awaited him, or how he would handle them should they arise. He also had no reason to trust Plumat or any of the other henchmen in the troop. They were Caledonians and Saxons, after all—not of his liking even on a good day. And there had been no good days since his father died and left him a ward of the Duke's court.

His hand went to the hilt of his dirk at the thought of an enemy bent on his own mortal destruction. "M'lord Plumat, do you think we will find this villain and bring him back quickly?"

"Bring him back?" Plumat answered laughingly. "Surely you jest, boy, to think we've come all this way to capture this knave. We'll bring him back all right—at least part of him. I intend to offer his head to the Duke, along with that of the old man and the woman, if we can bag them all at once."

Earl deLongait galloped up to his leader just then. "We *have* them, m'lord!" he shouted, bringing the turmoil of the entire group to a sudden stop. "They are no more than ten leagues from here, to the south and west. And with the roads muddy, I would guess mayhaps closer."

"How come you by this information?" Plumat demanded.

"One of the Caledonians ferreted out the news during the night. A wagon was seen yesterday on the road to

Abbotsford Priory. A boy, flaxen haired, drove the heavily laden cart—and a woman rode with him—dark hair, comely, just as the warrant describes. They can be none other than our felons."

"If we ride ten leagues in the wrong direction, I'll have you staked out in a peat bog, deLongait. Are you that certain this information is good?"

DeLongait shifted his beefy frame in the saddle, then made a sweeping motion with Draco, the giant battleaxe that was his trademark weapon. "Aye, m'lord. It is as genuine as two pieces of silver can guarantee, I'd wager my blade on that."

"Then get these misfits mounted and let's be off. With any luck, we can catch that lot before they reach the Clyde River. Perhaps then Draco can have a taste of Scotian blood."

An awful smell erupted from inside the tomb as soon as Novice John pushed the left door open wide enough to see inside. The air reeked of rotted wood, decay and something Daynin recognized distantly as the odor of a wet dog.

The Prior pushed the right door inward, then thrust his candlestick ahead of them, illuminating an entire wall of Latin prayers adorning the far side of the sepulcher. He crossed himself, stepped back, and bade the novice to take the candelabra. Two steps in and the novice's light revealed an elaborate wooden sarcophagus laid out on an ornate stone catafalque. The platform displayed all manner of Pictish images, Viking symbols and the distinctive royal seal of Dalriada.

"God help us," the novice whispered, having lost all concern for his vows of silence.

The Prior, too, seemed taken aback by the host of

heathen imagery. He began to sweat profusely and covered his nose to ward off the terrible odors.

Daynin stood there in awe. He had never seen the likes of the runes and ornate calligraphy the walls of the tomb contained. His eyes searched the text for information, but found nothing except prayers for the dead. Then he noticed a glint of gold in the darkness to his right.

Standing in the corner was a small but magnificent gilt and silver carnyx, a chieftain's war horn of the Pictish tribes. Mounted at the horn's base, an angry, stylized boar's head seemed to growl with all the menace its long dead maker could muster. Daynin shuddered at the boar's bright red eyes that almost spoke to him from across the ages, crying out in silent anguish, *At last—you have come at last!*

Chapter 15:

The Crossings

Clearly visible even in the thick morning haze, the drab stone spires of Hermitage Castle high on the bluffs north of the Hogshead ferry cast a pall over the peaceful river valley that lay before Kruzurk and Mediah. All roads converged on the landing with its small, but well-defended motte and bailey keep on the south side of the river. Fires from the gatewatch camp glowed in the half light, sending aloft a dozen lazy curls of smoke. A few villagers milled around outside the camp, having delivered their morning quotas of supplies to the Duke's men. A single ferry barge bucked against its guide rope that stretched across the wide and impetuous flow of the Liddle River.

"M'lord, they will likely have warrants for you in this place," Mediah warned as he reined in his steed. "Surely we must look for a less defended way across the border."

Kruzurk urged his horse off the road and into a sapling thicket, then dismounted. "We can't waste time looking for another crossing. According to the maps at Lanercost, this is the only good road for twenty leagues in either direction. Once we're across the river, we should be able to make excellent time." He tossed the half full waterbags to his companion and added, "Fetch these full from that stream we crossed whilst I cut some saplings. Then we shall put your artistic skills to work."

An hour later, just as the sun peeked over the ridge, the

first stirrings of the guard changing at the camp down below brought Kruzurk to his feet. "Take horse, Mediah, it's time to go. You know what to do. Make it look good. We've only one chance to fool this lot."

Mediah mounted, then turned in his saddle and said, "M'lord, if you really are a magician, methinks this would be the time to parlay that magic."

Kruzurk stepped up next to the horse and took Mediah's forearm in his. "We have leverage, my friend. The leverage of mathematical certainty and the powerful contents of these 'wineskins' are the best magic I can conjure. The rest is timing. Just remember, make for the ferry as soon as they break and run. Now go!" A hard slap on the horse's rump sent the animal charging down the slope with Mediah careening all over the saddle like a drunken hooligan.

The Duke's men saw the crazed rider heading for their camp and quickly spread the alarm, bringing even the Captain of the watch to see what was up. Mediah's animal had been reined in by the time the officer got to the road. The dark skinned "drunk" was dragged off his horse and thrown down into the mud.

Mediah kicked and flailed at his captors, screeching wildly at the top of his voice, shouting Greek obscenities one second and, "Don't let him catch me! Get thee gone, demon!" the next. He managed to get to his feet and struggled to turn in the direction of the road. Pointing and gesturing, he pleaded, "He's coming, I tell you! Allah help us all!"

"What the bloody hell is this idiot screaming about?" the Captain demanded.

" 'E's drunk as a miller's maid, m'lord," one of the soldiers crowed. " 'Ad two pouches o' brew on 'is 'orse, 'e did, and mighty fine brew it is, too."

The Captain grabbed one of the bags, sniffed it, and then gave it a mighty tilt. "This is good," he barked. "Where'd you get this, knave? Tell me, now, or I'll slit you from yer ass end to yer eyeballs!"

Mediah fell to his knees in front of the Captain and blurted out the second act. "Mercy, please, yer lordship. Kill me now, before the phantom comes for my head. Please, kill me and have done with it!"

By now, most of the guards had passed around the first bag so that all could have a taste of the addicting drink. The second skin was already being consumed as Mediah's crazed cackling continued.

The Captain, quite amused by the morning's entertainment and filled with more than his share of the mushroom swill, quickly turned from taskmaster to turnip head from the effects of the brew. Minutes later the rest of the gatewatch found themselves in a similar state, all of them having drunk enough of the liquid to bring on a nightmare they would not soon forget.

From the top of the bluff, Kruzurk could see his plan unfolding. The entire garrison seemed stoned on the potion, but not so looped that they were no longer a threat. His part in the great deception would have to be flawless to avoid an arrow in the back, or worse. He donned the makeshift breastplate Mediah had crafted out of sapling bark. From it, five very real looking arrow shafts protruded. Next, the hideous neck mask went on over his head, aligned so he could see forward through a slit, but covering his face entirely. The red ocher bloodstains Mediah had applied to the mask and breastplate provided the last element of authenticity.

To complete the ruse, Kruzurk rubbed a dozen of his special glow-in-the-dark pellets in the palms of his hands, creating an eerie green glow that he applied to the horse's mane and to his own front side. He would now appear to be a headless glowing corpse, riddled with arrows, charging through the midst of those just tipsy enough not to believe their own disbelief.

Kruze took a deep breath, drew his short blade, and gave his horse a sharp kick in the flank. The animal screamed, lurched forward, then bolted toward the enemy camp. Down the hill they came, pell-mell, the horse's eyes wide in stark terror at its own headlong flight. Kruze's flowing red magician's robe filled with the wind, making him appear twice his size and to those tanked on the Teller's wine, no doubt he would almost seem to be flying.

The two gatewatch sentries standing astride the main road got the first glimpse of the onrushing red specter. For a few seconds, they just stood there, unable to move as the phantom closed on them. As the horrible vision got close enough for them to see the enraged animal and its giant headless rider, the guards' terror erupted into wild cries of confusion. Throwing their weapons and shields aside, both men ran for the keep, screaming at the tops of their voices.

"Get thee gone, Cerberus!" one man shouted, ripping off his own helmet to aid his escape.

The other blabbered, "Demons! Demons are upon us!"

Every eye in the camp turned to the road in unison. The Captain of the watch was well past the point of any rational thinking. His head swiveled around in time to see the phantom bearing down on him, and he simply passed out stone cold in the ditch. Seeing their officer go down as if by magic, panic spread through the ranks.

Five men turned tail to run, but were hit from behind by Kruze's charger and knocked helter-skelter in the mud. Two more fumbled to load their crossbows, allowing the ghost to fly between them. Another man frantically waved a torch in front of him to ward off the evil host, to no avail. He too was knocked heels over head by flying hooves.

A dozen men were either down or running for their lives by the time Kruze reached the ferry landing. He reined in his animal and turned to retrieve Mediah, who was desperately trying to remount his horse. An arrow fired from the walls of the keep flew well wide of its mark and struck the wooden railing beside Kruze's horse. Another sailed harmlessly over his head. "Drat, they're not all drunk," he swore.

Once mounted, Mediah struggled with a drunken fool who tried all he could to hold onto his horse. He kicked the man in the face, regained the reins and rode down two crossbowmen that were still trying in vain to load their weapons. "Get aboard," the Greek shouted. "Don't wait for me!"

Kruze knew Mediah would make it now, provided the bowmen in the keep were typical conscripts who couldn't hit an ox at fifty paces. He ripped off his disguise and dropped to the ground. Taking the horse's halter, he guided him across the rough-hewn landing to where the ferry barge was moored. Another flight of arrows spattered the water to his right. He turned to see the keep's gate swinging open. That meant more soldiers, and this batch would be sober.

"Come *on*, Mediah," he yelled. Kruze leaped onto the heaving barge, then urged his horse to jump aboard. Mediah had just reached the landing when the first troop of soldiers crossed the motte, heading straight for them. More arrows scattered piecemeal in the water and on the landing. One struck Mediah's horse, bouncing off the saddle.

Quickly gaining the barge, Mediah tossed his reins to Kruze and set to work hauling on the heavy rope that drew the ferry across the river. "This will never work!" he shouted. "They will haul us right back over before we get across."

The magician had a quick reply. "Tie off that brake rope, Mediah. We'll cut the barge adrift and let the current take us across."

"Surely you jest, my lord!" Mediah roared. "This flow will tear the barge to pieces, and us with it."

At that instant, an arrow struck the barge rail and shattered. A whole flight of arrows sailed over the ferry from a different direction. More soldiers had come up from the village. There was no time to worry about the current. Kruzurk's blade flashed, and the rope groaned under the strain. Another slash cut almost halfway through, but still the rope held.

"Get back!" was all Mediah had time to shout before the rope came untwined like a hundred snakes heads all uncoiling in unison. A loud "crack" followed a high pitched whining noise. Then the rope separated, sending the barge crashing into the landing. The log landing dissolved into a thousand pieces of flotsam as it swept downstream pushed by the much heavier barge.

Within seconds the ungainly ferry and its top-heavy cargo swung in a wide arc out into the main channel of the river. The buffeting of the current threatened to toss the horses into the water, but Mediah held onto them with a conviction bordering on the mystical. Kruzurk lay at the feet of the animals, doing what he could to soothe their panic, all the while trying his best not to get trampled.

The ferry's guide rope, stretched almost to its breaking point all the way back to the north bank of the Liddle, acted as an enormous pendulum for the barge. As the current pushed the hapless boat further downstream, the rope held its ground on the far side, pulling the barge inexorably closer to the north bank and freedom. Kruze's mathematical leverage was doing the job.

"If—the—rope—holds—we'll make it," Kruzurk yelled over each successive swell of the roiling black waters.

Mediah could only nod his head in exaggerated agreement, his skill with the horses the single element keeping the barge from tipping upside down in the surging current. He wasn't about to change his focus to marvel at the Euclidian certainty by which Kruzurk's plan had been aided. To him, it was sufficient that the plan worked, at least as long as the rope held.

The main track out of Hafdeway dropped briefly into a winding trough of a sunken road, then abruptly reappeared at the southern entrance to the mill bridge. Ean's watchful eyes caught the flutter of the Duke's standard to his right, just as it disappeared into that trough. He quickly realized the troop of armored cavalry would soon have them cut off from the road to Ravensport. Unless he acted swiftly to slow them down, he and Simon would be sharing a cell or a tree limb by nightfall.

McKinnon galloped ahead to buy some time, still unaware that Troon had been pinned to his saddle by a crossbow shaft—a shaft that probably came from Troon's own hand, long ago created for the Duke's armory. A stone's throw from the northern bridge exit, Ean jumped from his horse and raced to a spot where the south entrance lay just within the cast of his longbow.

In his prime, Ean could loose an arrow every twelfth heartbeat and still be accurate at two hundred paces. He knew he would have to be faster than that today, if the enemy were to be stopped. Behind him, Sparkle trotted past, huffing under her load and barely keeping a running pace. Ean only had time for a quick look, and that's when he saw the blood streaming down Simon's leg.

"Get on with ye, Troon!" he shouted. "I'll hold this bridge to give you time to beat it out of here." Troon responded with a halfhearted wave, unable to do much else but run for his life.

Turning his attention back to the bridge, McKinnon drew one of Troon's specially designed, long-range quarrels from his brace of arrows and mounted it on the longbow. The heavy, square-headed crossbow bolt could knock a charger down, even at that distance, if he could hit it anywhere in the forelock. Ean drew the bow with all his might, released a long but steady breath, and waited for the first target to appear at the far end of the bridge.

"Thwack!" The longbow loosed the quarrel on its deadly errand. The arrow struck the lead horse just above the eye, sending it into an enraged spin and throwing its rider against the stone rampart at the side of the bridge. The horse reared up, then fell back in a confused heap on top of the man, half dazed from the fall. The animal screamed more like a gutted pig than a charger, exactly the effect Ean had hoped for, knowing that would throw the other horses into a panic as well.

In rapid succession, he let fly three more arrows. One struck its mark dead on and another, by happenstance, ripped the Duke's standard from the hands of its holder. More than confusion spread through the ten riders bunched up at the bridge entrance, especially after seeing their liege's colors go down. Two men at the back of the column broke for the village. Another leaped from his horse to aid his fallen commander. Still another let fly from his crossbow, falling well short of the target.

The thrashing animal Ean had brought down with the first quarrel did everything it could to right itself, but to no avail. In the process, it completely blocked the south end of the bridge and made mounted ducks of the rest of the Duke's men. Ean fired another quarrel. The horse he struck this time collapsed like a drunken milkmaid, spilling its rider into another soldier and further spreading the panic.

"Best be savin' yer own scrawny arse, now, McKinnon," the wily old man professed as he turned and ran for his life.

Three of the priory's stouter novices had spent the better part of the morning helping Daynin unload, catalog and store the bulk of the Blackgloom Bounty in the catacombs. All were somewhat dazed by the amount of booty they had cataloged thus far. The cart contained more gold, silver, jewelry, and intricately adorned goblets than anyone had ever seen in that part of the world. Books were in abundance as well, and there were still more boxes yet to be examined.

"When you return from taking those coffers down to the vault, finish listing everything in these two crates, and take them down as well. Leave the remainder of the booty in the wagon," Daynin ordered the novitiates. "I'll be taking all of that with me in the morning." The three nodded in silence and went back to work finishing their impressive list of manuscripts and plunder.

Suddenly Daynin realized he had forgotten to deliver Sabritha's breakfast. He made a quick pass through the refectory's galley to find something—anything—to offer her. He dashed toward the hovel and backed in the door without knocking, his hands laden with a tray of fried bread and wine. As he turned to set the tray down, Sabritha stood there before the fireplace swathed in little more than a shocked look, a few soap suds, and a modestly placed sponge.

"Damn, plowboy! Don't people in your clan ever knock?"

Flushed and almost blinded by the blood coursing through his brain, Daynin couldn't help but let his eyes linger a bit longer than he should have. The sight of her naked form was nothing short of stunning. Sabritha appeared even more beautiful than she did as the Seed's mistress—especially since this time, he knew she was the real thing.

"I-I-I-uh," Daynin stuttered, unable to even begin to think of a way to cover his blunder. The tray trembled in his hands, setting adrift the mug of wine.

"Better set that down before you lose my breakfast," she snapped. "Then you can get yourself *out* of here until I'm done with my bath."

"Of course—I—I'm sorry—the door—wasn't locked or anything . . ."

"Who locks doors in a *cathedral* grounds, for ninnies' sake?" came the sharp reply.

That sent Daynin on his way in a hurry. He didn't remember closing the door behind him, although he was certain that he had. He didn't even remember going down into the catacombs, yet that is where he found himself—standing in the entrance to the sepulcher. Treasure and books had been stacked against one wall, though he barely noticed, his thoughts lost in the glow of the candles he had somehow picked up in his blind rush from above.

"You fool!" he wailed. The cascade of echoes from a hundred directions seemed to mock him, making him feel even more ridiculous. "She's never going to take me seriously if I don't stop being such an ass!" A hundred S's hissed back from the dark corridors around him.

Mesmerized by visions of Sabritha, the treasure, and what the two combined might mean to his future, Daynin stepped inside the tomb wherein the Great Deceiver's casket had lain for half a millennium. The boy's mind went everywhere and nowhere, numbed by the cold and dampness. He picked up one of the ancient texts and placed it on the sarcophagus, allowing it to flop open to a velvet bookmark. Without thinking, he began to read aloud.

Daynin scanned down the page, stopping abruptly when he realized that he was repeating a conjuration likely written by a sorcerer's hand. Stunned, his eyes immediately skipped from the book to several rows of pictographs carved on top of the sarcophagus. Shoving the book aside, he feverishly brushed away eons of dirt, decay, and detritus, bringing the whole of a long hidden message to light. While his eyes scanned the markings, words formed in his head—almost like a chant—but different somehow, very different. Reading on, he could hear himself repeating lines left by an ancient Pictish priest who must have believed that Brude McAlpin would again walk in the land of the living, provided the right conditions prevailed.

"*Prima urbes inter—divum domus Dalriada,*" his chant began. "First among cities, home of the gods, Dalriada," Daynin translated aloud. He read on, "Oh child of Scotia, set me free—spirit to live, all eyes must see."

He swept the candles back and forth to decipher more, unsure exactly where his fingers were leading him. "Time and the teller's craft thy tools—say the words and bring the one who was destined to rule, back to the light, so full of might—all his enemies will fear the night."

The words spilled from Daynin's mouth as fast as his fingers could trace the runes. "*Amal Matrach, Dein Bei,* trappings of death fall away. Keen this crypt open, no time to delay, give Brude McAlpin his rightful sway."

For a few seconds, the words and symbols rattled around in Daynin's mind. He read the whole thing again, this time louder. He could feel his blood running hotter with each repetition, but there was no stopping. The words flowed like a song he had known since birth. Again and again he recited them, each time more rapidly and with more conviction until he reached a near frenzied state of mind.

The lid of the sepulcher grew hotter, or was it the mayhem in Daynin's mind that made it feel that way? He shook off the effects for a moment, then realized the whole tomb seemed hotter. He felt sweaty, confused and light headed. By now, the candles had burned well below the halfway mark. Panic set in and he turned to leave, his imagination only guessing at the consequences of being trapped in that awful place without a light.

He managed one faltering step toward the opening before five hundred years of tumult erupted behind him. A crackle like that of a great oak rent by lightning ripped the silence of the catacombs. Instantly, the casket exploded into a cacophony of noise, dust and debris. Daynin flew head first through the open double doors and sailed across the corridor, crashing sideways into the wall. His candles flew hither and yon, snuffed out by the blast, throwing the whole chamber into the blackness of unmeasured time. Mixed with the dying echoes of the blast, only a single sound could be heard in the gloomy darkness—the creak of bronze armor left too long to the ravages of rust and ruin.

Chapter 16:

The Unleashing

The sudden splash of hooves thrashing across the Tweed River ford unleashed every waterfowl in the vicinity, sending them flapping in all directions. Plumat's giant charger, Cauldron, led the troop with Miles Aubrecht, Earl deLongait and a score of Caledonians strung out behind them.

The troop had ridden hard and without halt since first light. Intent upon making good his boast of capturing the boy before the day was half spent, Plumat's horses were beginning to show the wear and tear of haste.

"My liege," deLongait roared, "we'd best be resting these animals, lest we lose some of our Caledonian minions."

Plumat reined in his stallion, turning sharply on the track to stem the troop's tide. "Damn these highland levies," he snarled. "I hated them in Ireland and I've no better use for them now."

DeLongait pulled up alongside and dismounted. "Aye, m'lord—a worthless lot they are, but we may have need of them. Most have little training on horseback, that's plain to see. God help us if we meet any real resistance in this sheep strewn swinebay of a country."

The rest of the troop straggled in, then scattered to dismount along the river bank, paying less heed to their mentors than to themselves and their mounts. In no time, cooking fires sprang up and the trappings of a day camp appeared. The Caledonians planned to go no further without their midday measure of bread and warm grog.

"DeLongait—take Miles with you and scout ahead as far as that yonder ridgeline. I want no surprises once we get this ragtag lot remounted and on the way again."

"Yes, m'lord," deLongait replied, snappily. He cuffed Miles by the scruff of the neck and shoved him toward his mount. "Let's go, boy—and no lagging behind or I'll swat you with Draco's duller edge."

It took the two riders an hour to reach the top of the steep ridge. Before them lay a narrow, rock strewn valley with Abbotsford Priory at its center, still a good distance away.

"Go back and fetch the troop, squire. That priory down there must be where our felons have taken refuge. Tell Plumat I have gone ahead, and for him to follow in haste. And stay on the track, boy—these hills are full of brigands who'll slit you from gut to grin just to steal your shoes."

Miles waved halfheartedly, then turned his mount to head back down the ridge. Barely out of shouting range from deLongait, his mind quickly leapt to thoughts of escape and freedom, but he couldn't help dwelling on that image of being slit wide open by some blaggard in the bush. He kicked his mount hard and pressed on, preferring the demeaning role of a live squire to that of a dead, shoeless freeman—at least for the time being.

A steady westerly wind whipped Ean's face, first with a measure of sand, then another of salt mist as he climbed up from the rocky Ravensport beach onto the boat. Troon was already aboard, the split in his thigh having been stitched together with cat tendons by a local butcher who passed for the village healer.

The sea remained in an uproar—far too menacing to allow the launch of the boat—even one as large as that McKinnon had hired to ferry them north to the mouth of the Clyde River in Scotia. It had taken all of Troon's spare supplies as well as the horses to bargain a way aboard, and now they were stuck with an evil wind blowing ashore, land-locking every ship in the bay.

"How soon?" Ean hollered, trying the best he could to be heard over the gale.

"Maybe soon, maybe sunset, maybe Sunday," came a well-practiced reply from the surly, self-appointed captain of the vessel. "You landlubbers got no 'preciation for the treacherous nature of the sea, and with this 'ere Irish wind a blowin', it could be days afore we get out of the harbor."

"Och! We dinnae *have* days to wait," Ean responded. "I paid you to get us from here to the Firth of Clyde, and by God I expect you to deliver!"

The captain spat sideways with the wind, turning his weathered face back to McKinnon. "Aye, old man, you can mess in one hand and pile yer ex-pec-ta-tions in the other—then see which one fills up first. But until this 'ere wind lays down a bit, we ain't gettin' as far as the headland out there. Got it?"

Ean gestured his disdain with a time honored single finger salute, then slipped below decks. There, Troon slept off the wine the butcher-healer had offered so freely. McKinnon knew it wouldn't be long before the Duke's men sniffed out their trail. After all, how hard could that be? Not many flatlanders trekked through Ravensport, and fewer still came pinned to their saddle by a Saxon crossbow bolt.

The wind had to change soon, otherwise Troon might have to be left behind, and the long journey north made overland. Satisfied that he had done all he could for the moment, Ean slumped back against a hogshead and allowed himself to sleep for the first time in days.

Wave after rolling wave swept down from the northeast, pitching the heavy barge up and down with each successive swell. The force of the water was doing its job, pushing the craft inexorably closer to the Liddle's north bank and freedom. But it was all Kruze and Mediah could do to steady the horses and keep themselves from taking a fatal, end over end plunge into the foaming mass of turbid water.

"Just a little longer!" Kruzurk cried out, more to convince himself than to steady Mediah, who seemed almost oblivious to their plight.

"Reminds—me—of—the—ocean sea," the Greek shouted back, his words rolling rhythmically with each new wave.

Kruzurk smiled despite the situation, causing a broad, mischievous grin to sprout from Mediah's coarse black beard in return. Nothing short of outright death seemed to rattle the Greek. That made him an invaluable ally in a land with nothing but bountiers, blaggards, and booty chasers roaming the roads north into Scotia.

When Kruze looked up, the steep, chalky cliffs of the north bank suddenly loomed closer, presenting a whole new threat to their survival. Unknown to him, the north shore of the Liddle sparkled with huge chunks of rock that had fallen from the cliffs above—a dead man's maze of crashing waves, jagged tree trunks and massive shards of stone. And they had no way to avoid them.

Kruzurk untied his magician's robe and stripped it off in one quick motion. In a second move, he shed his other clothes except for his breeches. "We'll have to swim for it. Those rocks will finish the barge. Tie everything to your horse, and let's jump whilst we still can."

Mediah's turban and robe came off first. In a heartbeat, he stripped naked except for his loincloth. "I'm a strong swimmer—you go first, and I'll follow, lest you should founder in that current."

Having stuffed and tied his goods as best he could to the horse, Kruzurk nodded in agreement. Without standing, he edged toward the barge's side and slipped quickly into the water up to his neck. The shock of the intense cold immediately overtook him. The old man lost his grip on the bucking barge and disappeared into the undulating brown mass without so much as a whimper.

Those in the church heard the deep rolling rumble far below the floor of Abbottsford's nave just before one corner of the pavestone foundation buckled. Violent shaking quickly spread from the floor to the huge columns that supported the roof of the church. Dust erupted from every crevice and corner, turning the yellow glow of a hundred candelabras to a ghostly brown and throwing the whole of the priory into the gloom of half-light.

"Saint Stephan preserve us!" Prior Bede bellowed, the quiet morning exemplum having turned to a maddened fire drill all around him. Novices and priests alike ran for the back door, fearing that the sanctuary's towering slate roof would come crashing down on them any second. "Stay yourselves," Bede ordered, his voice commanding their attention even as the rumbling from below subsided. "These walls will stand, but I cannae say for the roof of the refectory. If you go out those doors, you will likely be crushed."

The throng of black robes pushed and shoved their way into a single mass near the back exit of the sanctuary, unsure what to do next. To their left, an unearthly wail began to echo from the catacomb's wellkeep. A collective gasp filled the nave, the brethren turning in unison to focus on the Bede, their eyes pleading, "Protect us, Father, from whatever Hell has sent forth to reap our doom."

Prior Bede crossed himself, then shoved one of the toppled oak pews out of his way. "Get thee gone, all of you, brethren! I know not what comes from that wellkeep, but I know 'tis nothing mortal that wails so mournfully. Take shelter in my hovel and wait for me there." The Prior waved for the covey of frightened men to go, but before they departed, he added, "And pray, brothers—pray that whatever I find down there can be dispatched by prayers alone, for my cross of St. George may prove a pitiful shield against whatever it is the devil has sent from his realm to ours."

From the crest of the jagged cairn overlooking the priory's southern approach, deLongait heard the roar too, though he mistook it for thunder. He swept the visor on his helmet back, casting a curious glance at the darkening sky, but found nothing indicating an approaching storm. His charger neighed nervously as well, probably picking up the strong vibrations through his hooves.

"Bloody highlands," deLongait swore. "The further we travel in this God forsaken wasteland, the more curious our tale becomes, eh, Tantamede?"

At that instant, a great hubbub burst forth from the back doors of the priory church down below. It was as though a gaggle of giant blackbirds had all been released from their cages at once. More than a dozen monks broke out of the church's rear portal, appearing for all the world like Cerberus himself was hot on their heels.

DeLongait steadied his mount, looking on in amazement at the sight. Priests were, after all, a normally staid contingent, showing no emotion and very little excitement over anything short of an extra measure of beer after vespers. But this group seemed hell-bent to escape that church, whatever the cause.

Tantamede reared briefly, then drove hard down the slope with his rider slapping his flanks. If Plumat's felons were in the vicinity, deLongait intended to be the one who claimed the reward for their capture, and not some gang of robed rioters or Caledonian misfits.

Sparks jumped off the flagstone track from the horse's hooves in the headlong dash to the priory's gate, adding an entirely new threat to the already confused mass scrambling for cover in the Bede's hovel. One novice looked up at the approaching specter and ripped off his coif as he ran, screaming, "God help us, the flaming minions of hell are upon us!" Others followed suit, first with their head covers, then tearing at their robes to speed their escape.

The first monk to reach Bede's hovel burst through the door and toppled over a stool Sabritha had placed there for just such a sudden intrusion. Three more quickly added themselves to the confused heap on the floor, their surprise at seeing a woman only slightly less obvious than their fear of what loomed outside.

"Get out of here!" Sabritha screamed, dropping the pot of stew she had just readied for the fire. She was paid no mind, though, even by monks loath to enter a room with a woman in it, let alone one who screamed at them the way she had done.

A tenured monk reached the hovel last. Seeing the mass confusion, he tried to calm his flock and restore order. He gestured frantically for the men to quiet themselves, finally shattering a long unbroken vow. "Settle down, all of you!" Upon hearing Prior Stin's angry voice for the first time ever, the huddled group fell silent. "Calm down, brethren.

We must pray now. Prior Bede's life is at stake."

"What the *hell* is going on?" Sabritha snapped. "You people act like you've seen the gates of Gehenna open up."

Prior Stin flipped a thumb back toward the sanctuary and whispered, "We may well have seen exactly that, my lady. God forgive us, we may have seen exactly that."

The labored huffing of a charger could be heard just outside the hovel, bringing all conversation to a halt. Sabritha grabbed for her blanket, pulled it tightly over her head in the manner of an old woman's shawl, and growled "Well, is no one going to see who's *out* there?"

Expressions of fear, anguish and complete dismay spread across the faces of the monks, ending with each one looking to Prior Stin to speak for them. "That may be the devil's minion himself, my lady. His black stallion flew across the ground on a sheet of flame—I saw it myself—and that followed a great upheaval from the catacombs beneath the sanctuary just before the specter appeared."

"Goat's grunt," Sabritha replied, instantly showing her disdain for the cowardice of the monkish mob. "If it's the devil come to take us, why would he waste his time riding a horse in here? You people make me . . ."

Before she could finish the words, an enormous battleaxe protruded through the half open door of the hovel, followed by an even larger helm with an impressive black hauberk beneath it. "Yield, in the name of Duke Harold of Anglia!" the helm bellowed. "I have a warrant for three felons believed to be secluded here."

Prior Stin stepped between deLongait and the woman. "M'lord, this is a house of God. We harbor no felons here—just those who come to us sick in soul and stature. They share our bread like this unfortunate old woman. Besides, your Anglish warrant carries no weight with the Church of

Scotia. Now lower your weapon and sup with us in peace."

"I've not come a hundred leagues for gruel and beer, monk," the helm replied. A mailed hand shoved the prior aside. "Now get out of my way, or I'll cleave that bald head of yours!" The man inside the helm gave Sabritha a cursory glance, then turned his attention to the rest of the room. "Stand up, you lot, and remove the rest of those coifs that I may see your hair. You there—be quick about it."

Two of the younger novices received a curious, but peremptory inspection, then were shoved aside as deLongait eyed each of the others closely. "Where are the rest of your people? And where is the boy—the one with long hair? I warn you now, if you don't give him up, you will pay when the Sheriff arrives."

A collective gasp went up from the men in the black robes, visions of a hangman's noose looming large in their futures. "He's—in—the catacombs," one of the novices blurted out, a shaky hand pointing toward the sanctuary.

DeLongait grabbed the boy by the front of his frock and jerked him through the crowd, shoving him toward the door. "Show me, boy, and you may yet live to see the morrow."

Three hundred steps down into the gloom of the wellkeep, Prior Bede stopped. He waved the candelabra ahead of him in a vain attempt to clear some of the dust that floated in the musty air around him. He could make out just the hint of a strange creaking noise somewhere below him, its metallic echo grating on his already thinned nerves.

"Who goes there? Show yourself, whoever you are," he demanded, hearing nothing in reply but what sounded like a rusted hinge screeching in the wind.

"Ow," came a mournful groan in the distance. "Damn the dark!"

"Daynin? Is that you, boy?" Prior Bede stepped down onto the large circular floor that led to the dozen hallways. "Gimme a shout, boy, that I may find you in all this dust."

"Father—I'm here—uh—by the Pictish tomb. Something—uhm, terrible has happened."

The candelabra's light barely penetrated the heavy air ahead of him, but Prior Bede forged onward. "Stay where you are, boy. Don't move around. There are places in these catacombs where you can fall for half a day if you cannae see your way. I'll find you—just stay still."

Daynin rolled over onto his stomach, feeling all around him for solid stone to stand on and hoping to find what remained of a candlestick. Shattered bits of stone, mortar, rotten wood, and shards of metal were all he found. He pushed himself to his feet, still dazed and confused by what had happened. A flash of light in the sooty darkness caught his eye. Bede's candles reflected off what remained of the bronze plaque that had been attached to the doors behind him. One of the doors creaked on a single hinge, the sound sending chills up Daynin's spine.

"Over here, Prior. To your right. I can see your light. Tread carefully, the hallway has changed from when last you saw it."

"Aye, I can see that, boy. What the bloody hell happened, Daynin? Did one of the arches collapse? We felt the rumble all the way up in the sanctuary. Are you hurt?"

Before he answered, Daynin felt around on his tattered clothing. He found a warm wet spot on one elbow, but other than that, he seemed fine. "I don't know what happened, Father. One moment I was chanting the words written on the sarcophagus, and the next, some force threw me out here like a rag doll."

"Threw you?"

Bede crept along only a few feet away, picking his way through the rubble. Daynin could see the sweat on his brow reflected in the candlelight. Never had he been more happy to see a shiny bald head in his life than at that moment. "Yes, thrown, like a great force hit me. Like a—a—giant demon's breath, or, or—maybe a . . ."

"An *explosion*—that's what the Roman chroniclers called it, at any rate," Bede added, his voice somewhat winded. "It is said there are people in the east who can make such explosions, with a mixture of magic, bat dung, and charcoal."

Daynin stiffened when the light came near enough to reveal the carnage around him. "The big doors are splintered!" he gasped. "And the vault—my God, Father—the sarcophagus is split wide open and shattered into a million pieces!"

The Bede stopped in his tracks, viewing the damage in utter disbelief. "It's a wonder the whole bloody thing hasn't collapsed," he whispered under his breath. "Are you sure you're not hurt?"

Daynin turned in place, dusting off the debris as he allowed the Prior to look him over. The back of his leather tunic had been riddled and pitted with splinters, but none had penetrated. A small bloodstain spread down his frock sleeve and his boot lacings were all but gone. Other than that, the boy was in one piece, except perhaps for his nerves.

He took a step toward the Prior and stopped, turning and cupping one hand to his ear. "Do you hear that?" Far to his right, lost in the depths of the shadows and smoke, the noise arose again. This time, it seemed more measured—more alive. Daynin knew no hinge could make such a sound, especially since it was moving.

Chapter 17:

The Gathering

Swept half a league down the ragged north bank of the Liddle River, Mediah desperately clung to the mane of his horse. A vain attempt to rescue Kruzurk from the dark swirling waters had long since given way to despair for the normally stouthearted Greek. He allowed his mare to tow him toward the beach with little more than a backward glance at the black murky swells that had seemingly just claimed his only friend in the world.

Struggling up the bank ahead of Mediah, Kruzurk's stallion defiantly shook itself off, none the worse for wear after the arduous swim from the barge. The mare followed behind, barely managing to drag herself and her passenger to dry land.

Mediah collapsed into a muddy, shivering heap, his body scraped and bruised by the maze of sharp rocks that lined the Scotian bank. *"Insha Allah,"* he vowed, almost unable to force the prayer through his chattering teeth. "Forgive me, dear friend, for I failed you in your time of need. May *Allah* give your soul its rewards."

Before the words were lost in a rising easterly wind, a familiar though somewhat shaky voice sang out from behind him. "I guess Allah will have to wait a while longer for this old soul."

A surge of joy, energy and surprise propelled Mediah to his feet. "Kruze!" he cried out, seeing the spindly old man

144

teetering toward him on bare feet, a drooping breechcloth his only clothing.

The two ran together, embracing like long lost brothers. "I thought you had gone down for good, m'lord! You turned blue as soon as you hit the water."

"Aye. That water felt considerably colder than I expected. Fortunately it was not too deep, though. I'm glad you made it."

"As am I, m'lord. But we'd best be off. The Duke's men must surely have seen us from the castle ramparts."

Kruzurk cast a mindful eye to the battlements perched on the bluffs above the river, remembering the urgency of their mission. He broke into a half sprint toward the trees and shouted, "Bring the horses, Mediah. We must hurry. I sense something awful is about to happen to Daynin."

"You, below decks there—show yerselves."

The sudden breach of his dream world caused Ean to flinch, then reach for his *sgian du*. He drew the blade instinctively, years of practice having honed that reflex to a fine edge. He glanced at Troon and realized the arrowsmith lay fast asleep or still drunk from his session with the butcher. Either way, Simon would be of no use in a fight with the Duke's men.

Ean dragged himself up the fo'c'sle ladder, poked his head out of the hatch and almost blinded himself from the bright light. "Bloody hell," he winced.

"Aye. That's what I hollered at ya for," the captain said, smiling through a nearly toothless grin. "It's clearing off in the east, and we best be settin' sail straightaway, soon as that bloody tide changes in our favor."

"Then what's the problem?" Ean replied. "Get a move on."

The captain jabbed a finger through the air, pointing

back toward the beach. "Them's what's the problem, old man. For you, that is. Makes no never mind to me, but I figgered you might be wantin' to know. They's a dozen horsemen just dropped over the bluff from Ravensport less than half a league distance and riding hard toward us."

Clambering for a better view, Ean pulled himself onto the deck, then shinnied up one of the ratlines. "Och! I knew 'twould only be a matter of time. It's the Duke's men for sure, come to hang me and Troon."

"A hangin' is it?" the captain roared. "Not on my deck, it bloody well ain't. That's bad luck for a ship, ya know." He turned sharply on his heels and barked, "Make sail, you lot! Cut the mooring lines. Skim that anchor—we got the Sheriff's men comin' for a neck stretchin'!"

Ean disappeared below decks, quickly reappearing with his longbow and a brace of arrows to make a fight of it, even if it would be a brief one. "Those cocky Saxon crows won't be decorating your yardarms with this clansman, Captain— not without a fight."

The captain let out a boisterous laugh. "Hah-har! Stay yerself, you old warhorse. The wind's up. Unless that troop be ridin' animals what can fly, you got no worries. Put that weapon down and make yerself useful. Get up there and help the lads tack that mainsul. We've got us a fair easterly wind and I dinnae intend to waste it."

Nothing made for more noise and hubbub in an encampment than a band of rowdy Caledonians sharing their lard, lies, and lechery. Geile Plumat made every effort to block their commotion from his mind, that he might better concentrate on planning the dangerous task at hand. He knew the risks of traveling further north into Scotia with so few troops, but he would be forced to do so unless they were able to catch their prey soon.

Plumat had heard the tales of highland-dwelling madmen who would rush out of the rocks and slaughter entire cavalcades, then disappear without a trace. And then there were the yarns, though not well documented, of giant beasts swimming the lakes and rivers. It was said they could swallow a twenty-oared snekke in one gulp, crew and all.

Just as Plumat relegated those thoughts to the realm of myth, the sound of hooves on the rocky track brought him back to reality. He swept his helm off the ground and sprang instantly to his feet. Miles Aubrecht beat a hasty path straight toward him—alone.

"M'lord! M'lord! Come quickly!" Miles called.

Reaching out for the reins of the boy's horse, Plumat hauled him to an abrupt stop. "What's the matter with you, boy? Where is deLongait? Is there trouble on the road? Speak up, damn you!"

The hard ride had Miles so winded all he could do was point. "Church—he went—down there. Big rumbling noise. I couldn't see—something terrible—has—happened."

Plumat threw himself onto Cauldron's back, shouting over the din of the motley crew at the river, "To horse, men! We've a battle at hand!"

Whether enticed by plunder or blood, a dozen Caledonians dropped everything and grabbed their weapons. In less time than it takes for a rooster to crow the sunrise, the gang mounted and made ready for action. With Plumat in the lead, they were off toward the ridgeline, hell-bent for whatever might lay ahead. Plumat could only hope the Caledonians were as good in a fight as they were in legend, for he knew that they were all about to be tested like they had never been tested before.

★ ★ ★ ★ ★

For a novice suddenly cast into the midst of a scriptural nightmare come to life, and despite being dragged along by a man twice his size, Novice John regained his composure quickly. "There—through those doors," he said, gesturing toward the back entrance of the nave.

"You best be telling me the truth, cleric," deLongait growled, "or you'll have the devil to pay when the Sheriff arrives."

"He's down there, I tell you. He went there to find a place to hide his books."

"Books, eh? Is there booty, as well? What did these scoundrels bring with them?"

Novice John pointed to the miller's cart, tethered behind the refectory. To avoid the mortal sin of deception as well as protect the priory's part of the bounty, he hesitated, then replied, "I'm not privy to what is in their wagon—yonder, m'lord—but the brethren say the highlanders plan to take their real treasure to a place called Rhum."

A hard cuff on the back of his head was the novice's reward for that information. "Rhum is it? Your lot is sworn to tell the truth, boy. Breaking your vow of veracity will be the least of your worries if I find out otherwise." As if to further emphasize the point, deLongait delivered another sharp "thwack" across the novice's bald spot.

"Ven der vais der coomb di-ya?" came a voice like a rockslide.

Hearing such an unearthly growl only a stone's throw from them, Daynin almost leapt out of his skin. He wanted to break for the wellkeep, but his feet would not allow him to desert the Prior. They were both frozen in place with nowhere to run in the pitch black catacombs, and nowhere to hide.

Again the voice growled, *"Ven der vais der coomin?"* The words stretched out of the dark, rhythmically and plainly demanding to know something—but what?

Without thinking, Daynin blurted out a semblance of a reply. *"Vee nicht der coomin. Venez los alterstaygin."*

They heard no response except an awful screeching sound growing louder. Prior Bede thrust the candelabra out ahead of Daynin, hoping for a glimpse of whatever or whoever approached them. The light glanced off hundreds of metallic surfaces, each moving in unison with the massive physique to which they were attached. For an instant, the Prior smiled at the thought of a giant scaly fish marching straight at them, but his smile quickly gave way to a grimace of horror.

The dull black, heavily riveted shape of a helmet suddenly towered above them. Huge—larger than a ten stone pail turned upside down—its two narrow eye slits gave no evidence of the man's—or being's—identity. A sword the size of a small wagon tongue bounced menacingly against one enormous mailed palm, as if in anticipation of some imminent bloodletting. An ornate bronzish-red hauberk—wider than a waterwheel—came into view next, yet Daynin and the Prior could still make no attempt to escape.

"Tuvas vender yah?" Daynin asked, his voice trembling slightly.

"What did you ask it—er, him?" Prior Bede whispered.

"I think I asked, 'where do you come from' but he's speaking a Pictish dialect I cannae barely understand."

The being stopped far enough away to survey his adversaries. *"Vox cloistermahn commen Cruithni caltrap?"*

"Yes!" Daynin said knowingly. "He's Cruithni, Father—what all of Britain called the Picts before the Romans renamed them for their painted bodies. And he wants to know

149

what a monk is doing on Cruithni land."

Prior Bede grasped his St. Columba's Cross and slipped its chain over his head. He held it aloft so the candlelight might better display it to their inquisitor. In a version of heavily Romanized Latin he proclaimed, "We have been here for generations, protecting this hallowed ground."

"Bradden der foooo—beer—kah. Yah cloven stad ben fayler," the being replied, his vehement disdain for the cross evident to the Prior even without a translation.

Once again, the being's sword began to bounce ominously in his hands. Little doubt remained that the bronzed bully's patience was running out. Daynin decided to press his luck, for there were few options remaining at that moment. *"Prima urbes inter—divum domus Dalriada,"* he repeated from what he could remember of the Latin words carved on the sarcophagus lid. "Give Brude McAlpin his rightful sway," he added, then started to repeat the entire litany again.

The being lurched forward, grabbing Daynin's tunic with his free hand and jerking him violently off the floor. He pulled his face close to the darkened eye slits in the helmet, shook him like a dead cat, and bellowed, "How do you know these words?" The guttural English, delivered in conjunction with such a violent and unexpected attack, almost brought Daynin to tears.

"Stay yourself!" Prior Bede demanded. "This is sanctified ground. There will be no violence here."

"P-p-p-please," Daynin begged, "I meant no harm. You must be the Great Deceiver the walls of this tomb describe. Is that not so?"

"Vosh neg dekander bloch," the helmet replied, then added—again in near perfect English, "I am Brude McAlpin, son of Angus and grandson of Wredech the Bold.

My clan has owned this land since Dalriada was little more than a dun's keep."

The Prior's head snapped to the right at the same instant Daynin's snapped to the left. Their eyes met in disbelief that a dead Pictish prince stood before them. "How can this be?" Bede blurted out.

The giant's grip on Daynin's tunic relaxed a bit, allowing him to drop to his feet. "You Anglish *philkensud*. What know you of this land and my people? Cruithni ruled here when your tribes still squat to piss."

Daynin pushed hard against the mailed grip that held him fast. "I'm *not* Anglish!" he growled. "I'm a McKinnon, of the McKlennan Clans, sprung from the Regents of Rhum. My father was—"

"A whore's groom, no doubt," the booming voice howled with delight. "Think you, boy, that I care from what bastard Scotian line you come? If you are not Cruithni, you are not worthy of a stone to mark your passing. And since you have no tattoos on your body, know I that you are nothing but a heathen, likely come to steal whatever your thieving lot can drag home behind you."

Pulling hard and backing up two steps finally broke the giant's grip and gave Daynin a better perspective of his adversary. He looked up into the black helmet slits and decided on another bold gamble. "At least my father had honor, and died for it. These walls tell of a Great Deceiver, who apparently had no honor—a man who invited his enemies to supper at Scone, then when they were seated at long tables, pulled a bolt that cast them into a deep pit where they were slain like sheep in a well."

Prior Bede gasped at the boy's sudden brash defense. No doubt, he expected the colossal sword to swoop down any second and send them both to the next life. But the angry armored entity just stood there, sizing up its enemies.

"You know nothing of the history these walls tell, *hovel* boy. Cruithni courage is valued above all else. Had you the weapons, I would test your mettle. Then we would see who eats his enemy's guts for supper."

"Heathen!" Bede declared, defiantly.

McAlpin thumped Daynin hard in the chest, knocking him backward against the wall. He turned on his heels, sweeping the candelabra aside to face the Prior at close quarters. "Mayhaps there would be more skill to impaling your black robe on my sword, eh, prayer man?"

The Bede couldn't back down now, nor could he resist with much more than words. "The Norse believed the stature of a man was told by the valor of his enemies. Where's the honor in gutting a priest and a boy?"

"I fought the Norse, *cloistermahn*. My people fought them and the Anglish, then the Caledonians and the Scots. That tale the boy tells of Scone—those were *my* allies slaughtered in that pit. The Anglish dogs and their cowardly minions, the Caledonians, paid ten fold in blood for that day's treachery, as you and all who tread this ground will soon learn."

Brude's sword began to draw back ominously, ready for its first bloodbath in nearly half a millennium. His motion stopped suddenly, when out of the darkness toward the wellkeep came a loud order, "Yield, in the name of Duke Harold of Anglia!"

Chapter 18:

The Clashing

Brude pushed the priest aside, oblivious to the monk's presence now that a real adversary had arrived. "Anglish dogs! Brude McAlpin yields to neh man ner monster. Step forward and see what form your doom has taken."

At the base of the wellkeep, Earl deLongait hesitated, obviously unsure what he was facing, or from which direction that terrible boast had come. The heavy rasping voice seemed to echo from every direction at once. He plucked Novice John out of the lead and shoved him bodily back toward the wellkeep, careful to make sure the candelabra remained intact.

"Don't lose the light, boy, or we're damned for sure. That's no human voice we just heard, wager that. Be it demon, devil, or duke, Draco will deal with it as long as I can see what I'm facing."

Torn between running for his life and waiting to see what awful apparition had come from the bowels of the catacombs, the novice crossed himself, then took a step forward to close on deLongait's back, preferring the protection of that giant headsman's axe to a simple wooden cross.

"Bloody hell!" deLongait gasped.

Out of the corner of his eye, Novice John caught the flash of a sword singing its way through the dusty gloom. He ducked, allowing Draco to meet the full force of the attack just in time to keep it from parting deLongait's skull.

153

A loud "clang" rocked the walls of the chamber, sending sparks flying like those off a blacksmith's anvil.

The shock of the impact almost buckled deLongait. He must never have been struck with such force. Worst still, his attacker seemed to disappear. "Where is he, boy? Can you see him?"

Novice John waved the candelabra around them in a circle, to no avail. "A ddd—ddd—demon, for sure, m'lord. That was no human form."

"Demon my ass!" deLongait roared, turning a half circle to face the next attack. "Whatever it is, it swings that broadsword like a bloody battering ram."

"Look out!" the novice screamed.

Again the "whoosh" of Brude's double-edged blade fell upon them. This time it struck deLongait a glancing blow to the side of his helmet, sending his armored coif crashing across the chamber floor and bouncing away into the darkness.

Echoes rang out from everywhere, the din of battle deafening in the confines of the stone walled crypt. "Damn that hurts," deLongait swore, but he had no time to lament the loss of his helm. He shook his head, turned about once more, and there before him stood the largest adversary he had ever hoped to meet in battle. "You move with the deftness of a cat for one your size. Are you a man or the devil's minion?"

"Aye, a cat—a *Cruithni* cat—come to take your black heart, Anglish."

"Many a man have I sent to hell with one swat from Draco, fool. Now back off before you're added to the list! I've no quarrel with you this day."

The two moved in a wary semicircle, sizing each other up like angry bulls waiting for the other to charge first.

Then Brude spoke again. "There are ten thousand days for which your kind must pay, *philkin-grood*. Ten thousand days your people raped my land, but no more."

Whether deLongait was dazzled by the shining bits of armor dancing in the candlelight, or dazed by the whack on his head, he never saw Brude's next move coming. It fell with the swiftness of a lightning bolt, and nearly the same lethality. A resounding "crangggg" bounced from wall to wall as Brude's blade rent deLongait's shoulder armor in one horrendous blow, penetrating all the way to the flesh.

The Duke's man, though unusually large for a Saxon, crumpled under the vicious assault. Blood erupted from the breach in his armor, quickly turning his yellow and red tunic to a crimson collage. Novice John reeled in terror, then dropped to his knees beside deLongait to await his trip to paradise.

Brude poised his sword to send the monk to his rewards, then hesitated. "Are there more of these Anglish bandits on the way, blackbird? Speak up or I'll drop yer head in yer own lap!"

Terrified by that image, Novice John unclasped his death grip from the shaft of the candelabra and raised a shaky hand toward the wellkeep. "Th—th—th—there may be m—m—m'lord. Uu—up there. This one ssss—sss—spoke of others on the way."

"Stay your tongue, priest," deLongait managed to growl. Despite his agony, he remained a part of the Duke's legion, and would no doubt choose to die that way. "Tell this bastard nothing, or I warn you . . ."

Two steps forward brought Brude towering over his fallen enemy. He thrust his sword tip under deLongait's chin, stopping only a whisper short of a coup-de-grace. "How many, and how soon? Tell me, boy, or this dog's death is on your hands."

By now, the novice quaked uncontrollably, crying and nearly at the point of collapse. His training in the priestly arts had never prepared him for such a violent arena. It was all he could do to bow his head and mutter, "I cannot say, your Lordship. I—I—I just know he mentioned others."

"This better be the truth, *cloistermahn,*" Brude's thundering voice declared. A brief protest from deLongait ended with a large Pictish horseboot planted squarely onto the ghastly wound in his shoulder. "Anglish armor—good for court, but hardly worth its weight in a real battle, eh *fewgtik?*"

DeLongait squirmed under the awful pain, able to do little else at that moment. His head rolled from side to side in bitter anguish. He moaned, "That towheaded boy—my life for a damned plowboy."

"What boy?" Brude demanded. He pushed harder with his heel, as if to bring a faster response.

"Arrrgghhh. Damn you, blaggard. *That* boy, I should imagine!" DeLongait's good arm gestured back toward the Saracen arch where Daynin and Prior Bede had just appeared from out of the gloom.

"How know you this boy?" the torture went on.

"We have—a warrant—three felons—Duke Harold's enemies . . ." With a final gasp, deLongait's arm dropped when he passed out from the pain.

Brude turned to face the arch. "Is this true, boy? These Anglish—they are your sworn enemies?"

Daynin had no idea how to answer Brude's question. The sight of so much blood on the stranger made him queasy, as well as unsure what answer might keep him alive. He remembered what Kruzurk had told him about truth, and decided to follow the path of least travail. "I cannae say for certain, but my guess is he's come to hang me for the murder of the Marquis of Greystone, Duke Harold's cousin."

Prior Bede lurched backward in horror. "Murder? You said nothing of murder! My God, boy, what blacksouled deceit is this? You come to my priory with the stain of murder on your hands and ask for help?"

"It was a fair fight, Prior," Daynin sighed. "He attacked the woman, and I . . ."

"You took his heart, did ya, boy?" Brude pressed.

Daynin turned defiantly to face the Great Deceiver. "It's Daynin, by God—not boy! I'm seventeen—not that it matters to you, but I'm *tired* of being called a *boy!*"

"Hahaar," the giant roared, his delight obvious at seeing the lad's mettle boil to the surface. "Seventeen and already took a Marquis' heart in single combat—and an Anglish one at that. I had a feeling you kept more behind your eyes than I could scare out of you, highlander. You have the stare of one who's tasted the enemy's blood and liked it."

For the first time in his life, Daynin had been called "highlander" openly and it felt good—much more manly than "boy" and certainly a step up from plowboy. The moniker struck him like the hind leg of a skittish ass. *I am a man now,* his brain screamed. *Not just in my own mind, but outwardly as well. And it's high time I started acting like one.*

His chest swelled with a pride he had never been allowed to know before, except in his grandfather's hovel when the old man had told him of battles against the Caledonians, the Britons, the Irish, and the Norse. The passion of a hundred clan generations ran through his veins. Yet at that moment, only three things flashed in his mind—Sabritha and the Island of Rhum—and that humongous sword waving in his face, glistening with fresh blood.

Apparently conscious of the boy's anxiety, Brude stood his broadsword on its tip, allowing both of his massive gauntlets to rest on the pommel in a pensive pose. "The Cruithni have a saying, highlander. 'The enemy of my enemy wars as my ally.' So it shall be with you—for I have need of allies in my quest. But I warn you—at the first hint of treachery, I'll cut you in so many pieces even the crows won't find enough for a meal. And another thing. 'Daynin' is hardly a fit name for the slayer of a Marquis. I shall call you *Draygnar* as befits a warrior. It means 'the boy who would be king' in my language."

Daynin stared up into the hollow eye slits of the giant's helmet, still unable to discern any outward signs of humanity or of what lived inside that massive shell of armor. His heart told him that being in league with the devil's disciple would be nothing less than a mortal sin. However, the news that Duke Harold had come all the way to Scotia to find him, and worse—the possibility of losing Sabritha and the Blackgloom Bounty—made him think such an alliance might not be a bad plan. Besides, he might even persuade the giant to leave the church in peace, which did not seem at all likely unless he agreed to the coalition.

"You leave me few choices, m'lord. I'll join with you, but only until we reach Rhum."

"This is blasphemy!" Prior Bede gasped. "Daynin, you must not join in this diablerie. Turn yourself in to the Duke and plead for self defense, but don't give your soul to this devil."

"I'd sooner jump in a well, Prior. I've seen the Duke's justice firsthand. The choice is always the same—die on the rack before or after you confess."

"Haaaahaaarrr!" McAlpin reached out to slap Daynin on the side of his shoulder, nearly knocking him down.

" 'Twould seem things have not changed much while I've slept these many years, eh *Draygnar?*"

"It's Daynin. Day-nin. And what would you prefer I call you, m'lord, now that we are in league against the Duke?"

"You may call me Brude, as was the custom among my friends—those few who lived long enough to become my friends, that is."

"Then we should be off before the rest of the Duke's army shows up. I've treasure and a woman to protect, and a castle to rebuild."

Brude leaned forward into the Prior's flaxen face. "You tell the rest of the Anglish that hell is waiting for them, *cloistermahn*. And tell them to bring plenty of mourners."

With the Duke's man gone from the hovel, Sabritha took the opportunity to send her gang of cowardly visitors on their way. "It's time for you to leave now—all of you," she scolded. "That was no goblin. He's just a big oaf in chainmail that you could have bested, had you tried. If only I had a sword! Oh never mind—get out of here—you should be ashamed of yourselves."

Prior Stin stepped toward the open door and gestured for the rest of his brood to hurry along. He cast Sabritha the kind of baleful glare that only a cloistered monk can summon, then left her to rant alone.

Quickly, she gathered her things and dashed out onto the priory grounds. Determined not to be there when the Duke's man or his cohorts returned, Sabritha went looking for Abaddon. Daynin was nowhere to be seen, but at that moment, friends were hardly foremost in her mind. Escape from a long fall on a short rope filled her thoughts, despite an equally greater fear of traveling alone in a dangerous place like the highlands.

Already hitched to the cart, Abaddon waited patiently near the laundry ward, where she finally found him. A light misty rain fell as Sabritha climbed aboard and guided the old warhorse toward the north exit of the priory grounds. She hesitated inside the gate, then pulled Abaddon to a stop, allowing herself to wonder for an instant where Daynin might be. She swung around on the seat for one last look and couldn't believe her eyes. In the distance, a large yellow banner fluttered against the gray backdrop at the south end of the valley.

"Bloody hell!" she gasped. "The Duke's army is here!"

The Running

A howling southeasterly wind pushed the *Shiva's* ancient mast to its limits, and Ean McKinnon right along with it. His worry about soldiers had been replaced by a bout of seasickness in the choppy dash through the North Channel that separates Ireland and Scotia. Ean leaned over the stern rail and heaved his guts out once more, to the apparent delight of the captain who seemed intent upon running his ship at right angles across every new ocean swell.

"Fish gruel ain't so tasty the second time, eh old man?" the captain asked.

"Mind yer tongue, ya saltwater blaggard." Ean's weakened voice lost its sauce in the high wind, but not its intent. "Is nae but a wee job to cut yer bloody throat and toss ya to the fishes, ya know."

The captain scoffed, "Aye and *then* who'd be steerin' this scow through those headlands in the Firth of Clyde? None of this crew, that's for sure. They're as worthless as farts in a windstorm when it comes to navigatin', wager that!"

Aside from the taste in his mouth, Ean could think of little except the outline of the coast scudding by off to his right. *Scotia!* he mused. *Home again at last. Now if only I can find Daynin before the Duke catches him. Then we shall see if he has his father's pluck!*

Plumat reined Cauldron to a stop near the edge of the

priory's stony south bluff. Pushing himself up in his stirrups to get a better view of the target below, he yelled back to his squire, "I see deLongait's charger, but nothing else. Ride ahead to the church and tell him we are coming. The Caledonians are scattered out behind us like pigs in a pilgrim's parade. I'll gather them up and come ahead when we can make a show of force these priests will pray about for a fortnight. If there's trouble, bring deLongait here to regroup. And Miles, don't do anything to start a fight—you are far from ready for combat."

"Aye, m'lord." Miles kicked his horse sharply in the flank as he guided him down the steep southern approach to the cathedral grounds. More than a little anxious to be somewhere that offered a roof, warm food and a semblance of safety, he pushed the horse harder. The boy's thoughts of warmth only lasted an instant, for ahead of him a flurry of activity burst out in all directions.

Monks scurried hither and yon, driven by a fear Miles could only imagine. A miller's cart raced out from behind the church and sped toward the front gate of the grounds, scattering a small herd of sheep in its wake. Then, just as Miles reached Prior Bede's hovel, the biggest, most frightening figure of a giant his worst nightmares could have conjured barged its way out of the rear doors of the sanctuary.

"Whoa, beast!" he screamed, to no avail. Pulling hard on his reins, Miles almost catapulted over the horse's head as the charger reeled in terror and confusion. The squire hung on for a second then fell sideways off his mount, one leg entangled in a stirrup. In a twinkling, the horse took off again, scared out of its wits. Dangling upside down, dragged along in the mud, Miles could do little except scream for his life.

Sabritha watched the courtyard scene unfold with something approaching amusement until she realized the charger had bolted straight toward her and the wagon. She knew what would happen next—Abaddon would break and take her and the cart along in his mad flight. She made the decision to jump, instead. Being crushed under an overturned wagon seemed considerably less enticing than staying to face the Duke's wrath, whatever outcome that might present.

Having followed the giant up from the wellkeep, Daynin pushed his way around Brude's hulking frame and stepped outside the church just in time to see the horse and rider dash across the courtyard in front of him. A quick survey proved what he already expected—the Duke or the Sheriff's men, or both, were upon them. Whoever the rider had been, he presented little threat now, but that yellow standard on the bluff was another thing entirely.

"We have to go!" Daynin begged. "The Duke's men are here. And in great numbers, it appears."

Brude clanked out into the mist, drawing his broadsword in one enormous flowing motion. He waved it menacingly over his head, switching from first one hand, then to the other, all the while boasting to the sky, "Bring on the Anglish! *Droongar* of Dalriada, the sacred sword of my fathers, has much to avenge!"

Careful to avoid the whirling blade as he approached the giant's back, Daynin pleaded again. "We can't fight them all, Brude. I see at least a dozen horses. And besides, you agreed to go with me!"

"Go? You ask that I withdraw in the face of the enemy? This blade spilled the blood of the Ninth Legion when it fell to the Cruithni in the forests of Fortrenn. I will not sheath it now—not with the enemy in sight. You go, boy—take yer woman—I will join you later. After all, we are allies now!"

One look at that troop on the bluff convinced Daynin he had few choices. Demon or no demon, Brude could never stand against so many, and without a bow or sword, Daynin would be of little help either way.

"The mouth of the Clyde—near Glasgow—that's where we'll be. I'll find us a ship . . ."

In his flowing Pictish vernacular, Brude replied, "Get thee gone, *Draygnar*. Brude McAlpin will stand ye in good stead here. I will hold this ground at all cost."

Out of the corner of his eye, Daynin caught a glimpse of Sabritha leaping from the cart, her coal black hair flowing in the wind. Abaddon reared up in his traces, almost tipping the cart over backwards on top of her. Daynin's heart went into his throat. "No!" he screamed, breaking into a dead run for the front gate.

Miles Aubrecht's horse raced by the cart and out the gate. Tumbling for her life, Sabritha cried out, "God help you, whoever you are!" Obviously she could only offer the poor squire a few seconds of empathy with her own plight having taken center stage. Abaddon jerked hard against the wagon's foot brake that kept him from following the charger on its mad dash to doom. Behind the wagon, events of an entirely different nature were about to turn the otherwise peaceful priory grounds into total carnage.

"Lights ahead, m'lord," Mediah reported.

Kruzurk slowed his horse to a walk, overjoyed with a reason to stop after the long day's ride on the trek northward. "Yes, I see them. Looks to be a tavern. We'll stop and give the horses a rest, then move on before daybreak. Careful what you say here, Mediah. We've no friends in this country."

"Aye. A den of thieves for sure, from the looks of it,"

Mediah agreed. "I'll see to the animals whilst you sup. Mayhaps there's a swinekeep about who can pass the local gossip, but I'll be careful what I say in return. Not to worry."

Mindful of his backside when he opened the front door, Kruzurk was amazed to find a tavern built from half timber and half cave, seemingly sprouting from the solid rock face behind it. An ancient weathered sign out front had read *The Hole Inn The Wall*. Now he saw the reason for the label.

A long bar stretched across the whole of the cave mouth at the rear of the great room. Hollow echoes from every sound in the tavern could be heard bouncing back into the darkness. An ugly hulking quencher roosted behind the barboard, his stare more than enough to scare off even the surliest of visitors. There were no corners in the circular room for Kruzurk to settle in, so he decided to take a table in the middle, next to a round, crackling fire pit. Three scraggly men at the other tables barely gave him notice.

"We're out of ale, if that be yer want, old man," the quencher's woman screeched from somewhere back in the smoky, pitch black alcove. "I *can* offer you cold beer and an even colder gruel, if'n ye have coin and can pay."

"Beer and bread—how much, barkeep?" Kruzurk replied.

"That depends," the keep was quick to respond. "If'n ye be stayin' the night, I'd be chargin' a quarter-talen for the food, booze and bed. You'd be sharin' the bed with others o' course."

Kruzurk's skin crawled at that notion. The floor of the inn was littered with dead roaches and rat droppings. He could only imagine how bad the beds were, not to mention the bedmates. "Just bread and beer, keep. And I'll have the brew in a clean pail if you don't mind."

"If'n we don't mind, says he," the keep scoffed. "Would ya be needed a woman to keep ya warm, then? Or a sheep mayhaps? I've got both, and only a tuppence for either."

Mediah had just slipped in the front door. He quickly sized up the situation and eased onto the bench next to Kruzurk. "I've news," he whispered. "A blind man in the barn out back heard some of the local henchmen talking about a bounty for a boy and a magician. The gang headed north to Galashiels at first light this morning. Seems the Duke is raising an army of mercenaries there."

"That tears it," Kruzurk groaned. "We haven't an hour to lose." He stood up and approached the barkeep, three silver talens in his fist. "We need two fresh horses, keep— and I'll take the bread and beer as well. How much?"

"Horses, says you?"

"How much, damn it? I've no time to dilly-dally with you," Kruzurk snapped. He dropped two of the talens on the board and waited for a reaction. "We'll be leaving two good horses in trade. What say you, now?"

The barkeep swept the coins off the board faster than a hog swoops an acorn. "Bloody hell, for two talens, you could ride me old lady, if'n ya wanted to, sire. Take yer pick of those beasts in the barn. And tell that old beggar out there to tend to your trade-ins."

"Done! And one more thing. How many roads lead from here to Galashiels?"

A hearty bite on one of the talens was all the proof the barkeep needed to realize he had just made the deal of the month. "How many? Why, they's just one o' course. This 'ere road leads to Abbotsford Priory, then over the Moorfoot cairn to Galashiels. But that ain't no place for the likes of you pilgrims, 'specially at night, if'n ya be catchin' my drift."

Kruzurk did not respond. He turned and motioned to Mediah, who by now had the pail of beer and a large haunch of bread in his hands. "Let's be off, Captain Fludd. We must hurry if we are to join up with the bountiers."

A confused look spread across Mediah's face, then he took the hint. "Aye—uh—m'lord Beasely. These writs must be delivered."

The two were almost to the door when one of the ragtags in the bar spoke up. "Pardon, yer lordship, but if'n ye be ridin' all the way to Galashiels, ye'll be missin' the Duke's party for sure."

"And you would know this, how?" Kruzurk replied, skeptically.

"Fer one o' them fancy silver talens, a bloke could be persuaded to show you where the Duke's men are, if'n he had a good horse and a hefty swig o' beer to settle his innards, that is."

Kruzurk tossed a talen on the floor at the man's feet. When the ragtag bent over to pick it up, Kruze planted his foot squarely on the knave's hand. "A bloke could *lose* his innards meddling in the King's business, my friend. Now where was it you said we needed to go?"

Chapter 20:

The Blooding

Novice John held the goblet close to Earl deLongait's lips. The pungent odor of the priory's vintage wine was enough to rouse him from his stupor. DeLongait's eyes flapped open with a look of complete shock that he remained in the land of the living. "Bloody hell," he whispered, his voice weak from the massive loss of blood.

"We stopped the bleeding," the novice proclaimed. "But we can't move you just yet. You're too heavy to carry up the wellkeep without risk of opening that shoulder again."

"Find—my—troop, boy. Bring—Plumat. You must—warn—him—about—giant . . ." That was all he could say before passing out again.

Prior Bede shook his head and turned to leave. "Stay with him, John. Make him as comfortable as you can. We'll bring down the brazier and charcoal later to cauterize that wound. A hot iron and prayer is all we can offer him for the time being. I'm sure the rest of his group will be along soon enough. They can decide what to do with him. I must see what manner of evil that monster has brought to my church, now that he is loose on the grounds."

Fortunately for Prior Bede, he had no clue what transpired in the middle of the churchyard above him. At that moment, Plumat's troop prepared to launch a headlong charge down the slopes of Moorfoot, straight into mortal combat with the most fearsome foe any of the attackers would ever encounter.

Meanwhile, Daynin managed to steady Abaddon and get Sabritha to her feet. He thought about the bounty he'd just left in the shambles of the catacombs, and could only hope Prior Bede would salvage some of it from the ruins. A last look at the far end of the valley convinced him that they had to make a run for it. Eluding the Duke's men had almost become second nature to him by now, and this time he had a head start, albeit a short one.

After a slightly hesitant effort at brushing the sheep dung off Sabritha's backside he asked, "Are you all right?"

"Oh sure, I'm just fine," she snapped back. "I nearly get my neck broken, I smell like sheep dip and now I assume we're off on another wild jaunt to who knows where. Daynin—do you make this kind of trouble *everywhere* you go? And who is that—that—*giant* over there?"

Her weak gesture towards Brude quickly brought McAlpin's plight back to Daynin's mind as he helped Sabritha onto the wagon, then climbed aboard. "A friend, I guess you'd say—or an ally actually—I'll tell you more on the road. He may be joining us again up north, when we take ship for Rhum." A crack of the whip punctuated the last statement, as Daynin put Abaddon into motion to distance them from the coming carnage.

Sabritha fell backward against a chest in the rear of the wagon. "Ouch! Are you trying to kill me, you mophead?"

"Sorry—we have to move fast. Hell is coming to supper."

Sabritha righted herself and growled, "The Sheriff is at the far end of the valley, in case you didn't know it. I saw the standard."

"Yes, I know. If we can reach Lamington Leech before

dark, there is no way they can follow us through that maze of craggy canyons. We should reach the Firth of Clyde by midday tomorrow with any luck. Then we'll find a ship and be gone before they catch up to us."

Sabritha turned to see the drama unfolding behind them. "Are you leaving that poor fool behind to take on the Duke's army all by himself?"

Daynin stole a quick peek over his shoulder. Brude stood his ground defiantly, even as a dozen horsemen lined up to charge down upon him. "Aye, his choice—not mine. But McAlpin has the kind of courage my father had. It's the enemy you should feel sorry for," he replied, then lashed old Abaddon even harder.

"Men!" Sabritha jeered. "That fool thinks he's invincible and you actually think you can outrun mounted knights in a miller's cart. Where are all the *sane* men in this country?"

That comment brought a wry smile to Daynin's face, despite her sarcasm. *Och! She called me a mahn! First Brude calls me "highlander" and now this. Two firsts in one day. Now if I can just keep us alive long enough to enjoy the next "first" with her . . .*

Angry that he had seemingly lost both his squire and his trusted lieutenant, Plumat groused, "Where the bloody hell *is* that boy? And where is deLongait? We can't sit here all night."

Scarba cupped his hands over his brow to fend off the light rain. He gave the valley a long scan. "I cannae say for certain, m'lord, lest that be his horse makin' for the heath way yonder on t'other side of the valley. Looks to be draggin' something, or somebody. If it's the squire, we won't find enough left of 'im to fill a beer mug, wager on that."

Another of the Caledonians spoke up. "Forget the squire. Can ye not see what stands awaiting us in that courtyard? Has to be the biggest highlander ever fell from a womb, says I. That beast is taller than a jousting mount reared up on its hind legs, 'e is."

"Aye, and wider than Scarba's old lady," another man added, his jest falling on deaf ears.

"Blaggards," Plumat growled. "Have I hired an army of cowards, that you sit here trembling at the sight of one suit of armor?"

A look of disdain passed from man to man amongst the Caledonians, their courage having been sullied by a Saxon prince once again. Only the Duke's colors kept the seedy mob from cutting Plumat's throat right there on the spot. That, and the very real prospect that he would take several of them to hell with him, even in a lopsided fight.

"Are you with me, lads?" Plumat barked. "Five silver pieces for the man who delivers a killing blow to that Goliath, and ten extra for the boy's head. What say you?"

Loot spoke louder than honor to the Caledonian killers. Almost with a single voice, they proclaimed, "Death to the Goliath! Onward, lads!" and flooded down the cairn's rocky slope.

Plumat held back, knowing it might take half the troop to bring down that giant. He couldn't commit himself to that kind of frontal assault. After all, that's what levies were for—to provide the bloodletting. "Whoa, Cauldron," he said, tightening the charger's reins. "Not yet, boy. We'll wait for the minions to do their job. Then we shall see what kind of mischief there is left to be done in this place."

"Quickly, Mediah," Kruzurk said. "We've not a minute to lose. If the Duke's men left for Abbotsford this morning, they've likely already arrived. I only hope Daynin had the good sense to drop off his penance with those monks and keep moving. Elsewise we may be too late."

A seedy blind beggar sat huddled in a dark corner of the barn, his ears pricking at the overheard conversation. He stood up and tip-tapped his way into the horse pen, a knobby stick guiding his steps. Beside him, a nasty, mud-encrusted mastiff the size of a small pony dogged his every move. The animal stopped instantly upon seeing the two strangers in the pen. His snarling growl announced the beggar's arrival.

"Alms for the poor?"

"Call off your dog, beggar," Mediah warned. "I already gave you a tuppence for your information earlier. Now begone with you."

"Meanin' no harm, your lordship. Thor here—he's my eyes. He sees that which my cane cannot reach."

Kruzurk approached the beggar, proffering his half of the bread loaf they'd just bought. The move elicited an even more unfriendly growl from the dog. "Take this bread—it's all I can offer you just now. We have to be on our way."

"You're too kind, m'lord. Fergum is my name—Olghar Fergum. They call me 'Fermin' hereabouts, since my un-happy circumstances force me to live with the rats." The beggar held out his filthy mitt to receive the gift. "And don't mind Thor. He's only vicious if he senses there's harm coming to me."

Kruzurk sidestepped the dog's enormous head to place the bread in Olghar's outstretched hand. "We were told this road goes through Abbotsford Priory. Is that true?"

"It certainly used to go there, m'lord. Not being able to travel these ten years since my blinding, I can only guess the track has not changed much. But one must be very careful taking that route. There are a dozen thieves' dens along the way, so they tell me. Cut your throat just to watch you die, they will."

Kruzurk made sure Olghar had the bread firmly in hand, then turned to mount his horse. "Thank you for that warning. We will be on our guard. Now we have to go."

Olghar took a few halting steps toward Kruzurk's fading voice and added, "Meanin' no disrespect, your lordship, but uhm, I believe it's dark out and I wouldna make that journey 'til first light, if I was you. Many a pilgrim has tried to reach the priory overnight, only to get waylaid by a bunch of no-goods out there in the dark. I hear about these things, you know."

After offering Kruzurk a much-needed boost up onto his saddle, Mediah turned to the beggar and snapped, "We are *hardly* what you'd call *pilgrims*, Fermin. And we have to get to the priory straightaway. We've important business there."

"Greek, eh? Your voice—it has the ring of Greek to it, does it not?" Olghar asked.

Mediah cast Kruzurk a quizzical glance, who simply shrugged. "Keep that to yourself, old man. Sometimes it's best not to know too much about travelers."

Olghar's knobby cane rose up to point straight at Mediah's chest. "I know this much, Greek. There's a track through the Tweedsmuir bog that will save you a three hour ride to Abbotsford and keep you out of harm's way."

"Hog rot," Mediah scoffed. "The inn keeper said nothing of a track across the moors."

"Aye, the inn keeper—that nasty slug makes 'is livin' off the thieves hereabouts. You think he's gonna tell you the truth? I can get you to Abbotsford—fast and alive—but you have to take me with you. That's my price. I want to die on holy ground and none of these local blaggards will carry me there."

Kruzurk urged his horse forward so that he could lean down closer to the beggar. "How do we know you're not in league with these cutthroats? Guide us on some wild ride into the moors, then we never come back—is that your plan?"

Olghar stuffed the bread loaf into a leather pouch, then fished from inside his grimy tunic an ivory seven point cross as big as a horse's bit. He held the cross to his lips and kissed it with the reverence of an Abbot. "I swear on this cross of Saint Vladimir. When we reach the priory, you can have it in payment. Is *that* enough proof that I speak the truth?"

"Saddle another horse, Mediah. And leave an extra silver piece in that empty beer bucket for payment. It looks like we have ourselves a guide."

Prior Bede heard the giant's deep-throated boasting outside before he even reached the top of the wellkeep. "God help us if that monster takes out his wrath on the brethren."

Peeking cautiously through the crack between the nave's open back doors, the Prior knew instantly what the giant crowed about. Less than a hundred paces from the outer perimeter wall of the cathedral grounds, a squadron of mounted troops had drawn up in line. Despite having no training in war, Prior Bede knew a bloody brawl brewed right in front of him.

The Caledonians must have realized it too. Close enough now to see the true size of their adversary, the line of attackers had come to a complete stop almost as abruptly as they had started. A resounding "Whoa!" echoed down the line when each man came face to face with his own mortality.

"That's no ordinary highlander," one man bemoaned.

Another chimed in, "Aye, a ruddy great beast 'e is."

"Och! Look at that armor," Scarba growled. "I've nae seen scale armor like that anywhere but on the story stones of the Picts at Loch Ness."

"Ain't no more Picts, Scarba—been so for many a year, now," someone spoke out.

Scarba drew his Glasgow blade and gave it a quick once over. "Aye, but that beast yonder could be the last of 'em. And it will be us that all of Caledonia sings about at campfires a hundred years from now, if we can take 'im. Wager that."

Agreement about an ancient axiom "The bigger they are, the harder they fall," passed from man to man in the ranks. At the same time, a small tabour thumped somewhere in the group, as if the drumbeat would bolster the collective courage of the Caledonian horde.

"Let's do 'im!" Scarba howled, the Glasgow sword waving wildly in the air.

All at once, the horsemen lurched forward, giving ground to Scarba only long enough for him to enter the gate at their head. Three abreast, the horses charged through the gap in the wall, instantly churning the courtyard's neatly manicured grounds into a loblolly of muck and mire.

"Get 'im!" someone screamed as the column of horses bore down on the steadfast McAlpin.

In a move made so fast it became invisible, Brude dashed forward and threw himself under the first rank of horses. Animals, men and weapons collapsed in a mangled heap, almost burying the Pict in the mud. The second rank of three, with no time to change direction, plowed straight into the pile of bodies, adding themselves to the mound of debris. Behind them, more horses reeled in terror, throwing riders hither and yon like sheep shot from a catapult.

In a matter of seconds, six of the Caledonians fell with injuries so bad they were out of the fight. Three more struggled to right themselves from under their fallen mounts while the rest of the column split in two lines to sweep left and right around the melee. Scarba managed to gain his feet long enough to strike one hearty blow against Brude's helmet. Everyone in the courtyard heard the resounding "crang".

Brude struck back, delivering a savage backhand across Scarba's knees. The Pict's humongous blade rent Scarba's kneeguards like goat cheese. Blood splattered the Caledonians and their horses, mingling with the mud and gore. Scarba fell without so much as a whimper, dead before he hit the ground.

Simultaneously, three crossbow bolts dinged off Brude's armor. He barely noticed that he'd been fired upon. He whirled in the mud, lashing out at the flank of the nearest horse. The animal screamed, reared backward and tossed its rider with a loud "splunk" in the mud.

The remaining Caledonians circled their prey, much as a pack of Westmoorland wolves might do, having gained considerable respect for the damage one swat from the giant's sword could produce. Several cranked off crossbow shots, to no avail. Brude's armor was too thick to penetrate, even at twenty paces. Another man let fly with a sling but the stone glanced off with little effect. Quickly, it became clear that the giant had never heard of Goliath, and the Caledonians had no David.

The man-mountain seemed all but invulnerable until one of the levies produced a long tether used for dragging down wayward sheep. He fastened a loop in one end, then rode forward as close as he dared. He cast the loop, snaring Brude's sword arm in mid flail. McAlpin ripped at the cord angrily, almost toppling the horse and rider. Another rope came from the opposite side of the circle. It, too, made its mark, entangling Brude's other arm.

Both ropes were quickly drawn tight with the huge warrior stretched in between. The giant tugged at first one, then the other to escape, even as more ropes fell around his head and shoulders. In no time, the Caledonians had their enemy ensnared with six ropes pulled by six horses in all directions.

The fight had been brief and costly, but in the end the Caledonians prevailed by sheer strength of numbers. "Finish him!" several of the henchmen howled. More agreed, a frenzied blood lust having replaced courage and all sense of an honorable victory.

Prior Bede couldn't help himself. Demon or no, he couldn't watch the Caledonians slaughter a helpless being. He broke out of the nave doors holding his cross high that they might see it in the gathering darkness. "Enough!" he ordered. "The blooding must cease. You fight on sacred ground!"

"No one's blood has been spilled here but ours," one of the men growled back. "Be gone with you, Abbot. We've a right to collect our reward for this victory, and collect it we will, by God!"

Turning to face the loudmouth, Prior Bede leveled his crucifix as an archer would aim a crossbow. "I warn you, my son. Hell will be your only reward if you murder this—this—*man* in cold blood."

Satisfied the giant was finally defanged and helpless, Plumat urged Cauldron forward from behind the stone wall where he had watched the finale of the battle. "Take his sword and bind him," he ordered. "Then do as the Abbot says. No need to finish him here. We'll take this big bastard with us and hang him from the first tree we find stout enough to swing 'im. Half of you see to the wounded. The rest of you—find that damn *boy!*"

Chapter 21:

The Kindling

Miles Aubrecht's horse had nearly run itself to death in the panicked dash from the priory grounds. The squire had long since passed out from his upside down ordeal, and still hung precariously from the stirrup when Daynin and Sabritha happened upon him in the dark. "Whoa, boy," Daynin whispered, trying his best to get close to the squire without spooking the charger again. He barely managed to free the squire's boot before the horse shied away, then bolted into the inky black night.

"What are you going to do with this blaggard now?" Sabritha asked impatiently.

"We don't have any choice. We'll have to take him with us. I'm sure we'll find a place along the way where we can leave him. Besides, I would really like to have that chainmail and helmet he's wearing. They probably saved his life after being dragged half the night."

Sabritha dropped down from the back of the cart and raced to Daynin's side, her eyes ablaze with anger. "Are you *daft?* Not only will he slow us down, but when he wakes up, he's likely to cause all manner of problems. That's the Duke's heraldry he's wearing, you know!"

Daynin had to bite his lip to keep from smiling. *She's so beautiful,* he mused. *Especially when she's angry.* He stood up to see her more clearly. At that same instant she edged closer to where he had been kneeling over the squire. Their gaze embraced from only a hand span's distance, the deep blue of his eyes so warm and welcoming that the fire in hers turned from anger to passion before either of them realized it.

Nothing short of an avalanche could have stopped what happened next. Sabritha's hands went to Daynin's waist. His hands cupped the soft pink of her wind-burned cheeks, their lips meeting somewhere in between. Neither could have said how, but for a few magical moments, the two were totally lost in a passion they had never expected to share with another human being.

For the young highlander, that first kiss seemed to last forever. His mind raced from the breathtaking sparkle in her eyes to the taste of her lips and thence to the fire in his gut and back again. Not in his wildest night fancies had he imagined something feeling so good—so right—and yet so incredibly confusing.

A vivid image of that awful night in Blackgloom when the sorcerer used Sabritha's image to fool him popped into Daynin's head. *The Seed said he duplicated her down to the last detail. She was so beautiful, her naked skin so perfect—even though she was only an image then. But this is real—she is real—and she's kissing me!*

"Owwww!" Miles groaned. One arm thrashed out blindly at Daynin's ankle, the other groped along his belt, perhaps for a hidden dirk.

The sudden outburst startled the two lovers, instantly separating all but their eyes from one another. "See? I told you he'd bring nothing but trouble," Sabritha said.

Daynin sidestepped the squire's grip, then planted a foot firmly on the arm groping for the knife. "Take care, Saxon. You've had a bad ride. I wouldn't make any rash moves were I you."

"Curse the Saxons and all they stand for," came the squire's angry retort.

Dropping to one knee again, Daynin peered into a face that he had just come to realize was as young, or younger, than his own. "Who are you, that you bear the Duke's heraldry, yet curse his name?"

"The name they gave me is Miles Aubrecht. I'm a squire-in-training for Geile Plumat who was sent here by Duke Harold to hang some felons. Who are you?"

"No doubt, the very felons of which you speak," Daynin declared flatly. "But you've nothing to fear from us, provided you agree to cooperate. Elsewise, we'll be leaving you here for the wolves."

The squire attempted to right himself, only to roll back in the mud dizzily. "May as well kill me now, for my master will surely do so when he finds me."

"Daynin, we really need to go," Sabritha interrupted. "It will be light soon."

Daynin cast a wary eye to the road behind them, then up at the first pinkish hint of daylight glowing behind the peaks to the east. "Aye, we have to move. If you want to go with us, boy, you'll have to give me your warrant that you'll not cry out, try to escape, or otherwise cause me to regret taking you along. And I'll be taking that dirk as well. If you cross me . . ."

"No, no—take it—and take me along, please!" Miles begged. "I've nothing to go back to with that mob of bountiers. Nothing but more dirty work, clouts on the head and a life of indentured misery. I give you my word I'll not cause you grief. *Vincit veritas!*"

Sabritha threw her hands up in the air, spun around and climbed back onto the wagon. Daynin could hear her muttering, "Heroes, headaches and heretics—what the *hell* have I gotten myself into?"

Riding single file on the narrow, almost invisible track,

Kruzurk, Mediah and their beggar guide had traversed most of the distance to Abbotsford. Thin shards of pinkish daylight were just beginning to wriggle through the tops of the stunted and gnarled trees to their right. Wave after wave of putrid, dead-smelling vapors mingled with a dank fog rising off the moor, causing the tendrils of light to dance with a ghostly, ethereal motion. Not a sound could be heard except the huffing of the horses, and Thor's occasional growl at some supposed threat well out ahead of them.

Mediah shifted in his saddle to check the path behind. He saw nothing. He could barely see his own horse's tail, let alone any sign of the tracks they'd just left in the soggy dike. "I've heard of the blind leading the blind, but never have I experienced it," he sighed. "This fog reminds me of Thalos where my ship was rammed and sunk—Allah be praised that I yet live to tell that tale."

"Aye," Kruzurk agreed, his voice almost a whisper. "I've no clue how Olghar guides us. I can barely see the track with two good eyes. Perhaps this is one time being blind is an advantage."

Three horse lengths ahead, the beggar's mount stopped, allowing him to slide down from the saddle. From that spot, he tip-tapped his way on foot, leading his horse by its reins. That pattern had gone on for hours, half a furlong on the horse, another on foot and so on. Suddenly, Thor's growl echoed back a warning, stopping Olghar in his tracks.

"We've company ahead," he whispered.

Not daring to step even a forearm off the narrow path they followed, Kruzurk slid silently from his horse. He tied his reins to the lead horse's tail and made his way up to Olghar's spot. The blind man sniffed a light breeze from the north like some fawn in the midst of a wolf pack.

"Strange, m'lord. Very strange," the beggar opined.

"There's smoke in the air—lots of it—and a camp. I smell mutton and beer."

By now, Mediah had joined them. He took a cue from the beggar and captured a whiff of wood smoke with his rather prominent nose. "Campfire—must be a big one. That gang of bountiers, most likely."

Kruzurk sniffed the air. "I can't smell anything except this tenebrous brew of a bog. How far is the priory from here, Olghar?"

"Three furlong, m'lord—maybe less. Close enough that they will know we're coming if this breeze changes. We should go whilst the wind favors us. I believe there are some old ruins southwest of the priory where you can spy what's going on around the cathedral before you make your next move."

"Good plan," Kruzurk agreed. "Should we proceed on foot from here?"

Olghar nodded his agreement, then added, "Step only where I step, and keep your animals quiet. If we're caught on this track, we're finished. There's nowhere to run until we reach high ground. One false move in this bog and you'll disappear faster than a hog's hiccup."

Mediah stifled a laugh and quickly turned back to tend to his horse. Having tied a leather thong around his horse's snout to keep him quiet, he donned the short sword and targ shield he'd bartered for back at the inn. He motioned for Kruzurk to take a position behind him, then moved up to cover Olghar from any surprise attack that might come from their flanks. Somewhere ahead, Thor barked out a warning, only to go strangely silent after a single yelp.

Morning overtook the *Shiva* much faster than Ean had expected. The lack of sleep he had endured since leaving Hafdeway was beginning to tell on him. Sadly, Troon fared little better. His leg wound had turned feverish overnight and Ean could do little except ask for advice from the seadogs aboard ship.

"Tie 'im to a bleedin' ratline and 'eave 'im o'er the side—let the salt water clean the wound," one of the ship's crew had suggested. Another offered to remove Troon's leg, for a fee, of course. Ean had seen enough battle wounds to know it was far too early for such a drastic course of action. But salt water did have healing properties, so he'd heard, and now that they were in the shallow waters of the Clyde, they might just try that.

"You're gonna what?" Troon barked, having waked up to find himself tied in a net like a giant sea turtle.

"That sling will hold, you old coot. Then we'll drop you over the side so's the motion of the salt water will clean up that butcher job the healer did on your leg."

"Bloody hell you are," Troon argued. "I ain't one for taking baths and I damn sure ain't keen on bein' dragged along for every fish to nibble on. Ye've gone plumb daft, Ean McKinnon."

Ean motioned for two of the crewmen to step forward and take him. "Is nae a better plan than this, Simon. I cannae sit back and see you lose your leg on my account."

Troon struggled mightily for a small man, but could do little to avoid the restraints. "Feed me to the fishes, then, you old sot. If this net breaks, I'll haunt you till hell has its first snowstorm—count on it!"

The withered little arrowsmith remained awash in the sling until the sun peeked around the tip of the headlands along the coast. The crew was preparing to bring Troon aboard just as the ship's lookout let loose a bloodcurdling scream from atop the mast. "Sea beast—in our wake!" A dozen heads turned to see what the lookout had seen, and sure enough, there was a fin the size of a Viking sail jutting out of the water less than two ship's lengths behind them.

"All hands, turn to!" came the captain's order. "Run out that jib! Put all the sail on she'll hold, boys, elsewise we're goners if that beast catches us!"

Ean raced below for his longbow, hoping he would not have to use it. From time immemorial, stories of huge monsters in the Scottish lochs and along the shores had passed from one generation to the next among his people. Most clansmen believed few of the wild tales of sea creatures that could crush whole ships or swallow entire herds of sheep, but this time, the evidence couldn't be ignored.

Bow in hand, Ean clambered back on deck to find a good shooting spot near the stern, then suddenly remembered his hapless friend dangling like a giant minnow off the side of the boat. "Troon!" he hollered. "We've got to reel 'im in fast!"

The captain's head whipped around toward the stern. "Aye, that old coot's blood scent is likely what brung the monster. Cut 'im loose, boys! Give the beast what it wants."

Ean's blood turned as cold as a highland gale. Instant reflex brought an arrow to bear on the captain's pointed hat. Before the order could be carried out, an arrow sped on its way.

Thwack! It ripped the tricorn right off the captain's head from behind, pinning it to the mast in front of him. "Anyone cuts Troon loose, ye'll bloody well pay for it," Ean roared. "Now haul 'im in afore I lose my temper!" A half-hearted wave from the captain affirmed the order.

Troon came aboard dazed and blue, unaware of his narrow escape from the mouth of a mythical monster. The huge black fin wavered, then finally gave up its chase a quarter league from the shallow inlet that marks the entrance to the Firth of Clyde.

Chapter 22:

The Burning

Fairly soused from hefty quantities of the priory's beer, many of the Caledonian bountiers awoke still reveling in their lopsided victory as a new day dawned. Even a generous stuffing of charcoal mutton the night before and the interruption of a vicious dog circling in their midst had failed to dull the edge on their blood lust.

"Wake up, lads—it's time to string up that giant!" someone shouted.

That seemed to be a common refrain among the drunken lot as the men began to scrounge for breakfast. Most wanted revenge for Scarba's death. But they all knew an execution could only be carried out when their Saxon overseer gave the order. And that was not likely anytime soon.

Plumat busied himself interrogating clergymen on the other side of the cathedral grounds. He had spent much of the night watching the monks tend to Earl deLongait, then searching for felons and trying to determine where the treasure and his squire had gone—to no avail.

Brude McAlpin maintained a stony silence all night, hoping the enemy's attention on him would allow his allies to make good their escape. It had taken every length of rope, chain and cord the Caledonians could pilfer from the church to bind McAlpin tight enough to prevent his escape. Then they taunted and jeered at him like some hulking beast with its senses knocked out. They even slopped beer and sheep manure on him, secure in the belief that his will had been soundly broken.

The giant allowed the blaggards to continue their festivities. Despite his enormous strength advantage, he never uttered a word or made any real attempt to escape.

Apparently out of fear of rekindling their prisoner's anger, no one had attempted to remove the Pict's helmet that they might finally look on the face of their enemy. The armored giant posed a real enigma for such backward men—a prize to be sure, but not one to be enjoyed unwisely. Besides, they had plenty of time for sport. The day's revelry had just begun, or so they thought.

"One more time, Abbot. Where's the boy?" Plumat continued, having slapped an empty gauntlet across his thigh impatiently several times during the morning's inquisition. "He's a wanted felon, and I intend to see him hanged for murder. Tell me now, or tell me while you bleed—makes me no never mind. And if you think that robe will protect you, you best think again."

Trussed up in front of his own hovel like some witch set for a burning at the stake, Prior Bede's anger grew with each verbal lash from Plumat. "You Saxon blaggards have violated every tenet of the Church. God may forgive you, but I won't. And neither will I help you in your black deeds. Be gone with you, Anglishman. Enough of this blasphemy!"

Plumat motioned for one of the Caledonian henchmen to deliver another smack across the Prior's face. The man hesitated, unsure just how far Saxon justice would allow the torture to proceed.

"Hit 'im, damn you!" Plumat roared.

A solid slap fell on the Prior, followed by a second one. "I said loosen his tongue, you *drengleslob*—not knock it out!" Plumat stepped forward and shoved the Caledonian aside. "Tell me what I need to know, priest, or I'll let this blaggard build a fire and roast your fat ass for breakfast."

Prior Bede inhaled a deep breath and spit as hard as he could, landing a blob of bloody phlegm squarely in the center of Plumat's heraldry. "Get thee gone, Saxon, or I warn you, all the Caledonian henchmen in creation won't be able to save you from the fires of retribution."

Only his innate fear of killing a clergyman prevented Plumat from allowing his anger to override justice at that moment. He gritted his teeth and shouted, "Set fire to one of the outbuildings! We'll see how far this cloistered coven will go to protect a felon when they see their life's work going up in smoke."

"Why are you stopping?" Sabritha demanded impatiently, having spent half the morning trouncing along in silence in the back of the cart.

Daynin's eyes went first to the creek running alongside the track, then to the squire, sound asleep in the cart behind the woman, then back to Sabritha. "Abaddon needs rest, and some water and grain. It will take hours for the Duke's men to ferret out which trail we took through Lamington Leech. By then, we'll have made the coast. I only hope Brude can find his way there, else I may have to break my word and leave 'im behind."

"You men and your *word*. You'd think your word was more precious than life itself, the way you value it."

Having quickly unhitched Abaddon, Daynin turned to deal with Sabritha's latest tirade. "If you cannae see the importance of a mahn doing what 'e says 'e'll do, then there's damn lit'le point in trying to explain it to you."

Even Daynin seemed surprised by the tenor of his words and the heavy highland brogue his voice had just adopted, seemingly without thought. It felt like he had just quoted his father, word for word, accent for accent. He could tell that Sabritha had been taken aback by it, too.

"Well—I guess your stay among the Anglish has finally worn off, eh plowboy? Seems your language *and* your manners have reverted to their crude Scotian roots."

A hot flash rippled straight up Daynin's back. "Sabritha, I dinnae mean to snap at you. But if a mahn has no honor, he has *nothing*. I find it impossible to imagine that a woman as wily and intelligent as you are cannot understand that, or at least accept it in her mahn."

"Her *mahn?* Is that what you think you are now—my *man?*"

"Aye. I hope so, at least. I *want* to be your mahn, for sure. Judging from that kiss last night, I have good reason, do I not?"

Sabritha turned and climbed over the sleeping squire. She dropped down from the back of the cart and strode purposely toward the creek, tossing her long black hair and a sharp rebuke over her shoulder. "I'm gonna wash off this sheep smell, highlander. A good *mahn* might think about finding us a rabbit for breakfast whilst I'm doing that. A fire would be nice, too, so's we can cook it while I warm up."

Daynin's face turned so hot at that instant, he could have kindled a fire without a flint. Instead, he reached down and grabbed a handful of sharp rocks from the track, then marched off into the brush to find some small game. *She's going to be a handful, that's for sure,* he mused. *Just like my mother was for my father!*

The vast expanse of tombstones that defined the priory's southern boundary was more than a little frightening to the Greek. He had never before seen such an incredible array of death markers and cenotaphs, all in neat rows with idols, symbols, and strange markings decorating each.

Mediah's beefy hand reached out to stop Olghar's progress, pushing him gently to his knees behind a large tree at the edge of the bog. The ground ahead lay wide open to view from the church except for a head-high wall that encircled the hundred score of tombstones.

"What is it, Greek?" the beggar asked.

"We'd best be circling west, along the back wall of these grounds. We've nothing to cover us ahead. If we stay between the bog's edge and the wall, I think we can reach cover on the other side without anyone seeing us. I'll tie the horses here and then we can proceed."

Olghar sniffed the air, his guide stick rising almost imperceptibly to point at something his nose had caught in the wind. "Wood smoke, and lots of it—but not a campfire. Something large is ablaze."

Having helped Mediah with the horses, Kruze moved up and quickly dropped to his knees beside the beggar. " 'Twould appear the mercenaries are doing what they do best—destroying the church. Let's just hope that's all they've accomplished."

"Can you see Thor anywhere? He should have come back by now."

"No, Olghar," Mediah answered. "It's a bit too foggy to see very far, but I'm sure he's around, somewhere. Not to worry, we'll find him. With all this smoke, he likely can't pick up our scent."

"Aye, that could be it," the wretch agreed, though the catch in his voice told a somewhat different story.

The trio crept around the perimeter of the cemetery, careful to keep the wall between them and any would-be lookouts, though it seemed there was little concern for new arrivals. No guards, watchers or even the occasional stroller were in evidence anywhere on the grounds. It was too quiet—much too quiet.

At the far end of the wall next to the ruins of what had been a stable, a heap of old straw and sheep dung had been piled waist high. Mediah made a dash across the open ground, darted around the pile of straw and charged head-long through what remained of the stable's back entrance. The place stood empty. Outside, nothing moved. Even the breeze had stopped, allowing the acrid black smoke on the other side of the grounds to hang in an ugly low cloud.

Kruzurk took Olghar's arm and hurried him along to join Mediah. Once inside the stables, a quick look at Mediah's pained expression told Kruzurk something terrible had happened. Mediah gestured toward the window. His lips formed the word "Thor" but he did not speak aloud. Fifty paces across the yard, the big dog lay sprawled on its side, a crossbow bolt jutting out of his ribs. Mediah drew his finger across his throat to indicate the time worn symbol of death.

"Any sign of the bountiers?" Kruze whispered.

"None, m'lord. This place is quieter than the Duke's dungeon. They must have come and gone already. Mayhaps at first light."

"Can you see my dog anywhere?" came Olghar's pitiful query. "He's never run off and left me like this."

Kruzurk patted the ragged creature on the back and said, "We'll uh—look for Thor once we get you settled with the monks."

"Perhaps I should go alone," Olghar offered. "If there's trouble. . . ."

"No reason to expect trouble. After all, we *are* the Duke's men."

Olghar turned as if to look straight into Kruzurk's eyes. "M'lord, I may be blind, but I'm no fool. You didn't come all this way—at night—with a blind man leading you—to do the King's business. Of that, I am quite certain."

"You're right—you're no fool. The truth is, we've come to fetch a boy. These bountiers mean to stretch his neck if they find him first. And I'm responsible for the bounty on his head. That's why we had to make haste, but I fear we are too late."

A single grimy hand reached out for Kruzurk's shoulder. The beggar pushed himself to his feet, his cane divining a path toward the door. Tip-tapping in the general direction of the graveyard, Olghar said, "Fear not, m'lord. I've a feeling about these things. We'll find the boy and right the wrong done 'im. You and the Greek stay here and I'll see what's what. If all's well, I'll return for you shortly."

It was just past midday when the *Shiva* finally made its turn upstream within sight of fortress Dumbarton's ruins, high on the north bank of the Clyde. Though a mere five leagues from where Daynin and Sabritha creaked along in Kruzurk's cart, Ean had no way of knowing for sure where the boy was or even if he still lived.

"Make lively there, you lot!" the captain bellowed. "Watch your depth—and trim those sheets! We don't want to run aground in this bloody river. God knows, I've no wish to stay in this monster infested land any longer than need be."

Troon lay sprawled across a hatch cover, exactly where he'd been since being fished out of the sea. Ean couldn't tell if the wiry little arrowsmith was sleeping, passed out, or delirious from fever. He decided to leave him alone for the time being. Letting sleeping dogs lie seemed the best plan, especially when dealing with a grumpy old man who had just been dragged like a ballast log on the high seas. Besides, the longer he delayed waking Troon, the more time Ean had to figure out a way to keep the captain from tossing them both overboard at the next sandbar in the firth.

Having taken a position on the bow to watch for rocks ahead, Ean let out a wistful cry to the winds. "You're *out* there, boy. I can *feel* it. If only I knew where!"

Another hard morning's ride was again telling a tale on the backsides of the bountiers. Several straggled far behind the main body of Plumat's army. One or two disappeared along the way, either from fear or loss of interest in the Duke's campaign. The rest had fanned out to forage and bring in new troops to replace those lost in the battle, rejoining Plumat's main force just south of Lamington Leech.

Half a score of new men had been recruited since leaving the priory that morning. The jingle of silver played far louder than any trumpet or drumbeat when it came to enticing fools to risk their lives in a cause for which they had no allegiance.

"Hold!" Plumat ordered, his arm raised high in the air. Unused to the chore of commanding troops himself, he wheeled Cauldron about to make sure his minions understood what he expected.

They did not, of course. Some slept in the saddle. Some were distracted by the vast panorama of deep, winding valleys that lay ahead of them. And the rest simply had no training to act like real soldiers, mounted or otherwise.

"Hold, damn you!" Plumat shouted. That stemmed the unruly column only by the shock value of the command. Most of the cutthroat mob did not wait for further orders. They dismounted, slipping from their horses helter-skelter to immediately go about establishing a day camp.

Shaking his head in dismay, Plumat swung one leg over the high pommel of his jousting saddle to wait for the rest of the ragged lot to straggle in. He knew every man would be needed for the next stage of the campaign, and could not risk losing even one of the worthless troops he had with him.

Leaving deLongait behind had been a serious enough blow, and losing the squire as well. Now he faced an arduous march north into ever more hostile territory with men he neither knew nor could trust.

The last man in the column finally came over the rise, leading his horse on foot into the camp. "We've followers, m'lord," he said to Plumat with little enthusiasm, a thumb jutting back over his shoulder toward the road behind them.

"Followers? What do you mean 'followers'?"

"Dunno, m'lord. They's a column o' dust risin' in the south. Has to be riders. Comin' 'ard too, 'twould seem. And mayhaps a wagon or two, given the rumble."

"Why in the bloody hell didn't you come up and warn me before now?"

The levy trudged on by, barely taking note of Plumat's commanding presence. "This bleedin' 'orse o' mine 'ad 'is own mind, as you might say. I barely got 'im to walk up that bloody slope, I did."

Plumat's leg instantly swung over the pommel and back into its stirrup. He wheeled Cauldron around and dug his spurs in hard. "No one *moves* until I return, is that clear?" he shouted, not waiting for an answer from any of the confused faces.

Chapter 23:

The Tracking

Abbotsford's grounds were as quiet as the graveyard Olghar had just felt his way through. The only sounds his keen ears picked up other than the hollow tip-tapping of his cane were sheep bleating somewhere in the distance and the harsh grackling of birds feasting on something. Suddenly his guide stick thumped against an object that shouldn't have been sprawled in the middle of any cathedral grounds.

"Hello?" he offered in a low voice, hoping the large body his cane had just outlined would be that of a sleeping person and not a dead one. There was no reply.

"Alms for a blind beggar? Is someone there?"

Again, no response. But Olghar's raised voice seemed to have aroused the crows or vultures or whatever had been feeding in the distance. The birds raised a cry that could only be described as otherworldly, then abruptly left in an upward cascade of maddened wing flapping.

"Halloo?" he shouted.

"Are they gone?" a male voice whispered, close by.

Olghar's cane immediately touched on the body he'd found, and sure enough, he felt rapid breathing. "All is quiet, whoever you are, but I cannot say if there are others around. I'm blind, you see."

"Yes, yes," the voice said impatiently, "I heard you the first time."

Olghar's attention snapped to where the voice had just

moved. The man was now partly upright, but still sitting on the ground. "Blaggards," the voice swore. "I thought that first band of cutthroats would burn us out. Then a Saxon army came, and they beat and tortured us again. I feel for that boy, with so many bad people bent on his capture."

"*Boy* says you? One with a warrant on 'im? And a woman, too, mayhaps?"

Having managed to stem the bleeding on his forehead, Prior Bede laboriously rolled onto his knees and pushed his considerable weight from the dirt. His hand reached out for Olghar's shoulder to steady himself, but the blind man jumped back in fear, almost causing the priest to topple again.

"Hold still—I'm the Prior here! I mean you no harm. I need your help to get to my hovel. My head is spinning like a laundry maid's loom."

Obediently, Olghar stepped forward to offer himself as support for the much larger man. His free hand made a cursory examination of the Prior's robes to ensure that he had indeed encountered a priest. "I've come a long way with some friends who are seeking this boy you speak of. They say he's innocent."

On wobbly legs, the pair made a dozen steps toward the hovel. Prior Bede said, "That boy is hardly innocent. Misjudged perhaps, but he admitted to murder with his own lips, though he did profess it to be a fair fight."

"Aye, so say these others. And I believe them."

Inside the hovel, Prior Bede loosened his grip on Olghar's shoulder and collapsed onto his cot. "Believe this, old one. That boy—Daynin is his name—has more trouble headed his way than he can possibly imagine. You'd best tell your friends to head northwest toward Glasgow, and fast. That is where the boy and his enemies will meet and no amount of help is going to save him, short of the Almighty's divine intervention."

"Perhaps that is why I joined them, Father. Perhaps that is why."

Divine intervention wasn't exactly at the forefront of Daynin's mind at that moment. In a deep quandary over the squire, he couldn't decide whether to leave the Saxon behind or not, even though that would virtually guarantee the Duke's men would find them. Taking him along could mean they would be found out anyway, when and if a ship could be hired to ferry them all to Rhum. And doing the boy harm, he would not even consider.

"He has to go with us," Daynin said, sighing.

"What? Are you talking to yourself again?" Sabritha sniped from behind him.

"The squire must go with us to Rhum—there's no other choice."

Sabritha climbed over several of the large chests to gain a spot on the wagon seat next to Daynin. "I could have told you that. He'll tell the Saxons everything if you let him go. The only other choice is to tie him to a tree somewhere off the track and hope they don't find him."

"Cannae do that," Daynin replied, his language again reverting to its familial Scotian roots. "The wolves would have 'im afore we're half a league gone."

"Have *who?*" came a plaintive cry from the back of the wagon.

Sabritha's head whipped around, her gaze seeming to throw fireballs at the squire. "Keep your mouth shut back there—or it might be *you* we're talking about."

The boy turned a ghostly white, his fate suddenly all too

clear. "I won't make trouble for you, I promise. *Please* don't make me go back! I-I-I can cook, and tend horses—and clean armor." A dagger-like stare from the woman shut him up instantly.

Daynin eased the reins over, guiding Abaddon off the bumpy stone track and into a grassy meadow near the joining of two magnificent valleys. The smell of clover mingled lightly with the first hint of heather blooms in the cool air. Those smells generated powerful images in his mind, and reverie claimed him.

First, he thought of his mother, lost so long ago to an ague that still had no name. They had buried her in a place not unlike the one that spread out before him now, with clover, heather and teaberry vines growing up the slopes of two rocky cairns. She had always smelled of teaberry soap, and that special kind of heather she used when washing their clothes.

His mother had never been replaced by his father, so special had been their bond. Daynin envisioned that kind of union with Sabritha, if only she would have him. She had spirit, and guile, and intelligence, and all the other attributes he had come to expect of the woman with whom he would rebuild the McKinnon clan. She was perfect—except for one thing. She had never lived in the highlands, and that might prove to be too great an obstacle for their love to overcome.

Only time would tell, for the highlands could be a harsh land, especially for women. And doubly so for those unused to the cold loneliness of clan life, highland winters and the constant deprivations so commonplace among his people. Sabritha would have one great advantage over others—if she chose it. She would call Rhum home. No other place in all of Scotia compared to the beauty and peace of Rhum with Kinloch Keep at its center.

A large grain bag in hand, Daynin dropped down from the wagon to feed Abaddon. "The Duke's men will have found their way through the Leech by now. Could be no more than half a day behind us, or less. We'll rest for a bit, then break for the coast with all the speed Abaddon can give us."

Sabritha's gaze made a careful sweep across the valley road behind them. She observed no movement all the way back up the moor as far as the heavy mist would allow. "Is there nowhere we can hide, Daynin?"

For the very first time since he had met her, he heard a worried tone lacing Sabritha's voice. Daynin smiled and said, "Our best chance is to find a boat and beat it to sea before they catch us."

"I'm slowing you down," the squire spoke up. "That old horse can barely pull this cart, let alone the three of us."

"It might help if we all walked for a while, that's true," Daynin agreed. "I don't know how far it is to the coast, but Glasgow is only a few leagues further on. With any luck, we can find a fisherman with a boat big enough to take us aboard. Then we'll be safe. They cannae track us on water."

Miles climbed out of the wagon to stretch his legs, but stopped abruptly, as though something evil flashed across his mind. "Daynin—I just remembered—Geile Plumat—my master—he sent for more men to join him at Glasgow. They could be coming by sea from Carlisle. The Duke has ships there, and men. They—they—could be there already—ahead of us!"

Brude McAlpin's shackled frame had been carried face down across the bare backs of a wagon team, strapped tightly legs-to-arms like a load of sheep hides headed to market. He had seen nothing but the steady plod of the team's enormous hooves, yet knew exactly where they were, even after hundreds of years entombed in the priory's catacombs. Brude was home—on Cruithni land for the first time since leaving Loch Ness to war with the armies of Oengus, long dead King of Scotland and scourge of the seven houses of Scone.

What an undisciplined lot, he told himself, having yet to feel the need to actually speak aloud to his Caledonian captors. *No wonder these black hearted thieves were so easy for my kin to defeat in battle. They love the drink far more than the taste of blood.*

He knew sooner or later one of the bountiers would gain enough courage or drunken curiosity to come over and make a show of things. That's when there would be trouble, for the band's leader had yet to return, and without orders to the contrary, no telling what the mob might do next. *Give me a free hand, that's all I ask—just one hand—free of these bloody chains—and I'll make fish bait of this bunch.*

Brude didn't have long to ponder his fate. Bored with the wait for their taskmaster, one of the Caledonians took out a pair of dice. "First mahn to roll a thuu—teen, eh? Gets 'is choice of that bloody giant's armor. What say ya, lads? Who's ta wager with old Billy Bones? Come on now, put up yer booty—ye've all got some of that Saxon silver, and I aims ta collect it."

"You 'eard what the Saxon said, Spivey," one of the new men argued. "No one's ta make a move afore he gets back. You'll get us all a floggin' if'n ya stir up that giant."

"Who appointed you sergeant-at-arms, Kendal of Sleek? You was nowhere to be found when that beast over there cut Jack Scurdie in half. We won the right to finish this big bastard, and by God, I'll have my vengeance! Now who's with me?"

An uproar from both points of view spread rapidly through the ranks, threatening all-out war amongst the bountiers. Several men rushed to the team of horses and cut Brude loose from his defenseless position. He fell with a resounding clank on the rocky ground, still bound from head to heel in ropes and chains.

" 'Ang 'im says I," Spivey bellowed.

"Aye, string 'im up!" several others chimed in.

Just as Spivey bent over to jerk Brude's helmet off, one of the camp lookouts broke into a dead run from his position astride the valley road down below. "The captain's back! The captain's back!" he screamed, trying desperately to stay his cohorts from their ill-conceived plan.

"Bloody hell," Spivey and the others crowed, but they stopped anyway, having no desire to face Plumat's wrath or that of the Kensington blade he carried.

No sooner had they turned from their mischief than Plumat and his standard appeared from down in the draw. Spread out behind him came a column of men—all armored—and all showing the maize and scarlet of Plumat's master, Duke Harold of Anglia. The rumble of their heavy war horses literally shook the ground, bringing a tremble to the knees of every bountier.

From his tenuous position on the ground, Brude raised up enough to see the entourage heading his way. *Aye! Now we've an enemy worth the killing,* he mused.

"Why don't I go and check on Olghar?" Mediah whispered. "There's no warrant on me. They'll just think I'm another beggar."

Kruzurk shook his head in disagreement, his eyes fixed on

Thor's seemingly lifeless carcass. "Men who would kill an animal for sport have no soul—no honor. I think we'll wait, Mediah. Olghar will come fetch us when the time is ri . . . "

Disregarding Kruzurk's logic, Mediah was already on the move, dashing half way across the open ground between the ruined stables and the back wall of the sanctuary. He stopped for an instant next to the dog and quickly began gesturing for Kruzurk to come ahead.

"He's still alive!" Mediah cried out as Kruzurk approached. The Greek then stifled his own voice with a hand over his mouth.

"I'll tend to Thor. You go and find Olghar. We've no time to waste, if this dog is to see another sunrise. And Mediah—tell no one why we are here."

Back at the Prior's hovel, Olghar availed himself of what remained in the priest's stew pot. "So there were many soldiers, eh Prior?" he asked, having licked his grimy fingers clean.

"Yes, and Caledonian mercenaries. At least a score of the blaggards, maybe more. Apparently the Saxon lord that Daynin murd—er—*killed* was a Marquis. There is a large reward for the boy's capture."

"Reward, says you?"

"Forget it, old man. You've neither the skills nor the courage to go after that boy. Aside from the soldiers, there is a demon in their midst. I saw it emerge from the catacombs myself. No man will stand against that creature, and it made an alliance with Daynin."

Olghar reached inside his pouch for the St. Vladimir's cross he'd promised to Kruzurk. He raised it to his forehead, touching lightly the dirty bandage that covered his eyes, then swept it left and right, up and down, as though making the sign of the cross. *"Megda ya signavet doth ichperdum nicht, pajalista."*

"What blasphemy is that you're spouting in my hovel?" Prior Bede demanded. Olghar heard the sound of his head lifting off the pillow, then falling back from dizziness.

"I speak no blasphemy, Prior. Merely an ancient prayer to keep us safe from this creature of the catacombs. I am a priest—like you. Or, I was—in the land of the Russ, many leagues to the East, where spirits and monsters are quite common."

"The Russ have no priests. It's common knowledge they are a godless lot," Prior Bede argued.

Olghar cocked his head to the right, turning it slowly to fix the sound. "Shhhh, someone is coming."

"By the mark, three by 'alf," the boatswain bellowed. His depth reading in the shallow waters of the Clyde's upper reaches echoed like a town crier, bouncing from cliff to cliff along the craggy riverbank.

A quick glance at the boatswain's knotted rope and the *Shiva*'s captain motioned for the tiller to be turned hard over, abruptly bringing the bow to port, then into a half circle. In a matter of seconds, the ship had turned completely around in the middle of the river. "Trim yer head— easy—easy—that's it! Now, set the anchor. Lively now, lest that current drag us aground! We've gone as far up this bleedin' river as we dare ta go."

A loud splash announced the anchor's dropping. The *Shiva* swung heavily against the anchor rope, trying in vain to flow with the rapid current that would ultimately take her back out to sea. Ean lurched against the slackened bow stays, almost toppling into the rigging from the abrupt stop. He realized instantly that they had reached the end of the trip.

Of greater concern to him at that moment was knowing they had not seen another boat the whole way up the Clyde. That meant even if he could find Daynin and bring him out of Scotia, the *Shiva* would have to stay right where she anchored to guarantee a return voyage.

"Captain, a word if I may," Ean said, plaintively.

"Say what you will, highlander, then get yerself and that seedy old man off my ship. We can just make the coast afore nightfall if we beat it out of this river whilst the current's with us. Otherwise, we'll be stuck here like a floundering whale 'til dawn."

Ean picked his way over and through the maze of ropes and scattered gear at the bow, thrown all asunder by the ship's sudden stop. "Captain, you must agree to stay 'til the morrow. I have nae but a sense of where my grandson is, but I *feel* 'im close by. If you leave now, you may well condemn him to the gallows."

"Gallows, aye," the captain snorted. "And good riddance to ye, blaggard. Asked to bring ya to the Clyde I was, and so I have. You got what ye bargained for—now the deal is done. Be off with ya, or I'll have yer scrawny ass tossed over the side, I will."

Toward the west, the day was rapidly fading, but there were still several hours of daylight Ean could use for searching, provided he could get ashore. He also knew that no sailor ventured into shallow waters after dusk, no matter how skilled.

"I have an offer, if you'll just gimme a listen."

"Listen, aye. But there better be some spoils in this offer of yours, elsewise you and that old bowman are fish bait."

Ean pulled up his long shepherd's tunic, exposing the ochre and green tartan of the McKinnon clans that he had always worn underneath. He slipped the sock knife from out of its hiding place around his ankle and slit a small hole in the hem of the tartan. From a fold in the hem, he produced a shiny gold sovereign the size of a cow's eye.

"Bloody hell!" the captain roared, his head swiveling around to ward off any overly curious looks from his crewmen.

"This one now, and another when I get back with the boy. Is that a bargain you can keep?" Ean whispered, a sharp edge to his words. "And Troon stays here. When I return, we'll all be needin' passage elsewhere, if you've the stomach for it."

The captain yanked the gold coin from Ean's grip and took a mighty bite on it to ensure its bona fides. "Aye, stomach aplenty for this kind of booty. Mind you this—ye've only got 'til midday tomorrow. If yer not back by then I'll give your bowman the deep six and up anchor without so much as a by-your-leave."

The crafty highlander did not wait for the reply. He whispered orders to Troon, who was finally awake. Quick as a marten's mouse, Ean fetched his bow and brace and went over the side into the dory for the long row to the bank. All the way to shore, his mind kept repeating the same refrain. "God forgive me, Daynin. I can only hope your inheritance was well spent today."

Chapter 24:

The Looking

The sleek lion's head prow of the *Woebringer* slashed almost silently through the out-flowing rush of the Clyde. Ranulf of Westmoorland's orders were to check the firth for ship traffic, then land a dozen of his best men at Glasgow to watch all the roads to the north of Scotia. Having thus sealed off any potential escape route for the supposed assassins, Ranulf was to await Plumat's army joining him at the Clyde with their prisoners, then transport one and all back to Carlisle for trial.

"Trim the sheets," the *Woebringer*'s captain ordered, his voice more subdued than it normally might have been. "Keep yer rowing noise down. Sound carries for half a league in this firth, and we don't want these blaggards to know we're here."

A menacing fog had formed over the headlands of the Clyde, obscuring the crumbling spires of Dumbarton Castle to the north and casting an eerie pall over the dark slopes of the Greenock Peninsula on the south bank. Ranulf chewed the tip of a carrot, easing the tension in his mind and the rumbling in his ample, but unfed stomach.

Having heard nothing from the Duke or Plumat since taking ship at Carlisle, he remained uneasy with this poorly planned foray into Scotia. Being a prominent reeve of the Duke's, he disliked his subordinate role to Plumat. But a command had been given, and he intended to see the task through to completion.

Just inside the mouth of the Clyde, scudding along at nearly five knots, the *Woebringer* suddenly and abruptly ran hard up onto an object hidden in the dark waters. The object threw the whole ship into a stall, the bow rising high in the air, then listing heavily to port.

"Avast! We've run aground!" the lookout screamed.

"Impossible," Captain Coke growled. "Look lively, men—it's only a log or a whale. I know this firth. It should be ten fathoms deep here."

The *Woebringer* lurched low on the port side, her forward bulwark dragging water for several seconds. The starboard side rose higher in the air, momentarily throwing everyone to the port side of the deck in a confused heap.

"Bloody hell," Ranulf swore. "Get this ship righted, Captain, or we're goners for sure!"

No sooner had the words been spoken than the vessel pitched back hard to the right, dropping the starboard side into the water with a loud kaploosh. Then all went silent. Not even the men on deck made a sound. The *Woebringer* scudded on past whatever she'd struck, seemingly undamaged.

"Damned blackwaters in these highlands," the boatswain growled. "Cursed I tell ya. These waters is cursed!"

"I should have stayed in Carlisle," Ranulf moaned pitifully, the carrot between his teeth bitten nearly in two.

Having downed a stout measure of warm beer, Prior Bede finally sat upright to recount the terror his priory had been through. "He *was* a giant, I tell you—and not of human flesh, either. That ogre took to the boy like a bear takes to its cubs. He fought those Caledonian dogs with a skill and vengeance I've not seen in these highlands since I took my vows of piety."

Kruzurk wrung out the cloth he'd just dipped into a

bowl of tepid water. His mind drifted elsewhere at the moment, though the Prior's story did provide some interesting details. He draped the cloth over the bulging knot on Prior Bede's forehead and pressed his query. "So the boy and the woman made good their escape? You're certain of that?"

"Yes, I'm sure!" the Prior replied. With both his chubby hands supporting his head like an apple perched on an arrow tip, he continued. "They escaped before the courtyard battle ended. And none of the blaggards followed until much later. They contented themselves with ransacking my Priory instead."

Mediah finished the last bites of stew he'd fished from the Prior's pot, then pushed away the proffered pail of beer Olghar held toward him. "Thank you, old one, but I cannot indulge in spirits."

"Did Daynin leave anything behind, Father? A note, or perhaps some of his books?" Kruzurk asked.

"Aye. They's a stack o' books down in the catacombs, along with the rest of that heathen trash we found in the Pict's tomb. Take it—take it all. I wish I'd never seen that boy or his bounty. There's nothing but evil can come to those who covet that treasure, mark me well on that."

"Pict? This giant was entombed and has now come back to life?" Mediah chimed in.

Prior Bede swept the cloth off his face. "Have ye not heard a word I've said? He's a spirit, or demon, or some such beast, brought to life by ungodly events that should never have happened. He waited in that tomb for hundreds of years until that boy chanted him back to life. Now my Priory is in ruins and there's blood on my grounds, so take what remains of that heathen plunder and be gone with you—all of you!"

Kruzurk could tell instantly that Olghar's spirits plummeted with those words. He had nowhere to go, and without Thor, he would be at the mercy of every blaggard who crossed his path. "Prior, we brought Olghar here to live out his days with you. Can you not grant him sanctuary?"

"Gone, I said. You people *violated* my sanctuary. I've no place for any of you. Get out of my house! Take whatever you need but be gone by dark. I've had all of this fighting I can stand. I want my peace and quiet back." His final words fading, the priest slumped over in a dead faint.

Having gained enough information from the few novices they could find, Mediah and Kruzurk finally ventured down into the catacombs to see if Daynin had left anything behind that might be useful. Even in the poor light of the candelabra, the dark puddle on the flagstone floor ahead of them could hardly be anything but blood—and none too old from its appearance. Kruzurk motioned for Mediah to step lightly, then leapt over the gory mess. Sometime later and deeper in the bowels of the catacomb, the two found their way to the ruined Pictish tomb and what remained of Daynin's bounty.

"Never have I seen doors splintered like these," Mediah said, distantly. "Something terrible happened here, Kruze— the priest is right about that."

"I don't like this any more than you do, Mediah. But I believe we may find something here that will help us in our quest. We need an advantage to overcome the Duke's numbers and his speed, otherwise we'll never catch up to Daynin in time."

Mediah shoved the shattered wreckage of the doorframe aside and peeked into the inky darkness. Instantly, he lurched backward, almost knocking Kruzurk down. "Demon!" he screeched. "A red eyed demon!"

Kruzurk grabbed Mediah's frock sleeve to steady him,

probing ahead with the candles. He saw a pair of ruby eyes glinting back at him from the gloom. "That's no demon—but it may be something important." The magician hitched his long robe higher, then stepped forward and knelt down to examine the object closely. "As I thought. This surely belonged to the Pict who was buried here. It is a *carnyx*—a war horn used only by Pictish chiefs. The Scotians called them boar's horns, and now I see why."

"Please, m'lord, do not touch that foul thing."

Handing the candelabra back to Mediah, Kruzurk carefully brushed aside the debris that half covered the magnificent horn. "I'm surprised the Caledonians left this behind. It's much smaller than the ones I've read about, but it's covered with gold, and those two ruby eyes would pay a Duke's ransom."

"We should also leave it and go," Mediah begged. "I've no need for ransoms or rubies."

"No, this is too important—perhaps more than we realize." The elaborately carved horn in hand, Kruzurk turned his attention to the pile of books in the opposite corner. "Ahh! This is what I had hoped to find. I felt certain Daynin would leave behind that which we need the most."

Kruzurk propped the carnyx on top of the stone slab that had previously held the Great Deceiver's coffin. He dropped to his knees to examine the books from the Blackgloom Bounty, quickly sweeping through the first pile, discarding volume after volume. He started on the second pile, with the same result. Toward the bottom of the third pile, his hands finally stopped.

"This is it! *The Salomonic Monograph*! I knew it would still be here, for Daynin has no use for such a dangerous book, nor do any of these priests. He must have sensed that when he left it here."

Mediah held the candles closer to get a better look at the manuscript's ancient cover. "Those markings on the bottom—I've seen such markings before, m'lord—in Crete. They are heathen spells wrought by the unclean ones!"

Kruzurk's fingers traced over the inlaid letters of the book's Latin title, moving from there down to the Sumerian glyphs, thence to the corresponding hieroglyphs at the bottom. "These are all words, Mediah—the same as the Persian and Roman words, only much older. They are Egyptian most likely. This grimoire is said to contain charms of making and veils of mysticism that go back to the dawn of magic. It could be the one thing that gives us an advantage over the Duke's men—if only I knew how to *read* it!"

Plumat's army crawled along Lamington Leech like a serpentine snail, and moving about that fast. Cauldron neighed nervously, his enormous front hoof pawing the ground at the aggravating delays. "Steady, boy," Plumat urged, patting his charger on the neck. "These levies move like molasses in a morning frost, but they'll all be needed, and I don't intend to lose a single one."

Fulchere the Bowman drew his mount to a stop just behind Cauldron. He raised the Duke's standard and waved it back and forth to symbolize a halt for the column. "Camp here, m'lord?"

"No one ordered you to stop," Plumat snapped back. "We've a good while before dark and I want this lot to march as far as possible before they drink themselves into another stupor."

"Beggin' yer pardon, m'lord, but I was thinkin' of deLongait. He's been in that wagon since first light, and lost a lot of blood on the trek."

"Damn," Plumat replied. A hard jerk on his reins whirled Cauldron around in his tracks. He galloped toward the rear of the column, just now making its way out of the narrow pass through the Leech. The wagon loaded with supplies and deLongait trailed last in line. As he approached the wagon, Plumat had no idea what to say to his stalwart companion, now likely to be crippled for life thanks to the Pict's giant broadsword.

Much to Plumat's surprise, he found Earl deLongait sitting upright in the wagon, his feet propped against the hogshead of beer that Fulchere's contingent had brought with them from Galashiels. A loud belch preceded his slurred welcome for his leader. "Plumat, my *boy*," he said drunkenly. His good arm flailed about, seemingly without any control, the other one limp in his lap.

"You're drunk," Plumat growled.

"That I am, sire, that I am," came the reply. "Well and truly earned, I should—hiccup—say, sir."

Plumat cast the wagon driver an angry look. "Is this *your* doing?"

The poor man swept the chainmail coif from off his head, fearing the worst. He shrugged his shoulders and answered, "Seemed the best medicine, m'lord. He was in a fearful fret from the pain, and lost a lot of blood. I figured beer could be a good substitute for blood, and seems I was right—'e's much better now than this morning. Those priests patched his shoulder with a hot iron, but they botched the cauterizing, for 'e's still bleedin' some."

"Then he's well enough to keep on the trek?"

"Aye, m'lord. Right as 'e's gonna get. Least wise 'til we find 'im a bed, and that ain't too likely in this rat hole of a country."

Without answering, Plumat wheeled Cauldron around

and raced back to the head of the column. "Step it up, Fulchere. Get them moving again. No stragglers. I expect to see the spires of Glasgow by first light—understood?"

Ean McKinnon's bowsight peeked ominously through the tiny opening in the brush, poised dead center on the hated Saxon heraldry. Some impulse stayed his motion, causing the bow to unflex ever so slightly. He could see the young man clearly, and recognized the Duke's eagle even from ninety paces away. The shot was an easy one—yet he hesitated still. *Where are the rest of 'em?* kept pulsing through Ean's mind.

"Daynin?" Ean's own voice argued a truth clearly displayed below him on the open track. *He's with the Saxons? This cannae be!* Yet there walked his grandson next to a cart, looking none the worst for wear, conversing with a Saxon dog like they were long lost kin. Ean's heart sank. He eased the bow down, completely confused by what he should do next. Then he noticed the woman, and the fog between his ears began to lift. *Bewitched—they've beguiled the boy—turned him into a dimwitted stooge through the wiles of an Anglish wench.*

Ean's mind swept back to that fateful day in Hafdeway when Daynin brought home the Scythian Stone in that same cart, and left with a witch-faced hawker. He easily recognized the wagon, with its ancient solid wheels painted the color of the sky.

"Drat the luck—I should'nae let him leave with that blaggard magician! This is all my fault." Almost without thinking, his bowsight fell on the target again, this time shifting from the Duke's man to the woman's throat. He took a deep breath to steady his hands, now quivering from the prolonged pull on the bow. He whispered, "Move on, boy—just a bit, aye—one more step and I'll pin that wench to yer wagon like a fly stuck to pig droppings."

Down below, the squire stepped aside to allow Daynin and the woman to pass. Both their strides were considerably stronger than his at the moment, the long walk on a rocky track having taken its toll on Miles's legs already. "How far—to the—coast—do you—think?" he begged.

Daynin's head turned just in time to see the arrow's deadly flight. Without thinking, he charged into Sabritha, knocking her backward straight into the squire. They went down like ducks bobbing in a pond. A split second later, the hickory shaft struck the wagon's side right where Sabritha's head should have been.

"Down—everyone stay down!" Daynin roared. His eyes raked the hillside, expecting another flight of missiles to rip them to shreds. He saw nothing—no movement at all. Even the late afternoon shadows seemed to have taken a nap. He glanced up at the arrow, still quivering from the impact with the wagon.

"Troon?" blurted from his lips in disbelief.

Sabritha pushed the squire off her, having confused his gallant effort to cover her body with that of a drunken groper. "Get off me, you cherubic villain—and keep your bloody hands to yourself."

"Shhhh," Daynin shushed. "There's something strange going on here."

"Yeah, and this boy with the wandering hands is about to find that out the hard way," Sabritha growled. She pushed herself to her feet, then turned and delivered a swift kick to the squire's shoulder in payment for his attempt at heroism.

Daynin leapt to his feet as well, still staring in disbelief at the distinctive bands on the arrow's shaft. "Those are Troon's markings. This arrow came from my grandfather's friend!"

"Then tell the old fart to stop shooting at us," Sabritha said. "Is he blind as well as daft? Highlanders—I swear, you lot are all crazy!"

Daynin stepped away from the wagon, cupped both hands to his cheeks and yelled, *"Vincit, veritas!"* The echo bounced and rebounded a dozen times off the rocky slopes above them.

Sabritha's head whipped around at Daynin's strange words. "What does that mean?"

"Truth prevails," Daynin replied. "If Troon is up there, he will respond in Gaelic."

A cascade of small stones flowed down from the steep, brushy hillside, followed by a grumpy voice shouting, *"S'lange a vas!"*

"See? That means 'good health'—it's a friend all right—no doubt about it." Daynin's spirits were suddenly boosted beyond all measure.

The old man slipped and slid his way down the slope, landing a few paces from Abaddon and causing the horse to shy away. Sabritha steadied the animal, then barked, "Just what we needed—an old coot more ancient than this horse."

Ean righted himself and sprang at the woman's face. "Watch yer tongue, lassie—er you'll be eat'n it for supper."

Daynin stepped between them and grabbed Ean, lifted him off his feet and hugged him with all his strength. "Grandfather, I can't believe you're here! How did you find us?"

"You got some explainin' to do first, boy," Ean growled. "I come all this way to fetch you and by the luck of the lochs, I find you consortin' with this Anglish trash. What's got into you, boy, eh? Has this wench beguiled you or what? Speak up!"

Surprised by his grandfather's malicious tone, Daynin stepped back to start the conversation anew. "Grandfather Ean McKinnon, may I introduce you to Sabritha—uh—Sabritha?"

"*Kilcullen*, you dolt," Sabritha snapped back. "And if it matters, old man, I'm not Anglish. I'm Irish and damned proud of it."

Ean gave the woman a disdainful once-over with his eyes, his head shaking in complete derision, then he cast his hawk-eyed glare on Daynin. "Cavorting with the Anglish and the Irish, eh? Your father would cuff you from his grave, boy."

"I'm taking her to Rhum, grandfather—to marry her if she'll have me. I ask your respect and eventually your blessing. But either way, Sabritha is going with us."

The old man's voice ripped aloud, "Marry her, says he?!"

Sabritha appeared as shocked as Ean by that sudden revelation. Her pale skin turned the brightest shade of red Daynin had ever seen. "Well, it's true," he said. "If you'll have me, that is."

Silence hung heavily in the air for a few seconds, then gave way abruptly to the squire's horrified shriek as he dashed past the others screaming, "Noooo! Plumat! Oh my god, noooo—my master's found us!"

Chapter 25:

The Seeing

"How many and how far, you dolt?" Plumat roared, his patience wearing thin with the scout's less than detailed report.

"Half a league, your lordship—no more than that. And I cannae say how many for sure. They were at the far end of the valley, stopped in a narrow gap when I spotted the wagon."

"Stopped eh? In plain sight? Sounds like the makings of a trap to me. Fulchere, take two of your men and some of the Caledonians—scout the road ahead—then send someone back to report. I'll wait here for the rest of the column to catch up. Do not give chase to those felons, whatever you do. There could be a hundred of their henchmen lining that gap."

Fulchere waved to the men behind him to form up, then turned in his saddle. "We're not to give chase—aye, m'lord. We'll check the road and make sure 'tis no trap. And if they make a fight of it, what are my orders?"

"My guess is they have no intention of standing their ground," Plumat replied warily. "Glasgow and a boat are their objectives—but they are in for a surprise if that's their game. Now get moving before we lose the light."

At the far end of the valley, Daynin and the others had broken into a state of panic. Miles Aubrecht had raced ahead, screaming his lament for all to hear, his energy having been increased tenfold by the sudden appearance of the Duke's scouts behind them. Sabritha did her best to steady Abaddon, fearful that he might bolt and run off as well.

"Take the woman and go," Ean ordered, the rapid cadence of his highland brogue flowing almost too fast for Daynin to follow. "I'll make a stand here. That should stall 'em long enough for you to reach Glasgow. Take the right fork around the village and you'll find a boat waiting for you about two leagues north. The boat will only be there 'til midday tomorrow—so don't wait for me."

Daynin stared wide-eyed at his grandfather. For the first time in his life, he felt the need to directly disobey the old man. "I'm not leaving you here. Give me your spare bow and I'll stand with you, or we can get on the wagon, but either way, we fight or run together."

"*Och,* boy—those are the Duke's men, come to take yer bloody head. You've no chance to outrun them in this wee cart—can ye not see that? Now get on with ya!"

Seeing a neck stretching in her immediate future, Sabritha's patience had all but run out. "Can we go now?" she snarled. Receiving no reply, she climbed onto the wagon seat, leaped over into the bed of the wagon with something less than ladylike skill and ripped open the first large chest she came to. She quickly began rummaging through the treasure it contained, giving one trinket after another a cursory examination before tossing it aside.

A broad smile erupted across Daynin's face, having instantly realized what Sabritha had in mind. "Grandfather— we don't have to fight! We can *buy* our way out of this. Come on—help me." The two climbed onto the back of the wagon and began tossing silver goblets, coins and whatever else Sabritha handed them onto the road. "More!" Daynin shouted.

Ean watched in amazement as a king's ransom got tossed onto the ground without so much as a second thought. "Bloody hell, boy! Where did you get all this?"

"Never mind that now," the woman retorted. "Can you drive this wagon? I think it's time for us to beat it out of here."

"Aye, but Daynin should drive. My longbow will keep those blaggards off our tail better than that treasure, wager that."

Sabritha stood up, looked behind them and realized she couldn't argue the point. "They're *on* us, Daynin."

One look back and Daynin scrambled over the wagon seat. He lashed old Abaddon hard, feeling a fear tightening his throat he'd never felt before. "Get on with ya, you old war horse!"

Ean and Sabritha both fell into the wagon bed as it lurched forward. Ean quickly righted himself and made ready to fire. Two hundred paces behind them, Fulchere the Bowman and his contingent closed at full gallop, the hooves of their war horses clattering on the stone trail like a thousand blacksmiths beating the same anvil.

Kruzurk retrieved the grimoire from the stack of books, handling it as though it were the cherished bones of a long lost saint. He motioned for Mediah to step closer with the light, that he might be able to see better. He propped the manuscript open atop the catafalque, the spine of the book resting against the carved boar's head that adorned the lower end of the carnyx.

The *Monograph* had fallen open to a leather marker placed about two thirds of the way toward the end of the book. The pages at that point contained a series of lists in three columns, none of which Kruzurk could begin to decipher. "Perhaps we should take this and go, Mediah. The candles are nearly half spent."

"Aye, m'lord. My thoughts exactly. You can read it better in the sanctuary above us, I should think."

"Somehow I doubt that," Kruzurk said, sighing. "This script is unlike any I've ever seen." Having closed the book, his eyes were inexplicably drawn to the calligraphy etched into the carnyx's fluted shaft. Without thinking, the Latin words began to spill from the magician's mouth. *"Prima urbes inter—divum domus Dalriada,"* he recited.

Mediah had turned toward what remained of the crypt's doorway. Hearing the words, he turned about. "What does *that* mean?"

"Probably a Roman translation of a Pictish phrase. In Latin, it means 'First among cities, home of the gods, Dalriada,' though I cannot imagine why such a phrase would be inscribed on the horn unless it's a warning of some kind." Kruzurk's eyes scanned ahead to read the rest of the horn's inscription.

"M'lord, what is a 'dalriada'?"

"Not a what, my Greek friend—Dalriada is a place—the ancestral kingdom of the Picts. The very ground we stand on used to be Pictish land. This priory and everything north to Loch Ness were controlled by the Picts and fought over for countless generations. The Picts held off the Vikings, the Celts, the Irish and even the Romans for a time, until they ultimately fell to treason in their own ranks."

"M'lord—the candles . . ." Mediah started to say, but a second too late. The light wavered, then abruptly went out, victim to a strange gust of cold musty air moving rapidly across the chamber.

"Damn," Kruzurk swore. "Stand still, Mediah. Don't try to move—it's too dangerous here." With one hand on the book to maintain his balance in the pitch blackness, Kruzurk retrieved a small pellet from his robe with the other. He dropped the pellet onto the catafalque's damp surface and crushed it with his palm. Instantly, the tomb came alive with a soft green glow like that of a firefly reflected off a pond.

"You never cease to amaze me, Kruze."

"It's just a compound, Mediah—simple alchemy. True magic is the knowledge of the natural world we live in and nothing more. Sorcery, on the other hand, perverts the natural laws, but I am bound by oath never to knowingly avail myself of such pyrrhonist profundities."

Being rudely dumped at the side of the track by his captors, Brude's attention swept over the grounds, sizing up his options. He grew tired of the delays, and angry at being dragged about like a side of butcher's beef. He focused on an all-out fight to the death, determined to take as many of his blood enemies with him as possible. The fight would be short, to be sure, since he was outnumbered at least fifty to one. *Ah, but it would be a glorious finish,* he mused.

He tried wriggling his massive gauntlets against the binding chains, the Caledonians having left him all alone in the fading light. They busied themselves kindling their cook fires and tapping beer kegs, paying him little mind, especially now that they were outnumbered by Saxons and unable to complete his execution at their own whim.

One of Brude's gauntlets finally lurched free of the chains behind him, yet the other remained tied to his back. His arms were completely enveloped in ropes and chains as well, but with time, he knew he could slip free of those. Then suddenly, without warning, his attention left the

Caledonian camp completely, focusing instead on some ethereal image somewhere far away. He could see through someone else's eyes, seemingly peering straight into what remained of Brude's soul.

Vendernochla doch fennakuth mahn cruithni? Brude cried out in his head, but he got no answer. *Why is this man reading Cruithni prayers, if he cannot answer me?*

A dark chamber and weathered hands appeared in Brude's vision, with a longish white beard that seemed to be moving. Brude could tell there were words flowing from the bearded one's mouth, but he could not understand them at first. Finally, the image cleared and he could see a wizened old sage's reflection in the polished metal of a carnyx! The sage was attempting to form the words of Brude's ancestral tongue, but like all others of lesser blood, he could make no sense of the language.

Curiously, the old man began to glow—all green and eerie like. If Brude had still possessed his human face, a broad smile would have erupted from ear to ear. Sadly, he had yet to realize his body of flesh long ago turned to dust, and that now he existed as a lonely spirit clothed in rust-laden armor.

Ean drew another of his precious chert-tipped arrows from the quiver and took dead aim at the second rider bearing down on them. Neither the chert arrowhead, nor any of the others he carried, would penetrate chainmail at much over a hundred paces, but the chert would shatter on impact, driving jagged fragments of stone up into the exposed chin of the target. Many times Ean had sparked a panic in the enemy ranks with such a shot. He could only hope it worked as well this time.

"Thwangg" the longbow barked, loosing its deadly dart.

"Gotcha!" is all Ean had time to say before the arrow struck the man just above his heart. The effect was that of a battering ram—the arrow shaft and tip both shattered, throwing deadly fragments in all directions. The target catapulted backward over the rump of his steed, his horse turning almost sideways from the painful hail of splinters tattooed into its neck.

Pandemonium broke out among the rest of the troop. They scattered in three directions, some of them still bearing down on the slow moving cart. The fallen man went head over heels with a muffled scream like a clutch of cats crammed in a beer keg. His cohorts dodged left and right to avoid trampling him, and to make themselves less of a target for the next arrow. Ean didn't wait, having already drawn a bead on another target. That man went down equally hard.

The band's Saxon leader took the next arrow in his hand just as he rode upon the sparkling spoils Daynin and Sabritha had left behind. The man bellowed in pain, but his voice quickly changed from fright to delight with the realization that an incredible bounty lay scattered before him in the road. Off his horse he came, having jerked the arrow shaft through his hand as though it were a mere wood splinter. The others must have seen the booty, too, for they quickly changed course at full gallop to close on the riches.

By now, old Abaddon had met his best stride, covering a quarter of a league of their escape without yet breaking a lather. Daynin lashed him harder, eager to catch up with the squire who beat a dead run toward the timber bridge ahead of them.

"Jump on if you can!" Daynin yelled from several paces behind the boy. "But get out of the way—I've got to make that bridge."

The squire dodged sideways to avoid Abaddon, tripping

in the process. He tumbled in the ruts of the road, coming back to his feet in one graceful vault. Facing the enemy, he realized they had all stopped on the track behind him.

"What are they doing?" he questioned, just as a glint of light from the treasure gave him his answer. For an instant, Miles Aubrecht's feet almost took him toward the treasure trove, but reason regained command and he leaped onto the back of the passing cart.

"Blaggards," Ean scoffed. "Not a disciplined troop among that lot, else we'd be goners for sure."

Sabritha shrugged her shoulders in a mock display of surprise. "Those who chase two foxes," she said, "end up eating roots for supper."

Kruzurk's mind felt awash in images he could not begin to understand, yet his eyes continued to devour the strange words and pictographs, both on the horn and the wall behind it. "From the land of Oengus, in his great house—" his voice suddenly blurted out.

"Say what, m'lord?" The flowing, guttural cadence of Kruzurk's words were beginning to frighten Mediah. It seemed that someone else controlled the magician's mouth, for the words rang out unlike any the Greek had heard before.

Kruzurk didn't respond to him. He read on, unable to break the flow of the epic Cruithni poem his mind translated from the wall. "—the Well of Fears doth form in the south— and flows unseen from Gretna Green, all the way north to Hemloch House. Follow the markers, if you dare—or a creature will guide those who share. Find the Well's doors that lead to the light, your journey will be shortened by at least a fortnight. But mark ye this, those who have read—touch ye not the waters of dread. And fail to bring booty to the Watchman of the Well, get thy soul ready for its trip to hell."

"Kruzurk?" Mediah begged.

The outburst seemed to break the magician's reverie. He shook his head in confusion, turning toward Mediah with a blank look spreading across his face. "What the deuce? Was I asleep?"

Mediah stepped forward and lifted Kruzurk's hand from the *Monograph*. "A trance of some kind would be my guess, m'lord. You were spouting words that sounded like a song, but such words I've never heard in all my travels."

Kruzurk stared at his hands for a few seconds, disbelief in his learned eyes. "Unknowingly, I've opened a veil of some kind, Mediah. But to where or what, I cannot say. It was as though the Oracle of Delphi or someone with great powers was reading the words into my mind—showing me a secret path. There's a river under our feet—way down below the catacombs. It flows all the way to Loch Linnhe in the north. If we find it, we can reach Kinloch Keep before Daynin does, and warn him about the Duke's men."

"Something tells me they already know, m'lord. I just hope we're not too late."

"Take the horn and the offering, you fool. You must have both with you, or perish in the Well," Brude whispered to the sage's image playing across his mind's eye. The bearded one seemed to understand, but not completely. "Don't forget the offering! It must be in Saxon blood—or the Watcher of the Well will take your own heart in payment!"

Each time the bearded one removed his hand from the book, his image began to dwindle. Yet Brude knew he had to urge him on, else the whole effort would be lost. "Take it, damn ye! Take the bloody book, and be gone. And hurry—ye've no time to dawdle."

Several paces away, one of the Caledonians overheard

the strange Pictish ranting coming from their prisoner. "Our giant is awake, lads! Shall we do 'im now?"

A crowd quickly gathered, encircling the huge carcass like a wounded bull in a marsh mire. No one wanted to tangle with the beast, but all were eyeing that elaborate and expensive armor. Every man knew such a treasure would fetch a handsome trade in the markets of Glasgow, and they were all determined to get a piece of that action.

"Get back, you lot!" came a resounding rebuke from one of the Saxon knights. "This man is a prisoner of Duke Harold's and will be duly tried and executed by the King's Eyre in Carlisle. Now back away, or I'll string one of you up as a warning!"

Plumat heard the commotion from far across the camp, then raced to stem the hubbub. "What's your game, Sercey?" he bellowed at his Saxon companion.

"No game, my lord. These men were about to commit a foul deed on the prisoner. I merely reminded them that . . ."

Plumat shoved his way on through the grumbling crowd to confront Sercey helm to helm. "I don't give a damn what you were reminding them of, just remember who gives the orders in this troop. Now get you down to the valley and see what's holding up Fulchere and the others. I don't intend to spend the night on this bloody cairn when there's a perfectly good keep less than five leagues from here—and we're losing the light."

Sercey pushed the Caledonians out of his way, waved for his squire to bring his horse, and rode off in haste. The dust had barely settled from his departure when he galloped back into camp, heading straight for Plumat. "My lord! My lord, come quickly—the felons have escaped!"

The Boarding

Realizing their time in the catacombs was growing short, Kruzurk asked Mediah to go back up to the sanctuary and fetch Olghar and his dog—provided Thor was still alive. Before sending him on his way, Kruze added, "I doubt the priors did him much good with their patch and burn healing, but if he's alive, we'll take him along. Olghar won't leave without him in any case, and we can't leave Olghar here."

"Aye, m'lord. But where will *you* be?"

"I should read as many of these runes as possible. They must give some hint for the way down to the Well of Fears. Otherwise, we will be here 'til the next moon trying to find it. Take these phoslin pellets with you—just crush one in your palm when you need it and you will have sufficient light."

"Phoslin?" Mediah questioned.

"That is what my old mentor Merlin called them. The green light comes from a substance called phosphorus. When you heat it, it glows in the dark. Now hurry, my friend—we haven't much time!"

Mediah crushed one of the gleaming round pellets between his palms. The bright glow made the Greek smile like a child who had just discovered sunshine. "A wondrous thing, Kruze."

"Mediah—say nothing about any of this to the priors. They must never learn how we got out of these catacombs.

Best to leave them assuming we perished. When you return, bring a chalice of some kind—we must collect a goblet of blood from the floor of the wellkeep."

His hand back on the *Monograph,* strange images and words again flooded Kruzurk Makshare's mind. This time, they were intermixed with whimsies of men and horses and a great deal of shouting. Kruze became terribly confused and frightened at first, then realized he must be sharing the mind—and visions—of another. "Who are you?" he asked, but heard no reply. Just the refrain, "Seize the horn and the book and be gone," that kept repeating itself over and over again in his mind.

Chaos reigned in the Caledonian ranks. Sercey's unexpected return had thrown the whole camp into total disarray. The Saxon knights shouted orders, impatient to have their horses saddled so they could be first to join the chase. Squires scurried hither and yon gathering their masters' goods to break camp. Caledonians swore at each other and at their taskmasters, angry that the evening grog would again be missed. Everyone except Brude seemed entirely oblivious to those around them.

Lowland fools, Brude thought. *I could make my escape if I could but wrench these chains free.* His attention fell back upon the bearded sage reaching out to him across time and distance. "Go on, old man, read the bloody runes—and be quick about it—lest I perish while you're about it!"

The last three wagons at the rear of the column rumbled off the cairn, drowning out Brude's bellowing and leaving him in a huge dust cloud. Suddenly, the Great Deceiver was all alone and could bring his full attention to his escape.

Given the late hour and maddened pace of the column's

exit, it should have been no great surprise when, just after dark, someone in the column finally realized their Pictish prize had been left behind on the mountain.

"Damn you blaggards!" Plumat could be heard swearing all the way back up the valley. "Take a wagon and go fetch that beast!"

All the while, Fulchere and his men had been busily scooping up every coin and bit of treasure their horses' rumpbags would hold, giving no mind whatever to the magician's cart rapidly disappearing in the distance. Nor were they paying much attention to Plumat's pennon, approaching from the opposite direction. That is, until he rode up almost on top of them, screaming every foul oath he could muster.

"What manner of treachery is this?" he yelled. "Why have you allowed the felons to escape? Are you bewitched, stoned or stupid?"

Fulchere managed to find his tongue, but could hardly make a valid defense for his cowardly actions. "Treasure, m'lord—lots of it—a King's ransom to be sure . . ."

Plumat jerked Cauldron to a stop, dropped out of his saddle, and slapped a heavy silver plate from Fulchere's hand in mid stride. "Did it never cross your feeble mind that if you caught the bloody wagon, all of the treasure would have been ours? Idiots, ingrates and imbeciles. I'm sent to Scotia with an army of half-wits! If not for my pledge to the Duke, I swear I would turn about and leave this place before the sun rises again!"

At last Brude wrenched himself free of chains. He watched the confrontation with a mixture of mirth and concern. From his vantage point high on an adjacent slope, he could not know what Plumat and the others were talking about, or if they planned to return. One thing he knew for sure—left behind and able to escape, he wouldn't give the Saxons a second chance to seize him. With movement he found surprisingly easy—weightless, in fact—the Great Deceiver scampered over the crest of the hill and disappeared in a sea of giant boulders.

It would be long after sunset and several leagues to the north before Brude came upon a deserted shepherd's hovel overlooking the Firth of Clyde. He stopped not to rest, for he required none, but to see if the bearded green sage whose images clogged his mind needed any more guidance. Happily, the visions that played out were exactly what Brude expected. The old man had found the Well of Fears!

Weighed down by the horn, knapsacks, supplies and rumpbags from their horses, Mediah struggled to tote Thor's nearly lifeless body down the steep, winding stairwell. With Olghar in tow and more than a little trepidation, Mediah tried to bolster the blind beggar's spirits and his own in the process. "Just a little further, old friend—you can make it. And when we get to the Well, maybe we can give Thor some water."

Kruzurk stopped on the slippery landing ahead of them. "We can't touch the water, Mediah. The visions warned against that. I may have something that will ease Thor's breathing, but be careful on these steps—they are slick with all manner of gooey mess. There's light ahead, too. Maybe we've found the Well. Best keep your voices down from here on."

"Is 'e still alive, Greek?" came Olghar's plaintive whisper.

Mediah shook his head yes, then realized the beggar couldn't see that. "Breathing hard, but alive. Now we have to be quiet."

No sooner did the words slip out of Mediah's mouth than a gruff, demanding voice boomed out of the half light, "Who goes there? Who comes to the Well of Fears? If ye be mortal—a fair warning—for this is the place from which the worst nightsweats come. If ye be a wandering soul come to find respite from the stinking realm of the dead, there is no room for your kind either."

All three of the intrepid travelers froze. Only Thor's labored breathing and a kind of swishing sound like that of a mill pond sluice broke the silence from somewhere in the gloom ahead. The noise grew louder, echoing from the muck covered stones all around them. Olghar took a faltering step backward, but his forearm stayed firmly locked under Mediah's elbow.

"*Prima—urbes—inter—divum domus—Dalriada,*" Kruzurk recited, his words coming out decidedly on the shaky side.

"Bah! You are not of Cruithni blood," the voice growled. "I can taste Cruithni sweat from the air. All I smell from you is Saxon vomit."

"Aye, we are not from here, but we've brought you an offering, just as the runes say. That is, if you are the Watcher of the Well." Kruzurk thrust the goblet of day old blood ahead of him, swirling it around to make sure the entity could smell the prize.

That swishing sound grew louder, and definitely less human in origin, yet it seemed to move away from them, leaving a gentle gurgling sound behind. Thor must have sensed something very strange in the air. His head lifted up abruptly, both ears turned toward the sound.

"We've a journey to take," Kruzurk declared, having yet to see from whence the voice came. "The runes said you would show us the way."

"Runes says you? And how is it you can read the language

of the Picts? No one's been down here in three hundred years what could read the sacred stones. Not even those pesky monks from up in the light."

Kruzurk's head darted to the left from where the voice seemed to emanate, but there was no one there. The voice crept much closer now. Close enough in fact that Kruze could smell the foul being. It reeked—worse even than the goblet of gore he held in his hand. "Are you the Watcher?" he asked again.

"I ask the questions here, mortal. What have you brought me, that I may decide not to eat your heart for my supper? And what is that strange smell among you? Are you part beast, for that is animal blood I taste on the air."

Olghar rebelled at the gut-wrenching image of what might come next. "You can't have him! He's my dog and by God I'll fight you for him!"

A boisterous, "Hahaahahaaa," shook the flagstones beneath them. "I doubt you could fight your way out of a hay stack, you ancient sea bass, but I give you credit for courage. And as for your god, he has no power here. I rule the Well!"

Stepping forward, the beggar jerked his arm free from Mediah's grasp. He raised his cane in the voice's direction and began to chant, his other hand making the sign of the cross as he spoke. *"Palmanyee vosta shemya nachock. Voseem natzit crist y trag svoloch!"*

Kruzurk tried to stop the old man before he could utter another word. "Olghar, I beg you, say no more."

"He plans to eat my dog," Olghar responded. "He'll have to kill me first."

"Hahahahaaaaar," the voice bellowed. "I am much amused. You can keep your beast, old crotch. I've no taste for him. Besides, I haven't enjoyed this much mirth since the dying days of Dalriada. Now, where's my gift, eh? What bring you for my supper?"

Mediah and Kruzurk did a double take. A huge barrel-chested being, half again Mediah's height, and with a belly big enough to hold a full-grown calf, lurched into the light. The being's tallowed skin was adorned with tattoos, runes and pictographs from an ample waistline all the way up to his blood-encrusted beard. Deep reddish scars protruded in places from the Watcher's abundant and coarse black body hair. The magnificently gross body suited the smell that had preceded it.

A pair of enormous blacksmith's arms reached out for the goblet, taking the prize from Kruzurk and thrusting it under the rusty half-helm the Watcher wore over his face. Downing the chalice of thick blood, the Watcher let out the most enormous of belches, again rattling the cobwebs and crevices of the catacombs. "Bah, this blood is old!" he groaned.

"My apologies," Kruzurk spoke up. "But we had no other Saxon blood from which to choose."

"More's the pity," the Watcher replied. "If I could leave the Well and go up into the light, I could solve *that* problem damn quick."

Mediah began mumbling an ancient prayer under his breath. Kruzurk could tell that the putrid smell of the Watcher, combined with the nauseating aroma of death that pervaded the Well was making Mediah ill. Kruze hoped he didn't throw up right there on the spot, lest he might offend the Watcher. "We must reach Loch Linnhe as fast as possible. Is this something you can help us with?"

"Me? I am the Watcher of the Well, you sniveling snot, not some traveler's guide. I can show you the way, but first you must give me my reward. Or did you forget that, perhaps?"

Kruzurk looked around at the others, a surprised look on his face. "I—I have this book, and a Cruithni war chief's horn."

"Book? What need have I of books? I spit on your book. And that horn is of no use to me—only a Cruithni chieftain can use its powers. Now, what else did you bring me? Gold, silver, perhaps? Dragon's teeth, or something sweet? Out with it, old man, or this will be the shortest journey of your miserable lives!"

Olghar reached inside his ragged tunic to fetch the St. Vladimir's cross. *"Megda ya signavet doth ichperdum nicht, pajalista,"* he prayed, slipping the cross and gold chain over his head. Offering his prize in the general direction of the Watcher, Olghar mournfully added, "Take this, if it will buy our passage."

Despite his size, the Watcher fell backward in terror at the sight of the twin railed cross. "No!" he groaned, his huge belly shaking like a hog heaving out its innards. "Put that away, you fool!"

Kruzurk snatched the crucifix from Olghar's out-stretched hand and with a quick motion, stuffed it into the middle of the *Monograph*'s ample confines. "There—it's out of sight, out of mind—you need have no fear."

"I fear nothing, you chalk bearded crone. But the master of this place would make cinders of us all with just one hint of that seditious symbol in our midst. Now go, and good riddance to ye!"

"Which way, m'lord?" Kruzurk asked, his arm making a grand sweeping motion toward the downward sloping path. At least a dozen passages lay ahead of them, each one seemingly darker and more foreboding than the next.

"Follow the webs, you spindly Wiccan, for they will lead you to the boat. And mark you this—there are no return paths. Tread forward only, never back. Walk toward the water, and stay on the track. The rest will become clear, once the beast is near."

Without another sound, the Watcher seemed to crouch over and blend into the stone surface behind him, leaving only the empty mug in the spot where he had stood. Kruzurk and the others left quickly, the path ahead marked by a series of large spider webs leading off toward a bluish green light of undetermined origin.

Though it had to be well past midnight, Daynin urged Abaddon to keep up his steady, plodding progress toward the coast. A full moon provided ample light to stay on the track, and as long as the lights of Glasgow twinkled to his left, Daynin knew he would strike the Clyde River where his grandfather had indicated.

Sabritha, the old man, and the squire were all fast asleep in the back of the wagon, exhausted from the day's events. Beyond tired himself, Daynin stayed awake from the excited rush of their narrow escape and the flicker of realization that a day or two at sea would soon bring them to Rhum and Kinloch Keep, where they would be safe forever.

His mind played out a vision of the cozy north tower with its great hearth in the middle. The one place he'd been forbidden entrance by his father except on special occasions when the whole McKinnon clan gathered for feasting and story telling would soon yield to *his* commands as master of Rhum.

Grandfather Ean had explained it thus, "The master of the house and his mate come together to share their souls in that room, boy. They do so with nay a bit o' clothing on their bodies, and generally prefer not to be disturbed whilst sharing. Some day you'll be the master of Kinloch, and you will want that same privilege."

"Master of the House of McKinnon" had a nice ring to it, even though little remained of the clan and Kinloch Keep. Daynin intended to change all that, just as soon as possible. For now, he had to keep his attention focused on old Abaddon's backside, lest they tumble off the track and end up splattered on the jagged rocks below. His thoughts had barely leaped back to reality before Abaddon let out a great snort and reared up in his trace.

"Bloody hell!" Daynin cried out, his mind reeling in disbelief at the intruder who seemed to have risen up right out of the road. "Where did—how did you catch us so fast?"

Chapter 27:

The Evading

Plumat spat into the roaring fire, realizing that the time his army had lost trying to recapture the Pict had also cost him the greater prize—the boy and the Blackgloom Bounty. He could undo neither blunder now. His ragtag army had scattered like birds in a hailstorm with darkness upon them and with no idea if the cart had reached the Clyde. Most of his men were legs up, having spent what was left of their new fortunes in the local taverns, content to drown their miseries in local brew.

To Plumat's dismay, the Pict's escape had seemed all too easy. The giant disappeared without a trace, if the Caledonians were to be believed. Plumat simply had to clear his mind and deal with the fact that he'd been out-maneuvered by a boy and a brutish thug. "Neither of them have sufficient wits to fill a bat's earlid," he scoffed, the Glasgow Inn's fire pit his only audience. "I'll have them by midday, by God, or know the reason why."

No sooner were the words out of his mouth than a portly figure came barging through the inn's back door. Ranulf of Westmoorland looked like he had tangled with a shepherd's dog and come away the loser. His tunic was ripped, his chainmail spotted with mud and dung and he smelled of animal sweat mixed with salt brine and puke. "Ale, barmaid—and make it hot!" he roared. Three steps inside the door, he realized he had no one to shout at except Plumat. "Bloody hell. Where *is* everyone?"

Plumat shook his head at the miserable sight. Ranulf's feathers would be ruffled with Plumat's failure to report earlier in the evening. "Gone to bed, I should imagine, m'lord," he said with deference to Ranulf's rank, hoping to settle those feathers.

"Where are your men, Plumat? Surely you're not staying here *alone* in this heathen brothel."

"The ones I can trust are still out searching, m'lord. A few are next door in the tavern. Others have taken beds elsewhere in Glasgow, that they might talk to the locals and get news of our felons."

"And what news have you? My ship is anchored in the river, and my men are searching around Dumbarton and the northern roads. But I take it you lost your prey somewhere on the track, eh?"

Plumat stood up. He towered over the plump and slovenly Ranulf, giving him a much more imposing posture from which to reply. The time had arrived to establish his authority, now that the pleasantries were over. "They escaped, no thanks to these drunken levies we hired. But they can't have gone far. That wagon is heavy with booty, and they've only the one horse. What of ships in the Clyde? Have you done your job and closed off the river traffic?"

"That's not exactly a millstream out there, Plumat. Had you come to find me before dark, you would have realized that. We have but one ship, and there are hundreds of inlets. A Norse fleet could be in that estuary and we would be hard pressed to know it."

The sharpness of Ranulf's reply set Plumat back. Then he remembered that Ranulf's only duty to the Duke was as overseer for gathering grain and slopping hogs to pay the royal taxes. "My orders were to march here, find you, and have you transport my army back to Carlisle. Your duty is to provide me with support. Was that not made clear to you?"

Ranulf had turned to scouring the inn's tables for whatever scraps he could find to eat. Upon that rebuke, his head snapped around to face the much younger Plumat, one hand reaching for his dirk. "How dare you talk to me in that tone. Why—you're nothing but a . . ."

Plumat shoved a bench out of his way and stepped forward, straight into Ranulf's face, hesitating only long enough to wrinkle his nose at the man's smell. "I'm under the direct orders of Duke Harold of Anglia. You take orders from me. What part of that is not clear to you?" A measured bump of Ranulf's ample front side shoved the man back, completely disarming him and putting him in his place.

Falling backward into a bar chair, Ranulf of Westmoorland could do little more than issue a sheepish reply. "Your pardon, m'lord. I was told you would be in charge, but it is not my custom to take orders from the Duke's men-at-arms."

"Then get used to it, Westmoorland. We've a dangerous task ahead of us here and nothing but enemy all around. Follow my orders and you may yet return to feeding your swineherds. Fail to do so, and you'll likely end up as a main course, feeding some Scotian twit's hogs with your own guts instead."

The Watcher's parting words about a beast had Kruzurk genuinely worried for the first time since leaving Lanercost Priory. He could overcome, outmaneuver or outwit men and their machinations, but beasts were another thing entirely—especially with others to think of. And in such a foreboding place like the Well of Fears, he had no doubt that any beast would be something out of the ordinary.

Downward they trod, the slope of the stone pathway growing ever more slippery and steep with each step. Kruzurk turned about to make sure the others followed him and, satisfied, marched onward. The cobwebs he had been ordered to follow grew larger and more menacing with each turn in the path, though he had yet to see a single spider. The webs bulged with white cocooned bundles as big as pumpkins, evidence that something besides lost souls wandered the catacombs. *Rats,* he rationalized. *That's why we've seen no rats!*

A strange swishing and alternately gurgling sound emanated from somewhere below. The light around the intrepid band turned from a soft green to a more pronounced bluish tint, similar to the light reflected off an ocean at dusk. Kruze could hear what sounded like waves lapping against the hull of a boat. He knew they were close to the end of the path. Suddenly, a vista opened ahead.

"This cannot be," the magician whispered, for his learned eyes would not allow his mind to accept what he could clearly see. "This simply can't be."

Mediah, with Olghar in tow, came around the final bend in the path and stopped instantly as though struck dumb by the sight. Olghar fidgeted with his cane, anxious to move on, but Mediah wouldn't allow it. "What is it, Greek? Have we reached the end? I can smell the water, and fish, and rotting timber. Are we there?"

"Shhhhhh," Kruzurk warned.

"*Insha Allah,*" Mediah prayed. "This cannot be."

Even Thor came out of his stupor to see the incredible sight. His ears perked, his nose twitched, and somewhere deep inside him, an ominous growl began to form.

The wagon's sudden lurching stop tossed everyone

asunder. Daynin desperately jerked on the reins trying to calm Abaddon. The poor horse was terrified at the giant's unexpected appearance in his path. All the more so because of the Pict's size and the many sparkling plates that adorned his intricate armor.

"I had a feeling you were in this wagon, though I cannot say why for sure. Are you not glad to see me, *Draygnar?* We are allies, after all."

"You scared the boogers out of me and the horse, you big blowhard! How in the name of Scotia did you get here before us? Last I saw of you at the priory, there were ten men on top of you."

Brude stepped around Abaddon, running his huge mailed hand along the animal's back to steady him. "Plenty of time for war stories later, boy. You best be moving this chariot along afore the sunrise catches you on this road. There's no way off it 'til you reach the shoreline down below, and I assume you have a ship waiting out there somewhere, do ye not?"

"Aye, we have a ship," Ean interrupted, "not that it's any business of yours. Who the bloody hell are you, anyway, and why have you stopped us?"

Brude's enormous helm turned toward the sudden verbal assault from the back of the wagon. "I'm the boy's ally, you old fart. Now sit thee down and hush your grousing or I'll toss you over the cliff edge."

Ean almost came out of his shoes trying to scramble past Sabritha and the squire. His face turned a bright scarlet and his voice choked, so unaccustomed was he to being rebuked. Only the quick hands of the woman and Miles Aubrecht kept him from losing a very short, one-sided fight.

"You bastard!" Ean swore, trying with all his strength to get at the giant tormentor.

"Easy, grandfather," Daynin pleaded. "This is Brude McAlpin—he helped us escape the Duke's men. He's a—a—he's . . ."

"What the boy is trying to say is that I come from a time long past. Daynin here gave me life again—and I am bound to repay that debt."

"Life *again?*" Ean scoffed.

"Aye, 'twas a long time ago when I first walked these grounds and fought with your ancestors."

The old man settled back a bit, still agitated with the delay. "Then you claim to be a ghost, is that it? I dinnae believe in such tripe. 'Tis but tawdry tales told to test the talents of the tale tellers, says I. They's no such thing as ghosts."

Daynin turned around to face the old man, his eyes bright with the sparkle of absolute truth. "I saw my father at the priory, grandfather. Plain as day, he stood there for one blink of my eyes, then poof—slipped right through the wall of the nave. Prior Bede said such spirits do exist, and I believe Brude tells the truth. He, too, has a long score to settle with the Caledonians."

"And anyone else who dares transgress Cruithni ground," Brude added.

The squire's ears perked up at the mention of that word. "There are no Cruithni left—only myths. I read that the Romans destroyed them hundreds of years ago. They called them Picts, for their custom of marking their skin with tattoos."

The Great Deceiver flew into a rage. Before anyone could stop him, one gigantic glove reached into the wagon and jerked the squire out by his throat. The hapless boy's life hung in the balance. He looked for all the world like a lamb trussed from an oak tree. Brude pulled the boy's face close to the view slit on his helmet. "No Cruithni left, eh? Does this feel like a myth from your Roman history, or the real thing? Speak up, scholar. Beg for mercy the way your ancestors did, or I'll snap your neck like a charred chicken bone."

"Put him down, you big rusty rivet pile!" Sabritha snarled. "Pick on someone your own size."

Brude dropped the boy in a heap on the ground, having turned his attention to the woman. "Spicy bit of salt you are, eh? Mayhaps you'd like to tumble with me next?"

Sabritha's lightning quick movement to slap at the giant's helmet stopped when met by Daynin's equally fast response. He stayed her wrist, then barked, "Enough of this! We have to get to the boat before first light. Brude, if you travel with us, you must act like an ally—not some half crazed Cruithni conundrum bent on destruction. The Anglish—they are your enemy—not these people."

The brutish hulk stepped back from the wagon, content that he'd made his point. "Go on. I'll meet you at the boat. This cart and that miserable beast can barely handle the load now. I'm off to find the Anglish dogs who stole my blade at Abbotsford. When I do, then will I have reason to draw blood this night."

"Where does the light come from?" Mediah asked, probably without actually expecting an answer.

Kruzurk ventured a couple of halting steps toward the water, his fear momentarily overcome by the same curiosity Mediah had expressed. He knelt next to the water's edge, sniffing the pungent aroma that wafted off the surface. "This is fresh water, but it smells of fish—or slime—or . . ."

"That's the monster you smell, you old fool . . ." came a frail, but very authoritative reply from the shadows. "If you venture any closer to the water, you'll likely find out for yourself."

Kruze, Mediah and Olghar all turned as one, taken aback by the nearly invisible intruder. Barely as tall as Mediah's belt, a troll-sized being seemed to glide across the slimy stone surface with the ease of a shadow. His dark robe displayed all the trappings of a monk, but none of the piety.

"What did you bring me?" he barked. "I don't do this for fun, you know."

"Are you the guidesman?" Kruzurk replied.

"I'm Gandahar, keeper of the boats," the diminutive being snapped back. "Now, what did you *bring* me?" A tiny hand reached out to push back the wimple covering his head and shoulders.

Upon seeing the hideous blue-white skin on the being's oddly shaped bald head, Mediah gasped aloud. Olghar tugged at his frock sleeve and begged, "What is it, master— what's *wrong?*"

"I'm waiting," came another sharp demand.

"We, uh—we gave our offering to the Watcher," Kruzurk answered, apologetically.

"That's what they all say. He probably ate it, too, didn't he? That's all he thinks about—food and blood, blood and food. I was hoping for something a bit more—shall we say— substantial?"

Gandahar glided closer to Mediah and the dog, his beady gaze playing rapidly among the threesome, as though expecting some action on their part. "Is that a horse you've brought me, mayhaps? I've always wanted to see one of those, in the flesh."

Kruzurk stepped between the being and Thor's nearly lifeless body. "No—a horse is much bigger. This is a dog, and a badly injured one at that—he's hardly worth . . ."

Gandahar darted back into the shadows before Kruzurk could even finish explaining. "Take him away—take him away—take him away!" the little being wailed, his voice louder and more shrill with each successive scream.

"Thor won't hurt you," Olghar said, reaching out to stroke the dog's fur. "See, he's very friendly."

"Get in the boat, and be gone with you!" Gandahar screeched. His hand protruded from the shadows, pointing the way to a small scow moored some fifty paces down the stone jetty. "Take one of the staffs you'll find in the boat and touch the water with it. When you reach your destination, touch the water again. Now get thee gone, before I summon the beast myself."

Kruzurk waved to Mediah to follow, and together, they made their way to the ancient wooden vessel. Climbing aboard, the magician found a cache of wooden staffs stored near the bow. He selected one, then made sure his companions were safely settled amidships. Satisfied that they were ready, he touched the staff to the water's surface and held his breath. Nothing happened.

Several minutes passed while they waited, wondering what to expect next. The long arched tunnelway was unlike any they had ever seen. Intricate and finely carved stones fit together so perfectly forming the channel's vaulted roof, if indeed it was a channel, that no mortar showed between the stones. And the light—coming from nowhere and everywhere—reflected eerily from every surface, making the tunnel seem to move on its own in perfect rhythm with the water's ebb and flow.

Behind the boat, some distance down the tunnel, Kruzurk caught a glimpse of a dark humpbacked shape as it emerged from the water, then disappeared again, then reappeared. The creature repeated that motion over and over, like a giant water snake undulating along the surface. And it was fast—faster than any sea creature Kruzurk knew to exist. As the thing drew nearer, he realized it was huge. So large, in fact, that its last dive into the depths splashed water on them from three boat length's distance.

"My God," Kruzurk whispered. "Hang on—that thing may swamp this scow and us with it."

Holding their breath, all three men waited several long seconds until the boat finally erupted into motion. In a sudden acceleration, the boat leapt forward as if caught by a giant wind—yet with no sail, and no wind to push it. Instead, the boat rapidly gained speed as it almost literally flew down the tunnel. Traveling faster than any of the adventurers had ever expected to as mortal men, they left behind all thought or concern for their own safety and simply marveled at the heady rush forward.

The beast had taken the boat in its wake and moved at an unbelievable pace, first on the surface, then below, then again above water once more. Time and time again the motion continued until Kruzurk lost all track of how long or how far they might have traveled.

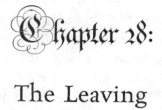

Chapter 28:

The Leaving

The Caledonian guard at the wagons never noticed his killer, so swift and deadly came the Cruithni's clandestine approach. He snapped the guard's neck with so little effort that it hardly seemed a worthy victory to Brude, though it had been necessary. Finding *Droongar* was his main objective at the moment—that and rejoining his allies at the boat. He didn't need or want a battle to fight, especially one in which he would be greatly outnumbered and, at the moment, unarmed.

Feverishly, he ripped through the baggage of the first wagon, without success. Moving on to the second didn't change his luck a bit. Finally at the third cart, he found his sword wrapped in a length of lavishly decorated damask brocade. "Ah, an elegant trophy for the woman," he bragged, completely unmindful how loud his voice sounded or how far it might carry in the still Scotian night.

A guard sleeping nearby came alive with a fury, screaming his head off. The cry, "To arms! To arms!" shattered the quiet of the wee hours. Within seconds, five of Plumat's men and an equal number of Caledonians had drawn up facing the Cruithni, torches and weapons at the ready.

"We've got yer bloody arse again, Pict!" Sercey crowed. "They's no place for ya ta run this time. Now yield or you're dead meat." Three of Sercey's bowmen took aim, knowing that at close range, their crossbows would penetrate any armor known to man. "What say you, knave? Yield or die!"

In a single lightning move, Brude cast the brocaded cloth at two of the bowmen and drew down on the third with his giant blade. Quick as a cat he slashed, but not as fast as the crossbow bolts that slammed into his breastplate. Two struck the front, then a third hit him from behind with a loud "clink", seemingly without effect. He looked down at the feathered shafts protruding from his chest, amazed that he yet remained standing. At that range, nothing could have stopped a barbed bolt from penetrating to the flesh—not even his vaunted scale armor.

The bowmen dropped their weapons and ran, having never seen a man sustain that kind of damage and live, let alone stand and face them. Sercey, too, made an instant judgment that this adversary would take more than he could offer. Clearly, the Pict lacked mortality, but existed as something else entirely. The Saxon waved his sword in a circular motion over his head to signal retreat. But the rest of his men had already taken flight.

In seconds, Brude stood alone at the wagon, his mind a tangle of outrage, anger, and confusion. An inescapable realization overtook him at long last. *I really am dead. You can't kill a corpse with crossbows!* In the deep recesses of his revived consciousness, he wanted someone to tell him the dream would end soon—that he would awaken to a steaming breakfast his matrons had cooked all night. Another wave of realization laced with horror swept through that hulking suit of armor. *Dead men don't eat. And they never get tired.* Reality quickly became his worst nightmare. *I'm dead, and nothing can change that. But how is it that I walk among the living?*

If he had been able to, Brude might have cried for himself and his people, now that he knew the awful truth. Surely all his kin were gone as well. Alas, there were no tears for the Great Deceiver. He could only grab the brocade and disappear into the shadows, satisfied for the moment that there existed a greater purpose for his resurrection. And that purpose had to be Daynin—there could be no other answer.

"Stand to yer ropes, lads!" the *Shiva*'s captain urged, his voice subdued from its normal volume. Given the placid nature of the firth at that early hour, the old salt didn't want to alert any potential enemies. "Up anchor, you scum— we've a cargo headin' our way and unless my eyes is failin', they be bringing a handsome booty with 'em."

The longboat heading toward the *Shiva* appeared overloaded with people and prizes. Daynin, Ean, and the squire did the best they could to row, having no training at all in the art of oarsmanship. Sabritha did what she could to help balance the cargo and steer the boat across a strong seaward bound current. All the while, Daynin kept a sharp eye toward the riverbank, expecting any moment to see the outline of that giant rusty being he had come to care about like a distant, but very human friend. Old Abaddon stood by the water's edge, all alone, unable to make the long swim to the boat.

Whummmp. The prow of the longboat echoed as it thumped hard into the side of the *Shiva*.

"Damned landlubbers!" the captain bellowed. "Hole my ship and I'll dump the lot of ye in the firth for the fishes to feed on."

Sabritha's quick tongue snapped back, "Then you'll never get paid, you piss-brained pirate!"

"Shhh," Daynin warned. Echoes of their dispute could be heard bouncing from one cliff face to the next, like a series of sentries giving the alarm all the way along the coast. A league and a half down the firth, several heads turned at the muffled sound. One was Brude's, another that of the nightwatch on the *Woebringer* and the third, a sleek dark shape, bobbing just at the surface of the water—waiting for breakfast to make itself known. All three heads moved at the same time, each with a different agenda but all in some way involving the *Shiva*.

The *Woebringer* came alive with activity. Crewmen jumped to their stations, warned that the ship should be ready for action on a moment's notice. Brude dashed along the south shore of the firth, rushing headlong toward the sound he recognized instantly as the hawking howl of Daynin's woman. Meanwhile, the gigantic dark shape turned slowly in the cold waters of the Clyde, its breakfast having finally made the fatal first move.

Roused from the best sleep he'd experienced since starting the expedition, Plumat had trouble shaking off the trappings of slumber. "What do you mean he was *here?*" he barked, incredulous at Sercey's report on the Pict. "You blaggards allowed him to escape—again?"

"Not exactly, m'lord. We uhh, well—we had to withdraw, as you might say."

"Ten of you withdrew from one man?" By now, Plumat had on his horse boots and armor, but still could not completely comprehend Sercey's message. "You knew he'd come back for that sword! I thought you had the trap set. Must I do everything in this army?"

Sercey bowed, his honor and courage both sullied. "That Pict took three crossbow bolts through his armor at point blank range and never even staggered, m'lord. In my opinion, we are not dealing with mortal enemies."

Plumat swept his helm from the table and growled back, "They bleed just like anyone else, Sercey. These Scotian dogs are wiry, but as mortal as you and me. Now fetch my horse and wake up the troops. Then get after that giant. I'll wager the Duke's pennon that big bugger will lead us straight to the boy and the treasure."

No sooner were the orders out of Plumat's mouth than one of the Caledonians burst through the back doors of the inn. "Your ship is making sail, Saxon! She's upped anchor—they are *leaving!*"

Scudding along at a speed Kruzurk could only estimate to be thrice that of a Viking snekke, the rickety old barge seemed to be holding together well, despite the constant buffeting from the sea beast's rhythmic motion. Olghar and Mediah had been reduced to little more than desolate human frames cast on the deck, seasick and certain of their impending doom.

"How much longer?" Olghar cried out from his pitiful position curled in a ball. Thor, taking a significant turn for the better, lay cuddled in his arms. Still, a whimper was all the dog could muster to echo his master's complaint.

"I have no way to tell," Kruzurk answered. "By my reckoning, we've come at least sixty leagues, and there seems to be no end to this channel, or catacomb or whatever it is. That beast just keeps dragging us in its wake like some big sucker fish. Surely Loch Linnhe cannot be far now. I may be wrong, but I hope we reach the surface and daylight soon."

"Master 'awkes—beggin' yer pardon, but do those pilgrims mean ta bring that bleedin' woman aboard with them?" the

Shiva's lookout squawked. Within seconds, most of the crew gawked over the ship's side at the sight of a female, aghast that she might actually come aboard.

"If ya mean ta bring that bloody wench with you . . ." Hawkes called out to the longboat, ". . . I'll not 'ave it—not for all the gold in the Hebrides, by God!"

Ean stood up in the boat, shaking his fist at the captain. "You made a bargain, you blaggard. Break your word and mayhaps I'll enlighten your crew of the deee-tails of our passage, eh?"

Captain Hawkes ripped his weathered headpiece off and trounced it on the deck, stomping it and swearing in three languages. "You lied to me, old man! There was nothin' said 'bout no wench on this here voyage—nary a word, mind you—'twas to be you, the boy and Troon!"

Already, Daynin had climbed the cargo net and with both feet planted firmly on deck, added, "We'll gladly pay extra for the woman's passage, the squire's, and possibly one more who's to join us yet. Is that fair enough?"

Hawkes moved closer to the boy's face, a gnarled finger pointing ominously at his nose. "You ain't got the plum for me to take a bleedin' wench aboard the *Shiva*, boy—no siree. You ain't got that kind of plum."

Just then, Ean dropped over the ship's railing, blade in hand. "Now look 'ere, you blaggard—we've the means ta pay ya and pay we will. A bargain made is a fair made trade, says I."

"Troon is here?" Daynin asked, shaking his head in confusion.

Ean responded, "Long story—leave it be for now, boy."

Sabritha appeared over the rail next, her spirited voice preceding her. "Cowards! You're all a bunch of seadog slugs, that you fear a woman's presence among you." By the time her feet met the deck, she was berating the crew with a cat-o-nine-tails verbal lashing the likes of which few of the seamen had ever imagined possible from a sprightly wench.

"How much booty you got in that boat, old man?" the captain jabbed. "And how far we got ta take this 'ere beast to collect it?"

Once again, Daynin stepped between Sabritha and a potential target. He stayed her gestures and tried to smooth her ruffled feathers with a broad, mischievous smile. A rush of passion swept over him as his hand touched the hot flesh of her wrist, forcing him to let go when her gaze darted to his hand then back to his face. "We can't swim to Rhum, Sabritha. And I won't leave you behind—not for all the treasure in Scotia—so please don't make things worse."

"Fine—then you best make that old fish fart shut his mouth and get this tub underway. I don't want to be aboard with this scum any longer than they want me aboard."

Daynin cringed at Sabritha's colorful language, even as he felt the urge to break into a hearty laugh at her cunning ways. In a single verbal assault, she had cowed an entire shipload of cutthroat crewmen. Most had probably never seen a woman like her, let alone heard one open her mouth with enough pointed rebukes to bring them all to their knees.

Behind them, the squire shoved the first of the treasure chests ahead of himself, barely managing the heavy load up the cargo net. "If the argument is settled, I could use some help down here."

Daynin nodded and replied, "Aye, lad—it's settled, all right." In his mind, he was answering an entirely different question. *She's the one,* he told himself. *I have nae doubt now. Never have I dreamt of finding a woman with my father's strength, my mother's beauty, and my grandfather's courage.*

Now, if she will have me—if I can prove myself to her—our life together will be what I've always seen in my visions. Clan McKinnon will rise from the ashes, once again to be what it was, and I will make my father proud.

Plumat shook his head at the mayhem around him. The long shadows of a new morning showed quickly that the *Woebringer*'s crew were far more adept at making sail than the Saxons were at getting boats off the beach to join her. Most of the Caledonians had left. Out chasing the giant, bent on retribution, they had abandoned the mission, which was just as well. They wouldn't have to be paid.

Plumat knew he had no way to catch the Pict, anyway, but that seemed of little consequence at the moment compared to the news that another ship had been heard in the firth. It had to be the boy's escape vessel.

"How's your shoulder?" Plumat asked deLongait as he conducted the man's litter down to the boats.

DeLongait delivered a gruff reply. "It burns like the fires of hell, Plumat." The man's fighting edge seemed to have returned after two nights of rest and more than an ample supply of grog. "Get my carcass in the boat and I'll do my share."

A smile crept along Plumat's lips under his visor, despite deLongait paying less than proper respect to his rank. He felt elated to have at least one man in his midst that he could trust for solid answers and a full measure of courage—even a seriously wounded man. "Not to worry, old friend—we'll have you at Carlisle in no time. Then you can take your pick of the wine and wenches."

Aboard the *Woebringer*, Ranulf paced the deck and swore to himself over the hubbub. "Can't they get off that beach any faster? For bloody's sake, the sun's almost up and that ship out there is probably halfway to the North Channel by now."

The ship's boatswain cast a weathered eye toward the longboats. "They's landlubbers, m'lord. Can't expect 'em to load all that gear and get aboard as fast as a salt-bred crew."

Back on the beach, Plumat gave his final instructions to the Saxon contingent returning to Carlisle overland. Then, stepping into the longboat, he roared at the oarsmen, "Row, you blaggards! There's booty to be had. Put your backs into it now!"

Chapter 29:

The Sailing

Having removed the last of the Blackgloom Bounty from the longboat, Daynin left the boat to trail at the end of its tether as the *Shiva* turned west, sailing with the Clyde's seaward bound current. Sunrise crested the ridgeline to the east, outlining Dumbarton Castle's ruined spires like some jagged set of teeth, smiling at the scene playing out below it.

In the cold dark waters of the firth, a real set of teeth scudded along behind the *Shiva*'s longboat, content to wait for deeper water to make its attack. And somewhere along the south shore of the Clyde, Brude McAlpin raced among the cairns and cockleshells, desperate to catch sight of the ship leaving him further behind with each new gust of wind.

I'll never catch them this way, Brude kept thinking. *If I cut across the peninsula—head south and then swim to meet them before they reach deep water—that should work.* It never occurred to him that swimming in full armor, even for a conjured spirit, might not be a practical feat. Cresting the first rise south of the beach, he suddenly realized he had far more to worry about than catching up with the boat. Arrayed below him marched a cavalcade of Caledonian horsemen, strung out in a line along the coast road directly across his path of retreat.

"Blaggards and thieves," he swore. Seeing no Saxons among them, he complained angrily, "Not a man in your midst is worthy of my time or valor. Yet, you stand in the

255

way, and that I cannot help."

Unsheathing *Droongar,* Brude decided to attack when the enemy least expected it. With the sunrise at his back, he would rush them, hack his way through their lines, reach the coast, and swim for it—or fall in the doing. After all, what could the heathens do to him that they had not already done?

The Caledonians must have been blinded by the sunrise or asleep on their horses not to have seen the giant hulk bearing down on them from the upslope. At a dead run, Brude slammed into the middle of the troop with the force of an armored tidal wave. *Droongar* flailed out of the half light, first low, then high, bringing down two horses and their riders before anyone could sound the alarm. Pandemonium flashed through the file of horsemen.

Unable to maneuver their horses en masse in the narrow and deeply rutted road-cut, the Caledonians attempted to take on the Pict one at a time. Horses and men fell with the precision of a reaper's crew. Brude's blade swung left, bringing down animals as fast as they could charge. Swinging right, he would drop another dismounted rider with a vicious and fatal blow.

Time and again, crossbow bolts clanged into his armor with no effect. Blood, gore, and serried piles of corpses quickly filled the road-cut, creating a scene of destruction even Brude found disgusting. He fought on, knowing the enemy would tire of the battle before he did, or run out of bodies to cast into the cauldron.

More horsemen appeared to his left, far down the road-cut. They hurriedly dismounted and formed up to charge on foot. Remembering the effect of those Caledonian tethers from the first battle, Brude chose to break for the coast rather than be overwhelmed by numbers. He ran, leaving a score of dead and dying men in his wake.

Hot on his heels, the bloodthirsty Caledonians hadn't seen enough carnage for the day. Some remounted, some followed on foot, but all were intent upon having that Pictish armor they knew would make them richer than even their wildest dreams.

The barge's sudden change in speed jolted Kruzurk from the rhythmic slumber he had allowed himself to enjoy. A sharp beam of light played brilliantly across the ripples ahead, heaving in the sea beast's wake. This time, it looked like real sunlight, just as the runes had said. "Wake up, you two—I think we're nearing the end of our journey."

Mediah leaped to his feet, startled by the ray of light and the heavy rocking motion of the boat. He pulled Olghar to his feet as well, then turned to view the sight ahead of them. "Another wellkeep?"

"Aye. That must be the Kinlochleven landing, which the runes foretold me to expect. We must climb to the top and find our way down to Loch Linnhe. From there, we are but half a day from Rhum by sea."

"But how can you be sure this is the right place?" Mediah asked.

"I know nothing for a fact. We shall have to go and see."

Thor must have sensed a change in the situation. For the first time since leaving the priory, he rolled over onto all fours and stretched himself. "Haarrroooof!" he woofed, sending gruff echoes bouncing in all directions.

Olghar reached down to pet his companion. "He's *well*, master! Thor's wound is healed! It's a miracle."

Kruzurk shrugged, unsure how or why the gash in the dog's ribs had healed so rapidly. "Perhaps when the water splashed on us—it may have healing qualities. Or—mayhaps those monks know more about healing than I gave them credit for." Remembering the boatkeeper's directions, Kruzurk leaned over the side and dipped his staff into the water to signal the beast to stop.

The barge slowed to the point that Mediah could toss a line over the side, snagging an ancient carved monolith standing at the end of an equally ancient wharf. "Dry ground again," he sighed, then jumped across the gap to pull the boat tightly against the dock by its mooring rope.

Kruzurk helped Olghar ashore ahead of him, unsure what to expect next, but satisfied they were making the right choices. A glance back over his shoulder told him that the sea beast had gone its merry way without so much as a look back. He had a sense that it was not the last they would see of the creature.

The trio's long climb up the wellkeep's winding stair ended at an exit through a pair of small doors into a clear highland morning. From their vantage point among the ruins above a steep precipice, they enjoyed a spectacular view. "There, *see* it?" Kruzurk crowed. "That village down there should be Kinlochleven. And there—to the north— surely that is Loch Linnhe, just as the images foretold. Now, if we can barter for horses, we can cut across the coast, find another boat and reach Rhum well ahead of the boy."

"Hold! Who goes there?" came a shout from the edge of the ruins. With sunlight glinting blindingly off his helmet, a leviathan of a man appeared before them, blocking the path down the escarpment with little more than his sheer girth. "You pilgrims are trespassing on Clan McKlennan hold- ings. Stand and state yer business, else I'll be obliged to toss you off this crag."

Mediah edged forward, placing himself between the

beefy sentinel and the others. "We mean no harm. We seek passage to Rhum—and we must make haste."

"Haste is it?" the clansman replied. His robust chest and stomach rolled with a brief, mocking laugh. "No need for ye to hurry to R-r-r-r-hum. Ain't been a soul on that bloody r-r-rock for many a year. Not since them black hearted Caledonians brought Clan McKinnon to ruin, that is."

"Aye, that's why we're here. We mean to help set that foul deed aright, if we can," Kruzurk answered sharply. "And time is of the essence."

"Set it right, says you? An old fool, a beggar and a—uh—uh—are you some kind of *djinni* or what, dark one? Come to make yer heathen magic on the Caledonians, is it? Or are ye gonna swat 'em with yer magic bottle?" Another, more raucous round of laughter followed, though more on the congenial side this time.

The man's laugh and his backhanded insult caused Mediah's hand to reach for his dirk, then stop. "I'm no *djinni*—I'm Greek. My name is Mediah, and this is Kruzurk the Magician. Olghar travels with us to Rhum."

"I am Maclaren McKlennan, son of Tavish McKlennan—heir to this keep and all the land ar-r-round it. And you three are trespassing, by God."

Seeing Mediah clench the hilt of his blade again, Kruzurk sidestepped the Greek to prevent any wasted bloodshed. "The Anglish and their Caledonian levies are on the way to Rhum to capture a boy who, like you, is heir to his clan holdings there. We mean to stop them."

"Och! That bloody hound of yours will 'ave a better chance of stoppin' Caledonians than you lads. These highlands are crawlin' with cutthroat scoundrels, all lookin' for fat pilgrims with easy plunder. Surely you knew that afore ya came here. Now what's yer real business? And how the bloody hell did you get up 'ere? Tell me the truth, or I'll be forced to smack ya down, old mahn."

Kruzurk turned to point toward the doors they had just passed through. Much to his surprise, they had disappeared into the cliff face. He realized he still carried the barge staff in his hand, but not wanting to look too much the fool, he answered, "We—uh—came here by boat."

"Aye, and a flyin' boat I s'pose it 'twas what brought you up 'ere onto the *Clach Leathad*, eh?" Maclaren scoffed. "Ain't but one way up here and you didn't take it, since me or one of me mates was on guard all night. The ruins of this keep are sacred to the McKlennans, and we don't take kindly to no pilgrims traipsin' about."

"I swear to you—we've come to help Daynin McKinnon, if that name means anything to you," Kruzurk offered. "We need a guide, and a boat as well. We can pay, if you've the stomach for a quest, that is."

Maclaren burst into an almost uncontrolled laughter, his pinkish skin turning a bright red as he laughed. "Stomach says 'e! Haharrrr! Can there be a bigger stomach than this 'ere one in all of Scotia? I think not, says I!"

"Then you'll join us?"

"Aye, old man, if ye've got the plum to back up yer boast of payment, I'll take ye to R-rrr-rhum. This Daynin McKinnon sounds like a mahn I should meet—if he's the r-r-real thing. For all I know, we could even be cousins. But to my knowledge, nary a one of the McKinnon clan escaped the death pits on R-r-rhum."

"Five talens for you and another five for the boat. Do we have a bargain, Master McKlennan?"

Proffering his huge hand to seal the bargain, Maclaren replied, "Aye, a bargain sealed with mah gr-r-rip, old mahn. Provided you call me Muck, that is. Everyone from these

260

parts knows me by that name. Not only am I the foremost mud wrestler in all of north Scotia, I hail from an island of the same name—not far from R-r-rhum in fact."

"Muck it is, then," Kruzurk agreed, extending his hand for the clench. "Welcome to the quest. I hope it turns out well for us all. Now, can we be off to Rhum?"

Riding the firth's ocean current and a stronger than usual land breeze, the *Shiva* seemed almost to be flying across the water. From his station near the stern of the ship, Daynin's gaze scanned from one shoreline to the other in hopes of catching a glimpse of Brude, but rocks and more rocks were all he saw.

"You're wasting your time. That clanking colossus is long gone," Sabritha said.

Daynin's head snapped around, his eyes aglow with something more than the usual desire for the woman. "He's not gone. He's out there somewhere and we're leaving him behind. I gave him my word, and now I'm breaking it with every league we travel."

"There you go with that 'word' thing again. When will you learn? You can't make a promise every time you plan to do something."

"Sabritha, if honor is not a part of a mahn's values, then he's nae a mahn in my opinion. And that goes for a woman as well. I would die for you, or my grandfather, or even Brude if it was required of me—yet I've never given any of you mah word on that. It's what an honorable mahn does. It is what my people do. McKinnons value honor above all else, and if you're to be happy staying with us, you have to accept that we are that way. There is little reason for you to stay otherwise."

Sabritha darted a glance toward the four large chests and

assorted smaller ones stacked on the stern deck, hinting at her motive. Then her gaze quickly settled on Daynin's face to proclaim the answer he wanted. "You can be as hard as hickory one minute, plowboy, and as gentle as a foal the next. That's one reason I'm here. But you offered me the most perfect sunrise in Scotia if I came along on this trip. Remember? I intend to make you deliver on that promise."

Even the "plowboy" jibe couldn't deter Daynin from believing every word Sabritha had just said. He searched her face and found more of what he longed for. The smooth, fine lines around her eyes and that inviting smile demanded that he take her in his arms and kiss away all her worries, past and present. Somehow, though, he could not—at least not yet. At that instant, Daynin realized the look in Sabritha's eyes had changed. Gone was the warmth, replaced by something bordering on terror.

"What the hell is that?" she blurted out.

A heartbeat later, the lookout at the tip of the mast bellowed, "Avast! Sea beast in our wake—and it's a big-un!"

Every head on the ship turned instantly, a collective gasp rising from the stern and spreading louder as it swept all the way forward to the fo'c'sle. "Mast on the horizon, dead astern, maybe two and a half leagues!" the lookout shouted again. "Bloody hell—she's huge, and from the cut of her sail, likely a Saxon!"

Word of pilgrims in the area spread rapidly through the moors and marshes around Kinlochleven. The arrival of strangers—especially those with silver in their pouches— brought every hidesman, whore, and heathen out of their hovels before midday. By the time Muck and his group reached the banks of Loch Linnhe, a crowd had gathered and set up a makeshift market, complete with every kind of animal, fish, and bird in Scotia.

Doing his best to keep pace with the measured stride of their portly guide, Kruzurk asked, somewhat out of breath, "Where did—all these—people—come from—Muck?"

His hefty size opening a path through the crowd ahead, Muck replied, "Never ceases to amaze me how folks seem to know what they know. I sent word to mah uncle, that he should join us at the loch. He's sailed to the Hebrides many times and knows boats far better than I. I can only guess that word got out, somehow. I cannae say for sure."

Mediah tugged harder on Olghar's sleeve to hurry him along, impatient to find a boat and get away from the horde of non-believers blocking their way. "Step aside," he snarled. "We've no coin to spend here. Now make way!"

Thor's naturally fearsome presence helped to open the path as well, now that he was back to his old surly self. The dog almost literally dragged his master along by the leash, making it harder and harder for Olghar to stay in step with the others.

From somewhere in the crowd, a voice shouted over the hubbub, "Hold up, Muckie boy!"

"Och, 'tis mah uncle," Muck crowed. He stopped in the middle of the path and turned around to shout back, "Over here, you old mugger. Come give us a kiss now!"

Mediah and Kruze saw the great hooded bird moving through the sea of heads first, then the diminutive person upon whose staff the bird perched. Muck's uncle had to be well on in years, yet stout as a Roman barricade to be able to heft such a load. With hair as white as a thunderstorm's crest and twice as unruly, he and the bird made quite an entrance. The color of the huge sea eagle's tail matched the old man's hair perfectly, but the enormous bird bore a far more stately demeanor, one that could only be described as regal.

"Muckie boy! I heard you wuz lookin' fer sailors, so I came at the run. Me and Talisman that is."

Muck leaned down to give the old man a bearish hug, careful to keep his head well out of Talisman's pecking range. "Either that crow of yours is growin' bigger, Uncle Eigh, or you've been turned into a troll. I cannae tell which."

"Call my eagle a crow again and I'll sic 'im on you, Muckie. He don't much like people no-ways, especially them what wears silly pots on their head." Eigh stretched on his tiptoes to deliver a requisite slap against the side of Muck's helmet.

"Aye, I remember poor Uncle Cor-r-rran the first time Talis-mahn laid eyes on his new armor. The bird came off that staff and nearly took Unc's noggin for a prize."

The two shared a hearty guffaw, unmindful of the people who could not tear their eyes away from the magnificent bird. Even with a hood on and his intense green eyes covered, a full grown sea eagle presented the most awesome of sights to villagers, who were unaccustomed to seeing any large birds of prey, let alone one with the wingspan of a man's height.

A sudden loud screech from Talisman sent Thor into a barking rage, scattering the crowd around them like deer at the first howl of wolves. It took Olghar and Mediah both to hold the dog back in the face of Talisman's enormous wings flapping and that awful, piercing scream.

"Shut that mutt's mouth, or by God I'll let Talisman take 'is eyes!" Eigh bellowed.

Kruzurk edged forward, holding the remains of a bread crust in his outstretched hand. Talisman's protest stopped almost immediately, as did Thor's. The bird and his razor sharp beak swooped down on the crust without being able to see it, so keen was his sense of smell.

"Bloody hell," Eigh swore. "I've never known Talisman to eat anything but meat. Who are you, pilgrim? And why did you offer him that crust of bread?"

"I'm Kruzurk Makshare, the magician, and I merely guessed that your bird might like it."

Eigh rudely slapped the rest of the crust from Kruzurk's hand. "Are ya daft, mahn? He *might* have *liked* yer bloody hand instead, ya damned fool. Don't try that again. This bird is no pet. He can snatch up a new-born sheep and carry him half a league afore rippin' 'im to shreds for 'is breakfast."

Kruzurk backed away, gesturing agreement as he moved. "I'll remember that. My apologies."

"What are you doin' with these strangers, anywho, Muckie? Why the bloody hell did ya bring 'em here? And where's this boat you wuz wanting me to spy for ya?"

By now, Muck had taken a healthy step backward as well, keenly aware of Talisman's reach. "We best talk elsewhere, uncle—they's too many ears here that dinnae need to know our business."

"Och, business is it? Then you're right on, Muckie boy—let's be off. No sense giving these blaggards an ear full, that's for sure."

Unfortunately, it was too late to worry about that. Well back in the crowd, a small, wiry man uncrumpled the Anglian writ he had carried with him all the way from Galashiels. He flashed it to his surly cohort, eliciting a wide, toothy grin from the man as they both realized the bounty of a lifetime stood a mere stone's throw from them.

"Get the boys," the blaggard said, his toothy grin full of a mischief that no good can come from.

# Chapter 30:

The Chasing

The lowland bountiers couldn't match the pace Brude kept up while crossing the rugged high ground that splits the Greenock Peninsula. He heard the Caledonians cursing below and behind him, but dared not take the time to see how close they were on his heels. They had dogs with them now—the one thing he had feared in life, and now feared because he had no time for fighting. If they caught him, he could fend off the animals, but that might mean missing Daynin's ship, somewhere out in the firth.

Reaching the crest of the ridge, Brude turned for a look at his pursuers before heading down the other side. His attention was drawn to two ships scudding along out in the Clyde, widely separated but with a strange wake between them, low in the water like nothing he had ever seen. "So, you Saxon drengs have a ship too, eh? Good. This fight may yet be worthy of my time. Many among you will be glad of your shields when first we meet—that much I can promise."

Brude's reverie filled with glorious images of mounted combat against a horde of Saxon knights, all bent upon his destruction. The moment would have given him great satisfaction if not for a well-aimed quarrel that chinked hard against the back of his breastplate. He looked down at his attacker and let out a boisterous laugh that echoed across the slopes. "You blaggards can kiss my royal Cruithni crotch!" A hearty shove sent an avalanche of rocks cascading down on the archers, scattering them among the boulders below.

Satisfied that he'd done all he could to delay the enemy, Brude rushed down the bluff, intent upon finding a good spot from which to hail Daynin's boat. Then the real work would begin, for Brude McAlpin—the Great Deceiver, warrior among warriors and heir to the Seven Houses of Scone—had never learned to swim.

Ean's crusty voice seemed to finally be getting through to Troon. "Wake up, you old war horse. We may have need of your longbow soon."

"What is it now?" Troon replied, both hands rubbing the sleep and salt brine from his eyes. "You ain't puttin' me over the side again, are ya?"

"Of course not—your leg looks fine. We got boarders and a damn sea beast in our wake, though," Ean answered.

"Boarders! Bloody hell—I hope they ain't from Tiree. Those blue water dogs are a surly lot, and they've got the best ships on the ocean sea."

"They're Saxons," Daynin said, flatly. "Come to offer me a long drop on a short rope."

Troon sat up abruptly, surprised to hear Daynin's voice, and gasped, unable to hide the searing pain in his thigh. "A rope is it, eh? And what did you do, Master McKinnon, that you should deserve a neck stretchin' by the King's Eyre?"

Daynin knelt down next to Troon and placed a hand on his shoulder. "Troon, I did what any mahn would have done in my spot. I sent a blaggard to hell for mistreating a woman."

"Did ya now?" Troon guffawed. "And this blaggard was a bloke who didn't wipe his own arse, eh? Blue blood, was he?"

Sabritha's sharp tongue provided the answer. "Not just any blue blood, but a Marquis—Duke Harold's own cousin, in fact."

Troon's head whipped to the right at the sound of a woman's voice. Both hands went to pulling at his scraggly gray hair, all in a muss from dirt and seawater. "And who might you be, missy with the raven black hair?"

"I'm Sabritha, the woman Daynin stepped in to help. Now we're all felons for that deed."

"Aye, felons in Anglia, mayhaps," Daynin rebutted. "But this is Scotia, and Saxon law means nothing here."

"Sabritha, is it?" Troon questioned, with more than a mild curiosity lacing his words. "Are ya by any chance Irish, little girl?"

"I'm a Kilcullen, of the Tandragee Glen Kilcullens . . ."

"Saints of Armagh! I knew your *family*, girl—I fought a campaign with your pap. Bloody ferocious sot 'e was, too. Tall as a haystack, with hair and beard ta match. He could drink a whole troop under the table and still hit half a hundred dead-centers the next day."

Hearing a tidbit of information about her father brought a tear to Sabritha's eyes. Since she had only a few fleeting memories of him from childhood, her mind raced and her heart quickened at finding someone besides herself had actually known him in life. And now to learn he had been an archer—exactly as she remembered him in her dreams. That meant her dreams were not dreams at all, but actual memories!

"I don't suppose you know what came of him after he left for Anglia—or of my mother?"

"Last I knew of yer pap, they listed 'im among the dead at the first battle of Wrexham. But the Saxons took plenty of prisoners that day, and none have been heard from since.

As for your mother, I only know your pap swore she was a saint."

"They're gaining on us!" the lookout shouted from above.

Captain Hawkes swung down from the ratlines, his face twisted in anguish. "Hard to port, pilot—take us into the shallows. That deep draft Saxon scow will tear her bottom out if she follows us in there." Almost as an afterthought, he added, "God help us if we run aground."

Again the lookout shouted, this time waving like a bear in a bout with bees. "It's turning! The beast is turning! It's following us into the shallows."

Standing knee deep in the shallows of Loch Linnhe, Eigh patted a hand against the hull of the boat bobbing next to him. "She ain't very big, Muckie, but this tub is sea worthy and should get you to R-rr-rhum, though I cannae see why you want to go there."

"It's those pilgrims who are goin', Uncle Eigh. I'm just the guide. They claim Saxons are on the way to take away Daynin McKinnon, heir to the McKinnon clan holdings."

Eigh waded back to the beach to retrieve Talisman's perching pole and said, "Aye, there was a Daynin in that clan. Only a lad as I recall, and bashed the same night as the rest o' them. I smell a r-r-rrat, Muckie boy."

Muck waved for the group to come on down from the hill above. "As do I, uncle. But I dinnae think this lot is lying. And besides, there's five talens in it for me."

"Five talens says you! Reckon they could use another hand in this venture?"

"We can use all the help we can get," Kruzurk answered, having come up behind them. "There's five talens in it for you, if you've a mind to come along, Eigh."

The old man showed both a willingness to go and a remarkable agility for his age. Talisman in hand, he clambered aboard the swaying *Pandora* with no help from the boat's crew. "For five bloody talens, I'd sail from here to the moon. Now, let's get goin'!"

No sooner were the words spoken than a hullabaloo erupted in the village on the bluff above them. "That's them! Down there!" someone shouted. Another yelled out, "Get 'em!" and a mad rush of people came pouring over the crest of the beach road. Armed with pitchforks, clubs and torches, a crowd of locals headed for the *Pandora*, each trying to outrace the other for a prize their grog and collective imagination had increased tenfold.

Mediah and Kruzurk jerked Olghar out of the water while Muck dragged Thor aboard. Eigh busied himself helping with the anchor so they could shove off the beach far enough to avoid the mob.

Eigh quickly realized that with no wind to speak of, they would never get out of the shallows in time. "Drunken sots," he swore, then turned to Talisman. Ripping off the bird's hood, the old man produced a pemmican lure from his pouch, pulled the leather jesses loose from Talisman's legs, and tossed the lure as far as he could, straight toward the crowd.

The effect was a sight to behold. In the twinkling of its huge eyes, Talisman's wings unfolded and carried him into flight. Down he swooped, then back up again—aiming dead as an arrow at the lure on the beach. The mob took one look at the giant winged predator bearing down on them and broke for parts unknown, their torches, tools, and tantrum left littering the sand behind them.

"Hahaharrr! Take that, you grubbers!" Eigh crowed. He put his fingers between his teeth and let out a shrill whistle.

Talisman turned back toward the boat in one swooping flap.

"Looks like we got our five talens worth, Kruze," Mediah said.

"Aye," Kruzurk agreed. "But I can't help wondering who they were after. We've not been here long enough to make enemies yet."

Muck swept the helmet from his head and wiped his brow. "If it's all the same to you, magician, we best not be stayin' ar-r-rround to find out. That lot will be back when they've had more grog, wager that."

The *Woebringer*'s lookout answered Ranulf from atop the mast, "They're draggin' somethin' astern for sure, m'lord. Whatever it is, it's huge, and low in the water, but I can't tell what it is."

"Keep a weather eye on that sail, lookout," Ranulf replied. "If it slacks the least, you give a shout."

Standing next to Ranulf, Plumat observed dryly, "It seems we're gaining on them."

Ranulf turned his head to spit with the wind. "Aye, gaining but not fast enough. If that scow reaches the open sea, we may never catch them. This ship is bigger and faster, but in heavy seas, we can't maneuver the way they can."

"She's turning!" the lookout barked.

The captain of the *Woebringer* rushed forward to a spot next to Plumat. He cupped his hands over his eyes and growled, "Damned highlanders—they're turning into the shallows."

"Go after them, Captain Coke—that's an order," came the resolute reply from Plumat.

"Bloody hell I will. That shoal is barely deep enough for

them, and we have twice their draft."

"Ranulf, need I remind you and your captain exactly who is in charge of this mission?"

Ranulf turned to the captain, a stupid, sheepish look spreading across his plump face. "Plumat is under direct orders from the Duke. Do as he says."

"You're all fools if you think we won't tear the bottom out of this ship. But if that's what you want, then so be it. Hard over, pilot! Bring us into their wake."

Two sails appeared one after the other, scudding along the headland to the right and bearing inland directly toward Brude's vantage point on the beach. Waving *Droongar* high in the air to attract their attention, he quickly dropped from the huge boulder into the icy waters of the Clyde.

"Come on, boy," he roared gleefully. "And make it quick, else there'll be hell to pay when those Caledonian dogs get here."

"Did you see that?" Ean cried out from his spot near the bow of the *Shiva*.

"See what, old man?" Captain Hawkes replied.

"Something flashed near the south shore—way down there. Like sunlight glinting off polished armor. Then it disappeared."

"More trouble, no doubt, with the way this trip is shaping up," came Hawkes' disgruntled retort.

"I saw it too, grandfather," Daynin added. "It looked like bronzed armor to me, as well. We'll know in a bit, soon as we round the headland."

Sabritha pushed her way through the crew to gain a better vantage point at the bow. "What if the Saxons have a trap set for us?"

"Then they best be able to walk on water," Hawkes

growled. "We'd see their sail if they had another ship waiting to cut us off."

"Och!" The tone of Ean's grunt could mean nothing less than trouble. He pointed to the cliffs facing the estuary. "Caledonians—lots of 'em—pouring over the bluff."

Hawkes turned to his pilot and screamed, "Hard over, Peckee! They've got us between the rocks and a sea serpent. Starboard now, or we've bought it for sure!"

Daynin's keener eyes told an altogether different story the moment *Shiva*'s bow swept past the headland. "No! Wait! That's Brude—there—neck deep in the water. They're after him, not us!"

"I don't give a render's puke who they're after," Hawkes yelled back. "Make for the main channel, pilot, and be damned quick about it. We're well within the cast of their crossbows."

"We cannae risk it, Daynin," Ean said, his voice laden with sympathy for Daynin.

"We *have* to, grandfather. I gave my word."

"You gave yer word to a spirit, boy—that ain't the same as givin' it to a real, live person."

"Man or mud hen, grandfather—I gave it and I bloody well intend to keep it." Daynin faced the captain and ordered, "Steer to port, captain, or I'll be forced to gut you where you stand."

The look of confusion on the captain's face would have been amusing under any other circumstances. He drew a large blade from his belt and braced for Daynin's attack. "You little snipe—I'll slit you from head to heel if you try anything."

Ean faced Hawkes too, ready to draw his blade to back Daynin's ploy, but he was already too late. Sabritha slipped up behind the captain, grabbed his wrist, and shoved his blade within a cat's whisker of his own throat. "I think you best be doing what Daynin says, eh, Captain?"

"Bloody hell! Sea monsters, sirens and sedition—this just ain't my day," the captain moaned. With his free hand, he motioned for Peckee to shove the tiller hard a-port, bringing the *Shiva* back into the shallows and headed straight for Brude.

Barely a bow shot behind the *Shiva*, the Saxon pursuers were actually enjoying the ungainly escapades of Daynin's ship. Between chomps on another carrot, Ranulf alternately laughed and expressed his opinions. "I tell you—she's out of control. No pilot in 'is right mind would steer a course like that, especially in these shallows. We'll 'ave 'er before she reaches the main channel, I wager."

Plumat grimaced at the slovenly manners Ranulf so generously displayed. Stepping upwind to avoid the man's odor and the occasional burst of carrot-laced spittle, he leaned against the railing to steady his gaze. "Would that you were right, for once, Ranulf. But look you! There—up on the bluff—our Caledonian minions have rejoined the chase. That is why the highlanders steer so wildly."

With the *Woebringer* not yet clear of the headland, those aboard could not tell that the *Shiva* had slowed almost to a stop while taking on a passenger. Their attention thus absorbed, none of the Saxons—not even the lookout—noticed the huge greenish black creature lurking low in the water dead ahead of them. The beast slowly turned in place, headed straight for the ship's prow.

"Hard over!" Ranulf screamed, his horrified realization coming a blink too late.

The *Woebringer* gave out a mighty groan and pitched forward like a stallion stumbling in a snake pit. A bubbling rumble sounded from below the ship's bow as it lurched high into the air, threatening to capsize the vessel. Every man aboard tumbled forward, only to be shoved violently backward when the bow came out of the water. The ship's mast twitched one way, then the other, its metal braces and fittings wrenching under the strain.

Ranulf, Plumat, and a dozen others ducked to avoid the host of ropes, chains and blocks flying hither and yon. Two men went down with ghastly wounds from wood shards and iron rivets fired like catapult bolts from the rigging. The mast swayed backward one more time, finally giving way to the mighty stress. A loud "crack" announced that the mast had splintered, sending the *Woebringer*'s crew tumbling wildly once more.

"Did you hear that?" Daynin cried out, his attention suddenly shifting from Brude's giant dripping frame to the awful sound echoing against the cliff face.

"Aye, boy. If those bloody Caledonians have a catapult, we're in big trouble," Troon's worried voice replied. All eyes and ears turned to see if they were about to be struck by a huge stone or a blazing ball of pitch from an unseen ballista on the peninsula.

Captain Hawkes' attention to the sound had been far keener than the others. "You landlubbers never heard a mast shatter afore, have ye? Look yonder—the Saxons have run aground!"

A score of heads came around toward the pursuing Saxon galley. Sure enough, she lay dead in the water, a shambles of broken mast, rigging and armored hunters who were about to become the hunted. A shout of "Hurrah!" rang out along the *Shiva*'s deck. Everyone aboard cheered the ghastly sight except Daynin. "How terrible—to die in the belly of a beast," he whispered to himself.

Just then, a hail of arrows rained high and low along the length of the *Shiva*. "Starboard," Hawkes bellowed. "Get down, you foo . . ." He never finished. A high arching arrow struck him square in the forehead, felling the man like a hundred-weight sack of meal.

The ship's pilot pushed the tiller hard over, putting as much distance between them and the shoreline as possible. The beach was crawling with Caledonians. A dozen torchmen ran hither and yon along a line of archers, lighting arrow tips. If the bowmen were in range, the *Shiva* was finished—she'd be a blazing hulk before the last arrow struck.

Daynin grabbed the arm of his colossal companion and shouted, "I dinnae care if you're a spirit or a saint, but if you've any magic in that black armor, now would be the time to use it."

Still dripping seawater, Brude shook himself off and strode deliberately toward the *Shiva*'s stern. "Brace yourself, highlander. Then will you know the true power of the Great Deceiver." His monstrous arms flapping like a giant grounded crow, Brude's visor flew open with a blast of wind that could have rivaled a Scotian spring storm. Instantly, the *Shiva*'s sail billowed out. The boat lurched forward with the force of fifty oarsmen all rowing in stride. Brude huffed again and the vessel scudded across the channel.

Well behind and unable to do anything but cling to the railing of the foundering ship and fume, Plumat watched the *Shiva* disappear in the distance. "I'll get you, boy! If it takes the rest of my life, I'll have your head!"

Chapter 31:

The Voyaging

The *Pandora* raced along Loch Linnhe's western shoreline, hugging the coast the way her grandson of a Viking captain had been taught to sail by all his ancestors. Loch Linnhe's surface, smooth as a priory's pond, glistened from the rays of a rapidly setting sun.

"Wake up, boy," Uncle Eigh urged, nudging his foot against the sleeping Muck's ribs. "We should see the opening to Lismore Slip any time now."

"Huh?" Muck responded. "Where are we?" he added sleepily, stretching his beefy arms out wide.

Eigh stroked Talisman's wing feathers to settle the bird and replied, "Not far from the channel that takes us west toward the Hebrides and Rrrr-rhum. You and those mighty lords of yours have been napping most of the afternoon. Good thing you brung me along to keep an eye on this cutthroat crew, else they mighta robbed you and tossed you into the loch by now."

Muck rolled to his knees and stood up, straightening the shiny metal pot on his head. He stepped back from Talisman's reach and shook himself like a giant walrus. "They ain't lords, Unc—leastwise as far as I can tell they ain't. One's a magician, one's a priest and t'other one claims to be a Greek, though I'd wager on 'im bein' a *djinni*, what with his prayer rug, beads and turban and such."

"Long as they got the plum to pay us what they agreed

to, boy, don't matter what they are or where they came from. We'll take 'em to Rr-rrhum, then have this skiff drop us at Coll on the way back. With ten silver talens to spend, we can live like clan chiefs in that pirate's hole 'til the next moon."

"Aye, that's a plan, Unc. We'll be paid well for our work, and deservin' of the spoils. The magician strikes me as an honest mahn, too. Who knows, he might even pay us a bonus if we stay on and help them bash a few Saxon heads."

"We'll have to see 'bout that, come first light, Muckie boy. We should be in sight of Rr-rr-rhum by then and know better what we're up against. For now, we best make for Drrr-imnin and wait for daylight. Sailing any further in these rocky environs at night is a fool's game, to be sure."

"Drimnin? But Unc, that bleedin' fortress is haunted, or so they say."

"We ain't meanin' ta go ashore, Muck. We'll just heave to in the harbor for the night. No harm to that, and a damn sight safer than nagivatin' the Slip when it's black as a bat's soul out here. Now go wake them pilgrims and tell 'em the scheme, else they be pitchin' a fit that we're stoppin'."

Looming out of the golden red glow of a gradually dying day, the north Irish coastline appeared more like an angry cloud bank in the distance than the solid rock cliff face Ean knew it to be. Off to his right, the flat spit of land called the Mull of Kintyre offered the last vestige of Scotian soil they would see for a while. And there was no guarantee they would ever see his ancestral land again, what with a dead captain aboard, a crew of surly misfits bent on who knew what, and more than sixty leagues of open water to traverse before they reached the safety of Rhum.

"Grandfather, what's bothering you?" Daynin asked.

"Och! You already know, lad. We've a treacherous crossing to make. Thirty leagues to the west is open water, and some of the biggest waves on the ocean sea, which this boat cannae handle. If we hug the coast, we're bound to run smack into the Thieves of Tiree, as they control the only safe passage to Rhum east of the Hebrides. Without a qualified captain to steer this ship, we dare not sail at night, and that means landing somewhere 'til first light. I'm no sailor, Daynin, but I've taken this sea route to Rhum several times and I cannae recall a single safe harbor along the way, especially with all this booty aboard."

"Why *can't* we sail at night?" Sabritha asked, her frustration at the thought of another day and night on the *Shiva* more than evident to everyone within earshot.

Ean cast an evil glance at the woman and snapped back, "Rr-rrr-ocks, woman, that's why. See that coastline there, to the east? It's a bloody harvest of giant rocks, layin' in wait for us. The only way to avoid them is by sailing west into the ocean sea, where even good sailors don't go in a tub like this. And we ain't got a good sailor among us, what with the captain croaked. Besides that, there's no way to tell direction at night without the sun to guide us."

Sabritha flipped her shawl over her shoulders to ward off the growing cold. "I can tell you which direction is west, even at night. See that first star—there—to the north— barely showing on the horizon? If you keep that star off your right shoulder, you will move west. My father taught me that when I was still too small to milk the goats. I should think you would know that, old man."

Daynin's hand went to his grandfather's shoulder, staying the stout highlander's angry motion toward Sabritha. "She means no disrespect, grandfather."

"Aye, she does, lad. She has *nothing* but disrespect for us. That's as plain as day old porridge. She knows nothing of the dense fogs these waters are known for, and what of her guiding star then?"

On his makeshift cane, Troon hobbled between Ean and the woman. "She's right about the star, Ean. Sail west and it will stay on your right. The problem is, we've no bloody way to tell how *far* west we've gone. We could sail right off the edge of the world if we're not careful. It's said there are demons out there the likes of which no mahn has ever seen."

"That's just a theory, Simon," Daynin declared. "A belief passed down for ages because no one has had the courage to find out the extent of the ocean sea, at least as far as we know. The answer for us is simple, though. We sail west until first light, then turn north. That should be safe enough on both counts. If there's fog, we drop the sail and wait 'til morning."

"Aye, good and safe all right. Straight into the Temptress of Tiree," Ean scoffed. "But that's better than ripping this tub open on the rocks, I suppose—or falling off the edge of the world. With luck and a good northerly breeze, we might be able to outrun those bloody Tireean snekkes afore their crews wake up for morning grog."

"Now if we can just get the crew to agree with our plan," Daynin added.

"I think I can handle that," came the quick response from Sabritha.

"Heave lads, heave! That's it!" Ranulf barked. The *Woebringer*'s crew gave out a loud "hurrah" as the remains of the shattered mast finally slipped sideways over the railing, ropes, rigging, and all. Plumat's fears of imminent death were momentarily distracted by the loud splash. Then he and his men turned to the more uncertain task of dealing with the sea beast and saving what remained of the ship.

The Saxons had fired a score of crossbow bolts into the beast already, and at close range, but with little effect. For hours, that giant black body had slammed into the *Woebringer*'s hull, then disappeared into the murky waters to unexpectedly reappear from a new direction. "We need to hit that bugger with something heavier than arrows," Plumat told his men. "Fashion a pike, or a heavy lance from one of the broken spars—that may be our only chance." Sercey and the others set to work immediately, cutting and honing a sharp point on a piece of wrecked crossbar.

"Give me a hack at that beast!" Earl deLongait cried out, having dragged himself and Draco from the fo'c'sle to the ship's railing. "My blade will put that monster down, by God, or I shall die in the trying!"

Plumat admired the man for his courage. But with only one good arm, and barely able to stand, deLongait hardly represented a formidable attacker. His giant axe, however, might prove a weapon of considerable value, if they could entice the beast to surface close by. With the light nearly gone, and no help from the Caledonians ashore, just keeping the vessel afloat had been an arduous enough task for the Saxons. Killing an animal as large as the ship itself might be too much to expect from any of them in the end.

"Ranulf," Plumat ordered, "have your men string up one of the dead men in a cargo net. Heave it over the side, but keep it out of the water and close by the hull of the ship. When the beast surfaces to steal his prize, we'll give him a whack with Draco. If that doesn't drive him off, maybe it will buy us some time to abandon ship."

"I'm not leaving this vessel, Plumat—orders or no orders. My family will be paying for the loss ten generations from now if I give up this ship. We have to make a fight of it, then repair the boat and try to make it back to Glasgow."

Plumat ducked as a cargo net full of beasty bait swung precariously past him. "We're not going back to Glasgow—not now, not ever," he snapped. "We're going after that boy, and I don't give a damn if we have to row this tub to do it."

The *Woebringer*'s captain spoke up just then. "M'lord, we've a main spar below deck. I think we can rig it as a temporary mast afore that beast holes the side. I need at least two hours and all hands to get the job done."

Plumat strode over to deLongait, knelt down and looked his old friend in the eyes. "Draco has a job to do, and I don't think you have the strength. Loan me your blade and I promise to bring it back when the deed is done."

"Take it, then, m'lord, and welcome to the task. Kill that slimy beast so we can be on our way, eh?"

The long hours of sailing into the endless expanse of water that led west to the ocean sea had been broken only by the momentary sighting of very distant lights far to the north. Clear as a monk's conscience, the night sky showed little hint of trouble. Sabritha's star stayed right where it was supposed to be—off the *Shiva*'s starboard quarter, keeping Daynin and his friends on course.

"You've done well, *Draygnar*," Brude boasted. He was somewhat more subdued than usual, his attention obviously drawn to the undulating surface of the sea.

His using that name pricked the hackles on Daynin's neck, but not wanting to confront the giant at close quarters, he bit his tongue and replied, "We're still alive, Brude.

For that, I am very thankful."

"*Penach ben venya grou,*" the brooding hulk whispered.

"What does that mean?"

Brude's helmet turned toward the boy. The darkened eye slits almost came alive as he spoke. "Some of us are alive, Daynin. Some of us are not so fortunate."

Daynin realized he had spoken without thinking. "I'm sorry. I—I—didn't mean to . . ."

"Apologies are for milkmaids and miztresses, highlander. A warrior should never have need of them. Do what you say you'll do, keep your word, maintain your honor, and save the apologies for the gods."

Something in the giant's words struck deep into Daynin's soul. The beast suddenly became much more than a rusting frame of ancient armor. He had become a being, albeit a being Daynin couldn't begin to understand at that instant. Without analyzing further, he scrambled up onto the ship's railing, eye to eye with the Great Deceiver, then reached out to flip open Brude's visor.

An enormous mailed fist tried to stay the boy's quick motion. Unfortunately it came too late. "Aaarrggg! Why in the name of Dalriada did you do that?" Brude growled.

Shaking from the painful grip on his wrist, Daynin peered into the helmet's cavernous interior. He wanted to cry out, or scream, or yell at someone that the armor contained nothing—nothing but an angry spirit bent on revenge. His voice failed—he could say nothing. Words would not come to him. With his free hand, he carefully closed the visor, and looking into the eye slits, whispered, "I'm sorry. Truly I am. I wanted to believe . . ."

"There you go apologizing again. What did I just tell you, *Draygnar?* Apologize to no mahn. Regret nothing. Live life as if every sunset is your last. And take nothing you've not earned with your own two hands. That is what the Cruithni believe—or—believed."

Daynin's mind leapt from Brude's words to the Blackgloom treasure stacked just a few strides away. "What of this bounty I took from the Seed? Did I earn that?"

"Spoils taken in war are paid for with blood, boy. If not yours, then surely someone else's. If you fought for them, you earned them. If not, then toss the lot overboard and be done with it."

"I cannae do that. I promised the woman I would take care of her. I've a keep to rebuild and my family's honor to rekindle. That will require every talen of that booty. And please stop calling me by that other name."

Brude's hand dropped onto Daynin's shoulder. "Does a hawk apologize if it steals the rabbit you chased for supper? Does the wind make apology if it blows down your tent? Do what you must, Daynin—but never apologize to anyone. The Romans had a saying, *'Ignoscito saepe alteri; nunquam tibi.'* In your words, that means roughly, 'Make excuses for others if you will, but never for yourself.' "

That hand on his shoulder sent a flood of images through Daynin's head. His father's beefy paws and warm smile came to mind, along with images of Rhum before the great fire. Those were all that mattered now—Rhum and Sabritha—and nobody could take them away from him.

The *Pandora* scudded quietly to a stop within a furlong of the sheer cliff face that formed Drimnin's imposing southern defensive wall. Spires, turrets, and merlons cut from living rock blotted out most of the stars above the ship, yet not a light showed from any of the windows. Every sound aboard the *Pandora* echoed from the cliff face, bounced around the rocky cairns lining the southern side of Lismore Slip, then mumbled again and again from one rock wall to another.

Kruzurk scanned the daunting battlements looming above him and couldn't help wondering if he had somehow missed "seeing" this particular aspect of their journey to Rhum. "This place is empty, you say?"

Eigh offered another morsel of fish to his bird, then turned to answer. "Aye. Been so since Viking times. They raided it, slaughtered all the defenders and burned alive the cadre of priests who built the place. No one's been here since, so the legend goes. No one but wandering spirits, if ya believe in such tripe."

Trying to ignore Talisman's agitated wing flapping, Kruzurk made another survey of the darkened walls over-head. His instinct nagged that he had been to Drimnin before, even though that was impossible, since this was his first journey so far north into Scotia. He had almost convinced himself to shrug off the nagging when a light flashed from one embrasure to another near the top of the wall.

"Did you see that?" Kruze asked, his boot rousing Mediah from a fitful slumber on the deck.

"Huh? What is it, m'lord? Are we there yet?"

"Wake up, Mediah. There's trouble afoot. I saw light where there should be none."

"What light?" Muck interrupted, his voice on edge.

"Way yonder at the top of the battlements," Kruze replied. "Someone is moving around—there, did you see it *that* time?"

"Och, bloody spirits on the move, that's all," Muck groused. "I wish we'd never stopped here."

Eigh set his winged companion on its perching pole. He made a long scan of Drimnin's upper reaches. Seeing nothing, he growled, "Damned pilgrims—you're all alike—

seein' things that ain't there. Now get some sleep and stop all this hubbub. You're keepin' my bird awake and he ain't gonna be fit to live with on the morrow."

Just as Kruzurk opened his mouth to respond, lights appeared again. This time, a dozen or more torches blinked from crenellation to crenellation at the top of the parapet, as though a procession marched along the battlements from one end to the other. "You best look again, Eigh. We've got company—and lots of it!"

The Tempting

On the slopes of the Greenock Peninsula, the rhythmic thumping of a tabour drum echoed off the bluffs, announcing the Caledonian version of "to arms". First light dawned aboard the *Woebringer*. Plumat and his men had labored all night helping the ship's crew jury-rig a mast and make needed repairs on the hull, all the while fending off the sea beast's sporadic attacks. Fortunately, the monster's ramming had ceased during the early hours of morning, the beast apparently convinced that Northumbrian oak provided more than a match for its own barnacled snout.

Even without more attacks, the Saxons still had a host of problems to overcome. The new mast could only be considered temporary at best, and dangerous in the extreme if the *Woebringer* encountered a storm at sea. Allowing nothing to deter him—not even the prospect of being swamped in deep water—Plumat worked the men as though demon-possessed. No longer was the venture one for lands and titles. It had instead become a quest for personal satisfaction, revenge and honor redeemed.

Staring up at the sharp slivers of light dancing behind the craggy peaks on the east side of the firth, Plumat finally felt he could ease up from driving his men so hard. "Ranulf," he said, "now that we're under way, you should take your men and go below for sleep. I'll keep watch with the captain and wake you around midday. We will be in deep water by then and safe from that ocean bound ogre."

"As you wish, Plumat," Ranulf replied, obviously yet to feel comfortable with the more correct response of "m'lord", in deference to Plumat's temporary rank. "Do you plan to go on with this insane mission, even with the ship damaged and seven of our men feeding the fishes?"

Plumat's head snapped 'round like a jousting target. "My plan was foolproof, Ranulf—catch that boy and his brigands *before* they could escape by sea—I just didn't know there would be so many fools in the mix. I intend to chase him to the gates of hell, now, if need be. You'll not see the spires of Carlisle again until the deed is finished, if that is what you are asking me."

Ranulf did not argue, knowing all too well Plumat's reputation with the sword. And he would be well within his rights to choose that option if Ranulf or anyone else aboard decided to commit an act of mutiny. "Very well then," Ranulf groaned, tossing the words back over his shoulder with the disdain of a prior's proclamation. Was he thinking he might better serve the Duke by waiting for another time to unseat Plumat? But all the Reeve added was, "Midday it is."

From their vantage point high on a precipice of the tiny island of Iona, the treacherous passage known as the Temptress of Tiree appeared to Daynin and his grandfather considerably less precarious than its reputation indicated. The narrow slot between two dark islets showed no signs of being a trap and the intervening waters were as calm as a frozen loch. "Nary a single sail since first light," Ean said, pensively.

"I think we've waited long enough, grandfather. The fog has lifted and we need to get back to the ship. The sun will be high very soon, melting the mist. If the pirates of Tiree were out there somewhere, surely we would have spotted them by now, don't you think?"

"Aye, lad, 'twould seem so. But a mahn shouldnae tempt fate this way. All I've ever heard about Tiree is that they are a blood-thirsty lot with ships faster than the wind. Once we set out for that passage, we'll be a bloody great duck, rr-rr-ipe for the pickings, and nowhere to rr-run."

"We cannae go around Tiree—not now. That would take days and give the Saxons time to catch up. We must reach Rhum and fortify what remains of the keep as best we can before the Anglish arrive and lay siege to our works."

Ean tossed a puzzled glance at the boy, then asked, "Siege, says you? You think those bloody Saxons are still after us?"

"Yes, grandfather. I'm sure of it. I feel it in my gut. And without help from somewhere, I haven't the first hint how we will withstand such an attack."

Between beefy puffs and gasps for air, Muck complained again, "I cannae see the point of scaling this bloody cliff, just to confront whoever 'twas toting those torches during the night."

Kruzurk's surprisingly agile pace up the steep, roughly hewn steps ascending the cliff wall had given everyone something to gasp about, but there were no more complaints. Nearly to the top of the battlements, Kruze, Muck, Eigh and Mediah sensed a strange, almost eerie hush to their surroundings. All conversation ceased. Even Talisman's irritated screeching gave way to stony silence without so much as a warning from Eigh.

Stepping through the gap at the top of the parapet, Kruze's staff jutted abruptly into the air over his head, stopping the others behind him. "Oh my . . ." he gasped, blinking from the sudden and unexpectedly bright morning light.

Muck craned his neck to see around Kruzurk. He finally moved ahead, breaking the silence with, "Aye, that would be Rrr-rrhum." As if to emphasize the point, when Eigh finally ascended the top step Talisman's enormous wings broke into a flapping frenzy.

The vista on the other side of the catwalk appeared endless. A profoundly blue ocean stretched almost to the horizon, capped by a misty, saddle shaped island that, on the one hand seemed to beckon "come hither" while on the other offered a warning that to do so might spell one's doom.

"Whoever you are, you are not welcome here," an ancient voice groaned from somewhere to Kruzurk's right. "I warn you—we are armed!"

Five heads turned as one. "You've nothing to fear from us," Kruze answered.

"Then why bring you swords and armor, and a great winged beast, if you mean us no harm?"

Talisman's high-pitched screech let the voice know that he did not appreciate being called a beast. Kruze waved to Eigh to silence the bird. He took a few halting steps toward the adjoining tower's darkened archway, still unable to make out the form of his inquisitor. "I can only tell you that I—er—*we* bring no evil intent. My friends and I journey to Rhum—yonder, across the water—to help a young boy defend his birthright."

"Then why stop you here? No one visits Drimnin. Not since the dark days of the Vikings," the voice demanded.

After taking several halting steps toward the tower, Kruzurk propped his staff against one of the crenellations so that he could pull the grimoire he'd carried with him from the catacombs out of his pack. The book flopped open to the spot where Olghar's cross had been hidden, bright sunlight giving the gilded cross an almost divine radiance. Well back in the tower's shadows, a collective gasp from a host of tiny voices rippled across the stone catwalk.

"Forgive me. I know not why, exactly, but I felt someone here might be able to translate this book for me," Kruzurk said, quietly as one praying for penance.

A low, melodic chant began to emanate from the tower, sending shivers up the backs of all four men. "Whence come you, pilgrim?" the one voice asked. "And where did you find that grimoire with the cross in it?"

"I did not find it exactly. You might say the book was liberated from a place called Blackgloom Keep. And the cross is not mine—it belongs to one who travels with us. He claims to be a priest of the Russ."

"Liberated? Then the Seed is dead?"

Surprised by that comment, Kruze hesitated before adding, "Aye. He is, and all his minions destroyed."

"Impossible!" the voice snapped back. "Neither man nor magic could best the Seed."

"All things are possible, given time and sufficient effort," came Kruzurk's well practiced reply. "But the Seed is dead, I assure you. I witnessed his demise myself."

"So, you are a sorcerer yourself, then, eh? For it is well known that the Seed's sorcery could only be overcome by a sorcery greater than his."

"Not so. 'Twas his own foul greed that destroyed him—not I."

"And what of the rest of the Blackgloom Bounty?"

"Most of it is safely stored in a priory," Kruzurk answered, having stepped several paces closer to the tower but still unable to see the shape of his host. "Might I ask who you are and how you come to know of the Seed and his treasure?"

The voice snapped back, "You may *not*. I will ask the questions, and you will answer. Or, you will return to your ship and be gone from here."

Kruzurk closed the grimoire, tucked it under his arm and said quietly, "As you wish."

"Now, tell the one with that bird to leave us. We allow no beasts here, especially predators. The others should leave, too, or toss their weapons from the battlements."

Eigh and Muck didn't hesitate, opting quickly to head back down the steps to the *Pandora*. Before they left, Mediah handed them his shield and short sword, determined to stay with Kruze no matter what.

Satisfied, the inquisitor pressed his query. "About this Russ—where is he, and why carry you his cross secreted in that evil book?"

"I beg to differ with you, m'lord," Kruzurk replied. "There are no evil books—only evil minds who interpret the contents for their own evil purposes."

Kruzurk went on to describe his encounter and travels with Olghar, hoping the tale might entice his inquisitor to step out into the light. That did not happen. Questions continued to fly from the darkened archway almost as fast as Kruze could answer, each one evoking a slightly louder chorus of chants from the inquisitor's cohorts, and a corresponding decrease in the magician's patience.

Finally, Kruzurk had had enough. He reached for his staff and strode purposefully toward the arch, anxious to force the issue or hasten his exit. He could make out hooded shapes in the shadows, but still no faces. "Will you show yourselves, that I may know who you are and why you ask so many questions?"

The murmuring in the background told him that a

conference had begun, and that his tales were the main subject. He prepared to turn and leave, then stopped as sunlight flashed brilliantly off the polished surface of a strange, conical helmet worn by the smallish robed cleric who marched out of the shadows towards him.

"Good morning to you," Kruze offered, satisfied that his trial by rota had ended.

"Tell me thy name, pilgrim," the inquisitor said, a more congenial voice having supplanted the previously harsh timbre.

Kruzurk sized up the cleric facing him. Long reddish gray hair and a fluffy beard fell in loose clumps around the man's shoulders, which seemed far too close to his waistline for a normal being. In one hand, the cleric clutched a crystal orb and in the other, a strange device resembling a fisherman's trident, except that it looked far too small to use for fishing.

"I am called Kruzurk Makshare. I hail from middle Anglia."

In the darkness of the tower, another collective gasp erupted, except this time it had a more discerning tone, as though his answer had been expected. The cleric's face shown with an enlightened expression as well. "A *palindrome*, indeed!" he exclaimed. "Exactly as our scribes have foretold these twelve generations. There can be no doubt—you come in the company of a Russ, you have the grimoire in your possession and I sense a knowing about you that cannot be a ruse." Turning toward the tower, the diminutive cleric raised the orb aloft and proclaimed, "He is the one, brethren. He is the one!"

Brude McAlpin, the Great Deceiver, had stood his silent vigil on the bow of the *Shiva* all night. Requiring no sleep or rest of any kind in his resurrected form, he played the role of sentinel for his shipload of mortal companions while Daynin and Ean were on their spying mission to Iona. Just then, the two highlanders came up against the *Shiva*'s stern in the longboat, reboarding without causing too much commotion.

" 'Bout bleedin' time you two wuz gettin' back here," Peckee growled. Although his newly gained position as ship's master brought little of the respect from his shipmates he thought he had earned, Peckee nevertheless had taken to the job like it was a birthright bestowed. "Can ye not see the sunrise is upon us, old man? Damned pilgrims."

With one hand on the stern rope to steady himself, Ean reached down and drew the *sgian du* from his sock. Daynin's boost from the longboat below lifted the old man past the tiller block to almost waist level with Peckee. Ean's eyes flashed upward with that red hot Scotian temper, his sock knife suddenly poised within a hand's span of Peckee's private parts. "Ahh was fightin' warr-rr-s afore *yew* were a wet spot on yer-rr-rr mam's bed covers, *boy,* and if ya value yer-rr-rr jewels, I'd stow that pilgrim talk and the attitude."

Peckee stepped back to distance himself from the razor sharp blade. His head spun 'round as his eyes caught a glimpse of the giant making his way sternward. Caught between a demon and a dagger blade, Peckee suddenly realized his captaincy had lost much of its luster. "Meanin' no disrespect," he pleaded, "I wuz just lookin' out for the good of the ship."

By now, Daynin had secured the longboat by its tether and joined Ean on deck, face to face with the frightened Peckee. "You're lucky we need you, captain," Daynin replied. "Elsewise grr-rr-andfather might slit ya from yer knees to yer nose, as I've seen 'im do ta many a mahn."

Ean almost snickered aloud at that remark. *The boy has grown up,* he told himself. *And in so short a time, I wouldnae thought it possible.* A beaming smile, mixed with mirth and a great deal of pride, spread across the old man's heavily lined face.

"What is all this uproar?" Brude demanded, only slightly lowering his voice from the normal booming bravado.

The three men wavered under Brude's sudden verbal assault, as well as with the swaying of the ship his movement inevitably caused. Ean turned about, not fully realizing he faced the giant's immediate presence. "Stay yerself, ya rusty relic. The situation is well in h . . ."

Only Sabritha's sudden appearance from below decks kept Brude from knocking Ean on his backside. Her long black hair and shapely figure instantly captured everyone's attention—even the Great Deceiver's. "What's all the commotion?" she snapped. "Why aren't we moving?" It seemed no one had a craving to answer her. It had become common knowledge aboard ship that to do so brought a hail of verbal barbs few men could stand against.

Peckee seized the opportunity to regain some of the power his position brought with it. "Avast, ya blue water beggars!" he barked. "All hands, lively now—to the sheets—up anchor—let's get the ladyship's barge under way!"

Plumat stared up at the jury-rigged mast, its ratlines and rigging straining heavily against the northeasterly gusts that pushed the *Woebringer* ever closer to the southern tip of Caledonia. There, Captain Coke had told him, the winds shifted to a southeastern quarter and would drive the ship northward into the ocean sea toward Rhum.

"So, tell me, Plumat, how do you know that prior was

telling you the truth? He could have picked any island name that came to mind. You have no way . . ."

Plumat cut him off sharply with, "Ranulf, that prior was just a boy, scared spitless by a hot iron held to his eyes. He spilled his guts like a bull blasted from a ballista. It's *Rhum* all right. That's where they're headed. I asked those in Glasgow for the location, and the captain confirmed it. Fifty leagues to the north, give or take a dozen leagues—that's where we'll find the boy and his band of brigands. That's where they'll meet justice. We're not taking them back to Carlisle. You were an agent of the King's Eyre—you can try them in place and we'll hang 'em on the spot. The whole lot will be done with and we'll have the treasure to bring home."

Ranulf cast a worried glance at the ship's tattered rigging. "Aye, if we make it that far."

Kruzurk and his companions sat quietly around the great stone table Perazelzeus and his brethren had set before them. A magnificent midday feast was laid out, replete with fresh fruit. Kruze wondered aloud. "Master Perazelzeus, how is that you have this wonderful fruit here in this clime?"

The modest little cleric smiled at that telling question. "Please, Master Makshare, call me Zeus. I rather fancy that less formal moniker. One of my brethren came up with it after reading about the Greeks and Romans. It suits me rather well, don't you think? As for the fruit, I can only tell you that we carry on a thriving trade here at Drimnin. In fact, it is one of our best guarded secrets. Traders come to us from the ends of the earth."

Having just enjoyed the taste of several new spices for the first time, Kruzurk crowed, "Ah, so it is possible to sail from Anglia all the way to the spice islands in the east!"

Perazelzeus sighed deeply before answering, "Well, not exactly—at least not yet. Much of the distance must be covered overland, through Persia. But I believe that one day soon, a great adventurer will find a way to sail west to the spice islands."

"West!?" Mediah gasped. "But what of the ocean sea and the monsters dwelling there? Won't a ship sail right off the edge?"

"Ah, that is the great question, my Greek friend," the cleric answered. "Can ships on the verge of the ocean sea fall into oblivion or continue westerly across the wide expanse of ocean I believe to be there? Sadly, no one has yet been there and back to tell us."

"Norse traders from the lands of the Russ have done so," Olghar professed. He had remained virtually silent all morning, preferring to listen and absorb what was said. His only comment thus far had been an expression of surprise at the invitation to join Kruze and Mediah, but now his creaking gristmill of a voice seemed anxious to engage the cleric. "That is how I learned my many languages—from those traders. They say there is another world to the west, but it is very difficult and dangerous to reach."

From the darkened regions of the great hall, a cacophony of cane rattling erupted. "Quiet, brethren! The Russ can speak. I will not have you being so rude to our guests!"

"Thank you, Master Zeus. So, tell me—what is it that traders trek across half the known world to seek from you here? Knowledge perhaps, or magic, or something even more powerful?"

Sensing that the Russ already knew the answer, the little cleric pushed his chair back, tapped several times on the table to stem the murmuring of his minions, and stood up.

Pushing his sleeves back, he announced, "Since you are traveling with the *One* we have been expecting, I will tell you, Olghar of Russ. But I warn you—this secret must never be uttered outside these walls, else you will bring such a cataclysm to mankind that your name will forever be damned by mages and mortals alike."

"Where are these fearsome Tireean pirates you keep fretting over, *Draygnar?*" Brude growled. "We're almost through the Temptress, and I've seen nothing of them."

Daynin's ears burned at the mention of that heathen name, yet to forestall another confrontation with the giant, he let it pass. "Aye, 'tis strange we've not seen a single sail since first light. Mayhaps it's market day and we've caught them all ashore, drunk as drengs in a harlot's den."

Simon Troon, now able to gain his feet with the help of the ship's railing, spit to windward and said, "Ya cannae assume a thing out here, lads. Tiii-rreeans is a sneaky lot, and those little snekkes they sail are hard to spot, even on a flat calm sea."

All heads turned as Sabritha picked her way from the stern block through the maze of ropes and regalia scattered pell-mell about the ship's deck. Reaching the prow, she cozied up next to Daynin and said nothing.

"You're cold," he whispered.

"I'm hardly dressed for an adventure at sea, plowboy. The air has gotten colder with every league we've traveled to the north. I hope this island of yours has a warm fire and a place to sleep."

"Aye, it does. Or it *will* have, once we make repairs. The main wall was badly damaged in the fire, but two of the towers still stood, last I saw of Kinloch Keep."

Sabritha snuggled closer for the warmth, mindful that a

host of eyes watched her every move. "These blaggards—I wish they'd keep their eyes on the sea instead of me."

"Ya cannae blame heathen salt water blokes for spyin' you with their peepers, missy," Troon said. "It's likely they've never seen a wench as sprightly as you. And at such close quarters, ta boot."

"Who asked *you* anyway?" she snapped, her somewhat mellowed temper suddenly reforged and directed at the old bowman.

"Please, Sabritha. A bit of rr-r-respect—Simon is my grandfather's oldest friend. Mine too, now that I think about it."

"Aye, boy, that I am. I been knowin' the both o' you since you was breast-high to a milk cow. And now look at you—all growed to a mahn!"

Sabritha's head turned back toward Daynin. "Well, al-l-l-most a man, anyway," she said laughingly.

Daynin felt the red hot embrace of embarrassment rushing through his body. His mind flashed back to Blackgloom and the image of Sabritha's perfect body. It was all he could do not to spin her around and kiss those lips until she was ready to take him below and finish the job of transforming him into a man.

Once again, that wonderful reverie fragmented as a shout came down from the lookout aloft. "Sail *ho,* mates! Three points off the larboard beam—she's roundin' the headland and scuddin' like a sea witch!"

"Now we've some sport at hand," Brude boasted. He drew that mighty sword and began brandishing it in the air, excited by the prospect of drawing more blood.

"Two sails!" the lookout shouted. "*Och*—and a third to the sou-west, behind us!"

Daynin's head went 'round like a potter's wheel, spying

first the sail in their wake and then the two dead ahead. "They're going to trap us in the narrows."

"Aye, lad," Troon agreed. "And this scow is too bloody slow to outrun them. I best fetch the weapons, for we've got a fight on our hands."

Sabritha took one look at the bowman's hobbled conditioned and said, "I'll get them for you, and I'll wake the others below."

From above, the lookout added to the litany of bad news. "We're doomed—there's a boom stretched across the narrows!"

Daynin cupped his hands over his brow to get a better look at what lay ahead. "What does he mean, a *boom*, Simon?"

"Likely a large rope or chain logger, stretched from one bank to the other. Sort of a cork in the bottle, as you might say, boy."

Just then Peckee emerged from the fo'c'sle and shouted, "What's all the hubbub? Why have we slowed down?"

"Tireeans, cap'n," Troon shouted. "Our worst fears is upon us—they've blocked the bleedin' channel ahead."

"Damn!" Peckee growled. "We never shoulda left Ravensport!"

The midday meal completed, Kruzurk and his friends were invited into the more formal surroundings of the great hall of books, inner sanctum of Perazelzeus. There, Olghar Fergum of Russ had been ceremoniously presented with an ancient vellum printed in raised letters, which he labored to translate aloud to one of the monks. Across the room, Mediah's horizons were being broadened from a game of merrels taught by another monk.

Meanwhile, Kruzurk's attention narrowed to a lengthy

and detailed conversation with Perazelzeus, whose questions kept focusing on the minutest details surrounding the Blackgloom Keep and the Scythian Stone. "Yes, yes," Kruze answered patiently, "the whole point of the ruse was to convince the Seed that we had the *real* Scythian Stone. Otherwise, we would never have been brought into his keep. The Seed not only needed the stone, he needed a virgin's blood to cleanse it, or so he thought."

"Yes, *exactly!*" Zeus pressed, his words and the occasional nervous fidget showing his excitement. "But how is it you knew what the stone looks like, that you could make it so convincing? No one has seen the genuine article in at least five generations."

Kruzurk hesitated, unsure exactly where the little cleric was going with his questions. "I merely created what I thought might pass for the real thing," he answered, avoiding any mention of his visitation from Merlin's spirit. "The Seed's greed did the rest."

"Ahhh, I see. Then you have no *actual* knowledge of the Scythian Stone, is that correct?"

Realizing he was about to be trapped between dishonesty and disbelief, Kruze chose the higher road. "You may not believe me, but I did have some help from the spirit of Merlin, who gave me a scroll and other information pertinent to the stone."

"*Pendragon's* Merlin? The Merlin of old? Surely you jest!"

Settling himself in his chair, Kruze thought carefully about his next answer. "Indeed—I was apprenticed to him at a young age. Long after his death, he came from the other side to tell me of the Seed's vile plans. As for the Scythian Stone, I could find no records at York or anywhere else detailing its actual appearance, or if it truly exists."

Zeus leaned across the table, coming almost nose tip to nose tip with Kruzurk. He whispered, "Oh, it *exists* all right. And you are the One we were told would fetch it."

"Fetch the stone? Impossible! I cannot delay my quest to Rhum. A boy's life is in danger, and I am the cause of it."

"Aye, fetch it you will. And to Rhum—take it you must—for that is to be the new seat of power in Scotia. That boy you talk of may even become the regent of this domain, provided you perform this boon. You must travel north to the Sconehaven donjon, about three leagues from here and there, do whatever is necessary to secure the Scythian Stone from its keeper!"

Chapter 33:

The Severing

Captain Peckee tugged at his grizzled beard, unsure what to do next. He glanced behind the *Shiva* and realized there was no turning back, no outrunning the Tireeans, and no way forward save straight into the boom that blocked their path. "Put all the sail on her she can bear, lads! You there—up forward—go below and fetch the boarding axes. Our one chance is to cut through that boom afore those bloody cutthroats are on us like locusts."

Ean and Troon had already strung all the bows they had with them, readied the quivers of arrows for rapid fire, and stood to the port quarter, sizing up the enemy. "We can put a hail of bolts on 'em from here, Ean, don't ya agree?"

"Aye, Troon," the elder McKinnon replied, "but we may need those arrows when they're closer. "If we had a fire lit, we might set their sails ablaze, though I doubt 'twould do much good in this spray."

Daynin admired his grandfather's mettle more than he ever had at that moment. Standing there, calm as a merchant in a market square, the old man shone with a courage few men could muster when so greatly outnumbered. "What can *I* do, grandfather?" he asked.

"Get that giant of yours to give us a hard blow, boy—like he did before. If we hit that boom right, the bow may cut right through it."

Seeing the need himself, Brude was already making his

way toward the stern of the ship. In a colorful and flowing rhythm, he shouted to the sky, "Cruithni honor begs a different ploy, yet allied I am to this Scotian boy! Thus do I make war with a mighty wind that he and his minions may live in the end!"

The *Shiva*'s ragged sail filled to its limits, jolting the ship forward so abruptly that not a person aboard could keep his feet. The ship leapt from the waves, almost flying over the surface of the water, hell-bent for the log boom and whatever fate awaited her there.

After two more blasts of air, Brude waved his sword and dashed toward the bow, ready to do battle if need be. Daynin and the others regained their feet, prepared for a bloodletting none of them was likely to forget. Sabritha hunkered behind the mainmast where she could watch Daynin's back and keep an eye on the treasure at the same time.

"This lot may go over the side with that loot, rather than fight it out," she whispered to Daynin.

"Aye, that they might," he answered with a grim laugh. "And if they do, 'twill give the rr-rr-rest of us more rr-rr-room ta fight!"

Daynin's bravado brought a proud smile to Ean McKinnon's weathered facade, amplified by an equally proud proclamation from Troon that, "You've done well with that boy, Ean."

Kruze stood in front of a roaring fire staring into the crystalline orb now securely attached to his staff's top. His mind went over the details of his task as Zeus had laid them out. "Within a few hundred paces of the donjon of Sconehaven," the cleric had told him, "you will find a bog surrounded by thirteen great white monoliths. A fearsome warrior lives in that donjon and guards the bog. This warrior wears a ring on a tether 'round his neck. No one out-side of Drimnin Keep knows the power of that ring. Securing it from him and combining its power with the orb I gave you will allow you to divine the exact whereabouts of the Scythian Stone."

Kruzurk now knew that the stone was real. In fact, it was the revered Stone of Destiny or Coronation Stone that every king of Dalriada, Scotia and the highlands had knelt upon since the beginning of time. Rhum had been the resting place of the Stone in times past, making it the only fit place for new kings to be crowned. But that had all changed with the Norse incursions, and sadly, told only half the story.

A rightful coronation, Kruze learned, needed a priest who could read the ancient runes emblazoned around the Stone's edges, as those runes bespoke the vows Scotian kings must pledge. Without saying the vows, a king became a king in name only, devoid of the power and knowledge of the Drimnin loremasters. For it was *they* who had main-tained the laws over the ages, kept the records, and would now provide a new king with his earthly right to govern. Even more important, a king of Scotia had to be of true highland lineage, otherwise corruption and contempt would be his only rewards from those he governed. Such was Kruzurk's fate—to provide the man who fulfilled the neces-sary criteria. But first, he had to find the Stone, and that promised to be no easy task.

Rounding the Mull of Kintyre, the *Woebringer* swung hard into the current that swept northeast toward Rhum. "Bugger!" Captain Coke swore. "She handles like a slug in a slop jar! You there—trim that head sheet or we'll lose her to landward!"

Three of the crew struggled to dog down the lines, tightening the newly rigged headsail and forcing it to fill with the wind to port. "That's it, lads! Now brace the mainsail to larboard," Coke shouted.

Plumat's stomach rolled with each new swell surging under the ship's bow. Half the night he'd spent wrenching his guts free of Caledonian grog and fried fish pies, which had proved hardly a choice meal for seafaring. Adding to his misery, the damaged *Woebringer* pitched and yawed badly instead of sailing the straight course she was designed for. "How much more of this heavy sea, captain?" he asked.

Captain Coke cast him an amused glance, then looked sternward to gauge the swells. Ranulf of Westmoorland lay there, doubled over near the stern blocks, himself a victim of the mortrews. "I told you lubbers to eat only biscuits for supper, didn't I? Sailing in deep water is nothing like scudding along that coastline. And with this half-assed mainsail ta boot, we'll be lucky the ship don't founder on some bleedin' Caledonian . . ."

Even in his stuporous state, Plumat heard the captain stop in midstream. "What is it?" he snapped.

"*Ships!* Two at least—way there in the mist—big ones—dracos I should think, judging from the cut of their sails."

Ranulf managed to pull himself up by the stern blocks, his wobbly knees unable to stand. "Aye, that would be Oswald, come to fetch us home."

Plumat shook off his lethargy and rushed to Ranulf's side. Tugging the fat reeve to his feet, Plumat growled, "Who is this Oswald, and why comes he to fetch us? I issued no such order."

"Oswald of Leeds—my brother-in-law—I sent him word of our campaign before leaving Carlisle. No doubt he comes looking for me, as we are aboard *his* ship, in a manner of speaking."

"Damn you, Ranulf! You told me this was *your* vessel! Are you indentured to this Oswald, or merely his dreng? What say you!?"

The heavy shaking at Plumat's hands was more than Ranulf's guts could take. He wrenched violently, then belched what remained of his stomach's contents all over the front of Plumat's tunic.

"Blaggard!" Plumat roared. Reeling in disgust at what had just happened, he shoved the man to the deck. "If you were not of noble rank, I'd throw your fat, slovenly ass over the side!"

Captain Coke kept his distance. "Should I heave to, m'lord, to allow those dracos to come abeam?"

"Yes, damn your eyes! And get me a bucket of seawater!"

"We're gonna hit that boom hard!" Peckee cried out to no one in particular, as all eyes were fixed on either the floating menace ahead or the equally menacing ships closing fast from the port side.

Twaack! Ean's longbow barked. The missile struck one of the Tireean crewmen square in the chest, toppling him backward in a heap of ropes and rigging.

"Bloody good shot," Troon crowed. "That was six ship lengths, I'd wager, and in this wind—you've still got the touch, McKinnon."

Sabritha cried out, "Wait! Shouldn't we at least make certain they *are* pirates?"

A hail of fire arrows from the first Tireean vessel quickly quelled her questions. Fortunately, all of the blazing bolts peppered the water well short of their mark.

Troon laughed aloud, screaming into the wind, "Bleedin' amateurs—you ain't worth the piss in a prior's pot!"

Counting the shafts left in six quivers, Daynin handed his grandfather another arrow. "How many men does a ship like that carry?"

One of the crewmen swung down out of the rigging to gain cover and answered, "Score and a half, at least, if they's fully loaded."

"That's almost a hundred men in three ships," Sabritha gasped, "and our numbers are less than twenty."

"Aye," the elder McKinnon vowed, "but it's thirty at a time, not all at once, and that we can handle."

Daynin added, "And we have Brude. I myself saw him tangle with a dozen of the Duke's mounted troops. These Tireeans will have hell to pay if they come aboard the *Shiva.*"

If the Great Deceiver had actually had mortal ears, no doubt they would have perked up from that spirited re-telling of the priory battle. The boy's words still warmed the giant's armor, making him feel almost alive. "Bring 'em on," he boasted. "*Droongar* shall feast on Tireean blood today!"

Casting a glance at the mainsail, then down at the boom now looming larger than he had expected, Peckee yelled a warning, "Hold fast!" but it came too late. The *Shiva*'s bow struck the center log with the force of a battering ram.

Crrrraaack! The boom crushed a huge dent in the ship's keel as the *Shiva* rode up and onto it. She settled in a pre-carious position, her barnacled bow as tall as a charger's back, sticking high and dry out of the water.

Miles appeared on deck from his sickbed below. "Bloody hell!" he screamed. "What happened? Are we sinking?"

"Go below, you sniveling snot!" Sabritha shrieked. "Get those men in the fo'c'sle up here to fight."

Captain Peckee's thoughts turned to jumping overboard,

so certain was he that the *Shiva* could never stay afloat. One look at the woman's baleful stare and he knew she would strangle him if he tried to jump. Motivation renewed, he tied down the tiller and ran forward to check the damage.

Brude had already leapt onto the log to assess the situation. "She's battered, but not sinking," he declared. With a single slash of his giant broadsword, a chunk of log peeled through the air and splashed into the water.

"That's it!" Daynin cheered. "Cut that bloody boom, Brude—you can do it!"

Arrows ripped into the rigging above Daynin's head, some alight, some not. Smoke began billowing from the mainsail as Troon, Ean and the others fired back. One of the crew screamed in agony, his throat pierced by a flaming bolt. Another fell from the ratlines into the water. Blood flowed freely on the deck, causing Sabritha to turn her head in horror.

The first Tireean vessel, now less than a boat-length distance, suffered heavy casualties from Ean and the other bowmen. Half her crew lay dead or wounded before the prow of their snekke struck the *Shiva* almost amidships. A muffled *caaarummpph* echoed in the shallow waters as the snekke's ram penetrated the *Shiva*'s portside hull.

"We're holed!" the lookout bellowed, an instant before the force of the impact tore his grip on the mainmast and he came tumbling down.

Peckee seized a broad axe from one of the dead and weighed into the Tireean boarders flooding over the side of his ship. Several of his crew joined him, momentarily stemming the tide of the onrushing enemy. More pirates clambered onto the *Shiva*'s railings, dropping aboard with daggers and short swords flashing in their teeth.

Ean felled two of the cutthroats with one arrow, the

range so short now he could reload and fire in a heartbeat. Troon killed another outright, as did Daynin with a well-aimed axe thrown with all his might. Seizing a sword, Sabritha fought off an intruder bent on stabbing Daynin in the side, only to be shoved onto her backside with a bloody lip for a reward.

Back at the boom, Brude's hacking stopped briefly as the second Tireean vessel scudded to a stop alongside the *Shiva*. He scanned the melee for signs he was needed, but decided the boom was the far greater threat. He hacked hard again, then again, and again, sending huge chunks of timber flying in all directions. Straddling the boom, he could feel it begin to separate from the *Shiva*'s enormous weight.

An instant before the log boom split, Brude swung back aboard the *Shiva*, his blade twirling faster than mortal eyes could see. "Bring it on, you blaggards!" he swore. Tearing into the onrushing crew of the second ship, he sent three men to their doom instantly. Gore, guts, and pirate pedigree splattered everyone in range.

A crossbowman in the second snekke's rigging fired bolt after bolt into Brude's armor, cursing when the giant would not go down. More pirates attacked Brude, all of them hacking and clanging away with axes and short swords, but to no avail.

Peckee and his men, having temporarily run out of enemies, suddenly realized the *Shiva*'s bow floated freely in the water. The captain shouted, "Quickly, men! Cut that snekke loose so's we can beat it outta here!"

Ean and Troon heard the cry but could not help. They were too busy targeting Brude's adversaries, now that the second ship's entire crew had engaged the giant. Single-handedly, Brude held the railing against all odds. Not one man had yet gained the *Shiva* from the second ship. A dozen of the snekke's numbers sprawled on her deck, dead or dying.

Peckee untied the tiller loop, doing all he could to get the ship underway, yet she still would not budge. With a snekke's ram embedded in her side and the log boom to her front, the *Shiva* wallowed like a mud hen in a midland marsh. Realizing the third snekke rapidly approached from the south, Peckee made a bold decision. "You men—come with me—we're gonna board the snekke and back her off with her own oars."

Miles heard the call and decided his fighting skills were no match for the heathens. Leaping over the railing into the mass of bloodied Tireeans, he grabbed an oar with the others and hauled away. The snekke groaned, but wouldn't move, stuck fast in the side of the much larger *Shiva*. To make matters worse, a fire had broken out aboard the Tireean vessel, dooming her and the *Shiva* as well.

Daynin leaned over the *Shiva*'s side and suddenly remembered what Kruzurk Makshare had told him about leverage. "Common sense and leverage," Daynin repeated from memory.

Barely hearing him over the din of battle, Sabritha pushed herself to her knees and cried out, "Daynin—look out!"

The treacherous walk through the rugged highlands north of Drimnin Keep had taken a toll on Kruzurk and Mediah. A misty, gray day hung about them like a bad dream, making the trek to Sconehaven seem twice as long.

"Did the cleric say how far this donjon was?" Mediah asked.

Kruzurk slowed his pace, then stopped to get a better

view of the land. "Three leagues, but it's difficult to judge distance in this mist. I wish now we had brought Eigh with us. Trudging about in this wilderness without a map or guide is wasting time, I fear. Time we cannot afford to lose."

"Indeed. The boy could already be at Rhum, if that Prior's story was accurate. And the Saxons as well. It's a good thing you ordered the *Pandora* to join us at Kinsley Spit—that will save us a long walk ba . . ."

Kruzurk abruptly thrust his staff in the air. "Shhhh—I hear something."

In the distance, the clanging of a blacksmith's hammer rent the air with its distinct "clink, clink, clink". The two edged closer to a bend in the track, careful not to show themselves any more than necessary.

Around the turn and down a steep slope, a small holding occupied both sides of the road. Black smoke from the smith's shop lingered in the heavy air. "We can't go around—it will take too long," Kruze whispered.

"Allow me to go first. If there's no threat, I will give a shout."

"No, Mediah. There's strength in numbers, even with two. We'll go together."

Hiking down the trail like they were neighbors coming for stew, the pair strode into the farm's midst and right up to the blacksmith. His rhythm interrupted, the smithy growled, "Who the hell are you?"

Mediah stepped forward, a broad smile his peace offering. "Pilgrims, m'lord. Come to visit Sconehaven. We were wondering if . . ."

"Go back wherever the hell you came from, pilgrim," the smithy replied, adding a menacing wave of his hammer for good measure. "Sconehaven ain't exactly a pilgrimage site."

"Beggin' your pardon, m'lord," Kruze intervened. "We were told of a place with great white stones and . . ."

"Damn it, pilgrim, are ye deaf? That bog is a demon's den, not fit for men. And stop calling me 'm'lord'—I *work* for a living!"

"Might we trouble you for directions, then?" Kruze pressed.

The smithy's hammer went up again, this time waving toward the road. "If you're that determined to die, then stay on this track. It takes you to Sconehaven. The bloody bog is beyond it a bit. But if you value your lives, turn around now and never look back."

An instant longer gazing over the ship's side and Daynin might never have seen another sunrise. Sabritha's scream turned him just as a blazing beam from the burning Tireean ship collapsed and fell onto the *Shiva*'s railing above Daynin's head. Once again, he found himself sprawled face down in Sabritha's lap, but this time, ashes and soot rained all around them.

"We've got to go below and push that rr-rrram away, or we're goners!"

"How can we do that?" Sabritha cried loudly, more to be heard than from fear of the battle.

"There must be a way," the boy answered. "At least you'll be safer there."

Dragging her by one wrist, Daynin ducked the flying ash and cinders, making his way through the tiny hatch that led down into the fo'c'sle. "Come on, I think we can use one of these oars as a lever. Kruzurk showed me how."

Sabritha shook the ashes from her hair and replied, "What the deuce is a *lever?*"

Daynin jammed one end of the huge oar between two of

the ship's side ribs, bending the other end like a longbow, hard against the tip of the Tireean ram. "Help me now—pull with all you've got!"

Their combined strength and the "magic" of Kruzurk's lever did the trick. The ram edged outward, ever so slowly giving way under the pressure. "Push, woman! Harder now!" Daynin shouted, his muscles strained to the limits. Sabritha gave it all she had, allowing the anger from that "woman" to triple her strength.

Suddenly, shards of crimson light erupted around the ram's edges. The darkened fo'c'sle lit up as the menacing mass eased its way out to sea, allowing light to flood the ship's hold. "We did it!" Daynin yelled. He grabbed Sabritha and hugged her, and would have done a high-lander's jig if not for the cramped quarters.

"Oh god, Daynin . . ." Sabritha gasped, her eyes focused through the gaping hole left by the ram's departure. "Our dimwit captain and the others are still on the burning ship!"

Daynin hurried to scramble up through the hatchway. The scene above was of total carnage. Ean and Troon had taken to pulling arrows from the dead that they might be prepared to fight the third ship. Brude's armor and the deck around him flowed with gore, so many of the Tireeans had met their end from his whirling blade. And just as Sabritha had warned, the other crew members were rapidly disappearing behind the *Shiva*, in the smoke and flames of the burning snekke.

"Grandfather! We're losing the crew!" Daynin shouted.

Ean turned in time to see the burning ship falling behind, even though Peckee and the others rowed like madmen in a vain attempt to keep up. "We cannae help 'em lad. The *Shiva*'s sails are moving her too fast. Take the tiller, boy, and guide us through the channel. Keep 'er midstream, and maybe we'll slip on through."

Dashing to the tiller block, Daynin did as he was told. He had watched the others steering the ship for hours, and now he practiced what he had learned. Skillfully maneuvering the *Shiva* away from the log boom and the other snekke, he steered a straight line for the clear passage he assumed lay dead ahead.

"HaaaaaHaaaarrrr!" Brude screeched, his hollow, booming voice full of a bravado heard all the way back to Tiree. "Bloody heathens! Know you now the extent of Cruithni courage!"

Daynin could only smile at the huge beast's display. Never had he witnessed the scale of carnage the likes of that delivered by the Great Deceiver. And yet, somehow, it seemed all too familiar.

The lengthy delay waiting for the other ships to come within hailing distance had driven Plumat near to rage. Nothing on his mission had yet gone right, and now, for all he knew, he was about to be subordinated to a man he didn't even know. "Can they not hear you?" he growled angrily at Captain Coke, who stood precariously atop the stern block yelling his lungs out.

"Apparently not, m'lord. In this wind, they'll likely have to bring over a skiff to parlay. Or, we can beat it into a bay somewhere and have us a talk whilst the crew replenishes the ship's stores. Water is low and so is the . . ."

"Damn yer eyes, Coke. I don't care how you do it—just get it done so we can be on our way. That boy gets further away the longer we sit here bobbing like a sea turtle in a slop jar."

"As you wish, m'lord. All hands make sail! Avast, ya worthless lot! We'll hug the coast, Plumat, then scoot into the Islets of Ismay. Should be safe enough there for the dracos to follow. And there's water aplenty, and wood for repairs."

Half a league down the track from the blacksmith's hovel, the crumbling spires of Sconehaven donjon towered majestically over the huge oak trees lining the road. "Looks deserted to me," Kruze said in a middling whisper.

"Mayhaps we should bypass it, m'lord."

"No, we cannot, Mediah. Zeus told me I would have to deal with this mysterious black knight, whoever he is. I'm sure he will be out and about somewhere on these grounds. We'll just keep walking for now. Likely as not, he will find us."

"M'lord," Mediah asked, "why is it that in your country so many evil persons prefer the color of black for their attire?"

Kruzurk laughed aloud, amused by his Greek cohort's innocence in such matters. "Black cloth is cheap, Mediah, as is black armor. Brighter dyes and shiny metals cost more. Those who hoard their gold rarely spend it on tawdry attire. And blood seldom shows on black, which can be an advantage for those bent on evil."

"Ah, I see. But you Anglish put such great stock in your heraldry and trappings. It seems amiss that some should choose black to adorn themselves, does it not?"

"White for good, black for evil, and everything in between is either less good or less evil—that is the way of it, Mediah."

"Beggin' your pardon, m'lord, but where does your red robe fall in that scale?"

"Dead center, Mediah. Magicians wear red to ward off evil, since black curses and black oaths are absorbed by the color red. White when mixed with red becomes a shade of red, no longer white. Ergo, red also protects one from potential danger at the hands of those who claim to be pure good. Plus, it helps if your attire does not show food stains. Bad for the image, you know!"

Mediah cackled aloud at that joke, instantly muffling his mirth with a beefy paw slapped over his jaw. "Forgive me," he begged.

Fifty paces down the track, the trail split in three directions. Clearly, one track led to Sconehaven. Another was the main road, while a third led down a gently sloping grass field to Kruzurk's right. The magician stopped and cocked his ear to the wind. "Get off the road," he yelled, just as Mediah came dashing past him, and not an instant too soon.

An enormous black stallion, as tall at his withers as a man's head, charged into the road junction. A god of a warrior reined in the beast, showering the two men with rock and dirt. As the dust cleared, Kruzurk knew instantly they had been intercepted by the one they had been sent to find.

"Prepare to die, pilgrims!" the warrior boasted.

"Hold, sir knight. We mean you no harm," Kruzurk replied.

"You are trespassing on my grounds. That alone brings a sentence of death!"

Kruzurk's eyes scanned the knight's elaborate armor. Large, razor sharp blades protruded skyward from his shoulder plates. A jeweled black hauberk showing no heraldry covered him from neck to knees, with heavy leather gauntlets protecting his arms all the way to the elbows. The knight's helm looked to be of Celtic design, its open cross slits allowing both mouth and eyes to be exposed. The man was handsome, regal, and frightening, all at the same time.

"Perazelzeus, the cleric of Drimnin Keep, told us we would find you here," Kruze continued. "We have need of your help."

The knight said nothing. His dark eyes leered through the helm's view slit and one hand tightly gripped his sword hilt. Only the charger's heavy breathing broke the silence. "Drimnin is no more," the black armored one finally professed. "You lie, pilgrim. There are no clerics there—the Norse saw to that in my father's time. It has been so ever since."

"No, it's true," Kruze replied. He raised his staff to show off the orb affixed to its end, causing the charger to snort nervously. "See this? I received it from Perazelzeus. We were told you could show us the way to the bog where the great white monoliths stand."

The knight steadied his horse and leaned out of the saddle to better view the orb. "So, you've come to visit Felgenthorn, eh? Hardly a place for pilgrims like you. It's not been used since my grandfather's time, when human sacrifices were carried out there."

Kruzurk took a step closer to the enormous horse, mindful of the giant hooves pawing at the ground. "Aye, Felgenthorn it must be. A stone of great value is buried in that bog, and we must fetch it to stop a terrible injustice."

"Injustice, you say? Of what nature? Is there, mayhaps, a fair maiden involved or great booty to be had?"

Seeing he had gained the knight's interest, Kruzurk bade him to dismount, that they might parlay further. The knight agreed, seeming almost hungry for conversation. Kruze soon learned there was ample reason for that hunger. The warrior had spent most of his life at Sconehaven, guarding the keep, scaring away pilgrims as well as the curious, and maintaining his father's assigned vigil over the bog.

After a long discussion, Kruzurk finally asked, "Will you take us to Felgenthorn, then, sir knight, that we may continue this quest? Our ship awaits us at Kinsley Spit, about five leagues from here."

The knight removed his helmet, presenting a handsome face, dark hair, and beard. He shook his long hair to loosen it from the helm's tight confinement and answered, "A ship, you say? I've never been on a ship. In fact, I've never been much further than the blacksmith's hovel up the road. I agree to permit you to fulfill your quest, but with one condition. You must allow me to help right the injustice you spoke of. You must take me with you to this island of Rhum!"

"You would quit your vigil here to come with us?" Mediah asked.

"Aye, and gladly so. If we retrieve this stone you spoke of, then I believe my destiny is to accompany it wherever it goes." The knight removed his right gauntlet, thrusting his arm forward for a hand clench. "I am called Ebon. My father was Ebon of Scone, descended from the Ebonite clans of Dundee."

Kruzurk shook the knight's hand. "Welcome to our quest, Ebon of Scone. I am Kruzurk Makshare and this is Mediah the Greek."

Chapter 34:

The Securing

A strong breeze swept around the northern tip of Coll, Tiree's island sister, pushing the battered *Shiva* out into deep water once again. Ean and Troon had worked feverishly below decks since the battle, attempting to patch the gaping wound in the ship's hull. Despite their best efforts, water still sloshed about almost knee deep in the fo'c'sle.

"I dinnae think that patch will hold much longer, Troon. We best start bailin' or this tub is a goner for sure."

Troon wiped the sweat from his balding head and scanned the fo'c'sle for something to carry water. "Ean, maybe we should be thinkin' about the longboat. There's room in it for all of us, and we should be no more than ten or twenty leagues from Rhum."

The elder McKinnon bent over to ring some of the water from his tartan. "We'd have to leave that *thing* behind. He's too bloody heavy for the longboat. Daynin wouldnae stand for that, having given his oath to the beast."

"Aye, that creature did save our skins, but if we stay aboard this tub much longer, we'll be swimmin' for Rhum."

"You stay down here and bail as best you can. I'll see to the others. Maybe that giant can lend a hand with the bailing."

"More that way," Daynin shouted, his head bobbing to the left to indicate which way Sabritha should pull the mainsail stay. With her help, and both hands on the tiller, he had managed to keep the ship's prow pointed in a more or less northerly direction toward home.

"I—think—they call that—*larboard*—Daynin!" She almost had to yell to be heard over the wearying wind.

Daynin's gaze wandered from the Scotian coastline far to his right, briefly settling on Sabritha's perfectly outlined backside. Salt spray had so drenched her clothes that there was little left to his imagination. *Saints of Argyle, she is the most perfect woman I have ever seen,* he mused. *Look at the way she stands the deck—proud, resolute, unafraid. Men were dying all around her and she never wavered . . . Oh no—Oh my God!*

Sensing that something was amiss, Sabritha lunged toward him. The ship's deck pitched her left, then right with each new swell, but even from a distance she could see the terror in Daynin's eyes. "What's wrong with you? You're as pale as that sail cloth!"

"I killed a man!" he blurted out.

"Another man," she corrected. "That seadog wasn't your first."

Daynin flashed back to the tavern and the black hauberk. He could see the brief scuffle, the blade flashing and what seemed like an ocean of blood on the barroom floor. "But the Marquis was an accident! This time I *meant* to kill."

"Daynin, you did what you had to do. We all did. If we hadn't, those cutthroats would have chopped us to pieces. I'm proud of what you did."

Her words seemed to drift in the howling wind. The boy's mind kept retelling the images his memory created. The axe, the man's face—he could even see the sweat on the Tireean's cheeks and smell the ale on his body. *I killed him. I killed a man.* But there could be no undoing that deed, nor any way to forget it.

"What the bloody hell's the matter with you, boy?" Ean growled.

The old man's gruff manner snapped Daynin back to reality. "Uhh, I was—there was a . . ."

"He was scolding me for not handling the sail right, that's all," Sabritha hissed. "Leave 'im alone, you old scab!"

"Since when am I takin' orders from the likes of you, wench?"

Her hand nearly made it to Ean's whiskered face this time, before he stayed her wrist in mid-strike. "Cross me one more time, woman, and you'll be learnin' just how good a swimmer you are."

"Let me go, damn you!" She jerked loose from the old man. Perhaps the stinging in her wrist had made her a wiser woman.

"You two stop it," Daynin ordered. "We've a long way to go to reach Rhum, and I won't have us fighting amongst ourselves."

Ean stepped closer to the boy, keeping a watch on Sabritha's every move. "She's gonna be trouble, Daynin. And so is this bloody tub. We're sinking, and no way to stop it."

Oswald of Leeds strode onto the rocky beach like an angry troll, waving his war axe with every gesture. "Ranulf, are you mad? Why did you not heave to in the channel? Could you not see our signals? Why have you come ashore here?"

Ranulf stepped away from Plumat, gesturing toward him as though to make introduction. "M'lord Oswald, may I present to you Duke Harold's commander for this expedition—Geile Plumat of Saxony."

In deference to Oswald's rank, Plumat shed his glove for a hand-clench. "An honor, m'lord," he said, his voice laced with just enough humility to avoid an immediate confrontation.

"Have you completed your task, Plumat?" Oswald growled.

"We have not. Our ship sustained major damage from a sea serpent, allowing the felons to escape. But I . . ."

"Sea serpent? Is *that* the best excuse you can come up with? Ranulf, what the bloody hell are you about? Is this some kind of joke? I've fifty men and a hundred talens invested in your return, and all I get is this saltwater charade about a sea serpent?"

Plumat struck while the iron was hot. "Do you not see the damage our ship has sustained? Do you not see that repairs are underway as we speak? I am under direct orders of the Duke to bring back those felons, and that makes you part of this mission, now that you've chosen to join us."

Oswald threw his chest out, slamming the flat of his axe against his leather breastplate. "This is my authority, boy! I don't take orders from wet nurse squires or Duke Harold. I've come to fetch my ship and its contents back to Carlisle, and that's all."

Plumat knew Oswald was right. He had no real authority over him, given the circumstances. He chose another tack. "Let's suppose you could treble your hundred talens by joining us—would that put a different agenda on the table?"

"And I suppose *you* have that kind of plum in your pouch?"

"Not yet, Oswald," Plumat replied. "But when we catch that gang of killers, there will be silver enough for us all."

Ranulf leaned forward hesitantly, offering a handful of

the treasure taken from Plumat's men as his bona fides. "See this, brother? Join us now and we'll split a king's ransom of such treasure."

"Bloody hell, Ranulf! Why didn't you *say* so? I'd make my own sister a widow for that much swag. Where's this band of brigands?"

Satisfied not only that his army had just grown by several score, but that its quality and fighting ability had improved measurably, Plumat turned to Captain Coke and bellowed, "Lively, captain! We've a gang of felons to fetch, and a fleet to get afloat. Every minute counts!"

Approaching the front gate of the great white wall surrounding Felgenthorn bog, Mediah stopped to assess the gargoyles looming overhead and allowed Kruzurk, the knight and his charger to pass him by.

"Are you not coming with us, Mediah?" Kruze asked.

"M'lord, this is an evil place. The faithful are taught that such places should be avoided at all costs—especially those adorned with heathen likenesses."

Ebon whispered to his charger, dropped its reins, and strode purposefully up to the gate. He tossed the iron chain aside and cast the doors open. "They used to make human sacrifices here, in times long past. Children were thrown bound and gagged into the bog, that a good harvest might be bargained from the gods. You've nothing to fear now. It's just a bog. I will protect you, if need be."

"All the same, m'lords, I choose to remain outside. To risk my entrance to paradise is not a choice I make lightly."

"As you wish, Mediah. We won't be long. With Ebon's help and the charger, I'm sure we can retrieve the stone and be gone before dusk."

Together, Kruzurk and the knight led the horse through

the gate and around the near side of the bog—the only side lined with trees. "Ebon, you carry a ring on a tether. I was told . . ."

"How do you know of my father's ring?" he snapped.

"The clerics at Drimnin told me. They also told me I would have need of that ring to determine the stone's location."

Ebon drew back, his defenses once again on alert. "I won't give up my father's ring. He gave it to me as it was given to his father and his father before him."

Kruzurk studied the immense vastness of the bog stretching out before them. "Ebon, it will take days to find the stone without your ring. Our quest will be lost and the stone's purpose defeated unless we act quickly. I will return your ring as soon as we find the stone, I promise."

The knight's desire to see the world seemed to outweigh his connection to the ring. He reached inside his hauberk to pull the ring from around his neck. After a moment of reconsideration, he held it out to Kruzurk and said, "You keep it, for now."

"Thank you, Ebon of Scone. Now, let's find that stone and be on our way. A great adventure awaits you!"

Brude McAlpin tipped the huge hogshead of seawater on its side, returning another mass of leakage to the ocean whence it came. He leaned back over the splintered hole he had chopped in the ship's decking and lowered the barrel for refilling.

"At this rate, we might just be able to keep this wreck afloat, Ean," Troon said.

Ean looked up through the hole in the deck, still uneasy about having to interact with a rusting relic from the realm of the dead. "Aye, he lifts this hundred weight like it's a dead mouse. It makes me clammy all over, havin' to depend on the likes of 'im."

Troon poured another bucket of water into the hogshead and replied, "Without 'im, we'd be fish bait about now."

"Damn, you old Irish liar, don't ya think I'm knowin' that? But can ya not see there's ruin at the end of this nightmare, if he is to be the prize?"

Troon stepped behind Ean's back. This time, he poured his bucket over the highlander's shoulders instead of into the hogshead. "There, ya old sot!" he laughed. "Now you've something else to piss and moan about!"

Up on deck, Sabritha and Daynin heard the ruckus erupting below. "What the deuce are they doing down there?" she asked.

"Dunno. Doesn't matter, long as that water level in the hold isn't rr-rr-ising. Every wave we cut through gets us one boat length closer to home, that's all I know. With any luck, we should be there before nightfall."

Sabritha slipped behind Daynin's back and let her hands encircle his waist to steady them both in the heavy, rolling swells. "This place means a lot to you, doesn't it?"

Wanting desperately to pull his hands from the tiller to hold hers, he stood to his duty instead. "My whole life was there. Everything I know of the world came from Rr-rr-rhum and my father. My mother too, but she died young. Then those black hearted bountiers came and asked for shelter from the snow storm. My father granted it, sealing the fate of Kinloch Keep. Little did he know the house of McKinnon would be destroyed by first light—except for grandfather and me."

"That's a sad tale, Daynin, but I think with the booty you have at hand now, Kinloch can again be a fine place."

"Aye, and it will . . ."

Sabritha's head turned to follow Daynin's gaze. "What is it?"

"An Sgurr—I think. See it there—in the mist off the starboard side—that bloody great crag is on the island of Eigg and to the northwest should be Rr-rr-rhum! We're almost home, Sabritha!"

Dashing to the bow of the ship, Sabritha side-stepped the giant and his huge barrel of water. She scrambled out onto the bowsprit to gain a better view, then let out a whooping shout. "I see it! An island—to the north—dead ahead!"

Her shout brought Ean and Troon clambering on deck, anxious to see if Sabritha's eyes were as keen as her temper. Both men threw themselves into the rigging, climbing as fast as old bones would carry them. Sure enough, the distinctive saddle back ridge of Rhum loomed out of the mist. There could be no doubt. They were home at last!

"We've covered nearly half of the east side of the bog, Master Kruzurk. Are you *sure* that orb of yours is working?"

"Well, no, I'm not. I must admit, Ebon, I haven't the first notion how I am to know when we've found the stone. I'm a magician, not a sorcerer, and this whole scheme smacks of the dark powers."

"Mayhaps you should put the ring *on*, instead of holding it in your hand."

"You could be right," Kruzurk answered, and slipped the ring onto his finger. The ring weighed heavily on his hand but within a heartbeat, it began to pulse. "That's odd." Kruzurk took a few more steps, the ring's pulsing growing stronger with each stride. "This thing is throbbing like a sore thumb. This way, Ebon."

Hurrying along the bank, Kruzurk abruptly stopped

under a large, overhanging bog oak limb. The ring throbbed so painfully against his fingers that he thought about removing it, but didn't. Gazing into the ring's reddish stone, he saw an image of the bog. He could make out the limb under which he stood, and there, hidden in knee-deep muck, the stone lay where it had waited for generations.

"Here! It's here, Ebon. There—no more than an arm span from the bank," he said excitedly, his staff pointing to the spot.

"I see nothing but mud. Are you certain?"

"It's there, I tell you. Quickly now—mount your charger and go back to the gate. Get my pouch from Mediah and bring that gate chain. We'll use it to drag the stone from the bog, and then we're off to Kinsley Spit."

Kruzurk plopped himself down against the trunk of the great bog oak to wait. Fatigue, mixed with an obscure anxiety, had suddenly overtaken him. "Merlin," he said wistfully, "wherever you are, guide me in this quest. I know not what this stone will mean to those who seek it, yet I am compelled, somehow, to pursue it no matter what."

Everyone aboard the *Shiva* had their eyes trained on the rapidly approaching coastline of Rhum. Everyone, that is, except Brude McAlpin. Having done all he could to keep the boat afloat, he now stood watch near the mast, his mind adrift in another place. The white bearded seer's images had once again appeared to him, this time in a very different place.

What is it you're up to now, old one? he mused. *Where is the book? Why sit you under a tree, a bog your only company? Why have you appeared to me again? Who are you, that your images come to my attention? Can you hear me ask these questions or am I doomed to wander this heathen world for eternity?*

Were my crimes so great that I am never to tread the grounds of Val Henna with my kin?

"I see the landing!" Ean McKinnon cried out. "Looks like they left the wharf intact. We can scud this tub right into the bay and unload with nary a wet legging."

Daynin could see the long stone jetty his kin had built when his father was still a boy. And sure enough, the wharf still stood, its image loosing a flood of painful memories. Sabritha was so accustomed to Daynin's thoughts now that she could read him like a templar's prayer. "Aren't you happy to be home?" she asked.

"Yes, of course. It's that wharf—my father taught me to fish from it. He threw me in the water there, when I was still a pup, so's I would learn to swim. I was afraid of the water back then, but he feared nothing. Seeing it now reminds me all the more how much I miss him—how much this place misses him and all the others."

"Memories are like monk's brew, Daynin. Sometimes, the taste is sweet, and sometimes bitter. I remember my father, but I can't even tell you what he was like, except that I thought he was a god."

Daynin turned to look into Sabritha's eyes. "Duncan McKinnon *was* a god to those hereabouts. They knew him to be true to his word, a friend who never shirked a task, and fea-rrr-ed neither mahn, monk nor monarch."

Sabritha's arms locked around Daynin's mid section, her head resting under his chin. She sighed and whispered, "I tell you what, plowboy, that big fire and warm bed you promised are sounding better all the time."

"Should we slacken sail, Plumat? The *Woebringer* falls further and further behind."

"Damn it, Oswald, I don't care if we lose that tub in the mist. Your brother-in-law and his crew are as worthless as six-day-old sheep droppings. Besides, I prefer that a ship the size of the *Dionysis* should take the lead, in the event we come upon our band of brigands. Your men look like they can handle a fight. Combined with mine, we'd bring a formidable force to a battle."

"Aye, these are good men. I can attest to that," Oswald boasted. "Some of yours have seen better days, though."

Plumat turned to face the much smaller man, his eyes barely level with Oswald's helm. "Were you to see what we have been up against, you would understand, I wager."

"Bah!" Oswald scoffed. "Never seen a man nor beast that couldn't be bested with a good axe."

His thoughts wandering back to the priory grounds, Plumat answered dryly, "Yes, if it is a man facing you, and not a demon giant."

"Haharr, *giant* says he. Forty years I've sailed the ocean sea and never laid eyes on such. Sea beasts and demons this boy has bested, and lived to tell about it, indeed. What a barroom story teller you are, mate!"

Plumat's hands suddenly went up to his helmet visor, cupping the bright light to improve the view. Excitement and trepidation laced his words in equal measure as he replied, "Prepare your men for battle, Oswald—there's a ship dead ahead! And she's on fire!"

Having discarded his armor and most of his clothes, Ebon of Scone stood next to the bog's bank staring down into the murky brown muck. "I never thought my vows would include wading in a bog up to my neck."

Kruzurk tied a line to the oak and replied, "It shouldn't be that deep, Ebon. I would do this myself, but I'm not sure you would know how to operate this hoist."

"Aye, that's a fact. I've never seen such a thing. Do you actually think those wheels—or whatever they are—can lift a heavy stone?"

"They're called pulleys, and yes, with that chain, we should be able to lift something as big as a wagon. I just hope the stone is not that heavy, else your horse may not be able to carry the load."

Ebon stepped off into the muck, sinking up to his knees immediately. "Not to worry about Castor—he can haul the stone or drag it. He has the heart of a lion and the wisdom of a fox."

Kruzurk pushed the end of the chain out over the bog with his staff so that Ebon could grasp it when the time came. "Just a bit further out and you should be able to feel the stone with your foot."

Struggling against the thick surface of the bog, Ebon pushed ahead, then turned toward Kruzurk with a satisfied look on his face. "It's here," he said. "It's a forearm thick and about as wide as I am tall."

"See if you can lift it," Kruze suggested. "We need a way to get the chain around it."

Ebon's arms went down into the muck. His shoulders strained hard, but to no avail. The stone did not budge. "I can feel markings on the surface. It feels like a great wheel, open in the center."

"Aye! That fits the description I have of the Scythian Stone."

Ebon shot out of the mud and scrambled back onto the bank, looking for all the world like some crazed demon. "Scythian Stone you say! Why did you not tell me what we were after? I'll have nothing more to do with the heathen thing."

Kruzurk placed a hand on Ebon's shoulder. "Those are just legends, my friend, that's all. A stone cannot be evil or good. Men who use stones for evil deeds are to blame. The stone itself is just a symbol. And I intend to return this one to where it belongs, that it might once again be used for that which it was intended."

"I must return to Sconehaven. I'm sorry, magician. Will you give me the ring back now?"

"Wait, Ebon. Tell me about your sword. Is *it* evil?"

Ebon glanced at his armor, piled in a heap against the bog oak. "Of course not. A sword has no power until swung by its owner."

"Ah, indeed. And so it is with this stone. Don't you see? There is nothing to fear. Now, won't you help me? I cannot do it alone. Besides, this is your bog. You are the protector here. I am only a visitor, completing a quest. Please, help me. Lives depend upon it."

Looking up at the sky, Ebon threw his hands in the air and blurted out, "Which is it to be, Father? Twenty more years of solitude, or eternal damnation for touching this seditious symbol? Forgive me, Father, but I must choose freedom."

Chapter 35:

The Straining

Oswald leaned forward on the *Dionysis'* railing, straining his eyes for any hint of treachery from the burning ship. "She's a bloody snekke, Plumat! This could be a Tireean trick. They never sail alone, but in packs of three. We should steer clear and leave her to burn to the waterline, if you ask me."

"Do you see any other ships, Oswald?" Plumat growled back. "I do not. We need to know if those brigands passed this way. That snekke's crew could save us days of sailing time."

"Aye," Oswald responded, his tone decidedly surly at the thought of Tireeans close by. "She might save us time or send us into a trap. That's Tiree over there on the horizon—see it? This draco is no match for snekkes, if there's a pack of 'em waitin' in the shallows."

Plumat motioned to his men to make ready, then donned his armor and helm. Oswald's crew did likewise as the *Dionysis* sailed within a crossbow's cast of the stricken ship's stern.

"Can you make out anything, lookout?" Plumat yelled aloft.

"She's afire all right—from stem to stern," the lookout reported. "That's no ruse. They's a handful of crew bailin' water, but they're losin' the fight. That heathen craft is a goner."

"Heave to, Oswald. We'll take the longboat and board

the snekke. No sense risking your ship."

"Aye, Plumat. That's the first thing you've said that we agree on."

Plumat flung the captain a dirty look as he turned and motioned for his men to follow. "You six come with me. We'll board that wreck and see if there's a tale to be told." Turning back toward Oswald, he added, "And you keep a sharp eye out for trouble. We may be coming back with all haste if this is a trick of some kind."

Aboard the flaming snekke, Peckee knew his men had lost the valiant fight. The one sided battle against the fire was rapidly coming to an end. Black smoke enveloped the whole vessel, making it almost impossible to see anything but flames and carnage. "Damn that highland lot, for leaving us this way," Peckee swore, his fist raised in anger.

Just then, Miles Aubrecht rushed to Peckee's side, wiping the smoke, blood, and grime from his face. "A ship is here—we're saved!"

"A ship, my ass," Peckee snapped back. "You're seein' things, boy. If there *is* one, it could only be that last Tireean, come to finish us off."

"I tell you, there's a big ship out there. She's no more'n a stone's throw from the stern—and there's a longboat headed this way!"

Peckee raced toward the stern block, thinking the *Shiva* had come back for them. His heart leaped into his throat at the sight of the massive draco. "Bloody *hell,* can this day get any worse?"

The day instantly worsened. "More ships—there—on the horizon!" one of Peckee's men cried out.

A dead calm settled around the snekke, the sea suddenly as friendly as a frozen firth. "We're done for," Peckee

moaned, his fear of Saxon seafarers far exceeding that of a
scuttling ship's fire. "Over the side, boys! Swim for it if
ye've got the grip, elsewise the Saxons will have you
swinging from a yardarm before supper."

The *Pandora* swayed heavily against her anchor rope, an
easterly breeze trying its best to push her from her Kinsley
Spit anchorage back out into the blue water that stretched
all the way to Rhum. Patience and time were both running
short. The ship's crew had not originally bargained for such
a long stay away from their home port.

"We'll give them damned pilgrims 'til the evening tide
changes, then we're headin' back to Loch Linnhe, with or
without them," Captain Ames declared.

Eigh stepped forward, pushing his much larger nephew
aside. "Mucky boy must not have made our plans clear
enough for ye, cap'n. We'll be waitin' 'til the pilgrims return,
elsewise ain't none of us gonna get paid for this little adventure. Now, what part of that do ye not comprrr-eee-hhhend?"

Ames glowered at his strange little tormentor, glad that
Eigh had his giant bird tethered to its perch, for once. "We
don't even know if he has the plum to pay us, now do we,
old man?"

"*Old* mahn, is it?" Eigh snapped.

Muck interrupted his uncle just in time to stave off a
bloodletting. "Ahh see 'em! Comin' down the embank-
ment—ther-r-re—to the left of that tall oak. See 'em?
They's a horsemahn with 'em and he's draggin' somethin'
behind his animal. The magician musta found what he was
lookin' for, sure enough!"

Brude McAlpin was the first to leap onto the aging stone
wharf, followed quickly by Ean McKinnon and Sabritha.

Daynin tossed the mooring lines to his grandfather, making the *Shiva* fast, then helped Simon Troon over the side. A light rain fell all around them, giving the ghostly quiet an even more sinister feel.

The craggy slopes of Askival loomed over the landing, its peak shrouded in an ever present wisp of cloud from which, it was said, spirits of long dead highlanders looked down on Rhum's human inhabitants. In the distance, the longing cry of a sparrowhawk rippled along the cliff face, adding its baleful tone to the less than friendly atmosphere.

"Good god, Daynin," Sabritha whispered, "I've seen dungeons that offered more warmth than this place."

"This is Rrr-rhum's only sheltered landing, Sabritha. The other side of the island, where Kinloch stands, faces the ocean and all its furies. We will trek through the Kuillins, then down the other side to Standguard Bridge. You will see the best of Rrr-rhum from there."

Sabritha pulled her cloak tightly against the dampness. "I hope these Kuillins have a warm fire and some stew in a pot. I'm so cold my goose bumps are bartering for blankets."

Ean and Troon both laughed aloud. "*Och,* woman—the Kuillins are these mountains, not some wayside tavern," Ean said. "The Norse called 'em that because so many of their kind perished in the takin' o' this island."

"Oh, that's just what I wanted to hear. So, there's no place to stay for the night?"

Daynin scanned the slopes of Askival, turning slowly toward Rhum's island neighbor of Eigg, several leagues to the southeast. "As far as we know, there's been no one on Rhum since Kinloch fell. Most people are afraid of this place now, and well they should be. The Caledonians slaughtered every living thing, including the red deer, the otter, and even the seals."

"*Seals?* What the deuce are they?"

Troon answered, "Think of a slug, girrrl, only much bigger. The size of a mahn, say, and that swims like a fish."

"You'll see, Sabritha. I'll wager the seals have returned to the island by now," Daynin added.

Turning to follow Ean's lead up the mountain pathway, Sabritha tossed a sarcastic, "Oh, I do hope so," over her shoulder to Troon.

Slinging a cargo net filled with the Blackgloom Bounty, books, and extra weapons over his shoulder, Brude clanked off after Troon, bringing up the rear of the column. Several strides up the slope, Daynin turned to look back down at the *Shiva*, his mind suddenly focused on Kruzurk Makshare. *We made it, Booze—er, Kruze. Thanks to you, I now have the wealth to rebuild this place and once again make it home. Too bad you cannae be part of that.*

Miles Aubrecht had stripped to his leathers, determined to make the distant shoreline any way he could. He took a deep breath, preparing himself for the plunge into the icy waters. An instant before his leap, a familiar voice wafted through the smoke, staying him on the ship's prow.

"Row, damn ya!" Plumat swore at the top of his voice. "Those blaggards are jumping ship like a pack of rats. If we don't catch at least one of 'em, you'll all pay with a lashing!"

"Plumat? Geile Plumat—is that you, m'lord?" Miles asked.

Dense black smoke obscured all but the lower portion of the snekke's hull, making recognition nearly impossible. "What the hell? Who is that? Who calls me?" Plumat cried out in reply.

" 'Tis I, your lordship! Your squire, Miles Aubrecht!"

The heat from the flaming snekke was so intense, they

dared not row any closer in the longboat. "Heave to, men!" Plumat ordered. "Jump for it, Miles! We're here on the larboard quarter. Swim for it, boy, as we can come no closer."

Miles took one last look around and seeing no one, leapt into the dark waters. He paddled like a dog for what seemed an eternity before someone grabbed his tunic from above. "Gotcha!" Fulchere the Bowman bellowed. With help from the other Saxons, Fulchere dragged the hapless squire aboard the longboat.

"What the bloody hell are you doing *here*, Miles?" Plumat growled. "We thought you were dead or lost in the highlands."

The squire heaved a mouthful of seawater, then, panting heavily, blurted out his story. "Captured—m'lord—my horse—threw me—priory . . ."

Impatient to get on with the more important details, Plumat snapped back, "Yes, yes, we know all that. I assumed they cut your throat and left you for the wolves. How did you escape? And how the *devil* did you wind up aboard a Tireean snekke?"

Miles pushed himself to an upright position, his mind whirling with details about his rescuers—and now friends— that he dared not divulge. "They, uhh—they *sold* me to these pirates. They were taking me to uhh, some island to uhh, be a court jester—but the ship caught fire in a battle."

The longboat broke out in a boisterous melee of laughter and back slapping at that comment. "Quiet, you lot!" Plumat ordered. "What of the boy? Where is he? And where is my treasure?"

To buy some time, Miles pretended to shake water from his ears. "Treasure, m'lord? I know nothing of that. I was, uhh, blindfolded much of the time—and—and, slung over a horse's rump."

Fulchere spoke up just then. "You lie, boy! Last time we saw you, you was high-tailing it with that lot in the wagon—them what was throwin' out the treasure."

Plumat grimaced at the very mention of that debacle. "Don't remind me how stupid you are, Fulchere. It was you who allowed the brigands to escape in the first place."

Miles took the opportunity to throw himself on Plumat's mercy. "I'm sorry, m'lord. Please forgive me. Please give me another chance—I, I promise I will do better this time."

"Settle down, boy. You'd think we were going to throw you back into the sea. You're my squire, so act like it and stop the sniveling. Now tell me about the boat and what happened to the others. Surely you must have heard them say something about where they were going."

"If you cannot keep that bloody charger from kicking at my men, I'll have to toss 'im in the sea," Captain Ames stated.

Kruzurk waded into the fray, concerned that Ebon of Scone might take matters into his own hand, accustomed as he was to dealing with people in a somewhat less verbal manner. "Hold, captain. May I offer a compromise? Perhaps if we tied Castor to the mast and then hobbled his hind legs—would that suffice for now? After all, we only have a few leagues to travel, and we desperately need Ebon's charger to move the stone."

"That's another thing," Ames said. "We never bargained to haul goods or animals. Not to mention more passengers."

Kruzurk produced three gold Byzantines from his purse, part of the spoils from Blackgloom. He put his arm around the captain and turned him to face out to sea, that no one aboard could observe the transaction. "Will these suffice to cover the extra baggage?"

Ames turned a rosy shade of red, having never seen such magnificent coins before. "Bloody hell, magician, you can *buy* a boat for that kind of plum."

Dropping the coins into the captain's outstretched palm, Kruzurk replied, "Ah, indeed. But then we would not have had your excellent captaincy to guide us, now would we?" A wink sealed the deal, and Ames turned about to shout his orders.

"Nicely done, m'lord," Mediah whispered. "I still can't believe how easily we got that stone aboard."

"The right kind of leverage can move mountains, Mediah," Kruze answered. "I just hope it's as easy to un-load as it was to load, once we reach Rhum."

By the time Ean and the others neared the top of the steep, winding trail leading over Askival's western flank, all were bordering on exhaustion. But with dusk rapidly approaching, the intrepid group had no choice but to forge ahead in hopes of reaching Kinloch Keep.

"How—much—further?" Sabritha managed to gasp out.

Trailing behind her, Daynin answered, "A league and a half, maybe. Rhum is only three leagues from end to end and side to side. It just seems much longer, climbing this side of Askival."

"Then the trail is all downhill on the other side?"

"Yes, Sabritha. But slippery and treacherous if you're not familiar with the path. Grandfather knows every false trail, so we won't have any problem, but strangers can walk right off a cliff and never see it coming."

"Remind me not to go wandering off, then," she retorted.

Ever since the landing, Brude had said nothing. His thoughts revolved around the white haired one whose "im-ages" came and went as time passed. *Vendernochla doch fennakuth mahn Cruithni?* he prayed over and over, asking in the ancient Pictish dialect for the stranger in his visions to reveal himself. Despite hearing no answers, Brude knew that the visions were real, that the robed one was on his way and that with him he carried the answers to all of Brude's questions.

"He dinnae talk much, does he?" Troon whispered loud enough for Ean to hear him.

Several strides ahead, Ean turned sideways and replied, "Aye, and it's a good thing. That big bugger-rrr gives me the shiver-rrs. I'd lead 'im off one of these cliffs, if ah didn't think he'd come back and cut me up fer-rrr fish bait."

Troon stifled a laugh, hurrying along to keep up with Ean the best he could on his bad leg. "Ya never apologized for tossin' me over the side o' that boat, Ean McKinnon. Nor have ya mentioned the plum yer gonna owe me for the weapons we've brung along."

Never looking back, Ean replied, "Weapons is it? Well, then I rr-reckon we're even for the amount of gold I had to pay to keep you aboard that scow. 'Twas a hefty sum fer an old used up bowman."

"Used up, is it? Well, then ya must be forgettin' them ten heathens I smote in the battle, eh?"

Before he could reply, Ean abruptly stopped ahead. Even in the growing darkness, he could make out the distinctive reddish walls outlined against the glow of the sea beyond. "Saints of Argyle," he said, wistfully. "Kinloch still stands!"

Safely back on board the *Dionysis*, Plumat pressed his inquisition of the squire, asking all manner of questions designed to catch the boy in a lie. As yet, Miles had held up under the blistering verbal onslaught.

"I tell you, master," Miles went on, "they are in league

with the pirates. They made a deal for safe passage to Rhum and threw me into the bargain. Then a fight broke out and our ship was set ablaze by an old highlander firing flaming arrows into the rigging."

Satisfied, at least for the moment, that the squire's tale held true, Plumat left the boy in the fo'c'sle and climbed back on deck. "Oswald, can we run this 'Temptress' at night, or should we go around it?"

Concerned both for his ship and the potential loss of the promised treasure, Oswald replied, "If it means booty, we can go straight through. To go around adds another ten to twenty leagues, and that's only if good weather holds. Rhum is the wettest island in the Hebrides and known for its stormy nature. The *Woebringer* will be in serious trouble in rough seas, as will the *Witch*, bein' smaller than us. Half a day's sailing could make or break us."

Plumat cast a worried eye at the other two ships. The *Witch* appeared sturdy enough, having caught up with them at the fire ship, but Ranulf's tub still lagged far behind. "We may yet need the *Woebringer* and her crew. How far is it to Rhum?"

"Damned if I know for sure," Oswald answered. "It's somewhere north of Coll, but I've never been there. Could be half a day's sailing or several days, depending on the wind."

His patience once again tested by unanswered questions, Plumat turned to Oswald and said grimly, "Heave to and wait for the *Woebringer* to catch up. Then we'll run the Temptress as a fleet of three. If there's Tireeans, a show of force from us may give 'em pause to attack."

Tired of pacing the deck waiting for the wind to favor them, Mediah finally sat down near the bow next to

Kruzurk Makshare. "M'lord, you've seemed quite pensive this evening. What troubles you?"

"I don't know, Mediah. This delay waiting for the wind to change—it's maddening when time is of the essence. I felt certain we would make landfall at Rhum by morning. Now that seems unlikely. Daynin is in great danger, but here we sit, bobbing about like a mass of seaweed. If we're too late, the consequences will be dire, not only for Daynin, but for us as well. And there is no turning back."

"Are you quite certain that is all that troubles you?" the Greek pressed.

"You are coming to know me all too well, my friend. It's the Stone. I know not what we are to do with it, nor even if we should do *anything* with it. For eons, that Stone has been the source of terrible legends, and now we have it in our hands. I'm not used to that kind of responsibility. In fact, I'm tempted to roll it over the side, where it will never be seen again."

"Do you not think those who controlled the Stone before could have done that, if they wished? Why leave it in a bog where it could easily be retrieved if it is truly evil as legend says? And what of Perazelzeus and his minions? Were they not told for ages that someone would come to them who was meant to put the Stone in its rightful place?"

"All good points, Mediah, yet it troubles me still, the thought that we could be causing some great rift in the world by bringing the Stone to light." Kruzurk pushed himself to his feet and stretched his arms wide like an eagle in flight. Much to his surprise, his robe suddenly filled with a cool land breeze. "Wind! The wind has shifted!"

Emerging from below decks, Captain Ames grunted, "Aye, I felt it from below. Now we can head west. Exactly where is it you want to land on that bloody rock, magician?"

"Land? Uh, captain, I have never been to Rhum. Have we a host of choices?"

Ames trudged off toward the stern block, mumbling aloud, "Bloody pilgrims. Always wantin' to go somewhere, yet never knowin' where." Kicking the backsides of his sleeping crew as he stepped over them, Ames took the tiller from his mate and shouted, "All hands, make sail! Nor-nor-west it is and lively now!"

Dusk rapidly enclosed Daynin's intrepid group. A cold rain added to their misery and made the risk of a fatal fall all the more real the longer they trudged down the slippery slopes of Askival.

"I'd pay a silver talen for one bloody lantern," Troon groaned.

"Save yer coin, Troon," Ean replied. "We've but a wee strrr-etch of this trail left afore we reach the brrr-idge. Then it's only a furlong to the gates of Kinloch. That is, if the brrr-idge is in one piece."

"And if it's not?" Sabritha hissed.

Ean stopped in his tracks and turned to face the woman. "Does nothing positive ever pass those bleedin' lips, woman? Ya've done nothin' but grouse from the first moment I laid eyes on ya."

Once again, Daynin stepped in. "Grandfather, Sabritha had little choice in joining this quest. She's tried to make the best of a bad situation. With a neck stretching her only other choice, I think she has some right to complain. After all, Rhum is not exactly Middlesex."

Throwing one arm behind him as if waving off an angry wasp, Ean moved on. He tossed a disdainful, "Good thing that wench is *your* problem, boy," over his shoulder.

The argument again brought home to Brude the awful

realization that he had no family, and never would again. His thoughts wandered back to the lochs, of scenes he'd not witnessed in hundreds of years, yet he saw so clearly at that moment he felt almost alive. Unfortunately, Ean's shout from ahead brought him quickly back to reality.

"Och!" the old man clucked. "The bridge looks ta be in one piece. We've made it, boy—we're home!"

Leaving Brude behind, Daynin and the others rushed forward to a wide spot in the trail next to Ean. Before them lay Standguard Bridge, its narrow confines stretching across a deep tidal chasm known as "the Willies".

Obviously not wanting to bring on another argument, Sabritha leaned close to Daynin's ear and whispered, "Looks rickety to me."

"Do you think it's safe, grandfather?" Daynin asked, more to allay his woman's fears than from any real concern.

"I guess we'll find out soon enough, eh, boy? I'll go across first and if I end up feedin' the fishes, then the rrr-est of you can circle 'round the other way."

One look at that bridge sent Brude's senses reeling. *Penochla doth ben fayler nost heygan gris!* his Cruithni roots screamed from some dark corner of lost memories. *I've seen this awful place before!* Although he'd felt absolutely no fear of anyone or anything since his resurrection from the tomb, Brude now froze in abject terror. He could *see* the bodies falling into the swirling waters below, hear the screams of his kin and feel the anguish in their hearts. *This is the place! Weggens Braga—where the great horn of Oengus was lost forever!*

Plumat paced the deck of the *Dionysis* like a jester without a jest. Even with the hint of moonlight overhead, the outline of the Temptress could only be judged by the sound of breakers crashing against her shorelines—first to starboard, then to port. And nowhere was the *Woebringer* to be seen.

"Send the *Witch* in first, captain. If there's trouble, she can turn about and warn us."

"Aye," Oswald agreed. "The *Witch* can maneuver better than us, and she's a shallower draft. I just wish the *Woebringer* had caught up before we try to run the channel. I fear the Tireeans will catch 'er afore first light, and that'll be the end of her for sure."

"We can't wait all night," Plumat growled. "I don't like leaving her behind, but this weather could turn on us anytime and then we'll never get to Rhum."

At that instant, the lookout came scurrying down the ratlines from his lofty perch. Not wanting to give away their position, he whispered, "Cap'n, they's a string o' lights to the sou-west. Three or four at least—likely bow lanterns. One is way ahead of t'others, but they're movin' mighty fast."

"Damn!" Oswald swore, instantly echoed by Plumat. "Signal the *Witch* to turn about—we've a fight on the way. All hands, to arms!"

The wind coming off the Scotian coast grew and faded alternately, as if a giant beast huffed and puffed from the mainland. The *Pandora* raced along for a while, then suddenly slackened to little more than rowing speed.

"Is it always like this out here?" Kruzurk asked of Captain Ames, frustrated.

"Aye. The Hebrides winds are like highland horses—ya can't trust 'em any further than you can ride 'em. We'll be lucky to make Rhum by first light at this rate."

Kruzurk turned away from the captain and strolled toward the bow of the ship. His mind would not allow sleep, so worried was he that Daynin and Sabritha had already met with a foul fate, and all because of him. He cast his eyes to the heavens and the myriad of stars winking through the wispy clouds above. A sliver of moonlight alternately lit the coastline behind them, its crescent reminding him of the symbols on Merlin's cloak.

What am I supposed to do, Merlin? Did you send me here to retrieve the Stone? Or was the destruction of the Seed all that you intended? Are these other events merely consequence? I cannot ignore my part in Daynin's plight, especially if it ends badly for him.

"Bloody cold out on this blue water, eh, pilgrim?" Eigh asked, his stealthy approach having gone unnoticed by the magician.

Kruzurk jumped slightly. "Uh, yes. Damp, too—with that breeze."

Eigh stretched to the limits of his tiptoes to spit with the wind and said, "We should be able to see the Kuillins afore long. By first light, for sure. Can ya see that dark shape, way out there to larboard? That would be Eigg, the island from which mah kin arose many a generation ago."

"Yes, I see it. The place for which you were named, I assume. But what are these Kuillins?"

"Mountains, my boy. A bloody great rrrr-idge of 'em what runs the length of Rrr-hum. Likely the cap'n will be scudding to the northeast coast to drop us off. We'll have to trek 'round the Kuillins the long way to reach Kinloch Keep. I've never been there, but Mucky says it's on the north coast, facing the sea."

"Why can't the captain sail straight to Kinloch?" Kruzurk asked. "Hauling that Stone over mountain roads without a wagon will not be easy."

"Rrr-oads, is it?" Eigh scoffed. "I wouldn't count on

havin' a road to travel, pilgrim. We'll be lucky if they's even a goat path to follow. I've heard the north coast of Rrrr-rhum is bloody treacherous—a haunt for pirates and sea witches. No doubt Ames knows that, too. Not likely he'll risk that route—leastwise, not in this slip of a boat."

A sudden freshening breeze filled the *Pandora*'s mainsail, snapping its braces taut as a dozen hangman's ropes. The ship lurched forward in a burst of speed, splicing through the waves and throwing salt spray high onto the deck.

"Now that's more like it!" Kruzurk crowed.

"Stand to those lines, boys!" came the captain's cry. "We've a hard blow comin'!"

With most of the night spent traversing the winding, seemingly invisible trail from Standguard Bridge, Daynin and his friends were more than delighted when they finally broke out of the forest onto the flat plain that stretched to the outer battlements of Kinloch Keep. Low on the horizon, a last glimmer of moonlight outlined the craggy crenellations running the length of Kinloch's walls. To strangers, the keep's battlements must have seemed extremely tall and foreboding—as indeed they were.

Without thinking, Sabritha let out another of her caustic comments. "So—this is what you people call home, eh?"

Ean turned to hush her, but Daynin had already done so with both a gesture and a determined look. "We need to be very quiet," he whispered. "There could be others lurking about."

Being the smallest in the group, Troon offered to go ahead, that he might scout the gate for any sign of trouble. Ean waved him forward, his bow at the ready. "Mind you well, Simon. I dinnae have time to pull another bolt from yer old Irish arse."

Daynin stepped up to accompany Troon, but his grandfather's outstretched bow stopped him in his tracks. "Wait 'ere, boy. And keep that wench of yours quiet. Watch for mah signal to come along, then be damned quick about crrrr-ossing this open grrrr-ound. We've no way to know who or what may be in the keep."

Despite his injured thigh and his age, Troon managed to cross the open ground with surprising speed. A stone's throw from Kinloch's first barbican, he dropped down behind a low hedge to observe the moat and drawbridge. Nothing stirred.

Troon waved his bow toward Ean, who waved his in turn to the rest of the troop, prompting them all to move toward the keep. Ean and Troon dashed across the open drawbridge first, quickly taking positions inside the gate. Trailing behind them, Brude McAlpin backed his way to the keep, ever watchful for any signs of attack from the rear.

Safely inside the first barbican, Ean took one look at his winded old friend and motioned for Daynin to scout ahead instead of Troon. "If the Scurrr-ry brrr-idge is down, give us a wave, boy. If it's up, get back here quick and we'll go rrr-ound to the east and see if the Seawall gate is open."

"Aye, grrr-andfather," Daynin replied. A fleeting look back at Sabritha's tired, anxious expression gave the boy renewed energy.

With daybreak already showing its first pinkish rays behind Askival, the young highlander knew he had to hurry. Even though he'd not been there for many years, Daynin remembered that being caught out in the open in the midst of Kinloch's formidable defensive lines was not an option.

Three distinct bands of outer works encircled the main keep, which stood upon a precipitous cliff jutting out into the sea. Assailable from the land only, each successive line of Kinloch's battlements got progressively taller, tighter, and trickier to attack. Each wall had its own moat, fed by seawater and protected by steep berms, slippery sandstone surfaces, and a host of other less obvious protective elements. In all of Kinloch's history, it had only fallen once, and then only to a deceit unthought in the highlands.

Visions of that horrific event must have clouded Daynin's mind on his way toward the second barbican, for he failed to notice the glimmer of a fine trip line stretched across the path. Although his attention was fixed on the wall ahead, his instincts screamed caution and he ducked. *Thhhwaannng,* a crossbow snapped, its echo ringing time and again against the barbican's walls. The bolt shot across the open ground, clinking against a distant rock.

Daynin froze, for in his exposed position sprawled across the path, he could do little else. He quickly scanned the tops of the wall, assuming the shot had come from there or perhaps the tower, but nothing showed—no movement, no lights—nothing. He shifted around to look back toward the first gate, hoping his grandfather would come to help, but realized they could not see him—at least not while he hugged the ground.

The idea of an arrow heading straight for his exposed backside gave Daynin's legs newfound strength. In a flash, he was up and running for his life, zigzagging all the way back to the first wall. Almost spent by the time he reached the others, he let out a loud whisper, "Someone—fired—at me!"

Catching the boy in mid stride, Ean dragged him to the ground while motioning for the others to get down. "I was afraid of this," Ean growled, his voice low and determined. "Some jackmonger has taken over Kinloch. Now we'll have to fight for it."

★ ★ ★ ★ ★

Perhaps it was the sudden change in weather, or the sight of two massive dracos bearing down out of the dark, but the Tireeans racing after the *Woebringer* suddenly turned hard to port, their lights disappearing in the gloom. Cheers went up aboard all three ships as Plumat's rescue arrived just in time.

"Signal her to fall in behind us, captain," Plumat snapped, his nerves raw from too much stress and too little rest. "Slow down enough for Ranulf's crew to stay up with us. Then put your carpenters to work building a siege tower and some ladders from the spare rigging. The tower should be at least twelve cubits tall. Build it in sections so we can assemble it on the beach once we get to Rhum. We may have need of one, and I do not want to waste time building it later."

Looking up at the strained rigging, Oswald replied, "As you wish, Plumat. I'll send the *Witch* on through the Temptress whilst the *Woebringer* catches up to us. If this wind holds, we can make a good run for Rhum. Depending on the distance, we could be there before nightfall tonight."

Plumat slipped out of his armor, dropping his helmet on the deck with a hollow clank. Glad to have the extra weight off his shoulders, he stretched and said, "Excellent. I'm going below for some sleep. And Oswald—have your smithy sharpen all the weapons."

"You expecting trouble, Plumat?" Oswald pressed.

"More trouble than you can even imagine, captain." Visions of the giant lacing his memory, Plumat added, "Very large trouble."

Chapter 36:

The Landings

"Heave! Heave!" Captain Ames shouted, glad to finally be rid of his strange passengers and their even stranger cargo. The sling Kruzurk had designed for the Scythian Stone worked remarkably well for Ebon's charger, though Castor seemed none too happy with his "flight" from the *Pandora*'s deck to the beach below.

"Steady, boy," Ebon said, smoothing the animal's back while Mediah untied the sling.

Eigh and Muck stood back, watching the process with something approaching amazement. "I wouldnae believed it, if'n I had nae seen it with mah own eyes," Muck avowed.

"Leverage, Muck—that's all," Kruzurk professed. "The same kind of leverage the Egyptians used to build the pyramids."

"The who?" Eigh asked.

"A great race of builders," Olghar Fergum answered, his dog Thor nipping playfully at Castor's enormous hooves.

Mediah began re-orienting the heavy rope sling so that Castor could tow the Stone on its makeshift sled. "This rig should work well, Kruzurk—even on these mountain tracks."

"Let's hope so, Mediah. We've no time to waste." Turning to scan the horizon, the magician saw the sun was just breaking out from behind the peaks on the Scotian mainland, many leagues to the east. Turning to the west, he could see only the dark slopes of Askival clearly against the pinkish sky. The treacherous path to Kinloch remained a mystery, along with the fate of Daynin and Sabritha.

"We must get moving." Tossing a small bag of silver up to Captain Ames, Kruzurk asked, "If you could return to this spot in a fortnight, captain, I might be able to match that purse with another for transport back to Loch Linnhe."

"No promises, pilgrim. But I'll do what I can. Good luck to ya!"

After laying low for what seemed like an eternity, Ean finally pushed himself to a squatting position. "We've got to make a dash for the gate afore the daylight makes us plum pigeons. Could ya tell if the drrr-rawbridge is down, Daynin?"

"Yes, it's open, grandfather. But if there are archers on those walls, we don't stand a chance of making the gate."

"Aye, boy. That's a fact. But I have a feeling that if the keep had troops in it, they'd be on us by now. There's only one way to find out, and time's a wastin'. Troon, you get to high ground—there on the left, so's you can cover us with your bow. Meanwhile, I'll beat it toward the gate. Daynin—you stay behind me. If I'm hit, you keep on for the gate."

Frustrated both from fatigue and the dangerous plan, Sabritha spoke up. "Why not let this big bugger go first? He's taken many a bolt in that armor so far, and never missed a step."

"HaaaaaHaaarr," Brude bellowed. "Now that's a plan worth its salt, wench!"

Ean, almost growling from having a woman question his orders, shot back, "Because woman, if it's mah kin on that wall, warr-rr will brrr-eak out soon as they see this creature coming toward 'em. If they see mah tarrrr-tan, we'll be welcomed with hot ale instead of a hail of arrows."

Satisfied with Ean's reasoning, Sabritha turned to Brude to settle him back down. "Best wait your turn, you big blaggard. The old man seems to know what he's doing."

The long shadows of daybreak outlined the three men as they broke for the second barbican. Troon found his spot first and set up a brace of arrows to cover Ean and Daynin. The elder McKinnon surprised his grandson, both with his speed and agility in the race toward the drawbridge.

An eerie silence was all that greeted them in their hurried approach until someone shouted from the battlements, "Who e're the hell you are, by God you're on McKlennan land and you'd best stop or face the consequences!"

Ean dropped to the ground with Daynin right behind him. "That voice sounds familiar, don't it, boy?"

"No, but it's definitely not Saxon. You think it's one of our people, grandfather?"

"Cannae say, boy. No one's called this McKlennan land since my grandfather Ethren married into their clan. It's been a McKinnon keep ever since. Give 'em a shout back. Your voice should throw 'em off, what with that bloody Anglish tilt it has to it now."

Daynin's brow wrinkled at that accusation, but he shouted anyway. "Hold your fire, whoever you are! We are McKinnons, come to reclaim our keep."

Several long moments of silence passed before the reply came. "Ah can tell a Saxon pup when ah hears one, y'Anglish puke. And there ain't been no McKinnons here for many a year. They all got croaked by them dog-eatin' Caledonians."

Ean waved for Daynin to stay silent. "I *do* know that voice. It sounds like old Wick McKlennan, but surely he must be dead by now. He was an old mahn when your pap was still a pup. Tell 'im he's a fisherman's fart soaked in seawater."

Daynin decided to throw caution aside and stood up, that he might be heard better. "Is that you, Wick McKlennan? Ean McKinnon says you're worthless as a fisherman's fart soaked in salt water!"

"Hahah!" came a low rolling laugh from behind the walls. "You must be McKinnons—no one knows that story but 'Evil' Mac McKinnon. Come forward, cherub, that these old eyes can spy you better. Mind ya, now—I've a dozen bowmen with yer head as a target, so nuthin' funny, eh?"

Daynin stepped forward, only to be stopped in his tracks by Ean's bow outstretched in front of him. "Take this, boy—for your bona fides." Ean slipped his *sgian du* from its hiding place and flipped it to the boy. "Mind ya, lad, he should know the pattern on the blade, if it's Wick. If he don't, you get yourself back here strrr-aightaway, and be damned careful with mah blade."

The small, heavy knife bore the worn but still distinct crest of the Regents of Rhum, Daynin's blood kin from the dark times before the Vikings and the Romans. He had never before been allowed to touch his grandfather's most prized possession. The importance of the moment did not escape him. "Aye, grandfather," he answered.

A dozen strides from the drawbridge, Daynin noticed that a very short, stocky man had taken up a station square in the middle of the gate opening. Though it was not yet full daylight, he could make out the orange and green of the McKlennan clan tartan. As he approached, the man's gnarled features grew clearer.

"Ahm Daynin McKinnon. Mah father was Duncan McKinnon and mah grrr-andfather is Ean . . ."

"Yes, yes," the diminutive figure barked impatiently. "Do you think me daft, boy? I may be as old as these walls, but I've not lost mah memory. Now, you best be stoppin' rrrr-ight therrrre, whilst I ask you a few questions."

Daynin did as he was told, stopping just short of the wall end of the drawbridge. A brief scan of the battlements revealed nothing. No bowmen, no lights from the arrow slits in the tower—nothing but his kinsman standing there like a troll from some clan fairytale.

"You said your grandfather is Ean McKinnon. I take it that old fish eater is still alive, then, is he not?"

"Aye, he is. Alive and well. He sends his greetings."

"Grrr-eetings, is it? I'll cuff 'is ears for bein' impolite, sendin' someone else to grrr-eet me in his stead. Is he with you, boy—here at Kinloch?"

"Yes, he's with me, along with some others. He's back there—no doubt with his bow drawn on you at this very moment, just in case there's treachery."

"Treachery, aye. Been a host o' that since he last supped in these walls, wager that. So, you are Duncan's boy, eh? And how is he doin' these days? Still sailin' the ocean sea?"

"I think you know he was killed here, along with the rest of mah clan. I've come to rrr-reclaim what's mine, and rebuild the keep."

"Oh well, yer high and mighty lordship! Why didn't ya just say so right away, and I woulda been layin' out the good silver for yer arrival."

Daynin's patience was wearing thin, both from the long trek and the old man's attempts to trip him up. He walked straight at Wick, his back stiffened and a new tone in his voice. "Enough of this banter, Wick McKlennan. I have my bona fides. We've come a long way and we've much to do."

Wick's eyes swept from the ground up to Daynin's face

when the boy finally stopped, the sock knife thrust forward in his palm. "Damn, boy, you're a tall one for a McKinnon. But you've got yer father's eyes. And your mother's grrr-it, for sure."

"Grandfather bade me show you this, that you might prove who you are. Do you recognize the design?"

"Bloody hell, boy. That's the Regent's crrr-est on that blade. Any fool from around here would know that. Now wave yer men on in. We've a lot to talk about and this ain't a good place to parlay."

Though it had been slow sailing all night, with the damaged *Woebringer* in her wake, the *Dionysis* at last broke out of a light fog into a new day dawning. Brilliantly lit up on the northern horizon, Askival's crown lay shrouded in cloud and mist, looking for all the world like some mislaid minstrel's cap.

"Rhum!" the lookout bellowed. "Three points ta larrrr-board."

Plumat's head snapped to the left, his hands forming a cup over his eyes. "Good work, Oswald. Now we've some sport at hand. Get the men ready for landing, and hail Ranulf to follow us in but stay aboard his ship to back us up in case there's trouble ashore."

"As you wish, Plumat. I'll send the *Witch* in first, to spy us a landing. That bloody island looks to be sheer cliff walls from here. We may have to stand off the beach a good distance with the *Dionysis*. She's two cubits deeper draft than the *Witch* or the *Woebringer*."

"I don't care how you manage it, Oswald, just get us ashore. If there's no landing, we'll use the longboats. And I want half your crew as levies—is that clear?"

Oswald turned the tiller block over to his mate, that he

might parlay with Plumat a little closer than half a ship's length. He strode into the Saxon's space with the defiance of a small bull, ready for discourse or recourse, whichever came first.

"Now you look 'ere, Saxon—you might be the Duke's almighty servant in this Scotian sortie, but by God, this crew belongs to me! They'll not be going ashore as your 'levies' as you put it, 'cause I know what that means. You'll send them in as arrow quarry whilst your men go on their merry way. Well, I ain't havin' it. They'll go ashore when I say so, and not before. And they'll be under my command, not yours—is that clear?"

A quick survey of the crew, most of whom were listening to Oswald's tirade, told Plumat he was once again in no position to demand anything. "Of course they will be under your command. I meant for them to carry the siege equipment—that's all. My men will do the fighting, if there's any to be done. We'll need your men to sail us back to Anglia, once we get this boy and his treasure."

Plumat's last word set the crew to murmuring from stem to stern. Apparently the Blackgloom Bounty had not been mentioned in their ranks before.

Oswald stepped closer to the Saxon and in a low breath, snarled, "Damn it, Plumat. Now you've let the cat outta the kettle. We may have a mutiny on our hands, thanks to that 'treasure' remark."

"Not to worry, Oswald. There's treasure aplenty. I've seen some of it with my own eyes. We could pay a hundred more like these men and still be rich as lords when we get back to Carlisle."

"Ahh, then you've no plans to turn the booty over to the Duke, eh?"

"With the bounty I'm told that boy took from the

Blackgloom Keep, I may *be* the Duke when this is over. And you can buy a fleet of dracos for yourself! Now, are you with me?"

"Aye—for the bounty—I'm with you!"

The beach trail quickly played out, branching off into two overgrown paths leading straight up the north slopes of Askival. Muck had gone ahead to scout the best track while the rest of Kruzurk's group rested for the arduous climb facing them.

Mediah stood scanning Askival's awesome features. "I fear the horse may not be able to handle the trek, Kruze. That sled is unwieldy on sand—it may be impossible to climb with it."

"Yes, I know, Mediah. And it will make our journey much longer. We may have to leave it here for now. Daynin's plight is my immediate concern. Disposition of the Scythian Stone may have to wait."

"Master," Olghar intervened, "are we anywhere near a cave?"

"A cave? Not that I know about, Olghar. Why do you ask?"

"There is something I must find. Something the monks told me about back at Drimnin. It is very important, should you see one on our journey."

"Muck is coming!" Eigh crowed, excitedly. Talisman let out a shriek to echo Eigh's voice, his enormous wings flapping against the restraints that held him to his perch pole.

Out of breath from the rapid descent, Muck rushed into the group's midst. "The path to the right is verrr-ah steep, but much easier than the left one. Ah went up as far as the left one would allow, and could see no end to it. It appearrr-s to go straight off a bloody cliff, though ah've no way to tell for sure. I don't know if the horse can handle either path, with that big load behind 'im."

Ebon of Scone spoke up to defend Castor. "He can handle it. We're not leaving him behind."

Kruzurk reached out to put a hand on Ebon's shoulder. "We'll take Castor. We just won't take the Stone."

A round of agreement spread through the group while Mediah untied the Stone's rigging. "I'll cut some of the brush and cover the Stone. No need to leave it out in the open."

"Good idea," Kruzurk agreed. "I think the rest of us should move on. Muck, have you any idea how far Kinloch Keep is from here?"

Muck swept the shiny pot from his head and wiped his brow. "Ah cannae say for certain. Mayhaps three or four leagues, but it may be very tough going. It could take us most of the day to get there." He tossed his head toward Olghar, not wanting to voice aloud what had already become obvious.

Kruzurk didn't have the heart to leave the blind priest behind, especially in such a desolate place. "Let's move on. Perhaps we'll find a cave for Olghar on the way."

"Ahh, that would be good, master," Olghar replied. Though blind, he was no doubt keenly aware of the situation they were in, and knew he would slow them down. "Mayhaps, if we find a cave, you could build me a fire and I could stay there whilst you go on to Kinloch."

"If that is what you wish," Kruzurk answered, glad that he didn't have to force the issue.

Brief introductions having been made inside the second barbican, Daynin's group marched in single file behind Wick McKlennan. They had been warned of a host of traps and trip wires he had spent years rigging in Kinloch's outer defenses, one of which they had already seen demonstrated.

"Mind yer heads," Wick warned. Ducking under the half raised portcullis on the main keep's gate, Wick waited while the others passed by, then began cranking the gate closed. From a single wheel counterbalanced by a giant lodestone, the drawbridge came up, the portcullis came down and the entrance to Kinloch was sealed.

In passing, Daynin asked, "Are you expecting trouble?"

"Nae, laddy. Ah hope not, anyways. Ah have to set the trrr-aps and close up the entrance because we dinnae want any visitors, now do we?"

Ean stopped long enough to admire the elaborate set of ropes, lanyards, and cables that all led to a central control box just inside the main gate. He had forgotten that Wick, in his day, had been one of the premier castle designers in all of the highlands. "I see you've not lost yer touch, riggin' these pitfalls and snares, eh Fish?"

Wick turned to Ean, his face suddenly flushed red. "Ah told you when you was a pup not to ever call me that again, Ean McKinnon. You ain't too big for me to turn over mah knee rrr-ight now, if'n that's yer bloody game."

"Mess with me, old mahn, and I'll turn this here Pictish beast on ya," Ean replied.

"Pict, is it?" Wick questioned. "Ah thought they was all worm meat afore my father's time. How is it this one survived?"

Daynin stepped in front of Brude to forestall any argument. "It's a long story, Wick. We are all very tired. Can we get a fire going and talk about this tonight?"

"Aye, they's a fire blazin' in the grrr-eat room, boy. Help yourselves to the pigeon stew. I s'pect you can find yer way there without me. I've more traps to check, then I'll join you."

Ean waved for Troon and the others to go ahead without him. "I'll be goin' with Wick. The rest of you get settled whilst we catch up on old times."

Sunrise had already begun to burn off the morning haze in the courtyard. Daynin led his group out of the bright light into the dimly lit great hall. An enormous fire, large enough to roast a full grown calf, blazed in the main hearth. A simmering pot of stew hung above the coals of a brazier fire on the other side of the hall. Between the two, a pair of ragged cots and a pile of clothing attested to Wick's prolonged and meager existence in the keep. Along the far wall, dozens of rusting arms and armaments stood at the ready, no doubt the remnants of Kinloch's once formidable arsenal.

Sabritha rushed to the oversized cauldron, more than a little anxious to test its contents. Having dropped his huge load of treasure with a resounding *craaaannng* that echoed throughout the keep, Brude amused himself with an inspection of the weapons, helmets and shields while Daynin and Troon piled more wood on the fire.

"I was beginning to wonder if we'd ever make it here," Troon said.

Daynin stoked the fire with an ancient iron prod that he remembered from his childhood at Kinloch. Feeling the familiar handle brought back memories of his mother drying clothes in front of that blaze, and her anger when sparks would jump out to burn tiny holes in the tartans. "I knew we would make it, Simon. I never believed it would be this difficult or that so many people would die before . . ."

Rudely interrupting the moment, a sharp protest was launched from the other side of the great hall. "Who the hell *are* you people!?" came a high pitched screech.

Every head turned as one. Outlined by the morning light

coming through the arched passageway behind her, the woman repeated her question, only louder. "I said, who the hell are you people, that you come into our keep unannounced and make yourselves at home?"

Daynin took several halting steps toward the long reddish hair, shapely figure, and sparkling eyes of a truly magnificent woman. "We *are* home," he declared.

Sabritha drew a heavy ladle from the cauldron, ready to use it if need be. "I thought you McKinnons owned this bloody keep," she growled.

"Quiet, Sabritha, please!" Daynin snapped back.

"McKinnons?" the woman replied in disbelief. "Then you must be ghosts. They were all laid low by a gang of cutthroats. I know—we buried them in the sea. My grandfather Wick McKlennan holds this place now, in their stead."

Risking a few more steps, Daynin lifted his cloak to reveal the tartan sash his grandfather had given him. "Aye, we are McKinnons. That is, I am. Mah grrr-andfather Ean is somewhere outside with your grandfather, making the rounds."

Just at that moment, Brude flew into a rage. "Bahh!" roared his voice inside his helmet. He slammed one of the long shields onto the flagstone floor and began stomping it like a madman. "Kellans!" he bellowed, continuing to crush the shield with his enormous armored horseboots. "This shield bears the Kellan crest—those bastard red shanks who murdered my kin!"

Daynin turned in horror, taken completely aback by the unexpected violence of Brude's tantrum. "What's wrong with you?" he cried out.

"Wrong?" Brude growled. His head turned toward the boy in a menacing fashion and with three strides he was in Daynin's face. One gauntlet seized the highlander like a dead cat and shook him violently. "You lied to me! If you are with these dogs, we are no longer allies!"

Gasping for breath, Daynin could barely speak. "I don't know—what—you're talking—about."

The woman disappeared through the archway. Sabritha and Troon both rushed to attack Brude's back. Brude shoved them aside with a wave of his hand. "Kellans—the dogs—they are the ones who set the tables at Scone. They are the ones who lured the Pictish chiefs to parlay, then threw the prisoners off that bridge of yours. And you are one of them! I would snap your neck now, if not for my vow."

Daynin struggled for breath, barely able to gasp out, "Put me down, damn you!"

Brude shoved him backwards against the wall. He reached for his sword, but stopped. "You gave me this life, *Draygnar,* and for that alone I will spare you. But from this moment on, we are enemies. From this day forward, if I meet you or any of your kin in battle, I will take your heads—you and your Kellan allies!"

Finding the battered *Shiva* tied to a stone wharf started Plumat's morning off in the best manner possible. Already, scouts from the *Witch* had surveyed the steep trail up the side of Askival and reported back that they had found tracks in the mud. There could be no doubt—the boy and the treasure had both come ashore at that spot. Now it was just a matter of trailing them to their lair so the Duke's mission could be brought to a speedy end.

"Get everything unloaded quickly, Oswald. I'll take twenty men and pursue our felons while you bring up the siege equipment. Have the *Witch*'s crew set up a camp here. From the looks of this place, there may not be another suitable spot."

"Aye, Plumat—as you wish. I'll send a runner to find you when we're ready to move and that may take a while. These salt bred scum don't take to mountain treks too well."

Plumat stepped onto the wharf, then turned back to Oswald. "Just get it done. We have these felons in our grip. They've no way off this rock, and they're outnumbered at least ten to one. This venture should be over by first light, tomorrow."

"There—just under that grayish outcrop—see it?" Muck insisted.

Kruzurk strained his eyes, but still could not make out the cave entrance. "Your eyes are much younger than mine, Muck. Why don't you lead the way up there and we'll get Olghar set up in a comfortable spot for the day."

Thor, now almost fully recovered from his crossbow wound, barked playfully from far ahead of the group. "My dog sounds well, doesn't he, master?" Olghar said, a major worry having been lifted from his heart.

Eigh couldn't resist voicing his disdain for all things canine. "Bloody hound. I wish he'd stop that barking. He's making Talisman edgy, and that ain't a good thing."

"Uncle Eigh, that crrr-ow of yours is always edgy," Muck teased.

Eigh turned about to deliver a playful slap to Muck's helmet, but stopped dead in his tracks. "Bloody hell—Vikings!" he shrieked.

All heads turned as one. The view from the high slopes of Askival was awesome. The group could see all the way down the mountain to an azure bay where a fleet swayed at anchor. Three large ships and a smaller one seemed to be unloading cargo. Scores of men and what appeared to be a gantry of some kind cluttered the beach.

Mediah spoke first. "Two of those ships are dracos. Not Vikings. I've sailed on 'em. They can hold up to fifty men and crew."

"Scotians?" Kruzurk asked.

"Saxons, I'd guess. They favor big ships," Mediah answered.

Kruzurk turned toward Mediah, his usual pink skin tone having turned almost ashen. "They've come for the boy, then. God help him, we're too late."

Mediah cupped his hands over his eyes to ward off the sun. He took a long look down at the beach, a mischievous smile spreading across his dark cheeks. "Perhaps not, Kruze. That's a siege weapon they're unloading. It looks like they are preparing for war."

Kruzurk turned to the others and said, "We must hurry. Muck, can you take Olghar to the cave, then rejoin us? The rest of us can work our way down to Kinloch faster that way. If we don't warn Daynin, that Saxon horde will be on him by nightfall."

Ebon patted his charger's nose to steady him on the steep trail, then suggested, "Perhaps Castor and I should go down there and take on those brigands. They appear to be unarmored. My sword and Castor's size would make quick work of them."

Wary of the young knight's apparent lack of familiarity with real battle, Kruzurk replied, "We shall have need of your sword soon enough, Ebon. No need to waste it on that rabble."

Moving on and climbing higher with each step, the group finally reached a crest overlooking the north coast of Rhum. To their left, way in the distance and sharply outlined against the sea, stood the distinctive red walls of

Kinloch Castle. Two tiny wisps of smoke could be seen curling out of the main keep, drifting toward the sea.

Kruzurk dropped his bag and waved for the others to stop. "I think we should rest here, eat something, then push on to the keep. The trail down seems quite steep. No need to risk an accident in haste."

The others seemed more than happy to heed his suggestion. The climb up had been much more difficult and dangerous than any of them had expected. Within minutes, Eigh and Mediah lay sprawled against their knapsacks and weapons, sound asleep. Ebon hobbled his horse, then removed the massive jousting saddle and sat down on the crest to ponder a world he never knew existed.

Noticing the ancient grimoire that had slipped out of Kruzurk's bag. Ebon asked, "Is that a book of magic?"

Kruzurk reached over to pull the manuscript from his bag. He propped it up on his lap and said, "Yes, I believe it is. But this grimoire also contains knowledge I can only guess at, for now."

"You can read it, then?" Ebon continued.

"In a way, I suppose. It is written in ancient languages and seems to contain knowledge from well back into the dark times before the Vikings, the Celts and the Romans." As if suddenly summoned, Kruzurk's thoughts left the mountain top. His gaze penetrated into a veil of shadowy walls, occasional flashes of light, and rapid movement. He was *seeing* someone else's visions again.

Far down the mountain, deep inside the walls of Kinloch Keep, Brude McAlpin felt the magician's presence. His mind was suddenly awash with visions of a keep from some high vantage point. *"Venochlan doch perlen dreis, yedor scoon?"* he groaned. "Where are you, wise one?" he shouted as he ran through Kinloch's darkened corridors, picking up speed with each giant stride. "I see your vision, yet it means nothing. Tell me where you are, and I will quit this place and come to you."

"South by west—look to the crest," Kruzurk moaned, though to Ebon, the words made no sense. A long, silent pause ensued until Kruzurk repeated the phrase several more times.

Finally, Ebon cried out, "Kruzurk? *Kruzurk*—what the devil is wrong with you? Kruzurk?"

Mediah leapt to his feet in an instant, half asleep but sword drawn even so. "What is it?"

Ebon pointed to the magician. "He's gone into a trance or—or something."

One look told Mediah what had happened. "It's that book again. This has happened before." Without thinking of his own peril, he knelt down and with his short sword edged the grimoire from under Kruze's hands, allowing it to drop to the dirt track. The effect on the magician was immediate.

Kruzurk blinked his eyes against the bright light and shook his head. "What the deuce? Did I fall asleep?"

Mediah answered, "Methinks you were seeing visions again. I *told* you that book is evil. I should cast it down the mountain right now, before it causes more trouble, but I fear touching that foul thing."

Jumping to his feet, Ebon now drew his sword and took a stance straddling the pathway. "It may be too late for that. Look down there! Unless my eyes deceive me, evil is on its way up to us!"

Finished with their rounds at the top of the south ramparts, Wick and Ean both saw what appeared to be a whirlwind racing through the first barbican, then the second and from there, out onto the rocky shoreline. The vision seemed to have flown over the outer walls, since both gates were closed.

"Did ya see that, Ean? Mah eyes must be givin' out on me."

Ean propped both elbows onto the top of the wall, that he might steady his vision. "Aye, that was real. I think it was that bloody Pictish beast we brought with us. If he left us, good riddance, says I. He's been nothin' but trouble."

Wick had already turned toward the main keep. He waved for Ean to follow and said, "Something's bad wrrrr-ong. Ah can feel it. We best get back to the others."

A last look told Ean that Brude had disappeared into the gorse and granite upslope of Askival. Unfortunately, he didn't wait long enough to see the reflections of sunlight off polished armor way at the crest of Askival. Those same reflections, however, did not go unnoticed from the south coast of Rhum.

"M'lord!" one of the levies shouted from back down the trail. "Did you see that light—way yonder—somethin' shining?"

Plumat raised his arm to stop the column of troops, snaking its way up the mountain at a snail's pace. "What light? I see nothing."

"I saw it too, m'lord," Fulchere the Bowman said. "At the crest—just below the cloud line. Looked like polished armor to me."

"Damn!" Plumat swore. "If there's an army bent on flanking our levies at the beach, they could rout them, burn the boats and strand us here 'til St. Bonafice day."

Fulchere spoke up again. "I can beat it back down the trail and warn them. Set up a defensive barrier, or get the ships to weigh anchor."

"Yes. Yes—*do* that, Fulchere! Have Oswald stand off the beach. Get all the bowmen and fortify that wharf. If you're attacked by overwhelming numbers, withdraw to the ships and wait for us to return. If nothing happens by nightfall, bring your archers and join us. We may have need of your bows at first light."

Plumat waved for the column to proceed. Determined to find the highlander's lair as quickly as possible, he urged his men to move at a speed that was reckless, since they did not know the trail or how dangerous it could be.

The point man's attention was locked onto the muddy tracks he followed. He turned to make sure the column was behind him, and that instant spelled his doom. Over he went off an almost invisible drop-off of Askival like so many hapless invaders before him. His screams were muffled by the brushy walls of the precipice. If not for the next man in the column being a bit more careful, the point man's loss might have gone completely unnoticed.

"Gelwin?" his follower cried out. "Gelwin!? Where the bloody hell *are* ya, mate?" There was, of course, no answer.

Word spread down the column. Every man stopped in his tracks, afraid to move, until Plumat realized that something had gone terribly wrong.

"Why are we stopped?" he yelled. "Get moving, you lot!"

"Gelwin's gone," someone finally offered, the sheepish reply rippling down the line to Plumat's ears. Hearing that, the Saxon shoved his way past the men ahead of him until he reached the first man in line. "What's wrong with you, Willem? Get moving!" he growled.

"They's nowhere to go, m'lord," the man answered. "It's a drop-off. Gelwin must not have seen it."

"Damn these highlanders!" Plumat swore. "Back—go

back, you imbeciles. The trail is a dead end!" he screamed, waving his arms like a man beset by bees.

Reversing the column's flow turned out to be more of a problem than Plumat realized. Laden with weapons, supplies, and worry, most of the men were either too frightened, fatigued or faint-hearted to follow orders. Half the morning was lost retracing the army's steps to a point in the trail that led off in a different direction. Even then, Plumat had no way of knowing if it was the right direction. Tired almost to the point of exhaustion, he decided not to risk another wild goose chase and ordered a halt.

"Miles, I want you to take two men and scout the trail ahead," Plumat ordered. "Take care to watch for pitfalls. Send a man back when you know the trail is good, then we'll join you. Is that clear?"

"Aye, m'lord," the squire answered, hesitantly.

"And Miles—take no chances. If you spot the enemy, do not engage them. Get back here with all haste, and try not to let the highlanders know you're there."

"Yes, m'lord. But—how far am I to go?"

"Somewhere ahead, there has to be a keep, or a village or some kind of landmark. Do not approach it when you see it. Send word and I will bring the troops." A hearty slap on Miles Aubrecht's backside sent the boy on his way.

Chapter 37:

The Converging

After the confusion of Brude's sudden violent departure, all Daynin could do was sit on one of the cots and contemplate what had gone wrong. He was devastated with the loss of his strongest ally, and worse, now they might have to face the giant's wrath from the sharp end of his sword.

"You can't dwell on this, Daynin," Sabritha counseled. "We have other things to think about. I, for one, would like to know what that woman has to say about our being here. *Is* this your keep, or have we come a long way for nothing?"

Troon offered his advice as well. "The lassie's right, boy. That beast was bound to be trouble. Your grandfather knew it, and so did I. Nothing good can come of a conjured spirit. We're better off without 'im."

Daynin took the bowl of stew Sabritha offered him, trying his best to maintain a strong, manly front for her. "Thank you, Sabritha. This stew smells good. It's been a long time since we've had a hot meal together."

"Yes it has," she answered, adding, "and a warm bed to sleep in."

A vivid image of her asleep in the Seed's cell, popped into Daynin's head. He felt a familiar flush racing through his face and hands, then straight down to his groin. "Ahem—uh, yes," he stuttered. "And yes, this is our keep, despite what mistress McKlennan or whatever her name is, says about it."

"Isa," Wick spoke up, having just followed Ean through the archway in time to hear Daynin's comment. "Her name is Isa."

"How appropriate," Sabritha said sarcastically. "Isa is the Celtic rune for ice."

"Sabritha, please—you're a guest here," Daynin responded.

Sabritha slammed the ladle back into the cauldron, splashing a full measure of stew onto the hot brazier. A loud hissing sound echoed around the room, not all of which was coming from the fire. Steam billowed up as well, enveloping half the chamber.

Marching into the great hall like a lord of the land, Wick growled, "Damn it, girr-rrl! Stay yourself and quit wastin' mah stew!"

For the first time since he had met her, Ean came to Sabritha's defense. "That girl is Daynin's intended, old mahn, so I suggest you offer some rrr-espect."

"I don't need *you* to defend me, Ean McKinnon," Sabritha fought back. Her sharp tongue had already proven more than a match for most of the men she had encountered, and this would be no exception. "As for me being a guest, *plowboy*, you can find your own damn cot to sleep on tonight!"

"*Och!*" Wick groused, "you McKinnons have nae changed in all these yearr-rrs. Full of spit and vinegar as usual and ready to fight at the drrr-op of a hannn-kee."

In an attempt to change the tone of the conversation, Troon turned to Ean and said, "We had a problem with the big bugger. I thought he was gonna squash Daynin, he got so mad."

"Yes, we saw him flying out of here like some demon unleashed," Ean replied. "What happened?"

Daynin took the lead at this point. "He claims we are in

league with the Kellans, whoever they are. Apparently, they are blood enemies of his people, and at some point, threw a host of 'em off Standguard Bridge alive."

"Kellans!? Bloody hell, boy," Wick argued, "they was on this island after the Fricians abandoned it and that was way before our clans claimed this bloody rrr-ock. In fact, our kin likely fought the Kellans to take this place. Did ye not *know* that, boy?"

"Had I known it, I would have argued with Brude. As it was, he gave me little chance. Now, he's our enemy, and God knows, we've enemies enough on the way already."

"Oh? And who else might I expect to be battering our gates?" Wick asked sarcastically.

Ean strode over to the pot of stew, taking his place very close to Sabritha. The look in her eyes had changed. Fear, laced with a hint of gratitude and warmth seemed to twinkle back at him. "Saxons, that's who. How's the stew, woman? Edible I hope, 'cause if Wick brewed it, it's likely laced with rrr-um."

"Saxons?" came the caustic response from McKlennan. "Oh, this tale just gets tastier by the tellin'! Giants, Saxons, Kellans and no tellin' what else. I shoulda shot all o' you at the gate."

"Who the bloody hell is that?" Eigh asked, having awakened and come to his senses from all the hubbub around him.

Standing between Mediah and Ebon, Kruzurk looked down the long, sloping trail at the strange entity closing on them. "That, my friends, is likely the being I've been seeing in my visions. Somehow, he is connected to the events back at Abbotsford and this grimoire I've brought from there."

"Whatever—or whoever he is, he's huge!" Ebon offered, his voice laden with anticipation.

Mediah glanced back at the grimoire, spread open on the ground behind them. He thought about the carnyx laced tightly against the back of his knapsack and wondered if it was also related. "Kruze—I have a bad feeling about this. That heathen book and the horn we brought from the priory—is it possible—?"

Kruzurk knew where the question was headed. "Yes, I think all of this is somehow connected. I've seen this creature's thoughts, or visions, or whatever they are. I am guessing he's a man, but unlike any we have ever seen before. And I believe the Scythian Stone is a part of what is about to happen next."

"Should we fight this creature, then?" Ebon wanted to know.

Kruzurk bent down to retrieve the grimoire, closing it up with Olghar's twin railed cross inside it, just as before. "I don't know what to expect, but it can't hurt to be at the ready."

From behind them came the sound of rocks cascading down the trail. "What's the parlay about?" Muck shouted, his voice again winded from the rapid descent. "I could hear you lot grousing from way up the mountain."

"We've company, it seems," Eigh replied. "We might have need of that big frog sticker of yours, Mucky boy."

"*Och,* a warrr-rrr, is it, eh? Lemme at 'em!"

A hundred paces below them, the strange entity stopped on the trail and shouted, "I seek the mage or seer among you. You there, with the red robe and beard like a snow peak, get thee down here."

Kruzurk stepped forward. He almost did a double take when he realized the sheer size of the armored giant below them. "I am the mage you seek. Are you the one with whom I've shared visions?"

"Visions, aye. Have you the book and carnyx?"

"We do," Kruzurk answered, flatly.

"Good. I may not kill you, after all. Are there Kellans among you?"

Eigh's bird suddenly flew into a rage, screeching and flapping its wings like a demon possessed. Unable to escape the tethers of his perch pole, Talisman put on quite a show until Eigh settled him back down.

Kruzurk held the book aloft, that the giant might see it better. "Here is the grimoire. There are no Kellans among us, whoever they are. As for the carnyx, we have it as well."

"Gut eating dogs, that's who the Kellans are," Brude answered, as he turned and pointed back toward Kinloch Keep. "There's a boy down there who's in league with 'em. The Kellans are my sworn enemies, as are all who war alongside them."

Kruzurk walked down the slope so that he might size up this new threat from close range. Though the giant appeared and acted human enough, there was an otherworldly aspect to him. Kruzurk, more keen to that realm than most, decided almost immediately that he was not dealing with a mortal being.

Lines from the walls of the crypt at Abbotsford Priory began flowing through the back of the magician's mind. "Are you the Great Deceiver? The Pict who has risen from his crypt?"

Almost before Kruzurk could get the words out of his mouth, Brude was upon him, staring down from those ghostly black eye slits in his helmet. "Cruithni, mage—not Pict! That's a Roman name, and if I hear it from you again, I'll gut you where you stand."

Trying not to show the terror in his heart, Kruzurk apologized. "Forgive me, m'lord. That name was all I had to go by, from the runes in your crypt. You are—or were, chief of the McAlpins, yes?"

"I am Brude McAlpin, chieftain of the Seven Houses of Scone—come back to this life to avenge my people. Why are you here, mage? And who are these peasants you've brought with you?"

"We're here to right a great wrong, m'lord," Kruzurk replied, knowing that any disrespect shown toward the giant might end in bloodshed. "That boy you spoke of is in great peril. A Saxon army lands on the other side of the island as we speak. They are bent on his capture and that is my fault, for I enlisted his aid in destroying an evil sorcerer."

Brude's huge gauntlet reached out and thumped Kruzurk square in the chest, all but knocking the magician down. "Then you are here to help my enemy, and that I will not allow!"

Muck stiffened but held back, as did Ebon. Any hostile move might spell Kruzurk's doom. Mediah had fetched the carnyx from his knapsack. He held it aloft and shouted, "Is this what you seek?"

The flash of gold instantly caught the giant's attention. He shoved Kruzurk aside, covering the hundred paces to Mediah in the blink of an eye. "HaaaHaaarrr!" he gloated, having grabbed the horn from the Greek's hands. "Now I can make war as a proper chief!"

An ear shattering *haaaaruuuuuuuhhh* rang out as Brude blew the carnyx with all his might. Every man in the group threw his hands to his ears to ward off the horrendous blast. Rocks shook themselves to pieces on the cliff face. Echoes resounded off Askival's slopes, bouncing hither and yon like an army of elephants trumpeting a charge.

On the south side of the island, the cacophony of trumpet sounds reverberated through the canyons and crevices, reaching Plumat's ears and those on the ships. "Holy

Benedict!" Plumat moaned, "that sounded like an entire army at the charge."

Oswald, his ships anchored off shore as ordered, also heard the trumpet blast. "Bloody hell, mates—sounds like the highlanders have massed an army in the hills. Plumat is in big trouble!"

Trudging along toward Standguard Bridge, Miles Aubrecht and his two minions heard the horn's roar coming up behind them. All three stopped in their tracks, thinking a highland army was about to pounce on them from the deep woods. And several leagues to the north, even the heavy stone confines of Kinloch Keep could not hold back the raucous renderings of Brude's great horn. The sound sent shivers up the backs of Daynin's assembled group as they sat around the stone dining table, pigeon stew at the ready.

The only word out of Daynin's mouth was, "Saxons!"

Wick threw himself away from the table and yelled at the top of his lungs, "Isa! Get you down here, girrrrl! We've a warrrrr at hand!"

Troon quickly gulped down two more spoons of stew and turned to Ean McKinnon. "I'll ready the bows. Should we stand at the first wall or the second?"

Ean looked to Wick, whose mottled complexion had suddenly turned bright red. "Are the barbicans still in good enough shape to delay an attack?"

"*Och!* Delay 'em, yes. Stop 'em—no. We can hurt 'em, though it would take a hundrrr-ed of us to man the outer barbican proper like. The inner wall is shorter and easier to hold, but the four of us cannae do it alone."

"Five of us!" Sabritha stated, bringing an approving look from both Ean and Daynin.

A resounding, "Six, by God!" rang out from Isa, coming down the stairwell.

All heads turned at the sight of the crimson-haired beauty, adorned in a form fitted armored tunic that was both beautiful and awesome. Her black leather helm tucked under one arm, Isa appeared for all the world like a goddess intent on war. "What?" she snapped.

"Nice gear," Sabritha offered, a hint of sarcasm in her words.

Wick tossed his stew bowl back onto the table and growled, "Girrrrl—ah've told ya before, it's nae a lassie's job to stand the walls with the men. Ah did'nae make that tunic with the notion you'd ever wearrrr it in battle. Now go and take it off, rrr-ight now!"

A bit embarrassed at how Wick's words sent a vivid image scorching through his brain and into the pit of his stomach, Daynin spoke up, "The Saxons only had about a score of men, last we saw of 'em. One extra bowman—er, uh—one extra *fighter* could make all the difference on the walls."

"The boy's right," Troon agreed. "If only to fetch arrows and load the crossbows."

Ean strode across the room, arm outstretched to clench hands. "Ah'm Ean McKinnon—your grrr-eat grrand cousin, I rrr-eckon. At least, you can call me that, if ya want to, girrr-lll. And that cherrr-ub over there is Daynin, mah grrr-andson."

Out of the corner of his eye, Daynin could tell that Sabritha's demeanor had changed markedly with Isa's reappearance. He swept around behind her, encircling her waist with his hands. "Would you like for me to find you a tunic to wear? Somewhere in the upper keep, if they were not lost or stolen, my father kept a trunk of my mother's clothes. They might be a bit large for you, but . . ."

Sabritha turned, coming face to face with Daynin. "I'm sure I won't look as good as she does, but any armor is better than none, when some heathen is trying to kill you."

Again, the sarcasm came through loud and clear, but Daynin didn't have time to deal with that problem, for the moment. "Perhaps you two should get better acquainted," he said in passing.

Isa's presence had obviously impressed everyone in the chamber except Sabritha. "I take it you're not from the highlands, then?" she asked.

Sabritha made a half hearted effort to engage the hand clench Isa had offered, then snapped back, "Hardly. I'm Irish—you know—where the sun actually shines and people aren't out to kill you every day."

"Yes, I've been there," came the response. "Lots of sheep on that island, as I recall. Sheep and more bloody sheep."

The verbal swordplay quickly bested the men. They hurried off to the upper chambers to gather weapons and prepare for battle, leaving the two women to finish their catty exchange.

Miles and the two Saxons stayed huddled in the deep brush just a few hundred paces from Standguard Bridge. They awaited their imminent doom in the midst of an imagined attack—an attack that never came. Finally, Miles ordered one of the men to return to Plumat. "Tell him we've gone ahead to scout the bridge, and that he should come with all haste."

Satisfied with that decision, Miles led his companion onto the trail and marched straight for the bridge. They stopped at the precipice, where the squire hesitated, wondering the same thing Sabritha had thought just a few hours earlier—will the bridge hold?

"You go first, Miller," Miles ordered.

"Why me?" the levy replied.

Feeling a bit heady from his new found authority, Miles ripped into the man. "Because I *said* so, that's why! I am the squire, you know, not you."

Miller spit into the dirt close to the squire's boots, mumbled something vile and proceeded across. He edged his way along the first part of the bridge, trying not to look down into the pounding surf that kept the bridge constantly in motion and ever so slippery.

At the halfway point, Miller turned to yell back at Miles, "Come along, squire—it's safe enough—if you've the grit for it."

Miles bent down and picked up his knapsack, preparing himself to dare the crossing. He looked down the length of the bridge, then shook his head in disbelief. Miller had disappeared!

"No, no, no!" he screamed, his voice all but lost in the salty sea breeze. "Miller! Where the hell are you?"

At the halfway point of the bridge, a gaping trap door screeched on its hinges under the walkway. Miles dropped to his knees to peer through the hole, but could see only wildly crashing waves pounding against the rocks far below.

"That's it—no more!" he swore aloud. Looking around, Miles ripped off the Duke's tunic and tossed it into the hole. With that and a single courageous leap, he freed himself from the Duke forever.

Olghar Fergum recited aloud the poetic formula given to him by the monks at Drimnin. "Three parts charcoal ground into paste, mix in sulfur, no more than a taste. Six parts bat dung, boiled to a trace, catch the niter in a cloth well placed. Pound it good, 'til it's black as night, then dry it well to test its might."

The fire Muck had started for him in the mouth of the cave felt good to the priest's weary bones. Thor must have thought so, too, for he had cuddled up next to the fire pit to sleep while his master labored to perfect the mysterious Drimnin "dazzle". "Won't be long now, eh, boy? That bat dung smells frightful, I know, but it's the only way to free up the niter I need. Then shall we see just how smart those Drimnin loremasters really are."

Further down the mountain's north face, Kruzurk and his band were still recovering from Brude's rude blast on the carnyx. The horn had boosted the giant's morale, thereby relieving some of his anger.

"So, magician—you've all come to save *Draygnar* from the Saxons, eh? How do you plan on defeating an army with this pitiful lot?"

Kruzurk looked puzzled by the question. "You mean Daynin?"

"Yes, Daynin—but I call him *Draygnar*. He and his wench and a couple of old men are all that hold that keep, and they are not well disposed to stand off a siege. How is it you think you can help them, with this rabble of yours, and not a warrior among you?"

Ebon thought briefly about challenging that statement, but let it go unanswered. The giant was, after all, as big as Ebon and his horse combined. "We will stand with them, whatever the odds," Ebon replied.

"Haaaaharrr," Brude laughed. "Have you training in battle, boy?"

Kruzurk raised his hands to quell the conversation. "Whatever we can do, we must do, and we must do it now. That Saxon army has had time to form up and march on Kinloch. We must do the same. If you are with us, Brude, we welcome you. If you are not, then I wish you well on your quest—whatever that is."

"Quest, aye. My quest is to find the Kellans, or their kin, and do them justice for my clan."

Mediah suddenly had a thought. "M'lord, might we ask a boon from the chief of the McAlpins—for—uh—bringing him the horn?"

Brude's helmet snapped around, his eye slits focusing on the Greek. "Boon? You would ask me a boon, when you've nothing to offer?"

To give Kruzurk the chance to reply, Mediah made a circular motion in the air with his hand, the other hand jutting back over his shoulder in the direction of the Scythian Stone.

"Yes. The Stone! Of course!" Kruzurk said, excitedly. "We brought something with us to Rhum. It is of great value, and can only be handled by someone of enormous strength, who is afraid of nothing. Might I impose upon you to retrieve it for us, m'lord?"

"You can, but for a price. You must swear upon your lives that you will then help me find the Kellans when I return. Agreed?"

Caught between a stone and their combined mortalities, Kruzurk put out his arm for a hand clench. "If you bring the stone to Kinloch Keep, I—we—will help you in your quest—but only after we deal with Daynin's plight. Agreed?"

"The enemy of my enemy wars as my ally," Brude recited. "Now, where is this bloody Stone you want?"

Plumat's patience was once again wearing thin with the long wait for word from Miles Aubrecht. "On your feet!" he ordered. "We're moving. Keep your eyes open and your mouths shut. Watch every tree and rock for signs of treachery. These brigands are here somewhere. I want no surprises."

The column had barely begun to move when the messenger sent back by the squire suddenly appeared on the trail. Nearly breathless from the long run, the man gasped out, "M'lord—they's a bridge—your squire said to come— all haste. The trail is clear, far as I know, though we heard war horns earlier."

"Yes, yes," Plumat barked at the levy. "We heard them too. These highlanders are a sneaky lot, but have not shown themselves yet. Now, lead the way. We'll find Miles and see what he knows."

"These six big ones trrr-ip the pitfalls outside the first drrr-awbridge," Wick explained to Sabritha. "If you see me wave one arrow, you pull a peg in this first rrr-ow and stand back—the rope will let go with a mighty furry, so dinnae get in its way. If I wave two arrows, pull a peg from this second row, and so on. If you see me wave this rrr-ed pennant, that means to pull this big lever and all of the pegs, fast as you can. Do you understand me, girrr-l? There cannae be a mistake, 'cause we only get one chance with this."

Sabritha nodded and said, "What should I do once all the pegs are pulled here?"

"You beat it inside the third gate and be ready to work the pegs there when we fall back. If we're overrun at the second wall, you close that bloody portcullis and find yerself a place ta hide, eh?"

Chilled by the thought that the Saxons might actually take the keep, Sabritha drew in a deep breath and let it out slowly. "Wick, tell me the truth. Can we hold this place, or is all of this foolhardy effort?"

Leaving her, Wick answered, "This keep has only fallen

to invaders once in all its days, and that was to trrrr-eachery from *inside* the walls. You just do as I tell ya, lassie, and we'll be fine, eh?"

Sabritha laced up the rest of her tunic, just getting used to the acrid smell of moldy leather. She reached for the short sword Daynin had given her and decided to move it from her waistline to a less cumbersome spot behind her back. She struggled with the broad belt and scabbard until a pair of helping hands jerked it into place behind her.

"There—better eh?" Isa hissed. "You can rrr-un faster with that sword behind you, I should imagine."

"I don't plan on running anywhere, Isa."

"Good," she snapped. "Grrr-andfather has worked many a year on these traps. Don't botch your job. And don't let that fire wane, either. We may have need of hot irons to close up some wounds."

"Yes, your majesty," Sabritha retorted, performing a dubious curtsy for effect. As Isa passed through the gate on her way out to the battlements, Sabritha shouted, "Keep your bloody head down, wench. That red hair of yours makes a target a blind archer couldn't miss!"

Out at the first barbican, Ean, Troon and Daynin had already taken up positions in the south tower overlooking the main drawbridge. The decision to leave the walls unmanned did not set well with Wick, but the logic of defending the south gate alone won out in the end, since there were only four of them to cover more than three furlongs of ramparts. The south tower also gave them a full panorama of the north gate approaches from the beach, should the enemy come from that direction.

"Wick, the water in the moat is low enough to wade across. Can you make it deeper?" Ean asked.

"Aye, but the time to deepen it is when the devil is

already knee deep in it, don't ya think?"

"What does that mean?" Daynin asked.

"You'll see, mah boy, when the time is rrrr-ight!" Wick replied, his response flowing like a melody. "But just in case, if somethin' happens to me afore we flood the moat, Daynin, you take this here pennant and wave it at yer woman back there. She'll do the rrrr-est."

Turning to look back toward the second barbican, Daynin saw Isa approaching. He couldn't help but admire the statuesque image she presented, especially in that black leather helm topped by a bevy of raven feathers. "I thought you told Isa to stay on the second wall," he muttered to Wick.

"Try tellin' that girrrl *any* damn thing, boy, and she'll do just the opposite to get yerrrr goat. We'll have to protect her, best we can, I rrrr-eckon."

Daynin's eye also caught the tiny figure of Sabritha, standing astride the second drawbridge in the distance, waving a scarf at him. He waved back, hoping it would not be the last time he ever saw her.

Fulchere's contingent of bowmen, levies and heavily armored Saxons formed up on the wharf, awaiting Ranulf's orders. Oswald had given the fat little reeve the unhappy task of leading the beach defenses, should an attack come from that direction, while he waited in safety aboard the *Dionysis*.

"It's been a long time since we heard that trumpet, m'lord," Fulchere observed. "Perhaps we should send out some skirmishers or a scout to see if there is a threat. I was ordered to . . ."

Ranulf pulled a carrot from his tunic and began chewing it nervously. "I don't care what you were ordered! We will need every man to defend this wharf if we're attacked. I'm not sending anyone out there in that gorse until we hear from Plumat. There could be thousands of those heathen bastards lurking about, just waiting for us to make the first move."

A few paces behind Ranulf, Fulchere merely shook his head. Outranked and with no authority to move, even though Plumat had told him to rejoin the main attack force with the archers as soon as possible, Fulchere merely replied, quietly, "As you wish, m'lord."

Kruzurk and his group's attempt to hastily approach the north beach had quickly been abandoned. There were simply too many pumpkin sized boulders littering the narrow passage for anyone to move rapidly. With a raging sea to one side and sheer cliffs on the other, that left little room for error.

"I think the drawbridge is up, Kruze," Mediah observed.

"Yes. We'll have to approach carefully. They must be aware of the Saxons by now."

The hair on the back of Eigh's neck went up at the thought of a Saxon horde somewhere in the area. "Mayhaps I should send Talisman ahead to give your boy Daynin a warning that we're coming. If they see my bird, surely they'll open the gates for us."

"You could be onto something, Eigh. Daynin cannot know we are coming, and if his friends are manning that gate, we could be in for a hail of arrows by approaching too boldly. Ebon, I think you should ride ahead and parlay with them. Your armor will protect you, as long as you stay well back from that wall. What say you?"

Ebon's foot had already hit the stirrup. "Aye! It's a task well turned to Castor and me. I'll ride up and let them know we're friends."

★ ★ ★ ★ ★

Olghar's cave had almost become untenable from the acrid smoke of his alchemy. His first two batches of the dazzle did little more than fizzle when ignited with a piece of cloth. The priest had only a limited supply of the sulfur given him at Drimnin, but he suspected that the dazzle would be of great importance before the day was over.

"We cannot fail, Thor," he told his dog. "I'll mix one more batch to see if it works, then we shall have to find more of this horrible smelling compound if we are to get suitable results." Thor merely rolled onto his side, content for once to be somewhere warm and dry. Little could he know his master was on the verge of creating history. Nor could Olghar, for that matter.

Brude covered the treacherous downhill trail leading back to the Scythian Stone in a matter of minutes. A brief reconnaissance uncovered the Stone's hiding place just as Kruzurk had described it. The giant quickly shoved the brush and debris away, preparing to grab his quarry and return to Kinloch as rapidly as possible. That plan came undone the instant he recognized what he had found.

"By the blood of all my ancestors," he sighed, almost in disbelief. "The Stone of Destiny! Oh, Val Henna! These fools have no idea what a treasure they've unearthed." To celebrate, he let loose with another ear shattering blast on the carnyx.

The Besieging

Within sight of Standguard Bridge, the Saxon column moved even more cautiously than before. Every man's eyes scanned the dense woods for the expected attack, and with the great chasm of "the Willies" blocking the path ahead, anxiety rose to a fever pitch.

"Take two men and scout ahead," Plumat ordered Saewold. "Find the squire and report back here. We're not risking that bridge until I know it's safe to cross."

"Aye, m'lord," Saewold agreed. He had no more than turned around to start the crossing when the thunderous roar of Brude's horn came tearing through the forest behind them.

"Damn these highlanders!" Plumat wailed. "Are they *everywhere?*" Already on edge from the long campaign, little sleep, and constant anxiety, the Saxon leader was almost at his wit's end, and his men knew it. "Saewold, lead the way—we are all going to cross now, before they hit us from behind."

The troop began moving right away, albeit with great trepidation at the constant swaying of the bridge. Half the men snaked their way forward. Though it seemed sturdy enough, Standguard's height above the sea was enough of a deterrent for those unused to its narrow confines. Then the open trap door was discovered near the center, and pandemonium broke out among the levies. Despite Plumat's best efforts to stem the panic, discipline became the first casualty of the bridge crossing,

The untrained levies began throwing their weapons and equipment over the side of the bridge, pushing and shoving against the men behind them, all the while being pressed ever tighter in the close quarters. Standguard's natural rocking motion increased violently and for an instant, Plumat thought his entire campaign would end in a catastrophic fall to the sea.

He drew his sword, determined at whatever cost to quell the mutiny on the bridge. "Hold you lot!" he yelled at the top of his lungs. One man attempted to shove him aside with a scaling ladder. Plumat parried the blow and hit the man square in the top of his head, splattering blood and gore on all those around them. The man's scream sent more shock waves through the throng, but stopped those who witnessed it dead in their tracks.

"The next man to run will share this fool's fate!" Plumat bellowed. For an instant, the tumult wavered.

Near the center of the bridge, Saewold and two of the other Saxons also drew their weapons. "Get back, you cockroaches!" came Saewold's order. The sight of drawn swords turned the tide. The unarmored levies, wedged between fear and frailty, allowed their frailty to win out.

Shoving one of the assault ladders across the gaping hole to allow passage, Saewold barked, "Now get moving, you gutless pukes—we've a war to wage and plunder to seize!"

Plumat stepped around the dead man, leaving him as fair warning for others who might be inclined to run. None did.

"Did ya hear that, laddy?" Wick asked, his head cocked toward the faint mob sounds wafting on the wind from Standguard Bridge. Daynin's attention was directed the other way—toward the north barbicans.

"Saxons, no doubt about it," Ean answered instead.

"Damn," the boy swore. "They're coming from the north, too. Look at that—a mounted knight!"

"No bloody way they coulda got horses to Rhum," Troon chimed in. "Especially chargers."

"A single mounted knight, with no archers or levies in support?" Ean scoffed. "These Anglish are too brave or too stupid to live. Either that or he's a distraction, to drrrr-aw us away from this gate."

Just then, Isa popped her head through the wooden trap door at the top of the tower, startling the men. "What knight are you talking about?" she demanded.

Daynin pointed to the horseman making his way carefully down the north beach toward the barbican. The man's black armor brought a broad smile to Isa's face. "Welllll," she purred, "perhaps I should go and see what this fellow wants."

"Good plan, girrrrl," Wick agreed. "You go and parlay with 'im, but dinnae open that gate, no matter what he says, eh?"

"Not to worry, grrr-andfather—I'll handle 'im all right. If I need any help, I'll wave my helm."

Ranulf paced along the line of archers, impatient and nervous at the same time. "Why don't they just *attack* us and stop blowing that bloody horn?"

Fulchere stepped in the reeve's path. "M'lord—it's almost midday. Plumat ordered me to return with these bowmen as soon as possible. He will need them if there's an assault to be made. We cannot *sit* here on this beach waiting for an attack when there may only be one shepherd out there in the gorse, keeping us pinned down with a bloody horn!"

"But—Oswald ordered me to hold this beach."

"M'lord Ranulf, if you have no bowmen, you could return to the *Woebringer*. The fault will lie with me, and ultimately with Plumat. Besides, there is nothing here to defend. If we capture the boy and the treasure, we can be off this bloody island on the morrow."

The safety of a ship and a warm meal quickly convinced Ranulf that Fulchere was right. "Very well. If you insist on leaving, I have no choice but to take my leave. I need two of your men to row me out. You can take the rest."

A score of bowmen was better than nothing, Fulchere reasoned. He turned and waved for his archers to follow him, and off they went to rejoin Plumat's group.

Watching what had transpired on the wharf and incensed that the beach had been left undefended, Oswald threw himself into a raging fit. "Hail the *Witch*. I want thirty of their men, all armed," he ordered his mate. "Lower the longboat. We're going ashore."

A crossbow's cast from the north gate, Ebon pulled Castor to a halt and dropped to his feet. His armor felt unusually heavy for some reason, perhaps because he hadn't had it on for nearly two full days. He led his charger to a spot close enough to hail the walls. "Halloooooo?" he called out. Only his echo answered. "We are friends here—come to aid Daynin. Will you open the gate?"

Isa had just reached the north tower in time to hear the last words. "Who are *you* that you demand we open our gates? Are you Saxons? We're well defended here. If you intend to lay siege, I warn you—you'll be glad of your shields this day."

Taken aback by both the tone and the anger in the response, Ebon wasn't quite sure how to reply. "We are not

Saxons. I am Ebon of Scone, come to aid Daynin and a fair maiden. I travel with Kruzurk Makshare and others. Now, will you open or *not?*"

"How do I know you're telling the truth?" Isa answered, her voice giving way to a bit more of the feminine side.

Realizing the voice was female, Ebon removed his helmet, a time honored sign of deference to the female sex. "I am a knight, sworn to the truth. Open the gate, m'lady, that we may parlay in peace. There is no treachery here, I swear it."

"If you move once that drawbridge is down, my bowmen will empty their quivers on you. Now drop your weapons and stand away from your horse."

Ebon did as he was told, wondering what manner of female could hold sway over an army of bowmen. Then he remembered what Brude had said about how few people there were defending Kinloch. Behind him, the portcullis slowly rose, creaking like an ancient grist wheel while the drawbridge groaned its way down into place across the moat. A hollow *whump* announced that the gate had opened.

Ebon turned to see a blade thrust right under his chin. "Hold!" he implored, eyes flashing. "Stay that blade!"

Though considerably shorter than Ebon, Isa's reach with her short sword was sufficient to make him totally defenseless. "You don't look so big now, sir knight. What *say* you?"

Just then, Mediah came out from hiding behind Castor. His beefy paw swept the woman's sword arm down and away from the kill zone. "Ease off, woman," he ordered.

Isa struggled, but in vain. "You bastard! You lied— you're no knight! Damn you, blaggard, let me go!"

Kruzurk stepped into Isa's vision at that moment. "I assure you, Ebon is a knight, and we are here to help Daynin.

I'm sorry we had to trick you, but time is pressing—a Saxon army approaches this place from the south and they mean to take no prisoners."

"We know that, you old crow," Isa snapped, her hands now free, but empty. "We thought you were part of their attack. Who *are* you people, anyway? Twelve years I've lived on this island without one visitor and now we have scores of you!"

Kruzurk motioned with his staff for everyone to move along. He could waste no more time with introductions. Reinforcing Kinloch's tiny but obviously determined garrison was far more important.

Over at the main gate, Daynin and Wick watched what was happening at the north gate while Ean and Troon kept an eye on the open ground surrounding the south barbican. At the very edge of the woods nearest the trail from Standguard Bridge, a solitary figure emerged from the thicket.

"Who's that?" Ean wondered.

"Bloody Saxon, from the cut of his garb," Troon replied. "Must be a scout, sent to ferret out our defenses. He's too far away to hit with my bow, but maybe he'll come closer."

Daynin's attention quickly shifted to the man in the clearing. "Wick, are there more traps out there like the one I tripped over?"

"Aye, lad. Trrrr-aps, pitfalls and a few other surprises those Anglish dogs will be sorry they've found. If ya know where to look, it's easy enough to see 'em, but if you don't, or you're in a hurry, that open ground is a death trap. You were mighty lucky, boy."

Straining for a better view of the lone figure, Daynin suddenly recognized him. "Holy Saints of Argyle! That's Miles Aubrecht!"

"Who?" Wick asked.

"Aye, Daynin, I think you're rrr-ight. Looks like 'im all right," Ean agreed. "How the bloody hell did he get here? And what's he doin' out there all by himself?"

Daynin pulled himself up on top of one of the stone crenellations, so Miles could see him better. He began waving his arms, then shouted, "Wait—don't come any closer, Miles!"

Ean reached up and dragged Daynin off the top of the wall. "What's wrong with you, boy? He's our blood enemy, likely sent to scout our perimeter for an attack."

"No, he's not, grandfather. He hates the Saxons as much as we do. We've got to let him in and find out what he knows." Before Ean could scold him again, Daynin bolted down the ladder and made straight for the levers that opened the gates.

Wick was still watching the events at the north gate, but the distance and a light haze screened most of the action. He heard the gate opening, and that was enough to set him off. "Somethin's amiss at the sea gate—ahm gonna go and see what Isa has done."

"Bloody bones!" Ean barked. "A Saxon army at the gates and everyone seems to have something else to worry with!"

Rushing past Sabritha, Wick only had time to yell, "Hold fast, girrrl—we've company at both gates."

Wick's mad dash through the corridors and courtyards of Kinloch was so swift, it would have given a Greek marathon runner reason to pause. He reached the last wall just as Isa's group hurried across the inner drawbridge. Astounded that she had allowed a group of armed strangers into the keep so casually, Wick drew his bow and took a position to fire.

First through the inner archway came a bizarre looking mage, his flowing white beard all matted and dirty from what must have been an arduous journey to reach Kinloch. Isa trailed behind him with a dark skinned man in a turban and two others of equally bizarre dress. Last in the group was the black knight Wick had seen at the gate, his horse in tow.

"Hold, you lot!" Wick ordered. "If ye've treachery in mind, you'll pay in blood, wager that." To quicken the point, Wick let loose a shaft into the wooden beam above Kruzurk's head.

That arrow almost unhinged the magician. Perhaps the long journey, or the stress of impending battle, or just the idea of being fired at set him off. Kruzurk lashed back with a verbal assault uncommon to his manner.

"Hold your fire, you roguish ass! We've come to help you fight the Saxons. Now stay your weapons and hear me out!"

"Ass is it, eh?" Wick barked back. "Another step and you'll have my bolt in your bloody ass, says I!"

"Grandfather—they've come to help," Isa added.

"Girrrl, I told ya not to open that bloody gate, and here ya've let a host o' heathens into the yarrrr-d with nary a worrrr-d to anyone. Have ye gone daft or what?"

From the long hallway behind Wick, a euphoric "Kruze!" rang out. Sabritha rushed to the old magician and threw her arms around him.

"I am so glad to see you!" Sabritha went on.

"And I, you," Kruzurk replied, somewhat embarrassed.

"I take it you two know each other, then," Isa intervened, shoving her way past the joyous reunion. "Can we get back to the problem at hand? There is an army out there, after all."

As if to agree, Talisman began flapping his enormous wings. "Settle down, you pretentious scoundrel, you," Eigh warned.

Wick stepped out of the shadows, anxious to meet the visitors and to find out how many men they had brought. A round of hand clenches solved the first problem, but alas, he was disappointed to learn that the whole contingent stood before him—all five of them.

"Isa, you should go back and close up the sea gate's defenses," Wick ordered. "Kruzurk, if I could impose—it would be good if one of your men would stand the firrr-st watch on the north tower, just in case."

Before Kruze could reply, Isa reached for Ebon's arm and said, craftily, "This one will do. I'll show him the way, grrr-andfather."

The rest of the group made its way into the great hall. As any good host would do, Wick offered them what remained of the stew and some grog, then left them with Sabritha to return to the north gate.

"Kruzurk, you have no idea how happy I am you've come."

"I had no choice, Sabritha. We've been chasing you ever since Abbotsford Priory. Those Saxons intend to hang you and Daynin."

"Yes, we know, but you should all eat, and rest—we'll talk later. I have to get back to my station at the gate. We will need every man, when and if the Anglish come."

Eigh stepped up for a bowl and said, "We'll be there, girrrl, and God help the bloody Saxons."

Meanwhile, just outside the south gate, Daynin continued waving and hollering at Miles Aubrecht, who seemed oblivious to the warnings. Fear of the Saxons behind him drove the squire further into the kill zone of the open ground.

"Grandfather, is he in range?" Daynin asked.

"Aye, boy. I can drrr-op 'im like a six point buck, but if he's a friend . . ."

"Shoot him, grandfather," Daynin ordered. "In the leg, or foot, if you can manage it. It's the only way to stop him before he falls in one of those traps."

No sooner had the words left Daynin's mouth, than an arrow flew from the elder McKinnon's bow. The distinctive *wheeeeng* of the bolt rent the still midday air, followed instantly by a plaintive, "Owww, my foot!" coming from the squire.

Daynin rushed out along the path, mindful of the trip wires. Reaching the squire, he scolded, "Damn you, Miles Aubrecht, did you not hear me? I begged you to stop. This whole field is strewn with death traps. A few more steps and you might have paid with your life."

Miles looked up at Daynin, his hands rubbing the spot where Ean's chert tipped bolt had struck him in the boot. "What does it matter, anyway? Plumat is here with an army. We are all doomed," he sniffled.

"Get up, Miles. I'll help you inside. We have an army of our own, and with you added to it, we can't lose."

The two hobbled inside the main gate and up into the tower, where Miles told the whole story of the fire ship and Plumat's rescue. He also relayed how many Saxons were coming, planting a seed of doom in everyone's mind. Then he sneaked away into the main keep.

"We cannae hold against a hundred men with siege ladders, Ean," Wick confessed, "especially if they have archers."

"Yes, I know. We can make them pay dearly, what with your traps and all. But they will eventually overwhelm this gate at some point, and then the next. Mayhaps we should take the women and abandon the keep. There are caves up on Askival where no one would find us."

"Leave?" Daynin gasped, incredulous at the very thought of it. "After all we've gone through to get here? I'm not leaving. This is my *home* and I will do whatever it takes to hold it. No one will ever take Kinloch from us again!"

" 'Tis good to have a brrr-ave hearrr-t, laddy," Wick replied. "But a brave mahn dies the same as a coward does, when he's gettin' 'is neck strrr-etched."

"Look 'ee there!" Troon cried out.

All heads turned toward the sea gate. "Brude! He's come back!" Daynin exclaimed. "But what is that he's carrying?"

Wick leaned on the wall and said, "Looks like a bloody great grinding stone to me."

Daynin climbed higher to get a better look. "No way! It's not possible—we *destroyed* that thing. But it looks—I swear, it looks just like the Scythian Stone!"

"In all the excitement," Wick said, "I forgot to tell you about the new arrivals. That must be the big bugger your magician friend talked about. Seems they sent him back to fetch something they had left on the beach."

"Kruzurk is *here!?*" Daynin replied, his head swimming with that news.

"Aye, boy—'twas them what came along with that big black knight whilst you was out savin' the squire. Brought a big fat mahn, and an old mahn with a bird, too—and a Greek, so I'm told."

Daynin jumped from the wall and flew down the ladder to the courtyard. "Thank God!" he sang out, dashing toward the main keep. "If Kruze and Mediah are here, we can hold Kinloch against a thousand men."

During their casual stroll to the sea gate, Isa felt satisfied that the black knight fit the profile of a man she might want to be with some day—though of course, she did not share that notion with Ebon. Instead, she probed him for information about the others he had come with to Rhum. Just as they closed the sea gate, Brude arrived outside with his treasure.

"Open the bloody gates!" he roared. "Brude McAlpin has returned to complete the bargain."

"What's that all about?" Isa asked.

Ebon stood to the drawbridge levers and began opening the gate. "A bargain the magician made—with a soulless being I cannot begin to explain. But whatever he is, the beast is huge and will fight well alongside us when the time comes."

"You mean—he's not—a mortal being?"

By then the gate had opened and Brude clanked his way across the drawbridge, toting the Scythian Stone over one shoulder the way a butcher might heft a side of beef. The woman immediately caught his attention. "Where's the mage?" he demanded with a gruff disdain for all things female.

Isa pointed toward the main keep, but chose not to reply. She helped Ebon close up the gate again, then trailed behind the giant as he made his way into the inner sanctums of Kinloch. Outside the double doors of the great hall, Brude slid the Stone to the floor, leaning it against the wall since it would not fit through the archway.

Striding into the great hall like some conquering hero, Brude ignored all of those present except Kruzurk. "I have done as you asked, mage. The Stone is here, so my end of the bargain is kept. Exactly what is it you intend to do with it?"

Kruzurk seemed puzzled by the question. "Truthfully, I cannot say, for I know not the specific purpose of the Stone. The Drimnin monks asked us to retrieve it and bring it here. What comes of it now is anyone's guess."

"Drimnin?" Brude growled. "My people destroyed that pestilent den of bookworms a thousand years ago. Mage, do you know the significance of that Stone? Have you any idea of its importance?"

"I know the legends, yes. But those are just legends, Brude. There is nothing written about the Scythian Stone that can be verified. Why? Was it important to your people?"

"You ignorant fools—that is the Stone of Destiny. Every king of Dalriada, Scotia and Caledonia has knelt on it since the beginning of time. That altar is bathed in the blood of a hundred generations. No man can become the legitimate regent of this land unless and until he has sworn his oath upon the Stone and recited the runes etched upon it from memory. That is why it's important to my people. It's no wonder the Vikings, the Fricians, and the Anglish have had their way here for so long—Scotia has had no rightful king since the Stone was lost."

A hush fell over the great hall like a thick fog. Those assembled had never heard so eloquent a speech. Though they knew the Great Deceiver to be a spirit and not of human flesh, he could not be disbelieved, so true did his words ring.

"Then the legends I've heard are true, up to a point," Kruzurk replied. "Perhaps that is the real reason we have all been brought here—to set a new course for—"

The cry "To arms! To arms!" broke the quiet of the great hall just then. Daynin rushed halfway down the spiral stairwell, screaming for all he was worth. "Saxons at the south gate—hurry!"

Due to the lack of skirmishers and archers, Plumat had waited to advance far longer than he planned. Now that Fulchere and Saewold had come up to support him, the assault could go forward. With half a hundred men-at-arms to employ, along with assault ladders and archers, the distant walls of Kinloch seemed much less formidable than they had when he first observed them from the forest's edge. Satisfied that all the elements were in place, Plumat waved his sword aloft to signal the advance. A single trumpet blew, sending the entire force out of the woods at a fast walk.

Half a dozen skirmishers led the attack, fanning out twenty paces ahead of two wings of heavily armored Saxon footmen stationed on either side of the path leading up to Kinloch. The unarmored levies struggled along behind them, lugging the assault ladders over their heads in a manner designed to protect them from arrows. Fulchere's archers brought up the rear, with Saewold and a dozen men-at-arms behind them in reserve.

For a hundred paces, the attack seemed to go flawlessly. Plumat could see no one defending the first wall, and for an instant he thought the keep had been left undefended. That thought vanished with an agonized scream from one of the skirmishers, cut down by a crossbow bolt at close range.

The Saxon line forged ahead, unwavering until a second casualty. A huge wooden plank fitted with iron spikes flung itself out of the ground as if by magic, impaling its target. Those who witnessed that grisly act froze in terror, not knowing what lay ahead or if they might be next. Very quickly, the coordinated assault began to break up. Some men turned to run while others lowered their shoulders, marching blindly forward.

"God, what I wouldn't give for a bloody horse!" Plumat railed, knowing that without leadership and orders, his ragtag army might easily crumble into mass confusion. "Fulchere—get forward and urge them onward. We must attack *en masse,* or this will turn into a bloody rout!"

"Aye, m'lord," Fulchere replied cheerfully. He dashed down the open pathway and made it almost even with the front of the columns before he hit the first trip line. Down he went, tumbling with such force that he rolled smack into a second trip. That, in turn, caused a gaping hole to open in the grassy pathway square in front of him. Fulchere dropped onto the row of sharp spikes lining the deep pit, meeting his doom without so much as a whimper.

Plumat saw the man go down, but could not tell what had happened. He got his answer when a sickening groan arose from the front ranks of the assault, almost immediately stopping the advance. A dozen of the levies dropped their ladders and bolted for the rear. Saewold and several of his men-at-arms tried to regain control by threatening with their swords, but to no avail. Seeing the levies run, the archers quickly lost their nerve as well, and in a matter of minutes the whole attack fell to shambles without a single enemy in sight.

Try as they might, Plumat and Saewold could do little but watch their grand assault melt back into the woods. Three more men went down in the retreat, and there was simply no way of knowing if any would stay to fight again, even if they could be rallied before nightfall.

"We should withdraw to the ships, Plumat," Saewold counseled, breathless from his dash to the rear. "Give these cowards some grog so they'll forget and then make another try on the morrow."

"I will not withdraw—not now. That will give the highlanders time to make their defenses even stronger. We must rally as many men as we can and hit that wall again before dark. I'll not be beaten by a boy with nothing but tricks and traps."

"That *boy* just killed a lot of good men, and he never had to raise a hand to do it. I think you've lost your edge, Plumat. Tomorrow's another day. Let it go for now. Fall back, regroup and give the men some time to . . ."

Plumat's sword flashed so quickly, Saewold never had a chance to defend himself. The tip of the blade sliced cleanly through the unprotected armpit of the Saxon's hauberk, piercing his heart and dropping the man where he stood. A dozen men witnessed the assassination, stunned at an act of treachery on that scale. Instantly, another uproar broke out, followed by a second mass exodus from the battlefield, leaving Plumat all alone to consider what he had just done.

To the ten people atop the south gate tower, what had just happened seemed nothing short of a miracle. No one moved, no one cheered. In fact, the silence was almost deafening until Wick finally whispered, "Bloody hell—did ya see that, Ean McKinnon?"

"Saxon dogs," Ean growled. "Ah've seen 'em rrrr-un like that afore. Lose a leader and they lose their bloody heads. They're trained to fight that way—follow orders or face the noose."

Daynin poked his head just above one of the crenellations for a better view. "They're gone. Those traps took the fight out of them."

"Aye," Troon agreed, "but they'll be back, wager that."

Relieved that a full fledged battle had been avoided, at least for the moment, Kruzurk stood up to study the panorama of war before him. "I've never seen a battle before. It's sickening."

"Sickening for the losers, eh?" Isa asked.

Muck took the opportunity to steal a peek over the walls. "I'd wager there's plenty o' plum in them dead men's pouches, eh Unc? Shame to let it go to waste, don't ya think?"

Eigh delivered a hard slap to Muck's groin. "Shut yer

mouth, Mucky boy. We've no time to be robbin' the dead. Those blaggards will be back, and much the wiser this time."

From his position below the tower, Brude had been unable to observe any of the action. "What say you up there? Are they coming or not? *Droongar* thirsts for Saxon blood!"

Daynin slipped down the ladder part way, still unsure exactly what Brude's motive for returning to Kinloch had been. From his spot on the ladder, he could look directly into the giant's eye slits, though, of course, he could see nothing. "I'm glad you're here. We will have need of your sword when those blaggards come back."

"Bah! I came not to help you, boy, but to keep my word to the mage. Once this is over, I shall continue my quest for the Kellans and their kin. If you get in my way, I'll cut you in half."

"Brude, I've learned that we are not now and never have been allied with the Kellans. In fact, my kin fought them for this land many years ago, long before I was born. Don't you see—those shields you found in the great hall are war trophies. That means we can still be friends!"

The giant edged closer to the ladder. His gauntlet rose slowly and ominously toward Daynin's face. "You, boy, I cannot trust. Nor will I ever trust the living again. That mage is the closest thing I have to a friend, and I'd sooner slit him wide open as look at 'im."

"They're forming up again!" Troon bellowed from above.

Brude stepped back from the ladder to draw his sword, ending the talk with a gruff, "We'll finish this parlay later, boy—that is, if you survive the day."

Chapter 39:

The Battering

Oswald and his thirty men reached Standguard Bridge just at the right moment to stem the tide of Saxon retreat. Standing like a small bull square in the middle of the bridge, his axe leveled at the oncoming flood of frightened men, Oswald's demeanor broke their flight in a single action.

"Get back, you lot! Damn yer eyes for bein' the cowards. What's wrong with you anyway? Where's Plumat?"

One man sheepishly pointed back to the battlefield, offering a pitiful, "Magic, says I—it was black magic what took our men down."

A dozen more of the retreaters buzzed with the same kind of childish rhetoric until Oswald shoved them aside to cross the bridge. "Magic my arse," he swore. "Black magic, red magic, or green magic, by thunder we're gonna find that treasure and get off this heathen island." He waded into the midst of the group huddled in fear at the far end of the bridge. "Are you with me, boys? There's great booty to be had! And women! And ale for the takin'. All you have to do is get up and act like men. Now stop all this sniveling and we'll be rich by nightfall!" A less than energetic "huzzzah" went up from the sheepish group, but they followed behind Oswald nevertheless, arriving back at the forest edge almost as quickly as they had left it.

Hearing some of Oswald's boisterous tirade wafting through the trees had renewed Plumat's spirit for the attack. He rushed down the trail to greet the men, anxious to push them straight into the fray again. "Forward men!" he cried out, waving his sword in the lead of the column.

Oswald stepped aside to allow the troops to pass, but they didn't fan out on the open ground this time. More a murderous mob than a coordinated attack force, the whole group surged forward down the narrow path, straight at the main gate of Kinloch. Trip lines let loose and traps sprung, taking a handful of attackers down, but onward the mob went, bent on the worst kind of destruction.

From the keep, Wick could see that his trip lines had done all they could do to thin the attacker's ranks. "We're in for it now, lads. If they stay on the path, there's nothin' to slow 'em down but the drrrr-awbrrr-idge."

"*Och,*" Ean said, "we'll thin 'em out best we can, then fall back to the second wall. That big bugger is a helluva fighter on foot. I'll wager he can hold the gate all by himself."

Seeing the mob spread out into a wider column as it neared the drawbridge, Wick seized on the chance to break their will again. He raised the red pennant high over his head and waved it round and round. Sabritha took the cue and began pulling pegs as fast as she could jerk them free. Tightly wound ropes tied to the pegs flew out of their coiled keepers, smoking with the sudden friction of motion.

Out on the plain, one after another of the stake-lined, dung-filled pits opened with resounding *whuuumps* just a few strides from the moat, festering hell holes for any man unlucky enough to fall in one. And many did.

Fanning out like a herd of sheep, half the first rank of attackers who left the track disappeared into the ground. Troops behind them tried to slow up or go around the traps, breaking the momentum of the assault. Some managed to get as far as the moat, choosing to wade across instead of waiting for the ladders.

All the while, Daynin and his friends pelted the enemy from the tower. Isa, Kruzurk, and Wick loaded while the others took aim and fired. Ean and Troon cut several men down with their longbows, lining the road with dead and dying Saxons. Eigh, Muck, and Mediah concentrated their crossbows on the closer targets, with deadly effect.

In the middle of the mob, Plumat could barely see what lay ahead, let alone what had befallen many of the troops on his flanks. He could hear the screams and knew they were paying a fearful price for the advance, but he had no way of knowing what else was to come. "Forward!" he yelled. "Onward, men—to the walls!"

Scattered groups of levies had retrieved their ladders on the way toward the keep. Archers set up to support them and the ground attack in hastily established lines just outside crossbow range. Hurriedly, the bowmen loosed a hail of arrows at the tower, but with little effect.

Those wading the moat, now knee deep in bone chilling muck, suddenly realized the water level was rising—and fast. A flood of seawater came pummeling down the stone lined moat like some giant salt water demon unleashed. The large wooden lever Sabritha pulled last had opened a coffer dam at the sea's edge, allowing a torrent of salt brine as tall as a mounted knight to sweep everything in the moat ahead of it. The swirling mass swallowed men and weapons alike as it gained momentum flowing downhill from the sea. It swept side to side, crashing violently against Kinloch's walls, then sloshing out of the moat's banks with the fury of a tidal wave.

Plumat watched with something bordering on fascination, then realized his entire assault force had either stopped moving or been wiped out. Arrows cascaded over his head, and somewhere to the rear, he could hear the rumble of the siege weapon being dragged forward by Oswald's men. "Finally," he sighed, knowing that at least one thing was about to go as planned. "Onward, lads! To the walls!"

With the moat flooded, Ebon left his position at the north barbican to join the battle at the main gate. He ran to Brude's side, determined to hold that spot whatever the cost. "Are we winning yet?" he asked the giant.

Brude cast his armored counterpart a skeptical look and answered, "We shall see soon enough. If they have a ram or siege equipment, this wall will never hold."

Ebon drew his sword and tapped it on the palm of his gauntlet, much as Brude had done back in the catacombs of Abbotsford. "I've lived my whole life for this day. Let them come."

"You're a damned fool, boy," Brude growled. "Get out now before it's too late. This is not your fight."

Realizing he had a chance to treble Brude's commitment to the battle, Ebon seized on the moment. "Yes, it is my fight. Kruzurk and I swore to help fight the Kellans once you brought the stone back. Half those men out there are Kellan levies, come to retake this place and burn it to the ground."

"Bahhhhh!" the giant roared, literally shaking the foundations of the south wall. With one hand, he drew his carnyx. With the other, he lifted his visor and huffed a huge breath, then let it out through the horn. The effect was deafening.

Waaaarooooooo! reverberated off the walls, stopping the entire battle in place. Enraged, Brude slashed the chains holding the drawbridge and portcullis in place. The drawbridge fell with a resounding *whump,* sending the portcullis up and out of the way. Tossing aside the massive beams that held the gate shut, the Great Deceiver shoved his way through the portal and out onto the drawbridge, ready for action.

"*Menal vendochla noch ben Kellan versa,*" he boasted, brandishing his sword aloft. "Come and meet your doom, you Kellan dogs!"

Half a hundred men took one look at the immense creature facing them and lost all heart for the battle. Even Plumat could not help feeling his blood run cold with the thought of combat against such an enemy. The archers behind him turned their full fury on the giant, hoping to bring the beast down with a cascade of arrows.

To the rear, Oswald had finally wrestled Plumat's siege weapon with its supply of hundred-weight stones into place. He too, saw the giant, and would not allow himself to believe such a creature could exist. "Get it loaded," Oswald ordered. "Hector will draw first blood, by the gods!" Somehow, the Trojan name Plumat had given the war machine seemed even more appropriate, now.

Glad that he had talked Plumat into building a mangonel instead of a useless siege tower, Oswald added, "If that's the monster Plumat told us about, our levies will turn and run unless we can bring 'im down with a hit from Hector. *Lively* now, boys, before that beast has a chance to move!"

For an untrained crew, the gang of seamen took to Hector like seasoned warriors. The first ball was loaded and on its way so quickly that even Oswald seemed surprised.

"Huzzahhh!" he crowed, watching the hundred-weight stone arc through the air toward the drawbridge. The round hit the back edge of the moat with a resounding *splunshhh,* doing little damage except splattering muck on all those close enough.

Quickly realigned, another round was hefted into Hector's sling, then lofted on its way. Brude stood his ground, though he could see the massive missile winging its way toward him. "Cowardly Kellan dogs!" he taunted, stepping aside at the last instant when the stone crashed down onto the drawbridge.

A roar went up from the Saxon horde, seeing their first signs of victory. Twenty arrows rained down around Brude, serving only to annoy him. From the tower, a dozen arrows and crossbow bolts were loosed at the attackers in reply.

With the drawbridge down, Plumat saw his opportunity to advance, despite the danger from the mangonel. He knew the giant could not stop them all if they rushed him in a group, so that became the plan. He waited until Hector's next round sailed overhead, then stood up to lead the attack. "Forward, men! To the gate—now's our chance—forward!"

Brude ducked the third round from the mangonel, allowing it to sail past him and on toward the wall. Hitting hard ground, the stone bounced twice and crashed into the tower just above the gate. The impact rocked the top of the tower, tossing Daynin and the others around like jousting dummies. Down below, Ebon's armor was all that saved him from being crushed by a shower of masonry and wood from above.

Out on the drawbridge, a mad rush of armored men flowed around Brude. Some stopped to ward off blows from the Pict's giant sword, while Plumat and a dozen more rushed the main gate. Only Ebon stood in their way, and stand he did. Slashing with all his might, the black knight dropped two of the Saxon men-at-arms before they could open their attack. Another man tried to dash past, only to be hamstrung by a vicious backward blow from Ebon's sword.

Five more Saxons squared up inside the gateway arch, ready to bring Ebon to his knees. They rushed forward in line abreast with Plumat and others hard on their heels. Just within sword range, two were suddenly felled by crossbow bolts fired through embrasures to their left. Daynin and Mediah slid down the tower ladder to join the fray, engaging two men each while Ebon blocked the main advance.

Behind them, Sabritha rushed forward with a pike and crossbow. She thrust the pike into one man's side, freeing Ebon to face the men to his left. Through the opening, Sabritha fired her crossbow into a Saxon's groin, bringing him down in a screaming heap.

Seeing the woman, Plumat urged his men on, knowing that if the highlanders were desperate enough to have women defending the keep, it was only a matter of time until his numbers would prevail. "Forward, men!" he yelled. "They've only a few defenders left!"

Back at the drawbridge, Brude's attention had turned completely to the dozen men hammering him from three sides. He knew they could not hurt him, but the distraction left him vulnerable. He turned to slash at two men who had managed to rush behind him and when he did, one of Hector's bone crushers struck him square in the back.

A sickening *cranngggg* rippled across the battlefield from the stone slamming into Brude's armor. The impact sent him flying off the bridge helmet first, his sword and carnyx cascading into the moat. The round bounced backward after hitting the giant, crushing a man on the drawbridge and finally coming to rest on the bank.

Brude ended up face down in the muck and reeds lining the moat. He tried desperately to push himself to his feet, but for once, his strength did not prevail. A host of levies pounced on the creature's back, pummeling him with swords, rocks, helmets and anything else they could find. The damage, though minimal, kept him pinned to the ground like a beached whale with no chance to right himself.

Another round from Hector rent the air with a kind of sickening moan as it passed overhead, striking the tower near its base. The effect was devastating. A hole the size of a miller's cart broke open. The rubble that filled the tower's core poured out, threatening to topple the whole structure into the moat. Kruzurk yelled for everyone to get out, though most were way ahead of him. The tower groaned ominously as more of its supportive insides spilled out, leaving the structure a weakened shell.

Down in the archway, Daynin quickly learned he was no match for battle hardened Saxons. The best he could manage was keeping their attention on him and not on the others. Mediah, too, had not the skills to wage war long, and Sabritha could do little more than parry blows with her sword. Outnumbered two to one, the defenders were losing ground fast and with more levies crossing the moat, the end game loomed.

"Fight, you bastards—kill them all!" Plumat railed.

Reinforced by Daynin's tower mates, his group momentarily held the edge in numbers, though they all knew the main gate was lost. Without Brude, they could not hope to stand in a pitched battle. Having used up all of their arrows and crossbow bolts, Eigh, Muck, and Kruzurk waded in

413

with their swords to help push back Plumat's group, giving Isa and the others time to fall back.

"Back!" Wick ordered. "Back to the second tower! Quickly now, girrrl!"

Isa swept past Sabritha, grabbing her arm and dragging her from the melee. "Come on—we have to ready the gate so they can withdraw. The tower's lost!"

Reluctant to leave Daynin's side, Sabritha nevertheless did as she was told. Wiping spattered blood from her face, she cried out, "Give 'em hell, plowboy!"

Halfway between the two walls, Troon and Ean stopped to retrieve some of the Saxon overshoots, then set up a firing position to cover the retreat. They had fewer than a dozen arrows stuck in the ground between them, but at close range, the effect would be deadly. "You ready, old mahn?" Ean asked, drawing a steady bead on one of the Saxon hauberks.

Troon looked to the rear to make sure the women had the second drawbridge in motion. "Aye, old fart! Let's give it to 'em."

Ean's arrow rent the air, striking a Saxon in the neck. Troon's shot merely grazed a man, though it put him to flight. "Bloody coward," Troon said. Another levy went down, Ean's arrow having gone cleanly through his shoulder.

"Make 'em count, ya old Irish blaggard," Ean growled.

Nearing exhaustion, Ebon realized they were being supported by arrow fire from the rear. He shoved one Saxon backward as hard as he could to disengage, then stepped in front of Daynin and the others to break up their melee. "Get out—now—I'll hold them!"

Kruzurk and the others, though hesitant to leave Ebon all alone, realized his armor would protect him better than they could. Their only chance now was to fall back and hold the second tower. "Go!" Kruzurk yelled, urging the others to get away. He stopped just long enough to pull a handful of phoslin beads from his robe. He rubbed three of them together against the wall, instantly creating a bright green glow in the darkened archway. The Saxons could do little but shield their eyes from the intense light, giving Ebon and Kruzurk time to make good their escape.

With everyone out of the tower, Ean and Troon used the last of their arrows to take out three more Saxons, then withdrew with the others to the second barbican. They got the drawbridge raised just in time to stem the tide of levies pouring through the partially collapsed front tower.

At the edge of the forest, Oswald had already decided that Hector would be of little use against the second wall unless he could move the weapon forward onto the open plain. "All right, you lot. Put yer backs into it. We've gotta move this beast for'ad so it's in range of that second line. Heave now!"

A dozen men pulled on the rope drags, inching the mangonel forward on its tiny wheels. "Come *on* now, lads," Oswald urged. "We've got to move faster than this, or the battle will be over afore we get this bugger in place."

Up at the first tower, Plumat huddled behind the wall of rubble with what remained of his men, uncertain how withering the arrow fire might be if they crossed the open ground to the second barbican. The Saxons had already lost nearly a third of their attack force storming the tower, and Plumat was in no hurry to die taking the next one.

He turned to one of the few ranked drengs left uninjured and said, "Cressey, with Fulchere and Saewold both dead, I make you second in command. Get Henri de Bracton and Robert Flud and as many levies as you can and take that second tower. Gather the ladders from out there and make your assault before we lose the light. We must hit them before they can reorganize—is that clear?"

Edlund Cressey, though a trained soldier, had never commanded an army in battle, let alone led an assault against a fortified tower. "Yes, m'lord," he gulped. "And you will be, uh, here in reserve, if we hit a snag?"

"Get *moving*, Cressey," Plumat snapped. "I'll be rallying the rest of the army to support you. We've got those highlanders on the run, and I plan to *keep* 'em running. No snags!"

"I think it's a good batch," Olghar told his trusty dog. "I'm not sure exactly how to test it, but maybe if I put it in this old mug of mine, it will burn better."

Having stuffed the ancient brass goblet full of finely ground dazzle, the Russ tore another long piece of cloth from his frock to make a fuse. He walked out of the cave into a brilliant afternoon sun, feeling the warmth on his face. He tip-tapped his way along the cliff edge until he found a suitable flat spot among the rocks. "This should be safe enough, Thor—at least if the dazzle works, it won't bring the cave down on us."

Olghar positioned the goblet on its side with the fuse trailing out several cubits. Then he recited one of his native prayers, sad that he no longer had his twin railed cross to bless the moment. *"Izvaneetya pajalista, Cristos Vanya, palmanyee nachock versa shemya voseem natzit crist y trag chetpalmanyee!"*

Satisfied that he had done all he could to ensure the outcome of the test, Olghar placed a burning branch atop the fuse, turned, and hurriedly tapped his way back into the cave. He sat down and waited for what seemed like a long time, thinking the dazzle had once again failed. Just as he got up to make his way outside, the most violent event he could imagine erupted in the still afternoon air.

An earth shattering *boooooom!!!* threw him backward against the cave wall. Rock shards and detritus flew in all directions, pelting the priest and old Thor with sharp fragments like a horde of stinging bees. The dog bolted, scared beyond its wits. Olghar could do little but lay there and try to contemplate what he had just done. He could hear nothing but a profound ringing in his ears, and could barely perceive the horrendous event he had just wrought. The blast had all but sealed the cave wherein he had brought the Drimnin dazzle to life for the first time in the western world.

The instant that distant *booooom, boooom, booom, boom* reached Plumat's ears, he knew his campaign was in trouble. Every face he could see, though hardened to war, deprivation, and the ravages of the sea, had turned milky white at the realization that something otherworldly had just occurred. All looked to the sky, hoping beyond hope that what they had heard was a loud clap of thunder, though not a cloud could be seen over Rhum.

All over the battlefield, those Saxons versed in religion swore oaths of protection. Veteran killers sank to their knees, wondering if the world was coming to an end. Archers stopped in mid draw, lowering their bows in awe at the unbelievable noise. Oswald's crew dropped the drag ropes and bolted for the woods, seeking shelter in the trees from whatever had created that sound. Out in the bay, Ranulf heard the explosion and almost swallowed his afternoon carrot whole. And somewhere on the north slopes of Askival, Thor ran for his life, following the scents he picked up on the trail down to Kinloch.

Even the defenders in the second barbican huddled against the tower walls, frightened from something none of them could begin to understand. None of them, that is, except Kruzurk Makshare who stood his ground, a wry smile spreading across his normally stern facade.

"Bloody hell!" Eigh swore. "What manner o' siege weapon makes a rrrr-acket like that?"

"Maybe it was Brude," Daynin offered.

"Not a cloud in the sky," Isa observed. "It wasn't thunder."

Ebon shook his head. "Last I saw of Brude, he lay face down in the mud with a host of men beating him unmercifully. I doubt he will be with us again."

Sabritha stood up to peek through one of the tower's crenellations. "Whatever that noise was, it scared the bajeebers out of the Saxons. They look like crows in a hailstorm, all hunkered down out there."

"Dinnae count that Pict out yet," Ean said. "He's one tough bugger. I saw 'im take many a crossbow bolt when we fought the Tireean pirates, and he never wavered. Not once."

Troon had been watching Kruzurk, trying to judge what was going on in the magician's mind. He finally asked, "You must know something the rest of us don't, master Kruze. Mind sharin' what it is?"

Kruzurk looked at them all hesitantly. "That sound was the beginning of a new age, my friends. An age none of us will be happy to be a part of, but it is upon us, like it or not. Rest assured, the Saxons have no idea what they just heard and hopefully, the fear they are feeling right now will make them far less bold when they press their attack."

Mediah quickly put the pieces together. "Olghar! That

was Olghar and the magic dust the Drimnin monks gave him, wasn't it, Kruze?"

"Alchemy, Mediah—not magic. The age of magic is over. The age of man's knowledge has just begun."

"Here they come!" Sabritha cried out.

Out beyond the first barbican, Cressey had done an admirable job rallying the badly shaken Saxon contingent. With Robert Flud and Henri de Bracton at his side, he led a horde of men past Plumat, through the rubble of the first tower and out onto the sloping plain separating Kinloch's defensive walls.

Meanwhile, a group of levies had chosen to take Brude as a prize of war after all attempts to finish him off had failed. They bound him with chains and ropes, strapping him tightly to one of the siege ladders. Though he was down, the Great Deceiver was anything but finished. The struggle to restrain him had already cost several levies their lives, but the prize of that armor overshadowed all reason.

Oswald, too, had rallied his men by now, and had dragged Hector into a suitable firing position. Some of the mangonel's missiles had been retrieved from the drawbridge, giving Oswald extra rounds to attack the second wall. And attack he did.

"Let fly!" came the command, followed by the groaning *swooosh* of Hector's tightly wound works. The hundred weight flew high over the first wall but fell well short of the second. Throwing up a torrent of dirt and rock when it hit, the round plowed a gaping wound into the lush green moss near the gate.

"Damn," Wick swore, "that currrr-sed thing will tear us to pieces."

"Not if I can help it," Ebon vowed. Trained to fight in

the open as a traditional knight on horseback, Ebon had already decided there was only one way to deal with the siege machine, and he was the only one able to do it. "I'll be back," he said, solemnly. With that, he disappeared down the tower ladder.

"Where the hell is he going?" Isa hissed.

"To attack that mangonel, I should imagine," Kruzurk answered. "We best give him as much support as we can from here, for if he fails, those Saxon besiegers will have our heads."

"We've only a dozen arrows and a few more traps ta slow that lot down," Wick added, grimly. "Ean, give yer shafts to Troon and let's you and me go below—we've just enough time to get the hot oil and lime ready. Isa, you and Sabritha beat it back to the keep and gather up anything we can shoot—even those old practice arrows from the jousting court. They'll hurt a mahn bad enough at close range. And be quick about it, girrrl—the Scurry gate won't hold 'em long."

Racing back to the main keep, Isa and Sabritha were almost run over by Ebon and Castor pounding by at a full gallop. He swerved just in time and reined his horse in. "Has the tower fallen?" he cried out.

Isa dashed to his side, shaken. "No, we're going for arrows. The Saxons are massed outside, but there are scores of them! You won't have a chance out there by yourself."

"I won't be alone, Isa," Ebon said, smiling. "Castor will scatter those levies like ducks in a courtyard, wager that."

"You men are all alike—so sure you can do anything! Here, take this with you, and damn you, don't soil it. I want it back, and without any blood on it, understood?"

Ebon raised his visor, leaned down and swept the lacy veil from Isa's hand. "Am I to be your champion, then?" he asked, laughingly.

"Just go do what you have to do and get back here in one piece, that's all I ask."

Tying the veil to his gauntlet, Ebon replied, "With this, my lady, I shall fight as a hundred men."

Sabritha grew tired of the bravado, not to mention the delay in doing their duty. "You two can court all you want later. We have a war to fight, lest you forget." Seeing her point, Ebon turned Castor around and galloped away to his destiny, leaving the women to scurry off into the keep.

Outside the second wall, Cressey's troops, mindful of traps and any sudden attack from the tower, crept along at less than a walking speed. The main body split into two groups, again taking either side of the path to avoid trip lines. Behind them, archers had already taken station along the top of the outer wall. The bowmen were too far away to be very effective against targets on the inner wall, but the morale boost of having Saxon arrows pummeling the highland defenses made them invaluable nevertheless. And out on the plain, Hector continued serving up his menu of hundred-weight killers with an accuracy that grew with each attempt.

"Daynin," Eigh shouted, "get down and open the gate! Ebon is comin'."

Shoving the gate open just in time, Daynin tumbled out of the way to avoid Castor's magnificent hooves. The charger galloped across the drawbridge, totally surprising the mass of troops on the other side. With the pathway wide open ahead, Ebon dashed toward the outer wall, setting off every one of Wick's trip lines as he rode.

Saxons went down in droves to avoid the triggered crossbow bolts zinging left and right around them. Some were not as quick or lucky as others. Archers on the wall let loose a flurry of ill conceived volleys at the knight, accidentally cutting down a few of Cressey's levies in the process. Robert Flud, alone, foolishly stood up to face the sable stallion and died under its hooves.

Seeing Ebon break through to the outer wall unscathed and pounding a beeline for Hector, Oswald, and his unarmored crew, a loud "Huzzzahhh!" arose from the tower's defenders

"What the . . ." was all Oswald had time to say before his crew fled their weapon, leaving him all alone to face the oncoming knight.

In another instance of foolish bravado, Oswald hefted his broad axe, planted his feet and waited for the black anguish to reach him. He, too, had only seconds to live. Castor slammed into the man with the force of a ten cubit battering ram, crushing him and scattering his armor like a basket of blacksmith's trash. Onward Ebon rode, not yet satisfied that he had put the fear of God into the Saxons. He killed one man with his swooping blade, then ran another one smack into a tree. The rest disappeared into the forest.

Turning back to the mangonel, Ebon thought of Brude, still wrapped and hog-tied on the side of the drawbridge. He swept a torch from a campfire near the edge of the woods and dropped it on Hector as he rode by. The heavily greased machine erupted in flames, ending its short but glorious career.

Back at the first wall, Plumat stood there in the rubble, shaking his head in total disbelief at what had just happened. "What black deceit is this?" he railed. "We cannot be bested by a handful of backward bumpkins and one mounted knight. We cannot, by God, I don't care how much sorcery they employ!"

No sooner were the words out of his mouth than Cressey and his men came streaming back through the crumbling archway, a beaten lot. Most were either wounded, dazed or bedeviled by all they had witnessed. The fight had gone out of them, that was plain to see. And there *was* no tomorrow, Plumat realized, finally.

"Withdraw!" he ordered, the word leaving a bitter taste in his mouth and a wrenching twist in the pit of his stomach.

Cressey limped by, waving for his men to follow. "We cannot fight demons, m'lord—try as we might. They must have a powerful sorcerer protecting this place. So many good men . . ."

"Yes, yes," Plumat barked back, "but not good enough!"

Out on the drawbridge, Ebon saw the mass of troops funneling through the ruined gate and thought perhaps his demise had come. He didn't have time to free Brude, and there was nowhere to run, even if he had wanted to. Resigned to his fate, he pulled Isa's veil from his wrist and stuffed it inside his breastplate. "Today is a good day to die!" he yelled, then spurred Castor forward.

What was left of Saxon pride and courage seemed to melt before Ebon's eyes. The whole army parted, allowing him to charge through their ranks without so much as a sword raised against him. He rode into and out of the first barbican and halfway to the second before he realized that he might live to fight another day.

As Plumat's column of beaten soldiers filed across the drawbridge, one man asked, "What about this big bugger?"

In disgust, Plumat ripped his helmet off and threw it into the moat. He answered, flatly, "I've seen all I want of him and this cursed island—shove him into the moat—let the crabs have him."

Chapter 40:

The Ending

"Open the gate!" Eigh cried out. "Ebon's back!"

Daynin slid the heavy oak beam out of the way and shoved the gate open. Sure enough, Ebon and Castor were standing in the middle of the drawbridge, covered in mud and blood. Daynin rushed out, thinking the knight had been injured. He grabbed Castor's reins to lead him through the portal, then quickly closed up the Scurry gate.

Isa and Sabritha had returned with their batch of arrows just in time to greet Ebon. "You made it!" Isa shouted. She dropped her load and dashed to the knight's side. Seeing all the blood, she, too, assumed he was badly hurt. "Let's get you down and tend to those wounds."

"Wounds?" Ebon replied, completely unaware that a crossbow bolt had lodged in his hip and another in his saddle, penetrating all the way to Castor's flesh. He turned, took one look at the bolt in his backside and swooned, almost falling from his horse.

From up in the tower, a series of "whoops" and "huzzahs" rang out amongst the defenders. They were beginning to realize that the Saxons had withdrawn, dragging some of their dead and wounded with them. On the field between the two barbicans, a dozen men lay dead or dying, many of whom had been felled by their own archers.

Further out, the plain between the south gate and the

forest had its share of fallen invaders as well, some that Oswald had claimed with Hector's indiscriminate hundred-weights. Away in the distance, smoke curled up from the mangonel's funeral pyre, to which the Saxons added, in passing, the bodies of unnamed and uncounted levies.

Out in the bay, Ranulf had already heard reports from the first of the returning deserters. He immediately sent boats ashore to pick up as many men as possible, all the while making ready to put to sea. With Oswald dead, the carrot-chewing reeve had just ascended a full rank in Duke Harold's hierarchy. He planned to waste no time sailing home to enjoy that new rank and remain out of harm's way as best he could.

Geile Plumat led what remained of his ragtag army down to the sea, their pride, prejudices, and battle pennants dragging behind them in the dust. Of the three score and thirty men he took ashore, the Saxon would only need room for half that many on the voyage home, a black mark on his honor he would not soon forget.

"Put the dead aboard that tub, set her afire and cut her loose," Plumat growled, as he and his rear guard marched past the *Shiva*, still at her mooring on the old stone wharf. "At least those highland buggers won't be able to get off this bloody island anytime soon."

Far up on Askival, poor Olghar struggled to gain his bearings in the pitch black rubble of the cave. Having lost his guide stick, he was forced to feel every rock. Unfortunately, the cave had changed so much there was little chance he would find his way out without help. Added to that, most of the cave mouth had been destroyed when the dazzle went off, making it almost impossible for anyone else to find Olghar, even if they knew where to look.

★ ★ ★ ★ ★

Back at Kinloch, the women tended to Ebon's wounds while Daynin and the others searched among the slain Saxons for anything that might be useful in the attack they assumed would come with the next day. They began stockpiling arrows, swords, knives, and all manner of armor, and had just made their way out of the main gate when all of a sudden, an enormous geyser erupted from the moat.

Brude had arisen! Still tangled in chains and ropes, the Great Deceiver lived again, though he had been underwater for a long time. Thrashing his helm from side to side to throw off the kelp and reeds, he finally blurted out, "Where the bloody hell have you been?"

Briefly taken aback, Daynin replied, "My God, Brude—I didn't know where you were. We thought the Saxons had you!"

"Saxons, bah," the beast bellowed. "They let one knight best their whole army. Ebon rode through them like a vestal virgin—twice—not one man daring to stop him. Now get me out of this mess, so I can go and finish the task he started."

Ean and the others stepped up to start cutting ropes and untwisting Brude's binding chains. The elder McKinnon told Brude, "It's far more important for you to help us rebuild the walls tonight, than to seek more blood. Those blaggards will hit us again at first light."

"Haaaaahaaaar," Brude laughed, "methinks not, highlander. They will be long gone by sunrise. I heard their leader say as much. They won't be back—not tomorrow, anyway. They're beaten, but I still have time to take some heads, if you'll hurry and get these blasted chains off me."

"Daynin," Troon offered, "perhaps we should leave things well enough alone, if you get my drift. Enough blood's been spilled here today."

"You blaggard!" Brude cried out. "Unbind me!"

"Perhaps you're right, Troon," Kruzurk agreed. "There comes a time when honor has done all it should do. Killing for the sake of killing then becomes a crime, and I think we've reached that point. The Saxons are beaten, for now. And besides, we have the Scythian Stone and the treasure to consider. We shall have need of Brude's wisdom for the disposition of both."

"Trrrr-easure, is it?" Eigh and Muck exclaimed, almost at the same instant.

Daynin tossed Kruzurk a disapproving look, then faced the two kinsmen he barely knew. "Uh—yes. We, uh, brought a bit of booty with us from Blackgloom Keep—to help rebuild Kinloch."

"Och," Eigh clucked. "This day just keeps gettin' better and better, eh Mucky boy?"

Muck's overstuffed frock pockets attested to the plunder of the dead he and his uncle had already begun. "Aye, Unc—mayhaps we'll be sharin' in a bit o' that booty as well, once we get done pickin' these stiffs. I mean, seein' as how we helped defend this place and all."

Mediah shook his head at their callous greed and replied, "No doubt there are ample spoils among the corpses. I, for one, will have no part of robbing them. You may have my share, and welcome to it."

By now, the giant had lost all patience. He struggled against the binding chains and roared in anger for his release, but to no avail. It took Daynin and all seven of his companions to drag Brude back to the great hall where reason might prevail.

Once there, Muck and Eigh quickly excused themselves to return to their battlefield enrichment efforts while

Kruzurk, Mediah and the two women worked on Ebon's wound. The knight had been laid out facedown on one of the cots in the great hall, that the crossbow bolt might be removed from his hip.

The others looked to Kruzurk for his medicinal knowledge, but he stepped aside, saying to Mediah, "You are probably better at this part than I—perhaps you should undertake the removal and I will prepare the poultice."

Mediah took to the task instantly. "Isa, please boil as much water as you can, quickly. Sabritha, I will have need of clean cloth—several cubits of it, and some twine or rope. We'll also need a hot iron to cauterize the wound."

Hearing that, Ebon tried to come up off the cot but was too weak from the blood loss. He passed out again. "Hurry, m'ladies—whilst he's out, we can remove that bolt," Mediah added.

From the corner of the great hall, Brude growled, "Release me, you fools, and I will show you how to remove the bolt. That boy saved all your lives—he deserves proper treatment."

Wick and the others ignored the giant, preferring not to give him any more reason for anger. Kruzurk was preparing a poultice with the things he had on hand, when he suddenly remembered Olghar. "Ean, we have a friend up on the mountain somewhere—he's a blind priest, and will need someone to bring him down who knows the trails."

"Och, 'tis nae a prrrr-oblem. Where did you leave 'im?"

"Muck took him to a cave—under a huge gray outcrop of rock. He can tell you better than I."

Ean began gathering his things to start the search. "On the north slope? Say, a half furrr-long from the summit? And the outcrop reminded you of a cow's upper lip?"

"Yes—exactly! You know the place?" Kruzurk said.

"Aye. Spent many a day there as a lad, making arrow points from the chert. That cave is full o' bats, you know. Not to mention the midlin' cats who sometimes make it their den."

Daynin's head snapped around. "*What* cats? What are you talking about, grandfather? And who is this priest, Kruzurk?"

Halfway out the door, Ean yelled back, "Too many questions, boy. When I get back with this monk, you'll have yer answers."

Kruzurk put a hand on Daynin's shoulder. "Your grandfather is right, Daynin. Enough questions for now—let's finish up here and get some rest. We'll talk in the morning."

The great hall hummed along with activity until nearly dusk. Ebon's wound was tended and cleaned and Kruzurk's poultice applied. Another big pot of stew was shared all around. After that, exhaustion quickly spread until most of the group found a place to sleep next to the big hearth. Muck volunteered to stand the first watch at the Scurry gate, and with Ean out searching for Olghar, that left Daynin and Sabritha the chance to be truly alone for the first time since Abbotsford Priory.

"You said before that there's another big hearth in the upper keep," Sabritha whispered. "One where we could—perhaps—lay out a blanket to sleep—uh—by ourselves?"

Somewhat taken aback by the pointed suggestion, Daynin answered, "Yes, of course. There's a bed, too. I'll get a scoop full of coals to start the fire. If you'll bring that big candelabra over there, I'll show you the way."

Though his body was tired beyond anything he had ever experienced, Daynin's mind was flooded with images of her body. He could barely contain his anticipation. Trailing behind Sabritha all the way up the main stairwell, he wished, for once in his life, to have had more training in the manly arts. Every step with his eyes on her shapely backside reinforced a growing desire for her, while at the same time building a wall of doubt that he might not know what to do and when, should the moment of his entry into manhood arrive.

"Left at the top," he guided her. "That long hall with the tapestries, that's where we're going."

Reaching the last step, Sabritha turned left and stopped. She waved the candelabra slowly from side to side as they walked on, marveling at the richness of the woven wall ornaments. "Oh Daynin, these are so beautiful—more beautiful than anything I've ever seen."

Daynin pried his eyes off her swaying waistline to once again appreciate the family heirlooms. "My mother brought those from Edinborough. They cost my father a year of fealty to the McTavish clans in their wars down south, but he always said the glow it gave my mother was worth every day of it."

"I'm surprised they survived the fire," she said, her voice trailing off to a near whisper.

"They wouldn't have, but they were in storage at the time, so the walls could be patched with new mortar. I guess the Caledonians didn't find them, else those thievin' bastards would have burned 'em or taken 'em along with everything else they stole."

Sabritha turned on her heels, the candelabra suddenly shining bright in Daynin's eyes. "There is so much history here. That means a lot to me, since I never had a real home. You'll have to tell me more. Especially about your mother."

"Aye," Daynin said, taking the lead. "With the Saxons gone, we should have ample time for that, whilst we rebuild the rest of the keep. Wick has done most of the work, but there's plenty left to do."

"Which room?" she asked.

"This one. 'Twas always a place I could'nae enter when I lived here as a boy. If you get lost up here, just remember it's the one with the double doors." Daynin shoved the doors apart and was surprised that the room not only had a blazing fire going already, but that someone had left his mother's wooden tub sitting in front of the hearth, ready for a bath. "Looks like the squire has been busy, eh?"

"Ohhhh my!" Sabritha purred. She twirled twice around in the middle of the room, admiring the well adorned chamber. "God, Daynin, this is beyond anything I ever imagined. It is so warm and comfortable—I feel so—so—at *home!*"

Without thinking, he blurted out, "You *are* home—that is, if you *want* it. And—no requirements—that is—you don't have to uh . . ."

For the first time since he had known her, Daynin began to see the softer side of the woman. Never before had she let her guard down to the point of admitting she wanted to be with him. The very idea made his head spin. He felt warm all over—very warm in fact. He spun about and tossed the scoop of coals into the fire, then turned back around. Sabritha had stepped so close to him, he could almost count her eyelashes.

"Uhmm—I should—uh—go get some more wood, I guess."

She placed the candelabra on the edge of the tub. Removing the scoop from Daynin's hand, she dropped it on to the hearth, both her hands sweeping upward to cup his face in her palms. "I *want* it, plowboy." Looking deep into his boyish eyes, she added, "I want it *all*, and I will give you whatever you want in exchange."

Tempted to kiss her, Daynin's mind reeled once again.

He felt his heart pounding like a tabour drum. His knees began to weaken and strangely, his ears rang so loudly, he could hear nothing else. He could see Sabritha's lips moving, though he had no idea what she said. Then she leaned up on her tiptoes to kiss him, not once, but several times, starting at his lips, his chin, each cheek and again on the lips.

The room really started spinning then. *Be a man,* his brain cried out, to no avail. His hands and arms swept around her, more to keep himself balanced than anything else, while his senses regained their composure. *She wants me! Oh God, is this real? How could I be this fortunate?*

Realizing that Daynin had suddenly turned from lively to leaden, Sabritha guided him toward the bed. "Are you all right?" she asked, helping him slide out of her arms and onto the cot.

Daynin slumped back and shook his head like some dullard just come from a clan drinking fest. "Dizzy," was all he could mutter.

Sabritha helped ease his legs up onto the bed, then began loosening his tunic and breeches. "You need rest and I need a bath. Get some sleep, plowboy," she said, soothingly. "Our new world begins tomorrow."

Unused to the strenuous climb up Askival's face, Ean McKinnon finally had to stop for rest. With only the barest hint of moonlight to guide him, he realized now that finding his old chert cave in the dark might have been a foolhardy venture. He sat down on a big boulder at a familiar spot where the upward trails split, scanning the north slope for any signs of the priest.

"Hellooooo!" he called out. Only his own echoes answered.

Rather than turn back, Ean trudged on, thinking the

432

priest must surely have a fire going. Just then, a rustling on the trail below caused him to draw his sword. "Come on out, ya bloody Saxon dog."

A dog of another kind answered with a hearty, "Wooof, wooof." Thor had come back to find his master.

"Well, I dinnae know who you are, boy, but if ya've a mind for company, we'll climb this bloody rrr-ock together. Maybe you can find this priest I'm to retrieve, eh?"

Thor rushed past Ean, charging up the trail like he had been raised on Askival. He led the clansman straight to Olghar's cave, though Ean would hardly have recognized the place on his own.

"Hellloooo!" he bellowed again.

This time, a faint reply seemed to come right out of the mountain. "Here—I'm here—in the cave—I can't see."

"Bloody hell, mahn—did the mountain cave in on ya?" Ean asked, as Thor went to work digging in the rubble.

"Yes," the faint voice replied, "in a manner of speaking."

Moving some bigger boulders aside, Ean helped Thor wiggle his way through a crack in what used to be the cave's mouth. He could hear the happy reunion inside. "I'm Ean McKinnon. I'll have ye out, quick as a marten's mouse."

Shoving more debris down the slope, Ean finally opened a hole big enough for the priest to crawl out of. With Thor in the lead, the two men began their slow descent down Askival. All the while, Olghar filled Ean in on Kruzurk's great adventure from Abbotsford to Rhum.

"So, you're the one that caused the big 'boom' we heard eh, priest? You put the fear o' god into those bloody Anglish, wager that."

"I *was* a priest—in Russ, where I hail from. Now, I am just a beggar, seeking a warm place to sleep. I'm happy I could help, though I must admit, I had no idea the dazzle would make so much noise."

"Sleep, aye," Ean replied. "For what you did for us, you'll never want for a bed, old mahn, long as I have anything to say about it. That is, if ya've a mind to stay here on Rrrr-hum."

"Yes, thank you. I would like that. Thor will appreciate it, too. You are very kind."

"Just don't be settin' off any more of that drizzle or whatever it was. You nearly shook the keep to crumbles."

Olghar laughed out loud for the first time since his blinding. "Not to worry—the dazzle is all gone, but I know how to make more, should we ever need it."

Early the next morning, Daynin awoke with his right arm numb. The smell of clean hair told him why. Sabritha's head lay across his arm, her back neatly fitted against his front as though the gods had molded them into a single being while they slept. And indeed, he actually felt that way. She was a part of him now, and he belonged to her, forever. His heart, his soul, his honor and his home—he had pledged them all to her in a single act of submission.

Now, with a new day upon them, Daynin realized he had no regrets for his actions. He lay there, his mind lazily replaying every image, every detail of the most intimate and wonderful night of his life. Through sleep deprived eyes, he could still see Sabritha's beautiful shoulders draped in an ebony tangle of hair, all wet from the bath with the roaring fire beside her. When she stood up to rinse herself, he had come fully awake, facing the tub and unable to make his eyes turn away. Her intimate curves, the perfect outlines of her back, even the creases on the backs of her knees all seemed so perfect.

She *was* perfect. The *night* had been perfect. And with her guidance, *he* had been perfect as well. He closed his eyes to savor the memory, to lock it in his soul where no one could ever take it from him.

A sudden and unexpected *bam—bam* on the chamber doors ripped Daynin from his reverie. In the blink of an eye, the doors were flung open by men with drawn swords. The Duke's heraldry flashed in the boy's eyes. Blood and screams erupted everywhere. He tried desperately to fight back, but his arms wouldn't move. He heard someone say his name, then yell it a second time.

"Daynin! Wake up, boy. Get some clothes on ya for pity sake," Ean growled. "We've work to do and it's already past first light."

Daynin shook his head, realizing Sabritha had gone. "Where *is* she? Where's Sabritha? What's happened to her?" he begged.

From the far corner of the chamber, Sabritha spoke up. "You've been dreaming, plowboy. I swear, if you'd had a sword in your hand, I might have had no head this morning."

Ean cast the woman a skeptical look, then turned his attention back to Daynin. "That trrr-easure needs to be put away, and those paid who warrant payment. Then there's that bloody giant of yours, who's making a nuisance of himself. I got the priest, by the way, whilst you was up here breakin' in yer bed last night. And there's lots of commotion about that cursed stone and its disposition. I cannae begin ta tell what the deuce that magician and his crew are goin' on about, so you best be takin' care of that, as well. And if that ain't enough, someone needs to be out shootin' us some breakfast."

"Yes, grandfather," Daynin moaned. "I'll take care of it.

Tell the others I'll be down soon."

"*Och!* I'm to be your messenger is it?" Ean raised a hand to feint a smack on Daynin's bare backside, adding, "You're none too big for me to be takin' a sea reed to, ya know, even though you're the new laird of this keep. Remember that."

Sabritha stifled a laugh from her corner, all the while continuing to comb out her long black hair. After Ean closed the door, she said, "I can see right now, this place is never gonna be dull."

Daynin rolled out of the cot and tiptoed across the cold flagstone floor. Though he was completely nude, he felt no shame whatever, standing behind Sabritha and running his fingers through her sable locks.

She reached back and touched his fingers, allowing her hands to wander over other parts of his naked flesh. "Hmmm," she whispered, "I guess I can't call you 'plowboy' anymore, huh?"

He leaned down over her head and kissed her with all the passion and love he had learned the night before. She kissed him back until finally, she pushed him away and said, "Enough of that, for now, highlander. You promised me a sunrise, remember?"

Epilogue

Aboard the *Dionysis*, Ranulf had taken to his new position as fleet commander with the relish of flies to a milk pail. Though not a skilled seaman, he still managed to get Plumat's army off the beach at Rhum and headed south for home. In the reeve's mind, a three ship armada made him every bit the equal of Plumat, so he took every opportunity to pay back his former commander with deception, dishonesty and disdain. Ultimately, his petty, small mindedness might well cost him dearly, but for now, he was, at least in his own estimation, the king of the ocean sea.

Though a beaten man, Plumat had enough anger in him to sustain him for a long time to come. He had already determined that the island of Rhum would some day be his eggshell to crush at will. That vision was to motivate Plumat in weaving and wrangling his way back into Duke Harold's good graces, so he might eventually craft a plan to seize Rhum and destroy it. That is, if he lived long enough.

For Duke Harold's part, once he had Plumat's detailed account of the disaster in hand, a mere mention of Rhum and the Blackgloom campaign would send him off into a rage. Fortunately for Daynin, the Duke would soon have much bigger enemies to consume his energies, though the death warrants for the boy, the woman, and the magician still very much remained in effect.

Meanwhile, all over Scotia, word spread rapidly of the

new laird in power at Kinloch. Speculation about this Regent of Rhum possessing great wealth, energy, and wisdom began to circulate to the whole of Anglia and as far west as Ireland. Even the Drimnin loremasters heard about it, bringing a broad smile to a certain diminutive little monk.

Back at Abbotsford Priory, the novitiate wasted no time in walling up Brude McAlpin's tomb, including the remainder of the Blackgloom Bounty. They left no door or other sign of what the sepulcher contained, choosing instead to seal the contents for all time behind a simple brick facade.

And what of Brude and the Scythian Stone? Ah, that's a tale too long herein to tell. But rest assured, this tome is but the end of the beginning for Daynin McKinnon and his friends. The rest, as you will no doubt see, is a story still being told 'round many a campfire where heroes and heathens abound.

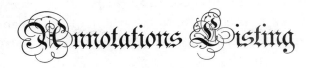

Annotations Listing

(Terms are arranged by
order of usage in the text.)

Caledonia: The Romans referred to Scotland as Caledonia, a name thought to have derived from the Pictish tribe Caledonii, but most historians credit Caledonia with a separate cultural identity.

Picts: Derived from the name given by Roman historians to most of the untamed tribes north of Hadrian's Wall. The name Pictii means, literally, "painted ones" for the Pictish practice of body tattooing.

Cruithni: What most non-Roman histories call the Picts.

Scotia: A generalized term for much of Scotland prior to its dominion under Saxon England.

King's Eyre: The king's traveling court in early medieval times.

A hide of land: Anywhere from 120–240 acres of land for tax purposes.

A league of distance: Roughly equivalent to three U.S. miles.

Coif: A round or hood-shaped cap worn by medieval clergy.

Nave: The principle area of a church, from the main entrance to the chancel.

Thegn, thane, teignus: A companion of the king or a military administrator and land owner.

Furlong: An ancient Roman measure of distance of about

220 yards, still used in horse racing today.

"Te Deum, non nobis Domine, nunc dimitis": A Latin prayer of thanksgiving.

Sgian du: An ancient Scotian sock knife, kept always on a clansman's leg for self defense.

Prime: The call to breakfast and prayers in medieval monasteries.

Stoat: Any of several small furry animals, similar to an ermine, prized for their pelts.

Vole: Any of several mouse-like creatures prized for their pelts.

Dalriada: The ancestral homeland of the Pictish tribes, consisting of much of northern Scotland.

Shetland: A reference to the Shetland Islands, northeast of the British Isles.

Arbalest: A type of long range crossbow often carried by Saxon light cavalry.

Promethean: From mythology-the giant deity who stole fire from heaven and gave it to mankind.

Fortnight: The medieval equivalent of two weeks.

Stygian River: The river that supposedly flows through Hell.

Catafalque: A raised platform upon which a casket is held for mourners to view.

Motte and bailey: A small wooden fortress built on a hill, and almost always surrounded by a ditch.

Euclid: A Greek geometrician who lived around 300 B.C.

Liege: A medieval lord and often a military commander.

Carnyx: A Pictish war horn, said to be the loudest wind instrument of the European Iron Age.

Levies: Typically, these are untrained mercenary troops used to fill the ranks of an army.

Hogshead: A large cask capable of holding well over 60

gallons of water, wine or other goods.

Exemplum: A lesson for the novitiate of a monastery, usually given by the prior.

Dagon: A medieval term for Satan or the devil.

Cerberus: Another name for Satan.

Vespers: A monastic service in the late afternoon or evening.

Gehenna: A medieval term for Hell.

Ratlines: Ladder-like ropes designed to allow sailors to climb up the sides of a ship's mast or rigging.

Snekke: A small, very fast medieval warship, usually of 20 oars and a single sail.

Dun's keep: A Scottish or Irish fort, usually built of wood with a surrounding ditch and stockade.

Coup-de-grace: The French equivalent of a "death blow".

Cloistered: A monk who lives within the confines of a monastery with no contact to the outside world.

Vernacular: The common or ordinary speech of a country or region.

Mastiff: A large, powerful dog brought to Britain by the Romans to guard their encampments.

Tabour: A small round drum carried around the neck and played one handed to accompany a fife or flute.

Heraldry: A family coat of arms or symbol, usually worn on a tunic covering a knight's chainmail.

Targ Shield: A round, leather covered wooden shield, typically mounted with metal barb-like cones.

Firth: The Scottish term for a long narrow bay or harbor, usually open to the sea.

Pommel: A protruding knob on the front end of a saddle. Used mainly for a grip when mounting.

Reeve: The chief tax collector for manorial lands belonging to a local lord.

Pyrrhonist: Medieval term for a non-believer.

Pennon: A long narrow flag attached to a knight's lance which bears the knight's coat of arms.

Estuary: The mouth of a large river in which the river's current meets the sea's tide.

Wimple: A cloth covering the head and neck, leaving only the face exposed.

Drengs: Free peasants who held a rank over land or property in exchange for military service to another.

Cast: The effective range of a bow or crossbow.

Grimoire: A magic book written in many languages telling how to invoke spirits, make magic circles, etc.

Rota: An ancient form of the jury system. Similar to a trial by committee.

Palindrome: A word, name or phrase that is spelled the same, either forward or backward.

Vellum: Fine lambskin used by monks or priests for preserving particularly important documents.

Merrels: A French game played with nine pieces on a side, using a cross shaped board.

Donjon: The original name for a keep or main tower where prisoners were often held for trial.

Mortrews: A pounded fish or meat paste made with bread and eggs, then sometimes fried.

Draco: A large warship capable of carrying thirty to fifty men and a crew.

Withers: The highest part of the back at the base of a horse's neck.

Hauberk: A long coat of chainmail, often elaborately adorned and marked with heraldry.

Barbican: A gateway or outworks defending a drawbridge.

Cubit: An ancient unit of measure the equivalent of a man's forearm length, or about 17–24 inches.

Portcullis: A heavy wooden or iron grating that can be lowered to prevent entrance through a castle gate.

Boon: A favor or request asked of a landowner or other party in power by those being governed.

Mangonel: A heavy slinging machine, similar to a ballista, used for throwing stone balls or rocks.

About the Author

JON BAXLEY is a freelance writer, novelist, historian, editor, and Internet entrepreneur from Hondo, Texas. His latest major work is a medieval fantasy that began as an award-winning eBook entitled *The Scythian Stone*, which ultimately evolved into the epic *The Blackgloom Bounty*, a Five Star Speculative Fiction masterpiece. More books in this series are to follow.

A 1969 University of Texas at Arlington graduate, Jon served with the U.S. Army, worked as a golf professional and consulted for the United States Information Agency in the former Soviet Union. Having been a full time writer and author for many years, Baxley eventually turned his attention to fiction writing and has never looked back.

When someone asks Jon about his writing experiences, he answers with, "Ask not what a publisher can do for *you*. Ask what *you* can do for your publisher." Baxley can be reached via his email address FiveStarAuthor@aol.com. Your comments on his works are both encouraged and invited.